"Then you should have what I'm here to do." Aaron

"Oh, I do. And I do…" Karen purred with a voice as thick as honey.

Aaron picked up the smell of wood, leather, and oiled iron all around him.

His *lupus* realized he was in a tight spot and wanted control. "**You really need to let me handle this**," it growled. This was the first time he could recall his new instinctive nature, his *lupus*, trying to save him, because he hadn't experienced this level of danger before. He turned control over to it. Although he was conscious of his actions, directed them, it still reminded him of his dreams with the black dog.

Howlers: Lupus Rex

Howlers: Lupus Rex

By
Tom Sutherland

Nicole,

Thanks for the hard work!
Remember – never show a
werewolf your moon.

Tom Sutherland

11/13/2015

First Printing: 2015

eBook ISBN 978-0-9962417-0-0
Paperback ISBN 978-0-9962417-1-7

Table30Press@gmail.com

To my wife, Angela.
Thank you for allowing me to indulge in this, my latest whim.

And to the *lupis* who almost got me…
Tag, you're it!

PART III—SUI DECEPTIO — 157

PART IV—RISE OF LUPUS SOLITARIUS — 245

PART V—LUPUS REX — 325

Acknowledgements

This is my first book. Well, it's the first one I've completed anyway. I've half a dozen more scattered around on various hard drives and floppy disks (yes, floppy disks). I would like to say I wrote *Howlers: Lupus Rex* all by my lonesome, in a closet, without any input from the rest of the world, but I would be lying. Too many people have given up their own valuable free time to read it and give me feedback. Some only made it a chapter or two, and some made it the whole way through. I don't blame those who didn't make it all the way. Their help and input was just as welcome and as valuable as those who did slog their way to the end. Proofreading a book is hard work. I didn't realize how hard it was until I finished the first draft on the last chapter. I suspect my volunteers didn't either when they first agreed to help me.

I am going to thank each and every one of these individuals here. Without them, this book would not be as good as it is. If I've forgotten anyone or there are mistakes found within, it is my fault and my fault alone, and I should be flayed for such an atrocity.

Angela (my wife), Anne Hood, Amy Storey, Becky White, Beth McClure, Beverly Nielsen, Cheryl Hogue, Chuck Rogers, Eric Curtis, Darlene Covich, Heather Smith, Jeff Jordan, JoAnn Hall, Keith Cleary, Kerby Pierre, Leah May, Marie Chase, Matthew Vaughn, Matthew Wilson, Megan Nieman, Michelle McLaren, Mike O'Neal, Pam Percle, Sasha Miller, Steve Conner (my Tai Chi Sifu), Stuart Spivey, Tim Clary, Tom Tweeddale, Tony Womack, Tracie Lenard, Vicki Christensen, Wendell Whitaker.

Antelogium

noun [an-tē-lä'-ji-əm]
1. Beginning.

Aaron Darveau, March 5, 1973

Bourbon Street, the most well know street in New Orleans, danced with thousands of bright, psychedelic Mardi Gras costumes. The aromas of fruity drinks, beer, and whiskey made up the light breezes that weaved up, down, and around the narrow streets and alleys, not quite covering up the bitter odors of sweat, urine, and vomit, because you can't have the former group of smells without the latter in a town that lets it all hang out once a year. The blues rhythm of picked banjos, spoons ricocheting across washboards, and sticks battering loosely-fitted snare drums echoed from all of the bars—bars which, luckily for Aaron, Jimmy, and Wendell, didn't heavily enforce the legal drinking age of eighteen.

Aaron had just lifted a jug of some particularly nasty, cheap brew to his lips when a half-naked woman carrying a paper bag full of groceries weaved through the revelers as she came up the street toward him. Her milky-chocolate complexion was tastefully camouflaged with long, flowing, pastel-colored scarves and accented with the tinkling, bangle bracelets associated with most Creole women. Just as a grin crept across his face, some drunk bumped into her, knocking her groceries to the ground. Most of the people around her ignored what happened and those who didn't pretended not to notice. Black or not, you didn't treat people that way; Aaron thrust the jug of beer into Jimmy's hands and rushed over to help her.

Some people have two imaginary friends to help them make decisions, a little devil and a little angel. Not Aaron. His spiritual mentor was James Tiberius Kirk, Captain of the *U.S.S. Enterprise* from the television show, *Star Trek*. He didn't let too many people know that though, as being from a small town in Louisiana, science fiction wasn't quite the mainstream hobby fishing or hunting was. Usually, when needing help on making a decision, he asked himself, *"WWKD—What Would Kirk Do?"* In this instance, Captain Kirk wouldn't want to look too eager by running up and skidding to a halt. As he neared her, his jog slowed to a stroll. "Can I help you, Ma'am?"

She looked up, amused. "Ma'am? *Asire w ase*, you da gentleman! Sho 'nuff! Helping out a lady like dis!" Her Creole tugged at his ears and kept him distracted from the fact she wasn't quite as young as he thought she was from a distance. She was probably mid-thirties, but he was bad at guessing ages. She might have been in her fifties for all he could tell. In either case, that musical accent stripped the years from her.

"Yes, Ma'am, I am," he spouted without thinking, inwardly grimacing at the stupid rhyme. He kneeled down next to the mass of spilt groceries. "My name's Aaron Darveau."

She handed him her bag. "I'm Jajine. Hold dis." As she refilled the bag, she remarked, "Dat's a Cajun name, but you not from 'round dese parts. And you can stop with the *Ma'am* bit. I ain't dat old."

"Yes, Ma'am. I mean, okay, Jajine." The bag was torn, so he shifted it around to keep its contents from falling back out. "And, no, I'm from Monroe. Me and my Junior ROTC drill team are marching in the Rex Parade tomorrow."

A thoughtful expression washed over her face, and she seemed to stare into him. "Rex," she muttered. "Well, ain't dat a coincidence." She quickly finished picking up the rest of her groceries and then pulled a damp business card from her bosom. She placed it in his hand, swapping it for the bag of groceries. "You come and see Madame Jajine tonight. Ah'll give ya a free readin' for helpin' me out like dis." Her bangles jingled—*ching, ching, ching*—in perfect rhythm with the back and forth swaying of her hips as she disappeared into the crowd. He held the card up and looked at it. It was decorated with various glyphs and astrological signs he had only ever seen in the horoscope section of the newspaper. *Madame Jajine, Fortune Teller, Dauphine Street* was all it said. He slipped it into his pocket.

Jimmy ragged on him without letting up for the rest of the afternoon. "You gonna go visit that black, gypsy lady? She'll put a hurtin' on ya!" Not only did Jimmy have the most facial hair of the three of them, he was also a little taller and much huskier.

Wendell, of course, decided to get in on the harassment too. "He ain't goin'. He's chicken."

"Both of y'all are just jealous," Aaron accused. "That's all. Y'all just mad I got the invitation and you didn't."

Wendell threw the empty beer jug in an already full trash can. "So, you gonna go or not?"

"Maybe later. Let's look around some." He shoved his hands in his pockets and looked up the street at a passing float, trying to show disinterest in the direction of the conversation. The bravado he showed when he first met Jajine quickly turned to shyness at the thought of meeting her in her apartment.

"Thought so," sniped Wendell, looking at Jimmy for back-up. "Chicken."

"I ain't chicken," Aaron grunted. "She's just too old for me."

"Looked good from where we were standing," Jimmy argued, teasing Aaron. "She looked like something out of *I Dream of Jeannie*."

"I ain't going," Aaron insisted firmly.

Both Wendell and Jimmy started squawking like chickens, "Bwak, bwak, bwak!" Wendell was the skinniest of the three and had the largest nose in school. When he strutted around like a hen pecking feed, he really looked like a chicken.

Aaron had to laugh at them, but secretly he was agitated. He didn't like being made fun of. "Fine! I'll go."

Wendell glanced at Jimmy. "I don't believe him." Then he looked at Aaron with a dare on his face. "We need to go along to make sure."

Jimmy grinned at Aaron. "Damned straight we do. Lead the way, hoss!"

They asked around for Dauphine Street and then searched up and down the block until they found someone who knew who Madame Jajine was. Their search ended in a bar. The bartender was a short, skinny guy, somewhere between twenty and seventy years of age—his face had a youthful air about it, but he was wrinkled like last week's history test paper.

Aaron cleared his throat. "I'm looking for Madame Jajine. Do you know where I can find her?"

Little-Old-Young-Man looked up from his duties behind the scratched and stained bar. His one, working eye settled on Aaron. The other one was glass and stared at everyone else at once. Aaron suspected that single, live eye had seen more than most other men's two eyes had together. He jerked his thumb over his shoulder. "Take da stairs. She be in number two. Just knock, and she'll be a answerin'."

They all stumbled up the squeaky stairs in alcohol-induced ineptness and found room number two to be the first door on the left. There was a poorly crafted, large wooden sign on it that was near-identical to her business card. The hallway was musty smelling and narrow with uneasy shadows along it because half the lights were out, and the ones that were working were too small to adequately do their job. Aaron raised his fist to knock, and the faded door creaked open just a crack but still enough to let the smell of burning incense, fried chicken, and cheap whiskey assault his nose.

Jajine's voice echoed from inside. "Who dat? Is dat you, Aaron?"

Aaron responded through the crack in the door. "Yes, Ma'am."

"Well, only you den. Your friends'll have to wait downstairs."

He grinned at his friends and reached for the doorknob, but Wendell stopped him with a low whisper. "Remember what Chief Ross said about getting rolled when alone. Gimme your wallet."

"Yeah. Here." Aaron fumbled his wallet out and handed it over. Wendell and Jimmy stumbled back down the stairs, snickering the whole way.

Aaron stepped into the apartment and realized with surprise there was no one near the door. He gently placed his fingers around the doorknob and slowly pushed the door closed. He was about to ask Jajine who opened it, but forgot about the question the instant he looked around the apartment. It reminded him of an old *Twilight Zone* episode, except it was in color. A massive snake stirred in a glass terrarium under the window, an old black-and-white television with the volume turned all the way down was sitting next to it, and mounds of newspapers were stacked everywhere. On the walls were pictures of what he assumed was her family. One showed a young Jajine in a frilly dress against a backdrop of a tropical island. "Where were these pictures taken?" he asked.

"Haiti. Dat's where I'm from," she yelled from the back of the apartment somewhere.

Jajine had numerous little trinkets scattered around the room whose purposes he couldn't begin to fathom, but before he had a chance to take a full inventory, she rushed in, wiping her hands on an old dishtowel. Strings of beads separated this room from the one she came from.

"So, you be wantin' your readin' now, huh?"

"Yes, please." Aaron shoved his hands deep into his pockets.

"Oh, Lordy. 'Please.' You are a polite one. I like dat about you, Aaron." She pulled out a stool for him to sit on, and then moved a stack of newspapers from a large and ornately carved chair to the couch. When she sat down on that large chair, she was the Queen Voodoo Priestess of New Orleans. It was her throne. She then put a rickety, old TV tray between them.

She laid her hand palm up on the TV tray and leaned forward just a bit. "Well, let me see your hand."

He held his hand out for her and flinched a little when she grabbed it. Her grip wasn't overpowering, but he certainly wasn't getting away without some effort. She rubbed her palm against his, uncurling his fingers as she did so. Her fingernails were long and manicured with a separate astrological sign painted on each one. "Mmm, yes, I can see it now."

"What?" He stared down at his own palm, trying to act aloof, but still attempting to see what she was seeing.

"You work hard for a living. This is rare for a kid these days." She looked back up at him. "What do you do?" Her Creole accent had diminished somewhat; it was tempered by something educated.

"I'm a small engine mechanic," he bragged. "Only part time though right now. I work a couple of days a week after school for a guy down the street."

"Yes," she whispered slowly and mysteriously, "I see dat."

Curious, he asked, "How?" and peered back at his palm again.

She cackled at him. "Boy, look at yo callouses! Anyone can see you don't spend yo time watching da devil box." He hadn't heard a TV called a devil box outside his family. His dad called it that from time to time in jest.

Aaron slumped his shoulders. "So I guess you aren't really a fortune teller, huh?"

"Not really, no," she said with a slight giggle as she gently released his hand. "I'm an educated black woman, living in New Orleans. Got my law degree ten years ago, but it didn't do me any good. I suspect all doze white men downtown think I'm too dangerous to work in one of dem high rises. So, I read palms and Tarot cards for the tourists to keep food on the table."

Aaron opened his mouth to reply but realized he didn't really know what to say. He was uncomfortable talking about race; he was worried he might say the wrong thing. He knew Nichelle Nichols, Lieutenant Uhura from *Star Trek*, was black, but that didn't seem to matter these days.

"Aaron, I'm going to ask you a few questions and I need you to be honest with me. Can you do dat?" She looked at him with an intensity that caused him to sit up a little straighter.

He remembered when Captain Kirk said, "*I don't like mysteries. They give me a bellyache,*" because he felt that way right now. If she wasn't a fortune teller, he was wondering why she lured him up here, why she wanted to ask him a bunch of questions. "What's this about?" He cocked his head somewhat to the side and slowly rubbed his clammy palms against his jeans.

She primped her hair and fluttered her eyelashes a couple of times while a pretty smile lit up her face. "Oh, just humor an old woman for a spell."

She didn't look that old to him, but he gave his okay with a small nod of his head.

"Do you like to get into fights?" she asked.

"Not really." He lightly shook his head. "When I was twelve, my dad wanted me to take Karate, but I chose Tai Chi instead."

"Why'd he want you to learn to fight?"

Aaron thrust his eyebrows up. "Oh, he didn't want me to learn to fight," he corrected her. "I have a temper and tend to lose my cool." He shrugged his shoulders. "I guess he thought it'd help me keep it under control. He got tired of me coming home all the time with a bloody nose and a black eye." He was surprised he was telling her this. It was really the first time in his life he had admitted it out loud.

"Does it?" she asked.

"I guess so. I don't get into nearly as many fights as I used to."

Jajine's laughter pleasantly rang out through the room. "You got self-control. Oh, dis is gonna be good! Now, have you ever killed an animal just for fun?"

That was a sick question. He narrowed his eyes and leaned back on the stool a bit. "No way!"

"You got compassion," she announced, slowly nodding her head. "Again, good. Just one more." She shifted on her throne, leaning toward him some. "Are you still a virgin?"

He was suddenly glad he was sitting down, because being in that small room with a moderately attractive woman, crazy or not, who was wearing exotic-looking gypsy clothes and talking about sex made him realize he had a hard-on. He leaned forward just a bit, to release the pressure of being bound up, and to hide any potentially embarrassing bulges. He was close to putting up some false bravado but felt a small compulsion to tell the truth. The lie forming in his mind dissipated like fog at sun up.

"Yes," he confessed, surprising himself.

"You're honest. Very good." She relaxed against the tall back of her throne and stared at him. She appeared to be trying to make a decision, tapping a fingernail on her front teeth. She sighed deeply and then asked,

6

"How big are you, boy, five foot two?"

"Five foot five," Aaron retorted, stung.

"And maybe 100 pounds soaking wet?"

"I compete in the Featherweight division during my Tai Chi matches. That's a hundred and thirty pounds!" He unconsciously pushed his chest out slightly to make himself look bigger than he was.

She sat up and clapped her hands together, smiling broadly at him. "And der's dat self-confidence I saw! Oh, ain't you da one. Yes, indeed. Yeah, you'll be able to take care of yourself, all right. But not today," she added derisively. She reached into a small, weaved basket sitting next to her chair. "Here, I have something for you." She held her hand up and Aaron saw she was holding a necklace made from a freshly cut leather thong with an inch and half long shiny fang, either a dog's or a wolf's, dangling from it.

He gingerly took it from her, afraid he might cut himself, and examined it closely.

"I want you to put dat necklace on and wear it," she softly commanded.

"This looks like silver," he uttered softly, in awe.

"Dat's 'cause it is, boy!" she exclaimed with a huge grin.

"I can't afford something like this," he protested with surprise. He didn't hand it back though, but continued to stare at it, fascinated with the way it glimmered in the light.

"Don't you worry 'bout dat none. It's yours now." She settled back into her chair again. "Now, Aaron, what I have to tell you is important," she explained with sincerity. "A few minutes ago I told you I wasn't a fortune teller. Dat ain't exactly true. I do have the gift of seeing the future on occasion, but not like most people think when they see what I do for a living. My mother had it, and all my grandmothers back as far as any of them could remember had it, too." She stopped talking and watched Aaron examine the necklace. "My mother and grandmother realized early on my gift was stronger than normal, and they spent as much time as possible teaching me everything they could about voodoo and the arts."

"Voodoo!" Aaron stopped looking at the necklace long enough to show his surprise.

Jajine chucked. "Yes, voodoo. But don't let dat scare you none. It isn't all black magic and zombies. Like any tool, or weapon, it's only as evil as those who wield it. I like my soul too much to use it for evil."

Aaron wasn't too convinced, but the necklace soaked up his attention.

"Well, I had one of my spells dis morning," she revealed. "It was about *Rex*, but not the parade. *Rex* means King. Did you know dat? Well, this was King Evil. Only…only it wasn't an evil like you would think about evil. It's more like…anti-good. When you told me you were marching in the Rex Parade, I knew it was about you, just as surely as I know the sun is hot."

Looking up from his examination of the tooth, Aaron asked, "What? You think I'm evil or something?"

"No, Aaron. I'm saying dat evil is coming for you. I can't protect you from it. Nobody can protect you from it. It's your fate dat you gotta face it. You'll need self-respect and courage. I see the potential for both of them in you."

"Then why the questions if you knew when you saw me?"

She smiled and clapped her hands again in delight. "Oh, you're a clever one, all right." Then she got serious again, and lowered her voice to a loud, conspiratorial whisper. "The questions were to see if you needed protecting. And you do. You're too innocent to be left to what dis evil would do to you if you didn't have protection. But as I said, I can't protect you. What I can do though is help prepare you for the day when it happens, help you develop the potential I see in you."

This all sounded like some con job to him. He was glad he left his wallet with his friends.

She must have sensed his disbelief, because she stopped the lecture and suggested, "Just wear the necklace. You'll learn soon enough what you need to do."

He wasn't sure why, but he felt an obligation to put it on. He tucked it under his shirt, and when the silver touched his skin, it was cold, colder than something that small should have been. It wasn't overwhelming though, so he left it in place. He then found himself getting up from his stool and staggering to the door. He wanted to say something, anything, but it was as if he was being controlled. He knew his legs were moving, but he couldn't stop them.

As he passed into the musty-smelling hallway, her voice echoed from all around him. "Remember to wear the necklace as much as possible. It'll teach you how to defend against this coming evil." He regained control of himself, but when he turned to the door, it was already shut.

Jajine traced a figure eight in the air, causing the door to close behind

Aaron. "Sweet dreams, boy." She turned and studied her snake as it slithered against the terrarium's glass, curling up against the end where she was closest. "Well, Luna, looks like fate may have smiled on us today." She stopped, as if listening for the snake to respond. "You don't have to tell me he's in danger. I know dat." She stopped to listen again. "No, I didn't put him in any more danger than he was already in. I'm helping dat boy out. But he's going to help me out, too. You just don't worry 'bout it no more." She stood up, went over to an end table, and turned a picture frame up that was face down. It contained the picture of a young man with strikingly similar features to Jajine's. "Joey, just a while longer, *mon cher*. Just a while longer, son."

Then she strode quickly into the kitchen, speaking to no one in particular. "*Lupus Rex*, my black ass. They want a *Lupus Rex*, I'll give 'em one their witches'll never see coming."

Part I—Paedagogus

noun [pe-də-gäg'-əs]

1. Tutor. 2. Guide.

Chapter 1—John Billings

Fall 1923-1928

John Billings ran down the narrow trail next to Sanderson Lake. David and Donnie Knorr and Hale Hopstein were right behind him, shouting for him to stop. It was late autumn, so most of the leaves had fallen off of the trees; there would be no hiding from his tormentors today. He jumped and skipped over rocks and dodged around trees and bushes, doing everything in his power to keep from falling. If he fell, they would catch up with him, and he would end up with another black eye or a ripped shirt. The black eye, he could handle. The ripped shirt would mean his mother would have to stitch it up while he listened to her complain about him playing too hard. They couldn't afford to buy another shirt.

David and Hale were both older and much bigger than he was. Donnie, or Little Donnie as everyone called him, was David's younger brother; he was smaller than John, but with David backing him up, it didn't matter. You didn't take on Little Donnie without David getting into the mix.

"We just wanna talk!" Hale yelled.

"Yeah, slow down, Johnny!" shouted David.

Yeah, right, John thought as he performed a perfect sprinting leap over a tangle of wait-a-minute vines.

John's day started out nice enough. He made it to school without running into them and managed to avoid them all day long. He almost made it home just as successfully. He usually survived the trip down the trail without running into them, but they surprised him today by jumping out of the woods right after he passed them by. He didn't think they were waiting for him, but it didn't matter; they were there now. Luckily, they were behind him and not in front of him—but they were still close enough that he couldn't easily get away.

He was listening to a couple of woodpeckers and enjoying the hard smell of the cold forest, and had made it about half-way down the trail, when a cracking twig and the familiar, sarcastic tone that could only be

Hale's voice broke John out of his daydream. John recognized his most avid tormenter before he even turned around to face him.

"Well, well, boys, what have we here?" Hale asked. " Johnny's lost. He's using our trail and he ain't paid the toll."

Little Donnie stuck his thumbs in his suspenders and rocked forward on his toes. His voice hadn't changed yet so it came out squeaky. "Yeah, he ain't paid the toll!"

David stepped up next to Little Donnie and put his hand on his shoulder. "He sure ain't, little brother." He peered back at Hale and winked. "Donnie, why don't you go and collect it for us?"

Little Donnie's expression rapidly changed from an arrogant smile to a gawking, wide-eyed, open-mouthed look of alarm. He looked up at David, swallowed a nervous lump in his throat. "Me?" he asked.

Hale laughed while he moved up and stood on Little Donnie's other side. "Yeah, you! You said you wanna be part of our gang. Well, you gotta earn your keep. Right now, you owe me and your brother a nickel each."

"That's…that's ten cents, Hale!" Little Donnie exclaimed. He turned to David and pleaded with his older brother, "David, Johnny ain't got no ten cents! He's poor!" He then timidly regarded John with that worried expression.

David declared, "You wanna be part of the gang, do like Hale said. I'm sure he's got something worth that much."

And that was all John needed to hear, and why he was now running down the trail instead of leisurely hiking down it listening to a woodpecker. So far, he had managed to stay ahead of them, but he knew Old Man Goetz's farm was right ahead. Open field. They would catch him, no doubt. He was better at maneuvering than they were in the twists and turns of the woods, but in the open, there would be nothing to dodge around. They would run him down like a pack of wild dogs.

He burst into the open field of the Goetz farm. The sun bathed his face in unwelcomed warmth—unwelcomed because it signaled his loss of forest cover. He scanned ahead across the low scrub and mounds of dirt from the recently harvested field. It might as well have been twenty miles to the other side. He knew he wouldn't make it. *Well, I might as well turn and around take my licks. Someone's gonna get something back though, I swear it!* Then Mr. Goetz's barn grabbed his attention. It was the only structure, and the only possible safe haven, between him and the other side of the field. It was a classic design, found throughout the Pennsylvania farming country. There would be a nice two-story loft in there.

He turned slightly to the left and put on another burst of speed. The pack of wild-boys continued their pursuit, hooting and hollering as they closed the gap between them. He was relieved to see the doors were open when he rounded the corner of the barn. That was good news; Mr. Goetz was probably close by. You don't leave barn doors open. He ran inside and quickly glanced around. He was alone except for the smell of manure and stored hay. He saw the ladder to his right and made it to the top and around a bale of hay just as Hale ran through the doorway.

"Johhnnyy, where arrre you…?"

David came in, dragging Little Donnie behind him. "If we lost him because you can't run, you're getting that black eye instead, Runt!"

Hale pointed up at the loft and yelled, "I'll bet he's up there! Ha Ha! We got you now, Johnny Boy!"

John quickly glanced around the loft for a way out. A dim light from the roof vents cast long shadows around the loft, but it was still enough to see by. The hay lift door was closed and bales of hay, stacked three high, filled the loft. He could probably maneuver around them and perhaps dodge one of the cretins, but not all three.

What's that in the corner? He ran over to it and saw it was a steamer trunk. He opened the lid, hoping to find some kind of weapon he could use to defend himself. All he saw was about a dozen quart-sized bottles of some clear liquid. He picked one up and felt its heft. *These might make for nice little surprise.* He picked up four and turned to listen for where his tormentors might be. The ladder creaked under the strain of someone climbing it.

"Here I come, Johnny Boy!" Hale teased. "Ready or not!"

John stepped out from behind one of the bales of hay and threw one of the glass jars at Hale's head just as it popped up over the edge of the loft. He told himself he was trying to scare them, but his aim was too accurate for that. He recognized too late the face that followed the top of the head. It didn't belong to Hale—it belonged to Little Donnie. John watched in horror as the jar flew through the air, hitting Little Donnie right in the nose. He cried out in pain and then screamed even louder when he fell and hit the barn floor. John grabbed another jar and ran to the edge of the loft.

He scolded them, "You cowards sent Little Donnie up after me?"

Little Donnie was on the barn floor holding a bloody nose. "David, it burns! It burns!"

David and Hale stared up at John. David threatened, "I'm fixin' to come up there and kick your ass for that!"

John sneered down at him, feeling just a bit more confident now that he knew he was in a position of strength. "Well, if you're feeling like you gotta do something, come on up. You'll only be able to do it one at time, though. I've got enough jars for each of you."

Suddenly, a loud voice boomed out, "Hold it right there!" Willard Goetz had finally arrived on the scene. John let a sigh of relief escape his lips as he saw the tall and lean man stomp through the barn doorway. He had his work hat on, but John knew he was balding underneath. He kept his face clean-shaven during the warmer months, but he was getting it ready for the cold season—a beard was partially covering his face.

Hale's bold demeanor withered into youthful vulnerability. "Mr. Goetz! Johnny up there threw a jar at Little Donnie here and done broke his nose."

David added, "He ain't done nuthin' to deserve it neither!"

Little Donnie was still crying, "It burns, David! My leg hurts, too!"

Mr. Goetz kneeled down by Little Donnie and examined him. "Well, his leg is definitely busted, and his nose is, too. And a few scratches on his face. He'll live, but he won't be running around soon." He pulled a handkerchief from his pocket and put it on Little Donnie's nose. "Hold this here, son. It'll stop bleeding in a few minutes."

John thought that if David could have found a hole to crawl into and hide, he would have. "He done broke his leg? Pa's gonna kill me!"

Mr. Goetz curtly nodded his head. "Well, I reckon that might be, but I doubt it'll go that far. More likely, you'll get the strap, if'n I know your pa." He then leaned over and appeared to be sniffing. He raised his head and squinted up into the darkness of the loft, up where John was standing, and saw the jar in his hand. "Put those jars back in the trunk. Don't need no damn revenuers running around these here parts."

As John returned the three unbroken jars to the trunk, Mr. Goetz said, "So, he didn't do anything, huh? I've seen treed squirrels and coons before. Looks to me like you boys done treed yourself a mean one today!"

Hale protested, "That ain't what happened, Mr. Goetz! Honest Injun!"

Mr. Goetz stood up. "Well, I'll let your fathers sort it out. In the meantime, Hale, there's a wheelbarrow under that tarp over yonder. Get it and tote Little Donnie up to the house while I go hitch up the buckboard.

We got to get him down to Doc Ellison."

He looked up at John as he came out from beside the bale of hay. "You can come on down, son," he offered. "I think you done made your point." He cast a stern gaze on David and Hale. "Ain't no one gonna bother you no more today, I reckon."

Mr. Goetz was right those five years ago. David and Hale acted like they were old friends of John's when he crawled down from that loft, and they all worked together getting Little Donnie into the wheelbarrow.

After Mr. Goetz and John dropped the cretins off at the doctor's house, Mr. Goetz took John home. Although Mr. Goetz didn't say anything, when they pulled up in front of John's house, John could see the sadness in his eyes. John and his mother were dirt poor and had been since John's father got killed when he tried to rob the bank down on Main Street. John and his mother lived in a two room shack so far on the other side of the tracks, they might as well have lived in the next town. The porch sagged from end to end, and they had placed large stones and scrap lumber under sections of it to keep it off the ground and out of the water when it rained. The front door's window was broken and replaced with a piece of scrap lumber. The roof's tar paper was ripped in a few places, and a poor man's patchwork of thin lead sheets was the only thing holding the elements at bay.

John's mother hurried out, twisting an old handkerchief around her nervous fingers, as Mr. Goetz pulled to a stop. People didn't usually visit the Billings since they were the "wrong sort." She was wearing a long work dress, and her dun-colored hair was up in a bun, sprouting out from various holes in a black net, torn from years of use. John jumped off the buckboard and ran up onto the porch and stood next to her.

Mr. Goetz climbed down and took off his hat. "Mrs. Billings, my name is Willard Goetz."

"I know who you are, Mr. Goetz. What can I do for you?"

"You should know your son helped a young boy to the doctor today."

His mother's eyes flew open in alarm. "Who was it?" She cast her attention questioningly down at John, eyebrows raised, and furrows of distress lining her face. "Is he okay?"

Mr. Goetz replied, "It was Little Donnie Knorr, and yes, Ma'am, he'll be fine. I just thought you should know what a hero you have for a son."

Now it was John's turn to gawk, eyes wide and mouth hanging open.

His mother stood a little straighter, and the years melted off of her. He saw what a beautiful woman she must have been long ago. Pride filled her face, and it was all shining on him.

Then with a start, she ripped that attention away. "Pardon my manners, Mr. Goetz. Thank you for bringing him home. Would you care for a jar of pickled red beet eggs? I just canned a batch, so they're fresh."

"Thank you, but no, Ma'am, that won't be necessary. I would like to ask a favor of you, though. With your permission, of course, if you don't think me too forward."

John's mother asked, "What could I do for you, Mr. Goetz?"

"Well, my farm needs looking after from time to time." Mr. Goetz ran his hand through his thinning hair. "I'm getting up in years, and it's getting harder to do all the things that need doing. With both my sons killed during the Great War, I just don't have the help I need." He stopped and tilted his head slightly, pointing it over toward John. "John here has proven himself to be honest and a hard worker. I would consider it an honor to have him help keep things running. Just until I get back on my feet, you see."

"I'm not sure. He has school and all, and—"

Mr. Goetz quickly interrupted her, "I would be happy to pay him a fair wage. I wouldn't expect him to work for free."

At the sound of the word "wage," Mr. Goetz got both John's and his mother's undivided attention. John spoke up first, "Ma, I can do it. It's on the way home from school, so I can work there 'til dark and then come home. His place ain't that far from here."

His mother didn't take much convincing. She kept busy with odd sewing jobs and seasonal farm work, but having some steady income would be nice. "Thank you, Mr. Goetz." Then she struck a somewhat regal pose, nose up and back straight. "But, if it doesn't work out," she decreed, "I want you to tell me immediately. We don't take charity, and we won't have you carrying us, either."

"Of course, Mrs. Billings." He turned to John. "I'll see you tomorrow after school, young man."

John smiled. "Yes, Sir! I'll be there!"

"I know you will." Mr. Goetz returned the smile. "Say, have you got some work clothes? Coveralls, gloves, and the like?"

John was crestfallen. Without the proper tools, Mr. Goetz wouldn't be able to use him. He was going to get fired from his first job, and he hadn't

16

worked day one. "No, Sir."

Mr. Goetz reached into his pocket and pulled out a wad of bills. He pulled a few of them off the top and handed them to John. "Stop by Hank's Dry Goods tomorrow and get yourself a good pair of boots, leather work gloves, and some denim coveralls." John gingerly took the cash as Mr. Goetz quickly glanced at John's mother and added, "This is a loan mind you, not a gift. I'll take it out of his first few pays."

Over the years, John outgrew those coveralls, and the next pair he bought, too. And the boots. Though the first pair was big to start with, they wore out before he outgrew them. With the money he made working for Mr. Goetz, he and his mother were able to get the holes in the roof and walls on their house repaired. They were even able to afford some meat once a week for a stew on Sundays.

Mr. Goetz was more than John's boss, though. He became the father John lost so many years earlier. Everything John knew about being a man, he learned from watching Mr. Goetz.

Five years, John thought. *It ain't seemed that long.* John finished locking the barn down for the night and headed up to Mr. Goetz's house. The old man worked you hard, but he was fair; you got paid for the work you did. He'd been working for him, doing everything that needed doing ever since that fateful day in the barn.

He knocked on the door when he got up to Mr. Goetz's porch, and then let himself in. Mrs. Goetz had just finished setting the table. The smell of freshly baked bread, candied carrots, and fried chicken made John's stomach grumble.

"Well, hello, John. It's good to see you this evening. I don't think I've seen you in a few days."

"No, Ma'am. I've been out in the south forty, fixing that fence. Them cows have been pushing—"

She corrected him; John figured *once a teacher, always a teacher.* "—*Those* cows. John, you're a man now. If you plan to make it in today's world, you need to learn proper grammar."

"Yes, Ma'am. *Those* cows have been pushing against the posts again. I think I've about got them all fixed now. Why they think the grass is sweeter on the other side, I'll never know."

She nonchalantly dismissed the current conversation with a simple, "That's nice." Then she handed him a basket smelling like fresh pumpernickel. "Here are some different breads and a bit of butter for your mother. Give her my best."

"Thank you, Mrs. Goetz, I will."

Mr. Goetz walked in with an envelope.

This was their routine every Friday evening. John would come in, make small talk with Mrs. Goetz, and get a basket of various food stuffs. His mother complained about it being charity the first couple of times, until John finally convinced her it was part of his pay. Still, she wouldn't let go of the notion she owed Mrs. Goetz something for it, so she knitted various articles for John to take to her—a hat, a scarf, or whatever she had the scraps for. Then Mr. Goetz would hand him an envelope containing his pay for the week. He used to give John the cash directly, but Mrs. Goetz complained about it being "gauche." John had to look that word up in the town library to understand what she meant.

John took the envelope and thanked them both. Suddenly, a bloodcurdling shriek tore through the walls and the windows. It didn't sound like a cow, but it didn't sound like a wildcat either.

Mr. Goetz looked at John. "Get the shotguns while I get my boots on."

John set his basket down on the floor and ran down the hallway to the gun cabinet. He pulled out the two shotguns Mr. Goetz kept handy for dealing with the larger, unwelcome visitors to his farm. They were both 12 gauge, side by side double-barrel breakdown models. He verified they were unloaded before shoving a couple handfuls of shells into his pockets. Mrs. Goetz kept her poise as she carried the basket back to her kitchen, but John could tell the shriek had her feeling uneasy.

John met Mr. Goetz at the front door, and as they stepped out onto the porch, the shriek split the night air again. It came from the north end of the field. The sun had just gone down behind the horizon, but the moon was full; they saw the barn doors were both closed.

Mr. Goetz asked, "The horses are stabled, right?"

"Yes, Sir!" John answered, his voice quivering with alarm and excitement. "I did it myself before I came up to the house."

They each grabbed a lantern off the front porch and lit them quickly. They trotted toward where the sound was coming from, but before they got very far a low and guttural howl froze them in their tracks. Both men gripped their weapons more tightly.

"What the hell was that, John?"

"I don't know, Sir. But I'll tell you, I haven't been this scared since the time you found me hiding out in your barn."

Mr. Goetz looked up at John with renewed respect on his face. "Well, John, if I had to have anyone with me right now, I'd want it to be you. It takes a big man to admit when he's scared. Let's go."

They headed out into the darkness. Although the moon gave them light to see by, the lanterns extinguished the shadows at their feet and allowed them to walk without fear of tripping over unseen obstacles. They could hear the animals shuffling restlessly inside the barn as they approached it.

Mr. Goetz muttered, "I would say it's a panther out there, but I'm not sure what that howl was."

"Maybe it's a panther and wolf fighting over something."

Mr. Goetz nodded his head. "That might-would explain things."

They hurried on past the barn and headed north into the field.

John whispered, "Shutter your lantern. I think I see something."

The lanterns had ruined their night-vision, but John's younger eyes still made out out something near the tree line. Whatever it was moved rapidly across his field of vision and disappeared down the trail he took as a child to get back and forth to school. He couldn't quite tell what *it* was, though.

Mr. Goetz quietly asked, "What did you see, John?"

"I'm not sure. It looked like a man, but it moved too fast. It seems to have dodged into the woods over by the lake."

Mr. Goetz peered over in that direction, squinting and trying to see anything out of the ordinary. "I don't see anything."

"It's gone."

"Did you see where it came from?"

"I think so." John pointed the shotgun in the direction where he first saw the shape. "Over there."

They unshuttered their lanterns and cautiously walked over to where John thought the shape had been. The smell of dead animal hit them in the face as they approached. A small Holstein calf with its stomach ripped open and its ropy guts steaming in the cold night air lay at their feet.

Mr. Goetz stated, "The only Holstein calves I know of around here are from the Widow Marley's place, up the road. How in the hell did it get down here, John?"

John looked around the monochrome-colored field. "I'm more concerned about what killed it."

19

Two months later, John and Mr. Goetz stared down at the deer lying at their feet. Its stomach was ripped open just like the calf from the month before last, and the pig from last month. Three months in a row there had been a fight followed by a howling that sent shivers up their backs.

"Mr. Goetz, the first one of these we found was weird. The second one in the same place like this? Coincidence. This third one tells me we got a critter that's taken a likin' to your north field. And it's big. Look at the size of the claw marks. I bet if we'd measured them from last time, they'd be a good match."

"I think you're right, John." Mr. Goetz stalked a circle around the carcass, kneeling down with his lantern every couple of steps, looking for any clue as to what they were up against.

John looked off to the night-blackened forest bordering the farm. "We need to find it and kill it. If it happens upon someone unprepared, it might kill them."

"The Knorrs are known for their tracking skills," Mr. Goetz pondered aloud. "Maybe we could interest them in this."

John winced at that suggestion. He'd had occasional problems out of David, Donnie, and Hale ever since the incident in the barn, but the last couple of years they'd pretty much left him alone. He suspected it was because he'd outgrown them all. Even so, he tried to stay clear of them. Mr. Goetz was right, though. Mr. Knorr was called in from time to time to help track down fugitives who had taken to the hills. David was getting good at it, too, if the rumors were right.

John looked back in the direction of the house. "I'll go get them."

Mr. Goetz shook his head. "Let's wait until morning."

"Why not tonight while the tracks are still fresh?"

"Whatever is killing these animals is big and mean. And deadly," Mr. Goetz explained. "I'd rather we didn't run into it at night. I reckon it wouldn't take kindly to us."

"Yeah, you're probably right."

"Come help me hitch up the buckboard. I'll give you a ride home."

John let out a sigh of relief. He didn't want to be out wandering around with that critter out there.

The next morning, after John finished his duties around Mr. Goetz's farm, they rode out to the Knorr's. They lived a few miles away, up on a ridge overlooking the town. It was a nice house, one of the nicer ones around, but it was old and not kept up. It had two stories, was made of brick, and had a tar and tile roof. Smoke coiled out of the chimney; the weather had turned chilly the last few weeks. Mr. Knorr's truck, a rarity around the Sanderson Lake area, was parked in front. He made good money running 'shine up and down the mountain.

Mr. Goetz rode up the driveway and four large hounds came running out to greet them, baying and barking. As the buckboard reached the house, David, Donnie, and their dad, William, came out. Mr. Knorr was a short and thin man with a scraggly beard that never seemed to completely cover his chin. His overalls were too large for him, making him look even smaller than he really was. He shouted in a baritone voice at the dogs and they quieted down, going from noise makers to friendly pets, wagging their tails and nipping at each other playfully.

John's feet had no more touched the ground and the dogs rushed over to him, sniffing, and whining, and begging for him to pet them. He kneeled down, showing some attention to one and the other three swarmed him, expecting their share.

Donnie called the dogs over. "Blue! Trailer! Get over here. Leave Johnny alone!" He went over and grabbed two of them by the collar. "Sorry, Johnny. They're just no-good hounds."

John smiled up at him. "That's okay, Donnie. I don't mind. I don't have a dog, but I like them." Donnie let go of the dogs and they crowded back around John.

After Mr. Goetz and Mr. Knorr shook hands, Mr. Knorr asked, "Whatcha got, Will?"

Mr. Goetz took his hat off and scratched his head. "Bill, I've got a problem I think only you can fix."

Mr. Knorr narrowed his eyes in interest. "Oh, yeah? What's that?"

"We got some kind of critter running around my farm. It's killed three different animals over the last three months, a calf, a hog, and a deer. It got the deer last night. I was hoping you might be interested in tracking it down and killing it."

"Whaddya 'spect it is? Wolf, cougar?"

"I ain't sure. It carried a calf from the Widow Marley's farm to my north field. It's got to be big, whatever it is. My first guess is wolf. Me and John there heard it howl a few times."

Mr. Knorr scrunched his eyebrows together. "Hmm. My guess is wolf, too, if'n it howled." He scratched his scraggly whiskers with dirt-encrusted fingernails. "Only a cougar would tote a calf that far though. It killed a deer last night, you say?"

"Yeah, we left the carcass there if you care to come take a look."

"Yeah, I'll come on down." Mr. Knorr turned to his boys. "Load 'em up."

David and Donnie leapt into action. David yelled, "Awright, Blue! Load 'em up!"

One of the dogs, Blue, ran toward Mr. Knorr's truck as he let out a small yip and a short howl. The other three followed him and they all jumped up into the back, barking and baying. They knew it was time to hunt.

Donnie ran toward the house. "I'll get the guns, Pa!"

Mr. Knorr yelled back, "And get my jacket!"

While Mr. Knorr examined the deer carcass and the tracks around the area, David and Donnie were standing over by the truck with two baying dogs each on leashes. It was all they could do to keep the dogs from running over toward the stinking deer carcass; something needed tracking and they were ready to get to work.

Mr. Knorr's brows creased in concentration. He asserted softly, "Will, this ain't no cougar done this."

John shuffled his feet while Mr. Goetz asked, "What was it then?"

"I ain't sure. Looks like a wolf, but it's the biggest damned wolf I ever seen."

"What next? We track it?"

"Yep." He quickly stood up, his face cheery with a large and confident grin. "Gonna make a mighty nice rug when I'm done with him." He went over to his truck, pulled out his rifle and started checking it. "Will, you and John better go arm yourselves. It ain't gonna like us walking up on it where it's done hid out."

By the time John ran up to the house and retrieved the shotguns, Mr. Knorr had found a clean spoor and had his boys come up with the dogs. They were nearly pulling the boys off their feet as they surged toward the source.

He waited for John and Mr. Goetz to get ready before slinging his own rifle over his shoulder and taking the leashes. With two dogs in each hand, he let them lead him where they would. He yelled to the lead dog, "Yeah, Ol' Blue! Hoot! Hoot! Come on, Blue! Hoot! Hoot!"

They all followed the dogs through the woods down an old animal trail until it got to Bodir Creek, one of the feeders for Sanderson Lake. The dogs lost the scent and snuffled up and down the bank for a few minutes. They were huffing and puffing so much in the cool morning air it looked like a steam whistle on a train. Mr. Knorr took them to the other side where they picked up the scent again. Whatever they were tracking jumped at least twenty-five feet, clean over the creek onto the other side. The dogs scrambled up the other side of the bank and their baying took on a renewed urgency as they crested the ridge running along it. They all but dragged Mr. Knorr down the other side and through the woods.

They followed the dogs for a good hour. Whatever they were tracking made phenomenal leaps and landed quite far from where it had jumped, and they spent precious time picking the scent back up.

They were starting to get to a thinner part of the forest when David spoke up. "Hale lives out round these here parts."

Mr. Knorr asked, "Where exactly?"

"Right where Ol' Blue is leading us looks like, Pa. Down the end of this ridge, up off'n Carson Road."

Donnie grabbed David's sleeve and asked with a shaky voice, "Do you think the wolf got Hale? We ain't seen him in a spell."

David comforted his little brother. "I don't think so, Donnie. Hale's pretty tough."

Sure enough, the dogs led the group right up to Hale's front door. Hale's dad, Ed Hopstein, came rushing out onto the porch with a shotgun in his hands. The approach of the baying dogs didn't appear to be something he was expecting that morning.

Mr. Hopstein looked out at the posse standing in front of his porch. "What's this about, Bill?"

Mr. Knorr held the dogs in check and looked apologetically back up at him. "Ed, we been tracking a wolf the last hour or so. Ya'll ain't got one in there do ya?"

Mr. Hopstein rested his shotgun over his shoulder and asked, "Now why in tarnation would I have a wolf in my house, Bill?"

"Well, I don't rightly know." Mr. Knorr looked down at his dogs, confused. "I'm not sure what they thought they was a trailin' if'n they come up on your house and not some wolf den."

Just then, Hale stepped out from around the house, and the dogs went into a near panic, pulling and yanking on their leashes. Before Mr. Knorr could get them under control, they broke free and rushed Hale.

What John saw Hale change into caused him to rethink everything he knew about the world and changed the direction of the rest of his life.

Hale let out a guttural howl. His face contorted and twisted, turning dark and hairy. His mouth and nose extended into a short snout with long, deadly fangs. The rest of his body elongated; his arms stretched out through his sleeves and his legs grew longer. His hands turned into a mixture between a human hand and a wolf's paw, fingers drawn-out with sharp talons on the ends. The monster ripped its clothes to shreds as it pulled them from its body. Everyone froze in their tracks. Only John and Mr. Goetz retained any semblance of self-control; this wasn't the first time they'd heard the howl. Still, they anxiously looked for a place to hide from the monster standing before them.

John found himself forcefully turned around by Mr. Goetz. He yanked the shotgun out of John's hands and yelled, "Get out of here! Just run, John! Run!"

John didn't need any convincing. He sprinted off into the woods. One of the dogs whimpered in pain and let out in a yip that was cut short either because it was dead or because it could no longer cry out. Gunshots echoed, shaking him out of his panic long enough to stop and steal a glance over his shoulder. Hale, or the monster he had become, picked up Mr. Goetz and bit him on the head, puncturing his skull with long, deadly fangs, and finally crushing it. Hale shook him like a rag doll and then tossed him against the house. Mr. Goetz's body lay where it fell, arms and legs twitching. John turned toward the only place of safety he could remember in his panic, Mr. Goetz's barn. The sounds of gunshots, baying, and men screaming in alarm, panic, and terror followed him into the forest.

John made it to the barn without much trouble. He knew the woods from a lifetime of running through them, sometimes running *from* someone through them. It may have taken them an hour to track the wolf, or

Hale...the monster, but it only took him about fifteen minutes to run back. The noises of the fight behind him slowly faded to nothingness as he crossed the second ridge. The only evidence of his dash back was the *crunch-crunch-crunch* of his footfalls and the *huh-huh-huh* of his breathing.

Just run, John! Run!

Mr. Goetz was dead and probably the Knorrs, too. Mr. Goetz had given him the precious moments needed to make it to the woods. He hoped the monster didn't see him as he made his escape. With four dogs and four humans—did Hale's dad help?—attacking it, perhaps it was too busy to think about John. He hoped so. He never clearly saw the monster on any of those nights, but what he did see that first night showed it moved fast. It wouldn't have much trouble running him down once it picked up his scent.

Just run, John! Run!

He cleared the edge of the woods on Mr. Goetz's farm and saw the barn. Safety!

The forest echoed with a muffled howl.

John didn't think it was close, but he knew it was after him. Like so many years before when he was running from David, Donnie, and Hale, he put on that little extra burst of speed. He knew this time though the barn doors would be closed. He'd closed them himself after turning the animals out and before everyone struck out this morning. He rounded the corner of the barn, raised the cross bar, flung open the door, and ran inside toward the ladder leading up to the loft. He climbed up and made a beeline for the steamer trunk full of moonshine.

He grabbed the handle on the side of the trunk and dragged it to the edge of the loft. The monster howled again only this time it wasn't deadened by the woods. It was clear, as if coming across the field. John threw several jars of moonshine onto the floor of the barn, breaking them and scattering the 'shine all over. He pulled out his box of matches, lit a small lantern Mr. Goetz kept up in the loft, and waited.

A shadow passed by the barn door, shortening as the monster slowly crept in through the doorway. It was on all fours, about the size of a pony, and sniffing. Its gaze fell upon John, and John knew it was coming for him. It slinked into the barn, growling, looking around for any surprises, and stopped when it got to the spilled 'shine. Moonshine isn't neutral smelling; it has a distinctive odor. It looked around the barn and up at John and then back down at the floor again. It sensed something was wrong and started backing out the way it came in.

John yelled, "Come on, you coward! You sent Donnie up here! You too yella to come up yourself?!" He launched a couple of the jars at it.

It dodged the two jars easily enough, snarled and growled at John, and then leapt for the ladder before he had a chance to throw the lantern. It was too fast! And it had avoided the spill altogether. John knew he had to get it into the moonshine somehow. He reached down for another jar, and as the monster showed its head above the edge of the loft, he let the jar fly. Just like Donnie so long ago, he hit it square in the face. The jar shattered, covering the monster's head and upper body in moonshine. It fell off of the ladder and into the spill.

John watched its eyes track the lantern as it shattered on the ground at its feet.

The monster, howling in pain and anger, and the barn, were rapidly being consumed by fire. John frantically looked around and realized in horror he hadn't planned his situation out too well. There was no way out. He looked back at the hay lift door. It was usually latched, but from the inside. He ran along the loft toward it, hoping he could get it open in time. The moonshine-based fire's flames were already licking their way up to the loft as the straw rapidly fed its voracious appetite.

He made it to the door, but the smoke was overwhelming, stinging his eyes and burning his throat and lungs. His fingers were pieces of cord wood as he tried to work the latching mechanism. The only light he had to work by was a skinny sliver of sunlight coming in between the doors, but it was too smoke-hazy to be of much use. A blast of heat on his back told him the fire was close. He looked over his shoulder and watched it dash toward his feet. He couldn't get the lock open! In a panic, he pushed against the doors, trying to break free from the lack of oxygen and the heat. He kept pushing the doors, rocking them back and forth. Finally, with a loud snap of wood and the squealing of nails and screws releasing their stubborn grip on the frame, the door flew open.

John saw the ground rushing up to him and knew this was the final moments of his life. He hoped his mother would be all right without him. He was remorseful he burned down Mr. Goetz's barn, but was just as happy he turned out the animals that morning.

As he landed in the pile of straw under the hay lift door, he heard Mrs. Goetz scream, "John, No!"

Chapter 2—Quadrivium

noun [kwä-dri-(v)(w)ē-əm]
1. Crossroad.

Aaron Darveau, May 1975

Aaron is having the nightmare again. It is as familiar to him as his own face in the mirror. He knows how it progresses and has no choice but to experience it as if it were new each time it occurs. He's never been able to wake himself up from it.

The dream always starts out the same way. He's in his back yard raking the leaves. It's hard keeping them in one area because the wind is blowing. He looks up at the gathering storm clouds and hopes he can get it done before his dad gets home. He has a date tonight, but he can't leave until his chores are done.

Aaron quickly sat up in bed, fully awake. It was still dark outside, but the cricket and cicada songs would have told him that even if his eyes were still closed. *Whoa! What's up with that dream?* Ever since his trip to New Orleans two years earlier, ever since Jajine told him evil was coming for him, he'd had it every couple of months.

The first time, it only got as far as him picking up his rake. Each time it came again though, it went a little further and turned more to nightmare than dream. It was baffling how the dream sharpened his senses, kept him alert. Whenever his senses relaxed, whenever he forgot about Madame Jajine's warning, the dream would return even more intensely, and his senses would be heightened again.

Aaron tried to get back to sleep but couldn't, so he went out and puttered around in his dad's shop for a couple of hours. When daylight arrived, he took a shower and then drove over to Master Chen's church for some meditation to calm down. The church was really a large gathering room, converted for use as a church, behind a Chinese restaurant. Master Chen was his Sifu, his Tai Chi teacher, and had been for over six years. Aaron meditated by standing in the Horse, Tai Chi's version of the seated Lotus position—arms hanging in midair in front of the body, knees bent and just covering the toes from sight if you looked down, chin tucked.

Unfortunately, Aaron couldn't get through his exercises without staring up at the studio's ceiling in agitation. The air conditioning unit had been making a racket all week, but today it was especially annoying. In addition to the squeaking and banging and rattling, it was giving off a particularly damp and sour odor—the drain line probably needed cleaning. Master

Chen told Aaron he was trying to get a repairman over to work on it, but like everything else in Monroe, Louisiana in the mid-1970s, if you weren't a local, getting help was hard. *I'll probably have to fix it myself. Again.* Aaron practically worked there at Master Chen's church, so getting up on the roof and performing the needed routine maintenance again wasn't a problem.

Master Chen had repeatedly tried to "officially" hire Aaron as an assistant Sifu. He didn't mind helping out when he was there for meditation and training, but he enjoyed his other pursuits too much—girls, fishing, girls, cars, girls, and some *Star Trek* when he could catch it on the family's devil box—to be tied down to that as a job. Besides, he wasn't sure his parents would have appreciated the fact he was working at a Confucian church, being Southern Baptist and all.

None of that mattered now though. He had graduated from high school and had already joined the navy. He had a job, or at least he would in another two weeks when he was scheduled to leave. He still hadn't told Master Chen. He wasn't purposely trying to hide the information, but he also wasn't sure how to tell the man who had turned him from a belligerent little boy into a confident young man that he was ready to strike out on his own. Whenever his Sifu asked what his plans were, Aaron sputtered and stuttered and changed the subject.

After Aaron finished his meditation, Master Chen came over and reprimanded him in a thick, broken Chinese accent. "Aaron, you look horrible! Form bad! Breathing bad! You not a beginner! What's your problem?"

Aaron sighed. "I had a bad dream again last night, Sifu."

"Again?" Master Chen asked as he raised his eyebrows. "You having bad dreams? Why you not tell me?"

Aaron shrugged his shoulders. "It wasn't that important. But last night's left me a bit shaken."

Master Chen bowed slightly to Aaron. "Honor me with your troubles."

Aaron hesitated, looking Master Chen in the eyes momentarily. "Okay, but don't laugh. Promise?"

"Promise."

"Remember that trip to New Orleans a couple of years ago?" Aaron asked.

"Yes," Master Chen answered. He ground his eyebrows together and slowly shook his head. "Pah! You gone for week. Got drunk. No Tai Chi practice. Very bad for you. Almost have to start over with lessons."

Aaron's eyes flew open. "How did you know that?" he exclaimed. "Never mind. It's not important." Aaron had learned to never question Master Chen on such matters. The conversation always ended up sounding like someone describing a dog chasing its tail, with Aaron being the dog. "Let's sit down, please. This is going to be a long story."

Aaron took a deep breath and related the events surrounding Madam Jajine to Master Chen, leaving nothing out. "And that same night," Aaron finished, "that very night, I started having the dreams. Do you think they mean anything?"

Master Chen slowly curled a lock of his greying beard between his fingers. "Everything in life means something to someone," he proclaimed. "What do *you* think they mean?"

Aaron shrugged his shoulders. "I have no clue. It's probably just Madam Jajine's weirdness getting in my way. But it's been over two years!" he exclaimed. "I've tried calling her to find out if she had any clue, but her phone's temporarily disconnected at her request. I can't get in touch with her." Aaron sighed. "Why am I still having them?"

Master Chen sat quietly. His eyes were slightly squinted while he observed Aaron, the rest of his face dark with concern. "Dream scary?"

Aaron thought for a moment. "Not really, no."

Master Chen stopped stroking his beard. "What is it then?"

"It's…it's more like the fact I am having them that is scaring me. Madam Jajine seemed honestly concerned with me. So even if I believed in all of this voodoo crap—which I don't—and she had something to do with them, I don't think she's purposefully trying to scare me. I do think the dreams mean something though. I just don't know what, and I'm tired of waiting to find out."

Master Chen chuckled. "Yes, you most impatient student I ever have." He then quieted down for moment before asking, "You know Tai Chi when you come to studio first time?"

"No."

"Why?" Master Chen asked, the Sifu in him taking hold. This was a test.

"I hadn't traveled the path yet."

"Good," Master Chen stated with a smile and a slight nod of his head. "These dreams, they new path for you. You must walk path and find end. I think you find crossroads at end. Your choice, it affect whole rest of life."

"From a dream?" Aaron asked.

"Yes."

"You've taught me all paths have crossroads," Aaron maintained, "but you've never mentioned anything about traveling them in dreams. What makes you think this one is so important?"

"Because dream make you forget how to breathe." Master Chen stood up in full Sifu mode. "Pah! I not sure how you survive in navy without me to watch you."

Aaron gasped. "You...you know I'm going into the navy? How?"

"Ha ha! Mother call." Master Chen smiled gently at the surprised look on Aaron's face. "Now, do meditation again. And this time, breathe!"

Chapter 3—Bill and Glen Benson

Spring 1977

Howard "Howie" Benson was a north Georgia redneck with strong ties to what he called "his hillbilly cousins up a ways in Tennessee." He was an early and ardent supporter of the Libertarian Movement, and back in the 1960s, that movement found its way into America's living rooms through televised protest marches against war and as the free love movement.

Howie had two girlfriends, Carol, a portly, green-eyed redhead, and Betty, a skinny, brown-eyed, auburn haired beauty. They didn't see this movement as free love. All three simply loved one another, and that was all there was to it.

Howie and his two girlfriends had fourteen kids over a ten year period before he decided enough was enough and went in for a vasectomy. That kind of operation wasn't common up around where he was from, but he had buddies in the Army who had it done. The two oldest children were Bill and Glen, born in 1959 and just one month apart from each other. Bill, the oldest, was born to Carol, and Glen to Betty. Howie jokingly insisted that neither of them were his because they both had heads of curly, wild blond hair and blue eyes; his hair was black as coal and his eyes were hazel. Bill and Glen, being the oldest, eventually took on some of the responsibility of caring for the rest of the children while their father worked.

They all lived in a rather large house on a couple acres of land up near Dawsonville, Georgia just south of the Tennessee border. They had various neighbor friends around, but they mostly kept to themselves. Folks mostly left each other alone unless asked for help.

What their father did for a living wasn't legal, even in the loosest sense of the word. He grew pot and sold it to a group of trusted dealers in the surrounding states. He never sold locally, and even though it took every penny he could earn to keep his brood clothed and fed, he kept his prices low and his distribution small so he could keep the police from looking too closely in his direction.

Howie had many different fields in Georgia and Tennessee where he grew his product. He usually worked up to four of these fields at a time, depending on the season, and spent quite a bit of time on the road tending them. His best fields were in the Chattahoochee Forest, and it was there he developed his own variety of pot he called "Howie Wowie."

The Wowie strain had a short growing period and a short stalk that was hard to spot from a distance or from an airplane. It would also grow in different lighting conditions and had a higher tolerance to cold. Howie Wowie allowed him to rapidly put a new field into production if he believed the cops were paying a little too much attention to him.

The boys approached Howie one day and told him they wanted to help out with the business. They were fifteen and said they were ready to get out of the house and actually contribute. Howie agreed they were old enough, so he let them ride along with him on his "business" trips tending the fields.

Howie started getting pressure from some of his customers to expand his network. He figured the boys were ready to make some moves on their own, so he gave them their own field to work when they turned sixteen. He didn't want to put his boys in contact with his existing customers, though; he didn't want to chance a snitch leading the law—or worse, hostile competition—to his front door. So he made arrangements for the boys to meet with a new player in the area, La'Man. Howie only asked for twenty percent of what the boys made.

The boys turned out to have their father's business acumen; they had a steady client base of their own by the time they were eighteen years old.

"How y'all keep getting away with what y'all do?" La'Man asked during a sell in Rome, Georgia. "Every one of my suppliers 'cept you boys done got caught." His dark brown skin glistened in the Georgia sun, and he pulled a handkerchief from his back pocket to wipe his forehead. "The fuzz has been crawlin' all up in our asses lately."

"Simple really. We keep our heads down," Bill explained.

Glen added, "Yeah. And we don't deal drugs. Only Wowie. Big H and coke is out." He went over and took a look at La'Man's car. It was gold colored with gold tire rims, fuzzy dice on the rearview mirror, and purple fuzzballs lining the rear window. A light coating of brown dust covered it because he had to drive it down a dirt road a ways for the meet, up to an old cement factory that had gone out of business years ago. Glen crinkled his nose and asked, "What the fuck is that smell coming out of your car, dude?"

Bill revealed, "That's lavender, bro. I think it smells nice."

La'Man showed a big, gold-crowned smile. "Thank you, Bill. Your brother don't know shit about what it takes to make a lady horny, does he? Lavender does it every fuckin' time."

Glen scoffed. "Don't need lavender. Just some Wowie. How the fuck *you* don't get caught pimping around in this big-assed car is beyond me. This thing just squeals, 'Pull me over!'"

"I just make sure I ain't carrying, that's how," La'Man crowed. He turned to a woman who had followed him in a nondescript Chevy sedan. "Open the trunk, Melon Tits! We ain't got all day, dammit!"

Bill laughed, "Melon-Tits? Seriously, La'Man?"

"Yeah, so what?" La'Man asked bluntly. "Her name's Melon-Tits. I got another called Brown Sugar. And another called Tiger Ass."

Bill's eyes widened, and a snarky grin crossed his face. "You actually call them that?" he asked.

La'Man's chin tucked toward his chest, and he stared blackly at Bill out from under drooped eyelids. "I sell drugs and pussy," he shot back jaggedly. "I don't know their real fuckin' names. Don't fuckin' care either just as long as they stay on their backs keeping those fancy-assed lawyers downtown happy. You got a problem with that?"

Glen broke in, trying to cool the situation down, "No, man, we ain't got no problem." He hurriedly loaded the plastic bags into her trunk. "Anyway, you can still have a good time, man; just don't brag about how good of a time you're having. That's all we're sayin'."

La'Man relaxed and fashioned a large grin. "Sure, sure. I guess that's why you two fuckers run around in that rusty ol' redneck 'Cadillac,' blaring your hick music all day long. And boys, you need to get yourself some real mufflers. I think those done got fucked. Shit, man, y'all make a lot of bread. Why the fuck don't y'all spend it on something nice?"

Bill got a pained look on his face, and humorously squealed, "Man, don't talk about Bertha like that. She'll hear you. She was our first, rescued from the salvage yard." He glanced over at his and Glen's Dodge pick-up truck. It was a little rusty, but that was character as far as he was concerned.

Glen closed the trunk on the woman's car, and La'Man handed a paper bag to Bill. Bill took it and threw it to Glen. La'Man asked, "You ain't gonna count it?"

Bill laughed at him. "Dude, we ain't counted it since the first time you paid us too much."

"Mutha fucka, I ain't never overpaid for shit in my life," La'Man protested.

Glen asked, "Would it make you feel any better if we did count it?"

"Fuck no!" Then La'Man showed that gold grin again. "I'd think you boys didn't trust me."

"Then why you bustin' our ass?" Glen asked.

"'Cause that's what I do! You boys take care. Catch you in a couple of weeks."

Bill and Glen climbed into Bertha and drove off, Johnny Paycheck blaring from the speakers. Business was good for a couple of small town rednecks.

Bill took a long, deep toke off of his doobie.

"Stop bogartin' the doob, dude," Glen complained. The doob was from a special breed Howie was working on. They were sitting on the tailgate of their truck, watching the dirt road leading up to their field. It was fairly isolated where they were at, slightly off the side of the road, but they still had a good view and would have the time to react if trouble came their way. A tall stand of pines stood off to the right of the road and about one hundred and fifty yards past that was their field. Spring was in the air and the smell of honeysuckle and pine was strong.

A small, beat-up boom-box playing the last few notes of a Merle Haggard song sat next to them on top of a couple of pig spears. The spears were made for hunting wild animals—namely pigs—with a cross member mounted twelve to eighteen inches below the point to prevent something from running up the shaft and harming the bearer. They usually hunted pigs on their field to keep them from rooting up their plants.

"Sorry, man. Here." Bill passed the doobie over to Glen. "That La'Man scares the shit out of me sometimes even if he does crack me up." Then mimicking La'Man perfectly, "I sell drugs and pussy. You got a problem with that?"

Glen started laughing and then choked as the smoke clogged up his throat. "Dude, don't do that shit when I'm toking. You're gonna kill me someday."

Bill chuckled back at him, then got serious. "You hear what he said about his other suppliers?"

"Yeah. Bummer." Glen reached over to the player and flipped the cassette over. He took another toke off of the doobie and passed it back to

Bill.

"You think they looking for us?" Bill asked.

"Shit, man, probably." He reached up and wiped the sweat off of his forehead with his shirt sleeve. "I don't know. Why? You think it's time to move again?"

"I'm not sure." Bill took a long, hard toke off of the doobie and slowly blew the smoke out. "We've had a good run here at the Daffodil field. Howie said we needed to keep moving around to different fields, though. He ain't never been caught."

"Yeah, okay, man. After this last harvest, we'll move." He reached over to Bill. "I told you, quit bogarting the doobie, man!"

Bill pulled the paper bag out as Glen finished off the roach. It was time to count the cash. Something they never did was count the cash in front of a repeat customer because it showed a lack of trust and kept your attention diverted from what was going on around you. Sure, you might get stiffed, but you could deal with that later. The important thing was to make the exchange and then get back on the road.

Bill turned the paper bag over on the tailgate. The cash fell out, four stacks of twenties, neatly wrapped in rubber bands. *La'Man sure is polite.* Something else that fell out of the bag, too, and Bill picked it up. It was a small plastic hobby box. The kind you find down at the electronics store. The kind people put radio transmitters in. He threw it on the ground and stomped on it, smashing it under the heel of his cowboy boot.

Glen jumped down, too. "Did La'Man just drop a dime on our ass?"

"Fuck! I don't know. Time to go."

A car came thundering up the dirt road as they sprinted around the sides of their truck heading for the doors. They both scowled over their shoulders at La'Man's Cadillac as they grabbed Bertha's door handles—it blocked their path out of there. Howie had taught them they needed a minimum of two ways out of any situation. They planned to take the back road out, but as they scrambled up into the cab of their truck, they saw another car coming up that one, too. They were trapped.

Bill yelled, "Get the shotgun!" while he jumped behind the wheel. Glen twisted in his seat and yanked the 12 gauge from the gun rack on the back window. It had a magazine extension filled with ten rounds of buckshot in it. Glen usually rode "shotgun" because he was left-handed, and it made maneuvering the gun easier.

35

Glen yelled, "Go!" and Bill dropped the transmission into four wheel drive; it wasn't fast but it would grab the ground and take them over anything they wanted. The truck was also equipped with oversized buckshot mudders, giving them a few extra inches of clearance. Getting the axle stuck on something wasn't going to be a problem. Bill turned the wheel sharply to the left and took off down the hill into the lowlands to the south of their field.

Glen looked over at Bill. "I can't believe La'Man would gig us like that. We're cheaper than anybody around."

Bill reasoned, "He's either working with the fuzz, or he wants our field. Or working with someone who wants our field." He glanced in the rearview mirror. "Doesn't look like they're coming down after us." He briefly stopped talking to concentrate on vaulting Bertha over a few stumps. They landed with a huge, four-wheeled splash, rolling through a small creek and throwing mud in all directions for yards. They cut this route out a few months back to go mud hogging. He never thought he would use it as an escape route. "Shit, Howie's gonna be pissed."

"Fuck Howie!" Glen roared. "I'm pissed!"

Bill scowled and nodded his head in agreement then checked his rearview mirror again. The truck was bouncing around something fierce, but what he saw made him widen his eyes. "Them pig spears still back there?" The tailgate was down when the boys bugged out, and Bill was afraid the spears might have slid out.

Glen boosted himself up in his seat and scanned the truck bed. "Yeah. Why?" Then he saw what Bill saw—three dogs were chasing them. "Never mind. I see them."

Bill marveled aloud, "Those are the biggest fuckin' dogs I ever seen. And we ain't gonna outrun them."

With the truck bouncing around it was hard for Glen to see exactly what they were. "They look like some kind of weird-assed mutant Doberman. I see three of them. And them bastards are fast, too. You're right, we ain't gonna outrun 'em. Find a flat spot somewhere."

"Fuckin' A!" Bill knew Glen wanted to crawl into the truck bed, but he couldn't do that with the truck bouncing so much. He found a spot about twenty feet long and headed to it. "Get ready!" He slowed to a near stop and yelled, "Now!"

Glen opened the door, reached around and grabbed the roll bar, then swung himself into the bed. "Go!" he yelled to Bill. Bill punched it again.

They had left the section they had cleared out and were now in raw underbrush and saplings. Going was slower, and the dogs were getting closer. Glen saw the dogs leap completely over obstacles Bertha had trouble with. He scooted up against the cab of the truck and waited. The dogs were so close behind the truck that Glen could hear them, even over the slapping of the branches against Bertha's sides and the loud mufflers, but couldn't see them. Suddenly, a head popped up over the tailgate, but the animal couldn't easily find a purchase for its claws. Glen stared open mouthed into its face but didn't see a dog; in the split second between first seeing the beast scrambling to pull itself into the truck and the almost involuntary squeeze of the trigger, he was aware of thinking that he had never seen anything so evil in his life. His full load of buck-shot hit the dog point blank in the face and spun him backwards and headless into the air.

The other two howled as they ran. Glen didn't have a name for the terror that hit him in a deep and primitive part of his brain. "Hurry the fuck up, Bill!" He wasn't sure if he yelled it out loud or just heard it in his own head.

"What the hell you think I'm doing, bro? I think there's a road up here somewhere. Just keep shooting!"

Glen shot at the two animals that were getting closer and closer to the truck but kept missing. It did slow them down some, but it seemed they understood when he was about to pull the trigger and would dodge at the last possible second. *Dogs can't fuckin' dodge!* The dog closest to them put on a sudden burst of speed, and before Glen had time to realize it, it was running alongside the right side of the truck. The dog was so close to it that Glen couldn't get a shot. *How the hell did it know to do that?*

In sheer desperation he pointed the barrel of the gun at the inside of the truck bed toward where he thought the dog's head might be, said a prayer, and fired his remaining two shots. He saw the headless body of the dog rolling along the ground behind the truck.

"Buck shot, mother fuc—"

Without any warning, Glen was thrown up and against the back of the cab as the truck lurched into the air. Bill bellowed, "Hang on!"

"Don't you know a stump when you see one? Shit!"

When the truck settled back down, it rolled to a stop, a grinding noise from underneath telling him Bertha wasn't going any further right now.

Probably bent the damned driveshaft. He jumped to the ground and spotted the third dog standing and looking at the headless body in the makeshift road behind them. He grabbed the two pig spears from the truck bed and tossed one to Bill who caught it in midair. "Come on. It's time to stick this fucker!"

Bill ran around to the back of the truck as the dog skidded to a stop no more than three feet from Glen. It eyed the spear as if it knew what a spear was. Bill ran up next to his brother, weapon at the ready, and realized what he saw was no dog. He didn't know what it was. He'd heard stories out of the local Cherokees about skin walkers, those who could shape shift, but those were supposed to be benevolent and helpful. This thing oozed evil. The word *werewolf* came to Bill's lips unbidden but certain. Ten minutes ago he would have laughed at the idea, but now without knowing how, he knew what he was looking at was a werewolf.

The werewolf was on all fours, but as Glen aimed his spear at it, it rose up on its hind legs and took two steps toward Bill as nimbly as any man. Its hands had long fingers ending in sharp talons, and it was covered in short, wiry, almost black hair. Its face was clearly that of a wolf, but it was at the same time somehow distinctly human. It had a short snout containing long and deadly looking fangs. Its eyes were a dark blue. There was no denying that there was a cunning intelligence behind them. It was muddy and smelled like a wet dog that had recently rolled in something three-days dead. It showed its teeth and growled low, deep in its throat. Its eyes shifted between Glen's face and Bill's spear.

Bill moved around to the right and Glen to the left in unspoken agreement. They'd chased enough wild hogs that their teamwork unconsciously took over. As soon as they were on either side of the monster, it seemed to sense what was going on and backed off three quick steps, refusing to be flanked. Not wanting to lose the opportunity, Glen rushed it, screaming to get its attention. The monster turned its attention to him, allowing Bill get a solid blow to its midsection, sinking the point up to the cross member. The animal howled in pain and tried to back off. The barbed point stayed firmly in place, Bill's strength anchoring it where it stood.

Realizing it was stuck, it rushed Glen, pulling the spear out of Bill's hands. Glen dropped to his knees and set the butt end of his spear into the ground at the last possible moment. The werewolf tried to dodge out of the way, but Glen managed to direct the spear until it found purchase deep in its shoulder. The werewolf howled again in pain while it tried to back off, but Glen held on with all of his strength. The monster then rushed Glen again, forcing him backward. Glen dropped the butt into the ground again, and when he did, the strength of the monster's shove snapped the wooden handle of the spear in half.

Seeing the broken weapon, Bill scrambled even harder to get a hold on his again, to keep the werewolf away from his brother. He dove for it and managed to get one hand around the shaft. The werewolf dragged him along the ground, forcing leaves and decay-smelling mud into his mouth and nose, while he continued to try to get both hands on the spear.

Through the mud in his eyes, Bill saw Glen set the butt of the broken spear shaft, the piece not impaled in the werewolf, on the ground in a last ditch effort to keep the monster at bay. It worked, though not as he had probably intended. As the werewolf ran itself onto Glen's improvised spear, the monster's momentum levered it up into the air, dragging Bill along with it. Bill unexpectedly found himself standing up on both feet with both hands on his spear.

While the werewolf was momentarily in the air, Bill used his own strength to drive his spear through the werewolf's body and bury its point in a tree, leaving the werewolf pinned.

Glen ran over, grasped the spear shaft, and yelled, "Get the fuckin' shotgun and blow this bastard's face off!"

While Bill ran back to the truck to get the shotgun, the werewolf seemed to recognize its predicament and started struggling, trying to free itself from the shaft embedded in its body. The barbed hooks held, and the cross member prevented the monster from working its way down the shaft toward Glen. It gave up on that tactic when it realized its situation and started slashing at the hickory shaft instead.

Bill ran up with the shotgun and pointed it at the animal's face. It stopped its flailing and growling long enough to sedately stare into the barrel of the gun, waiting on Bill to pull the trigger. The click of a firing pin hitting empty air echoed all around them.

The werewolf resumed its attack on the shaft.

Bill muttered, "Oh, shit," and started checking his pockets for ammo. "Where's the ammo, Glen?"

"Fuck! Left front pocket!" Bill rushed over to him and dug around in the pocket. The shaft was starting to give.

Bill pulled out the ammunition and put two rounds into the shotgun. He pointed the gun at the werewolf's head and pulled the trigger. The shaft of the spear broke just as the werewolf's head disintegrated.

Bill and Glen stood there and watched the werewolf's body change into a human body. It was male and it was black. A tattoo of a skull and crossbones smoking a doobie was clearly visible on the left shoulder.

"What the fuck, Glen?" Bill asked. "That's La'Man's tattoo!"

"I don't know, bro, but we need to get the hell out of here."

Bill tore his eyes away from La'Man to look at Glen's wounds. He had long gouges on both arms that looked deep but were more oozing blood than actually bleeding. "You okay?"

"Yeah, that sumbitch got me when my spear broke. Thanks for the back-up."

"Sure thing, bro."

They both picked up their empty shotgun casings then threw them into the back of their truck. "How bad is Bertha?" Glen asked.

"Pretty bad." Bill cringed at the thought of what he might have done to her. "I landed on a stump. I think I broke the front axle."

"Let's look."

They both crawled under the front of their truck, dragging what few tools they kept behind the seat with them, and found that the u-joint was bent on the front differential. They disconnected the forward drive shaft from it and from the transmission.

They crawled back out and Glen warned, "It's two-wheel drive until I can get her back to the shop, so be careful." He turned around and looked in the direction they were originally travelling. "How close you think we are to that road?"

"It shouldn't be more than a hundred yards or so. You walk in front, find us a way out. I'll follow along behind you."

Chapter 4—Luto Via

noun [Lü-tō()(v)(w)ē'-ə]
1. Dirt Road.

Aaron Darveau, January 5, 1983

Aaron's in his back yard raking the leaves. It's hard keeping them in one area because the wind is blowing. He looks up at the gathering storm clouds and hopes he can get it done before his dad gets home. He has a date tonight, but he can't leave until his chores are done.

He knows what's coming next and dreads it. He spends a little extra time raking the stray leaf or two into the pile just so he won't have to look up and see the large, black dog trotting toward him up the driveway. There are a few strays in the neighborhood who know him as an easy mark for some scraps or a belly rub, but this one is a stranger. Not a stranger to Aaron though—he's dreamed of this dog for years—but a stranger to the neighborhood. It doesn't belong here. It is larger and in much better shape than the local mutts. Its coat is solid black and doesn't shine at all; it absorbs light like an old chalkboard. Its claws spark against the concrete like steel knives. It growls as it gradually and deliberately stops in front of Aaron.

Aaron Darveau, January 28, 1983

Aaron was lost. He was up north of town trying to find an old junkyard that supposedly had every Mustang part made. He ran into a guy, Kyle Bronton, at a car show a month or so back who told him about the place. Lil' Red, Aaron's dilapidated '66 Mustang, needed a few parts, and he had been sniffing around the show hoping for some free help. Kyle, it seems, was well known in the Mustang circle as he had restored several Mustangs for other people. Everyone Aaron talked to said he should go talk to Kyle.

Aaron tracked him down in the parking lot. "Are you Kyle Bronton?"

"Yep! The one and only!" He sounded cocky, but he had a pleasant smile on his face.

Aaron smiled back. "I'm Aaron. Aaron Darveau. I hear you know Mustangs."

"Yeah, I done replaced a headlight or two. Whatcha got?"

Aaron and Kyle were friends from then on. They spent the next several hours talking Mustang lore. Actually, Kyle spent most of the time talking, and Aaron spent most of the time listening. But Aaron never got bored with his part of the conversation. Kyle was a natural story-teller and knew the history of every Mustang model ever made, all of the official variants, and quite a few engineering stories that never made it to the public ear. He turned Aaron onto an old junkyard he knew about up north of town.

So, here Aaron was, up north of Orlando—somewhere—following some road Kyle said to follow. Aaron's two friends, Rick and Tracy, had tagged along, and they were razzing him about being lost.

Rick was the worst. "You're from Louisiana, right? I thought you knew how to follow back roads like this?"

"The directions are messed up," Aaron complained. "Kyle said to drive five miles down this dirt road. 'You can't miss it!' he said. I think we missed it."

"No kidding!" Tracy prodded. "Maybe we ought to turn back before it gets too late."

Rick snatched Kyle's hand-drawn map out of Aaron's hand and turned it upside down and sideways, trying to make sense of it. "It's probably after closing time anyway."

Aaron conceded. "Yeah, y'all are probably right." He pulled Lil' Red to the side of the road and turned her around. The front left tire blew out before he could get up to speed, jerking the steering wheel to the side. If it wasn't for the dirt on the road and the slow speed they were traveling, they would have ended up in the ditch.

"Son of a bitch!" Aaron bellowed as he came to a stop. He got out and glared at the tire. "Damn it! We get lost in the middle of fucking nowhere, it's getting dark, and now I've got a flat tire. What else can possibly go wrong tonight?!"

Rick got out of Lil' Red and went around and looked at the tire. "Chill out, Aaron," he coaxed. "It's not the end of the world. Shit, man, it's just a flat."

"Yeah, you're right. Sorry." Aaron sighed. Tai Chi training or not, Aaron liked surprises as much as sleeping babies do and had since the doctor slapped his ass for the first time to kick-start his lungs. Accepting interruptions to life and letting things take their natural course was something that took years to learn, and he wasn't entirely there yet. Still, accepting the unexpected didn't make it any more palatable.

They all peered down the road into nothingness. It disappeared into the woods like a train track down a tunnel. Tall trees lined it on either side, blocking out everything except the darkening sky above. Loneliness gripped Aaron from back the way they had come. If it hadn't been for the silvery band of sky overhead, they wouldn't have been able to see anything. The road up ahead curved around to the right so they couldn't see much sky in that direction.

Aaron opened the trunk to get the jack and the spare out. A slight breeze kicked up and brought the smell of old swamp to his nose—damp leaves, mud, and the occasional whiff of stale water. Tracy held the flashlight while Aaron worked the lug nuts off of the tire. Aaron had just dropped the flat tire to the side when a series of howls—at least three different ones—wailed from somewhere deep in the swamp. Something stored deep in the men's genetic memory put their hackles at attention before their conscious minds registered the danger. Rick stared wide-eyed at Aaron while Tracy swung the dim flashlight in a wide arc toward the sound.

"You're a country boy," Rick blurted. "What the fuck was that?"

"It's probably just some wild dogs." Aaron tried to sound calm. He didn't need Rick and Tracy panicking. He needed to get them out of here though. He'd trampled through the woods and swamps of northern Louisiana his whole life, and he knew he'd never heard anything like those howls. He'd heard wolf and coyote howls before, and he'd heard humans howl in cheap imitation. These howls were—different.

He slammed the slightly mushy spare tire onto the hub, and his fingers moved like machines spinning the lug nuts on. Howls shattered the moonlit silence again, closer than the first time just as he spun the lug wrench on the last nut. Aaron had run coon dogs before, and he could judge distance pretty accurately. He realized these howls had come from something less than half their original distance. Whatever was making them covered at least half a mile in less time than it took to change the tire. *Whatever they are, they aren't on leashes, and they're running all out. Not good.*

Rick was rooted to the ground, staring off into the night.

Tracy painted the trees with the flashlight, trying to see what was out there. "Hurry the fuck up, man. This shit ain't funny. It's time to boogie the fuck out of here."

"Well, shine the fucking light back over here so I can see what the hell I'm doing," Aaron shot back. He cranked the jack back down once Tracy gave him some light to work with. "Look guys, if whatever is making that sound is wild, they won't come close to us. They're more afraid of us than we are of them. We should—"

"I doubt that shit," Rick blurted out. "Just hurry."

43

"There're probably some coon hunters out tonight running dogs. That's all." *Dogs with a howl I'm not familiar with.* He knew there *were* all kinds of coon dogs, and he knew he didn't know them all.

The instant Aaron slammed the trunk closed, howling and growling exploded from the same direction as the original howls, followed a split second later from the other direction. The three men were surrounded. More disconcerting was the howlers were communicating. He didn't know how he knew that, but he knew it as clearly as he ever knew anything in his life. These weren't dogs, and there were no coon hunters.

Aaron's Tai Chi training and his experience spending a life in the woods kicked in as he tried to make sense of what he was facing and what he needed to do to face it. Either another pack of these howlers slipped up from the other side of the road or the original pack separated so they could cover both sides. They were fast and sneaky because Aaron didn't hear them approach and didn't know they were there until they started 'talking' to each other. Whatever these howlers were, they were crashing through the woods. Aaron felt like a deer being driven by a bunch of deer hounds.

Kirk ordered, *"Take cover!"* but he was too late. Aaron had already ordered, "Get in the car!" *You're getting slow, Kirk!* Tracy dove into the backseat from the driver's side while Aaron jumped behind the steering wheel. He jabbed the key into the ignition and twisted it, praying the car wouldn't decide it needed a break. The crashing from the woods on both sides of the car grew so loud Aaron expected the trees to fall across the road at any moment. The howling and growling rose to their own unnerving levels.

Rick started to race around Lil' Red to the passenger side, but the crescendo increased on that side of road. He skidded to a halt and backed up toward the driver side door. He shrieked at Aaron, "Get out so I can get in!"

Aaron fought the instinct to remain in relative safety inside the car but stepped out anyway just enough to let Rick scramble past him. Rick wasn't moving fast enough, so Aaron pushed him the rest of the way over the center console. He jumped back into his seat and punched the gas pedal before he closed his door. Lil' Red's engine screamed as its tires kicked up large amounts of dirt and gravel, straining to find purchase on the road. What Rick and Tracy saw over their shoulders and what Aaron saw in the rearview mirror shook them to their cores.

44

Tracy, in his rush to get into the car, had dropped the flashlight. There wasn't an abundance of light behind them, but there was enough to see what stalked them. Three of the largest wolves Aaron had ever seen jumped onto the road. They couldn't see any details in the darkness, but the glow from the flashlight made their shapes and movements unmistakable. That was all they had a chance to see, because Lil' Red finally found traction in the dirt and kicked up a red fog, taillights in the dust. Aaron kept the gas pedal on the floor until he saw the speedometer reach seventy.

The only sounds in the car were the tires on the road and the rattles from Lil' Red's loose exhaust pipes as they drove back to the base. No one spoke; they were trapped in their own thoughts, trying to make sense of something that didn't make sense. *Couldn't* make sense. But there was no mistaking it. They had witnessed something that was not natural, and they knew they had barely escaped with their lives. The three men didn't take a deep breath until they saw the lights of Orlando through the windshield.

Chapter 5—Venor

verb [vē'-nōr]

1. Stalk.

Aaron Darveau, February 10, 1983

Aaron's in his back yard raking the leaves. It's hard keeping them in one area because the wind is blowing. He looks up at the gathering storm clouds and hopes he can get it done before his dad gets home. He has a date tonight, but he can't leave until his chores are done.

He knows what's coming next and dreads it. He spends a little extra time raking the stray leaf or two into the pile just so he won't have to look up and see the large, black dog trotting toward him up the driveway. There are a few strays in the neighborhood who know him as an easy mark for some scraps or a belly rub, but this one is a stranger. Not a stranger to Aaron though—he's dreamed of this dog for years—but a stranger to the neighborhood. It doesn't belong here. It is larger and in much better shape than the local mutts. Its coat is solid black and doesn't shine at all; it absorbs light like an old chalkboard. Its claws spark against the concrete like steel knives. It growls as it gradually and deliberately stops in front of Aaron.

Aaron has experience caring for and training dogs; he knows one thing you never do is move suddenly when faced with an aggressive one and this one is definitely aggressive. He also knows you never look into their eyes; they take it as a challenge to their dominance. Aaron looks at the ground in front of the dog.

The dog's ears are up and pointed toward Aaron, and its tail is out straight. It's leaning on its front legs; a dog exerting its dominance will do that. Aaron knows the dog is going to attack when its growl turns into a snarl, just like the dozens of other times he has stood face to face with it.

Aaron Darveau, April 2, 1983

Karen Argali took Aaron utterly unaware the first time he saw her. She captured his attention as if she were the only woman in the bar. Although she never moved from her table, she was always sitting where he was looking, regardless of where he was. She was dark complexioned, Italian if he had to guess, with gentle, brown eyes, and long, black hair falling to loose curls just below her shoulders. Her petite hands had perfectly manicured and naturally colored nails that proudly shone every time she took a sip from her drink. She had a small gap between her two front teeth. A gap like that turns some people off, but it fit her in a Lauren Hutton kind of way. It wasn't so wide as to be obnoxious and turned her from just another pretty face in the crowd to one that plucked a man's attention at first glance like a well-tuned guitar string. Even sitting, she conveyed an exotic, physical beauty that didn't belong in the Trail Boss Country and Western Dance Hall and Saloon. She looked like a woman who knew what she wanted.

Karen's table was along one of the walls near the front door. Aaron saw she was by herself, but he figured she either had a boyfriend somewhere else in the bar or she was on the prowl. In either case, she was way out of his league. This was a woman and not the usual girl who came here. He spent the next few songs studying her; several times men approached her asking for a dance, but she turned them all down with a simple shake of her head, a modest smile, and a polite, "No, thank you." He kept turning in her direction, his eyes being cooperative hostages to her beauty.

Aaron wasn't sure what made him think she would dance with him, especially after all of the other refusals he'd witnessed. But one thing he did know was it never hurt to give things a shot. He stepped up to her, held his hand out in relaxed invitation, and asked if she would care to dance.

Aaron had a rule that you never asked a woman more than twice to dance. That bordered on harassment. They were usually polite the first time they turned him down. But the second time, they would let him know his advances were unwelcome, if indeed they were, by being rude. Karen was never rude, and he even caught her watching him a few times. He took this as an unspoken invitation to ask again. Still, she turned him down with a simple, "No, thank you," each of the four times he asked.

Well, Kirk never gave up, and he wasn't going to either. He marched up to her a fifth time. "This is the last time I'm going to ask you. If you say 'no' this time, I swear you'll never see me again." He paused for effect with his hand hanging out in no-man's land. "Would you care to dance, Ma'am?"

She looked up at him. "All right." Her reaction didn't instill confidence, but it placed her in his arms, so he took it.

They danced every two-step and swing song that night until their clothes were soaked with sweat. Her curls were long gone by the fourth dance, so she tied her hair into a messy pony-tail with fine tendrils of hair on her neck hanging down over her collar. Aaron was fascinated that she was confident enough in herself that she didn't need to primp after every dance to maintain that *just walked out of the beauty salon* look—it came naturally to her. He'd met a number of women there at the Trail Boss who, no matter how many beers he'd drank, couldn't have passed for lumberjacks after a few fast songs on the dance floor. Not Karen, and he liked her all the more for it.

When last call was announced, they stood and nervously glanced at each other like two kids at their first mixer, trying to figure out how to make skin contact, shuffling their feet and keeping their hands in their pockets. They gave each other a chaste hug through unspoken agreement, said thank you, and turned toward the door. He didn't want this night to end, but he was in new territory here. His evenings at the Trail Boss had never made it to closing time; he was usually long gone by now, already out the door with some woman, or he'd left early because the fishing was light. Right then he was thinking *WWKD*. Honesty is the best policy.

"Karen, I don't want this night to end." He was surprised those words sprang past his lips. They weren't suave or debonair. In fact, they came close to broadcasting desperation.

He was even more surprised when she turned back to him. "Me either. I'm having fun! Where are you from?"

"Monroe, Louisiana," he spouted out fast enough that he was afraid it might have made him sound more desperate than his last line. Then a little slower, "I'm in the Navy, stationed over at the Orlando base." His answer was just long enough to see them through the door together.

The cold wind blew through their sweaty clothes as soon as they stepped outside, making them feel like they were walking through ice water. Seeking shelter from the wind, they dove into her car, as it was the closest to them. It was a land yacht of some model Aaron didn't recognize.

Slamming the car's door against the wind, Aaron asked, "Where are you from?"

"Buffalo, New York."

"Heh! I bet you thought you'd left the cold behind, huh?"

"Yeah," she beamed followed by a little laugh. "I hate the snow! Don't get much of that down here."

"No, we don't. I don't mind it, but then again," he shrugged his shoulders, "I've never lived in it. So, what are you doing down here?"

"I'm an office manager for a meat wholesaler," she replied as she turned the engine on. "I just moved down so the owners are letting me live with them until I get on my feet."

"That's nice of them."

"Yeah. What do you do at the Navy base?" She turned the heater controls to "Hot."

"Nothing really. It's my shore duty rotation. I'm in charge of the kids who get kicked out of nuclear power school and are awaiting orders to the fleet. It's just busy work. Relaxing though, after spending the last five years on a cruiser."

"How long have you been in?"

"June twelfth will be eight years," he told her. "Then my tour is done."

She looked him directly in the eyes. "You getting out then?"

"I'm not sure. I don't have anything waiting for me back in Louisiana. Both of my parents died a couple of years ago, shot during a robbery. I'll probably stay in."

The outside lights to the bar went out and Karen looked in that direction, scanning the area around the building. It was too dark to see much so Aaron wasn't sure what she was looking for. He took the opportunity to admire her profile. There wasn't much moonlight, but the constant twilight of the town put a hazy-blue glow on her and made her look even more beautiful.

She looked back at him. "Sorry to hear about that," she murmured softly.

"Oh, it's okay." He shrugged his shoulders. "It's been a while. Thanks, though."

"Did they catch the guy who did it?"

"Yeah. He's in Angola Prison in Louisiana, death row, waiting on execution."

They both ran out of things to make small talk about, and Karen looked down at her hands in nervous insecurity. Aaron decided it was time he asked the question he felt always needed answering. "You got a boyfriend or married or anything?"

She snapped her gaze up at Aaron and asked curtly, "Would I be in this car with you if I was?"

"Maybe," he insisted matter-of-factly. "Some women would be. I'm not saying you're like that, but I like to know what I'm getting into."

"Well, you aren't getting into anything tonight. You–"

Aaron cut her off by kissing her. She fought the kiss just long enough for him to consider breaking it and leaving—but then she relaxed and returned it. After a few more minutes of heavy kissing and clumsy groping, he surprised himself by suggesting, "Let's get a room."

She surprised him even more when she pulled back with a lustful smile. "Sounds good to me."

She drove them up the street to one of the cheaper hotels, where Aaron went in and got a key. Neither of them talked as they took the stairs up to the room. There was nothing to say.

She took the key from him and opened the door, leading him into the room. Aaron displayed the *Do Not Disturb* sign and then closed the door. He turned to her, and she took the lead again by putting her arms around his neck and kissing him. When they pulled back for air, her eyes captured his soul. Something wild peeked back at him, and he wanted to be part of it. He wanted her. He gently grabbed a handful of her hair and held it to his nose, taking a deep breath, inhaling her scent. Although there was a light scent of sweat, it was not an unpleasant smell. There was something else there though, something deeper. She even smelled wild, like that smell you have when you've been out hunting all day. The smell is organic and earthy, natural. She had the smell of a huntress about her.

They say smell triggers memories, no matter how long ago the brain stored them. Events and places believed to be long dead can bubble to the surface in the most unlikely places and from the most distant past. He didn't have to search for this one. Her smell brought back memories from barely two months ago. His memories of the dirt road, the flat tire, the howling, the wolves, they all came crashing back to him. He suddenly found himself back on that road, only this time he was frozen in place and unable to react.

Chapter 6—Prensio

verb [prǝn'-sē-ō]

1. Capture.

Karen Argali, April 2, 1983

Karen was shocked she was in a hotel room with Aaron so soon after meeting him. Her plan was to watch him, not sleep with him. But when he came up and asked her dance, and she got his smell, all of her plans ended up rattling in the bottom of a trash can. She kept saying, "No, thank you," thinking he would stay away, but that wasn't what she really wanted. She *wanted* him to keep coming back. She guessed he finally had enough *noes* for the evening because he threatened not to ask her again. She knew then she had to make a decision, right or wrong, and once he held her in his arms, she knew she made the right one.

After growing up in a life where single women in dingy bars were looked at as one-night stands, or worse, she swore she would never be that kind of woman. No, this would not be a one-night stand. This would be a *first*-night stand, because if her previous life taught her anything, it was that if a woman prudently uses what she has to get what she wants, the man would come back. She planned on Aaron coming back again and again. It would be a balancing act though, because his confidence was astounding; he would be hard to hold onto. He might not need her as much as she needed him. Being told *no* did not turn him off. He didn't crawl into a hole and hide or float away like a piece of driftwood. She needed that. She needed him.

Of course, being here with him now had its advantages. He was good looking in his own way. He carried himself such that he seemed taller than he really was. His hair was cropped short, probably navy rules or something, so it was hard to tell if it was blond or light brown. He had full lips—kissable lips. The one thing that captivated her the most was his blue eyes. Baby Blue Eyes, as her mother would call them. And she didn't even want to dwell too long on how his scent weakened her knees. His body was inviting, too, charging the air between them with his strength. She could feel the muscles in his arms while they danced. He wasn't bulky like a body builder, but slim and cut. There was no denying she found him sexy.

When he put those arms around her, any reluctance or fear drained from her body. Just as she was relaxing, starting to feel the moment, those arms went lax. He'd grabbed some of her hair and smelled it and then froze as still as a statue. She leaned back and saw him focused on something in the distance, something only he could see. A little taken aback, she asked him, "Are you still with me?"

Aaron blinked twice and came back from wherever he had drifted off to. "Yes," he replied abruptly. "Your smell brought back a memory of something that happened a few months ago." He then gave her a hug, wrapping his arms completely around her again, protectively. "That's all."

"Good memory or bad memory?" she teased.

He broke the embrace. "I need a drink of water." He got up and disappeared into the bathroom.

Does he suspect? I hope I haven't lost him!

The sink faucet ran for a couple of minutes, and he came out with a freshly dried, red face. He sat down in the chair. "Sorry about that. I'm not sure where that came from."

Concerned, she sat down in his lap. "What happened?"

He laughed nervously. "Me and some friends were chased by a pack of wild dogs," he explained. "Damned near got us! When I smelled your hair, it brought back that memory for some strange-assed reason."

Karen was torn between needing to keep things under wraps and telling him the truth. Her mind screamed, *"That was me, Aaron! That was me! I've wanted you since I first saw you!"* In the end, all she could muster was, "My hair smells like dog?"

"What? No! No, not at all!" he exclaimed. "I was changing a tire so I got a little sweaty. I guess the smell just triggered that memory." He leaned over and kissed her on the cheek. "No, you do *not* smell like dog. In fact, I kinda like the way you smell."

With that, she kissed him again, pulling away only to stand and lead him toward the bed; her need was primal. Through willpower alone, she stopped and forced herself to gaze into his eyes. "Are you sure this is what you want? Are you sure you want me?" Her voice was low and husky, just above a whisper and focused just for him.

She saw him calculating. Most men would have simply said, "Yep, let's jump in the sack!" He was thinking about how to answer this. She had seen him do that before they left the bar. He didn't blather some asinine one-liner. He spoke from his heart and meant every word he said. He might be an animal of emotion like all men, but something in his mind had final say.

"Karen, you're the most beautiful woman I've ever seen. I'm not sure how I ended up here with you, but I'm here because I want to be. I want this. I want you."

She laid her head on his chest and whispered softly, "Good."

They tore each other's clothes off. She pressed her bare chest to his in an embrace and an intense, burning coldness raged between her breasts, forcing her to lurch away. "Ow!" she exclaimed.

He stepped back, alarmed. "What's the matter? Did I hurt you?"

She looked at his chest, at his necklace, at the silver fang hanging there. "Your necklace, it…it scratched me. Can you take it off?" She looked down at her wound, a silver burn. It wasn't too bad. In the dim light it would look like a scratch.

Aaron took his necklace off. "Sorry," he pleaded. "It's just some hippy necklace I got off a crazy fortune teller in New Orleans about ten years ago. It's never scratched me. You okay?"

"Yeah," she boasted, "I'm a big girl." She tilted her head to the side. "Hippy necklace?"

"I just call it that," he confessed through a sheepish grin. "It looks like something you would see in some New Age store downtown. Don't you think?"

She creased her brows. "Let me see it?" He handed it to her, and she made sure not to touch the silver shard, holding it by its leather thong. It was a canine fang made from silver. She watched the fang twist and glint in the light. "Tell me about this fortune teller."

He took the necklace from her and tossed it onto his pile of clothes. He turned back to her with a big, lustful grin. "Later," he promised.

The bed sprang up and engulfed them both.

Aaron Darveau, April 2-22, 1983

Neither one of them got any sleep that night. They were still at it when the sun came up. They alternated all night between rough and rowdy to gentle and tender, her leading and then following. He couldn't get enough of her, and she willingly took everything he had to give. When he thought he was too exhausted to get aroused again, she proved him wrong. At one point, when they were perfectly synchronized, he felt her gouge scratches in his back. They weren't too bad, though; when he checked the next day, they were already healed up.

During the next couple of weeks, virtually every minute Aaron had available away from the base found him with Karen. They took day trips on the weekends and visited all the local amusement resorts, got sunburned on just about every beach on both coasts, flew down Alligator Alley at breakneck speeds, and drove to the ends of the Florida Keys where they both swore they could see Cuba. A whirlwind of passion fueled their nights, and it didn't matter where they found themselves when the mood hit them—hotels, beaches, the backseat of Lil' Red when they were out of cash, under a boardwalk, her place—they rode the whirlwind.

Aaron knew he wasn't a Don Juan, but he could find female companionship when he wanted it. Karen was something different, though. For the first time he could remember, he honestly thought he could spend the rest of his life waking up next to the same someone every morning. It was obvious he was addicted to her, but he didn't care. Like a junkie who can't wait for his next fix, he would glare at the clock on the wall at work, cursing it for not moving faster, counting down the hour-long minutes until they were together again. He was rarely spending his nights on base by the end of the first month.

Karen lived with her employers, Craig and Lisa Minor, at their estate. She was their office manager and they were kind enough to let her live there until she could get on her feet. The first time Aaron met the Minors, they went out of their way to make him feel comfortable. Craig was in his mid-fifties and appeared to be in good shape. He was of average height, but because he didn't have the belly most men his age had, he projected a younger image. He had pale blue eyes and a full head of grey hair he kept neatly trimmed off the collar and ears. He wore nice clothes, even around the house. He wasn't much into jewelry but did have a large ring on his right hand with the letter 'M' in Old English script and a wedding band on his left.

Lisa was a couple of years younger and fighting the middle-aged spread with a vengeance, constantly walking the estate for exercise, and working to keep her hair its original color, blonde. She had piercing blue eyes, and when she looked at you with them, it was as if your soul stood bare before her—she stared right into you. She liked to laugh and tell little jokes, but you could tell she always had something else on her mind.

Other than the gardener, Frank, and the maid, Maria, they had the house mostly to themselves during the week because Craig and Lisa were often out of town on business. He was uncomfortable staying there the first few days but in short order began to think of the place as home.

Aaron had never seen such a place as what the Minors owned. It was a large estate completely surrounded by trees about an hour north of the base and a good ten miles to the next nearest neighbor. The house, and that was an understatement, was a Roman villa, open and airy, built entirely of stone. Instead of a full garden in the courtyard, there was a swimming pool with native plants around the edges separating it from a covered walkway. The open, inner edge of the walkway—Craig called it a loggia—was lined with columns that reminded Aaron of some of the more ancient sites he'd visited in Italy; they had natural-looking cracks and lent an authentic feel to the surrounding construction. The villa had sixteen bedroom suites accessed via large, double oaken doors along the outer wall of the loggia. Each suite had a king-sized bed, a sitting area, and a bathroom. The bathrooms came complete with a stone-walled, double-headed shower, a hot tub, a toilet, a bidet, and twin sinks. He found a sunken living room as large as some of his high school classrooms. There was a well-stocked office, complete with a fax machine and two electric typewriters. The filing cabinets were hidden in the oaken walls to maintain the antique look. The den included a wet bar and was set up as a small movie theater. The kitchen continued the classic design but it contained all the latest appliances. A large arched foyer provided the only access to the front yard and main drive. A second, less intimidating entrance led to the backyard where the servants lived in separate houses larger than the house he grew up in and just as luxurious as the rest of the villa.

The interior décor was Greco-Roman, but it didn't feel too much like a museum. Each of the four corners in the loggia had an alcove carved into the stone, and in each alcove was a small statue depicting someone from Roman mythology—Diana the Huntress, Mars, the God of War, and Romulus and Remus, the founders of Rome. They were only about four feet tall, but as each stood on their own pedestal, they rose above Aaron's shoulders. Clearly no expense was spared in the lavish appointments found throughout the estate. Aaron decided the meat wholesaling business paid considerably better than he thought it did to support a place like this.

One afternoon, he and Craig were sitting by the pool drinking a fancy rum drink. Aaron asked, "This house seems way more than you and Lisa need. Why all the room?"

"We like to entertain," Craig explained. "It's quite a drive back into town for our guests to find a hotel, so the extra rooms are useful."

Craig and Lisa had their own distinct hobbies, and as Aaron was becoming a fixture around there, they took the extra effort to include him in their activities.

Craig's passion was sake.

"Every civilized man should be exposed to sake," Craig told him one Thursday evening. "Sake is a Japanese alcoholic beverage made from fermented rice. You may hear some people call it wine, but it's really more like beer because of the way the fermentation occurs." He then commenced a lengthy dissertation on the intricate details of the process, giving Aaron hands-on-experience in his homebrew sake room. At first, Aaron wasn't too impressed with the sour smell, but the more time he spent in there, the more he liked it.

Aaron asked him, "Where did you learn all of this?"

"I spent some time in Japan during the Korean War," Craig replied. "I learned it there."

Karen must have had a sensitive nose because she never did develop an appreciation for the process. "You smell like Craig's sake room!" she complained one night. "Take a shower before coming to bed."

Lisa's passion was cooking—or more specifically, barbequing. Every weekend Aaron spent with them, she had something in the smoker—ribs, brisket, steaks, fish, or chicken. As a meat wholesaler, they had access to some of the finest cuts of meat available, and Lisa knew how to cook them to perfection.

She told him, "You need to be able to cook the meat without burning or undercooking it. You also need to learn to make your own sauce." One Friday night while Karen was swimming, Lisa had Aaron in the kitchen teaching him about how different ingredients were used to make rubs, injections, and bastings, and how they affected different types and even different cuts of meat. "If you learn how to make a good sauce, the smoker can be forgiving. If your sauce isn't any good, no amount of smoke is going to fix it."

When they later went out to the smoker for some instruction on how to set the dampers on the smoker, Craig said, "When Lisa was growing up, her entire family thought she would be a great chef someday."

Aaron blinked at Lisa. "Really?"

Lisa shot Aaron a look of mock indignation and asked, "You don't think

I could have done it?"

"No...I mean, yes," Aaron stammered. "Wait, I was asking 'Really' because I thought it was cool. I think you'd make a great chef. Why didn't you? Go that route, I mean."

"I chose Craig instead."

Craig added, "Yes, and I'm glad, too." Then he leaned over and kissed her on the cheek.

Aaron was comfortable with these people, and when he wasn't with them, he was homesick. They filled a hole that opened the day he found out his parents died.

Chapter 7—Imaginatio

noun [i-mä-ji-nä'-tē-ō]

1. Dream, Imagination.

Aaron Darveau, April 23, 1983

Aaron's in his back yard raking the leaves. It's hard keeping them in one area because the wind is blowing. He looks up at the gathering storm clouds and hopes he can get it done before his dad gets home. He has a date tonight, but he can't leave until his chores are done.

He knows what's coming next and dreads it. He spends a little extra time raking the stray leaf or two into the pile just so he won't have to look up and see the large, black dog trotting toward him up the driveway. There are a few strays in the neighborhood who know him as an easy mark for some scraps or a belly rub, but this one is a stranger. Not a stranger to Aaron though—he's dreamed of this dog for years—but a stranger to the neighborhood. It doesn't belong here. It is larger and in much better shape than the local mutts. Its coat is solid black and doesn't shine at all; it absorbs light like an old chalkboard. Its claws spark against the concrete like steel knives. It growls as it gradually and deliberately stops in front of Aaron.

Aaron has experience caring for and training dogs; he knows one thing you never do is move suddenly when faced with an aggressive one and this one is definitely aggressive. He also knows you never look into their eyes; they take it as a challenge to their dominance. Aaron looks at the ground in front of the dog.

The dog's ears are up and pointed toward Aaron, and its tail is out straight. It's leaning on its front legs; a dog exerting its dominance will do that. Aaron knows the dog is going to attack when its growl turns into a snarl, just like the dozens of other times he has stood face to face with it.

Aaron knows the rake is useless against the dog, but he also knows he would feel better if he had something, anything, between them. He carefully shifts the rake so it's in front of him while he—just as carefully—places his other hand on it. His Tai Chi training kicks in and he bends his knees to give himself some balance. It's easier to move quickly if he doesn't have to spend precious time shifting his weight. The dog starts circling him, so Aaron starts circling it back, refusing to let the dog get behind him.

Aaron decides to chance a look into the dog's eyes. He knows what he's going to see but does it anyway. The eyes are like empty sockets, a vacuum ready to suck his soul into Hell. They chill him to the bone as if it's the first time he's seen them. He knows what he has to do. If he stands any chance of saving himself, and his soul, he has to defeat this dog. It wants to possess him. Aaron knows he has to kill it. He'll have to give more than he receives and he knows a flimsy yard rake and all the Tai Chi practice in the world won't help him.

He senses more than sees the pile of leaves scatter as a cold wind picks them up. Suddenly, a spot of ice forms on the center of his chest. It spreads throughout his body. He doesn't need a mirror to know what's happening. He's changing into an anti-version of this dog. In the next few moments, he becomes a mirror image of the hellhound in every respect. When the hellhound steps forward with his left foot, Aaron steps forward with his right. Where the hellhound's left ear has a notch from some previous battle, Aaron's right ear is notched.

The dream usually ends here, but not this time.

This time they clash in a black hurricane roar as Aaron refuses to yield his soul without a fight....

Aaron jerked awake shivering and staring at the ceiling; he was lying on sweat-soaked sheets—a recently-revealed byproduct of these night terrors. He moved a little closer to the edge of the bed, seeking a warmer, or at least drier, place to lie. His fingers slid across his wet scalp as he ran them through his hair.

Tonight was close, he thought. We'd never attacked each other before. One night and one night soon, I'll have to finish that fight. He knew it would be a spectacular battle. Still, he did not relish the thought, even though he wanted to see what would happen next. The suspense usually kept him wired for hours after waking up—he was afraid this was going to be one of those times.

He got out of bed and quietly made his way to the dresser. The Florida sun was peeking through the window, so there was no need to turn on the light and wake up Karen. She was grouchy if he woke her up before midmorning. He reached into his ditty bag and pulled out his shaving kit. He rummaged around inside it until his hand brushed against his hippy necklace. Holding the fang in the early morning sunlight, he ran his fingers over it, feeling the smooth sides and the sharp point. He sat down on the edge of the bed and continued to watch the sunbeam twinkle off of it while the dream slowly faded from his consciousness. He looked up from time to time to watch Karen sleep. The sunbeam slowly moved across the bed, and it wouldn't be long before she would turn over, grumble about the light, and try to steal the covers. He hoped she wouldn't roll over into the sweat-soaked spot he left there. Damn, she's beautiful. You're a lucky man, Aaron. Don't screw it up. Although he knew Karen didn't like the necklace—she still insisted it scratched her—he put it on anyway. He could take it off again later. He just felt naked without it sometimes. Then he dug around in his overnight bag until he found his shorts and t-shirt, trying not to make any noise.

Usually, if he found himself out of bed early in the morning, he would enjoy the view from the backyard. He never considered himself a morning person, but the Navy schedule tended to convert most people. His heart was still racing, burning off the adrenaline from his dream, though. *Time for some Tai Chi. I need to calm down.* Master Chen would be proud of him for continuing his studies so long after leaving Louisiana.

Craig came out with a cup of coffee about half-way through Aaron's third performance of the Wu Form and sat down to watch. Aaron had long gotten over his bashfulness while doing his forms in front of others—mainly by reaching a state of meditation where nothing existed but Chi, the energy that flows through all living things. *Damn Lucas for renaming it the "Force."* He was certainly aware of his surroundings, but anything other than himself was just another source of Chi to absorb and mold.

The Wu Form contained over one hundred stances and positions and took nearly twenty minutes to complete. Holding his body in one pose while transitioning to the next was physically strenuous, and combined with the humidity, drenched him in sweat by the time he made his closing move.

The grass under his bare feet and between his toes relaxed him and helped to keep him centered, and he let out a sad sigh at the loss of its touch when he stepped onto the patio. He threw his towel on the table and sank into a chair next to Craig. "Good morning."

"Morning, Aaron," Craig said as he lifted his coffee cup to his lips. "So, that's a martial art? Sorry, but I don't see it."

"It is. There are some who think Kung Fu is based on Tai Chi, some who think Tai Chi is based on Kung Fu, and there is a stubborn faction who believes they are separate and aren't related at all. I don't agree with that one, though; there're too many similar moves between them. Tai Chi's better for meditation, though. Kung Fu is a hard style—hits and kicks and lots of jumping and screaming. Tai Chi is considered a soft style—redirections, mostly."

Craig chuckled. "I would think that is something kids would like to do, jumping and kicking. How did you get into Tai Chi? Seems too sedate for the younger generation."

Aaron laughed. "My dad wanted me to take a harder style, but I chose Tai Chi just to be obstinate. Master Chen, my teacher, was especially patient and firm with me." He picked his up towel and wiped his face and neck. "It took about a year before I discovered I enjoyed the forms. Been doing it for about fourteen years now. I would really like to open up my own studio someday." He shrugged his shoulders. "Master Chen says he would sponsor me. I don't know, though. It's probably just a pipe dream."

He wrapped the towel around the back of his neck, letting the ends fall to his chest. "But you're right. Tai Chi is usually studied by the older generation. Less stressful on the joints and all. But I think I could teach it to kids, especially troubled kids. It's helped me. I know it would help them."

"What rank are you? Black Belt?"

"Tai Chi doesn't have ranks in the traditional sense. We have beginners, intermediates, advanced, and masters. I'm in the advanced category, but it sounds conceited when I say it out loud. I just tell people I'm a student." He smiled. "We're all students, so I'm not lying when I say it."

Lisa came out, leaned over and kissed Craig on the forehead. "Morning. How many are we expecting tonight?"

Craig answered, "About twenty."

Aaron asked, "Party? Need any help with the smoker?" He was confident that if she wasn't smoking something with twenty people coming over this evening, then she probably needed to be in bed and forced-fed chicken noodle soup.

She smiled. "You betcha! In fact, since you're all sweaty and haven't had your shower yet, you can clean the smoker out for me. You know where the brushes are."

That afternoon was humid and still with a hint of the approaching regular, four o'clock, fifteen minute Florida rain shower. The clouds weren't pregnant yet, so the occasional ray of sunshine didn't have any trouble sneaking through. Aaron and Karen were lounging around the pool sipping their beers while the smell of meat cooking on a low, smoky fire promised everyone in the courtyard a relaxing evening of good food with good friends. Word got out Karen was no longer considered single, and all of her and the Minors' friends were coming over later that evening eager to meet the man who had captured her.

Aaron had just settled back into his chair after checking the temperature on the smoker when Craig came over and joined him. "Excited?" he asked.

"About what?" Aaron asked back.

"About meeting everyone," he explained. "Everyone's looking forward to meeting you."

"Oh. Yeah, I suppose," Aaron muttered. "I'm more nervous, though. Y'all keep talking about this get-together like I'm auditioning for a movie or something."

He grinned like he was holding a prank back. "In a way, you are."

Aaron sighed and took a long swig of his beer to hide his frown. *WWKD? Express his displeasure, of course.* "Man, you know I don't like surprises. What are you up to?" Craig's only answer was another wide, toothy grin.

Karen giggled, and then with a sing-song tone, teased Aaron, "You'll have to wait and see-ee." Then she took his hand, lifted it to her lips, and kissed it with a loud smack to let him know it was okay to relax. "You'll like it, I promise."

Aaron took a long gulp from his beer.

Chapter 8—Frank Mason

Frank Edward Mason, Jr. finished making his run around the estate. It took most of a day to do so, but that was his job. Tonight was a big whoop-de-doo, what with all of Craig's friends coming over for some big party. Frank was gardener, grounds keeper, and forest ranger, all rolled up into one. If it grew out of or ran across the ground it was his responsibility, and had been for eighteen years. Craig liked to keep most of it wild so it didn't require much maintenance. Still, it had to be checked every couple of days. Craig gave him quite a bit of leeway on how he handled things. If something came up that needed his attention, Frank did it. If it was more than he could handle, he brought in wildlings to help. *That's what they're for, I reckon.* He loved this piece of land as if it were his own.

He stopped by his quarters to get dressed and then went and found Craig in the courtyard. "Boss, the grounds are clear," he reported.

Craig smiled. "Thanks, Frank. Tell Maria to keep her temporary help until tomorrow for clean up."

"Yessuh, Boss. Will there be anything else for me tonight?"

Craig shook his head. "No, I think that's it. Good night, Frank. Thanks."

"Night, Boss."

Frank found Maria on the back patio and relayed Craig's message. The "extra help" meant wildlings, of course.

Frank grew up in Virginia Beach, Virginia, about a fifteen minute walk from the Atlantic Ocean. It was a old, rambling two-story house perfectly suited for him, five younger brothers and sisters, and their parents.

It didn't take long for Frank, Sr. and his wife, Christine, to start their family once he finally got home from the war. Frank, Jr. was born in 1946, exactly ten months after his father returned home from Europe. Frank, Jr. found himself with five younger siblings within eight years.

Frank, Sr. had been a mechanic for the Red Tails, the all Negro aerial combat squadron that served with distinction in Europe. He planned to use that hard-earned knowledge and experience to start his own airplane repair shop. Negroes were permitted funds under the G.I. Bill, but the process to procure those funds was littered with red tape making it nearly impossible for him to receive them. If it hadn't been for the hardships he endured just earning the right to serve his country, he would have given up. So while Christine ran the house and the kids, he opened his shop at the end of a local airstrip used mostly by crop dusters about a twenty-minute walk from his home.

The business struggled the first few years. Frank Sr. was a black man living on the edge of a mostly white area and the locals were slow to trust him to work on their airplanes. In time though they learned he was as honest as they came and did great work, and his business grew.

Family-owned businesses relied heavily on family labor in the forties and fifties. Frank, Jr. and the other boys spent their free time at the shop helping the mechanics with whatever they could that didn't require training. From the time they could carry a box of rags, they were earning their keep. The three girls worked just as hard around the house helping their mother.

Somewhere in the middle of his high school years, Frank, Jr. found grease-blackened fingernails and wrench-busted knuckles were not to his liking. He understood it was a family business and knew where the food on the table came from, but he made up his mind he wasn't going to be a mechanic all of his life. He was still wearing his graduation cap and gown when he finally got up the courage to tell his father he wanted to try something other than turning wrenches.

His father hid his disappointment, but offered to let him stay at the house—for cheap rent. "A man has to make his own way. And a Negro has to work twice as hard while doing it," he reminded him.

Virginia Beach was a sleepy little coastal town until the ships docked and sailors eager to spend money poured down the gangplank with their paychecks in hand. Their money was welcome in the restaurants and bars, and the police did their best to keep a positive, public image on the town. If a sailor got too drunk and caused too much of a ruckus, the cops would typically put him in a cab back to his ship rather than putting him in jail.

After the war, inlanders, as the locals called them, found Virginia Beach a welcoming tourist stop between New England and Myrtle Beach. It was already suited to welcoming outsiders—sailors—so when the tourists started showing up with their out-of-town money, it was a perfect fit. The restaurants, bars, and hotels welcomed this new source of cash with open arms. The city council and its economic development committee offered incentives to all businesses, especially those along the waterfront, to keep well-manicured lawns and well-maintained building facings. Virginia Beach suddenly found itself no longer a sleepy little coastal town but a jumping hotbed of tourism.

Frank found work for one of the lawn maintenance companies that sprang up to maintain the town's new look. He found working outdoors suited him more than working in a garage. The smell of freshly cut grass was ambrosia to him, and the look of a neatly trimmed shrub was something he could appreciate. A repaired engine didn't look any different than one that was broken, and he found he liked seeing the fruits of his labor and took pride in his work. It took him a few months, but he managed to save up enough money to move out of his parents' house and get a place of his own.

He rented an "apartment" a few blocks from home. It was actually the attic above one of his friends' parents' garage, but it was home to him. He dreamed of a place on the "strip"—the road that ran parallel to the beach— but no one would rent one of those apartments to a Negro back then, even if he could have afforded it. The apartment wasn't fancy, but it did come fully furnished. His entire family helped him move in one Saturday afternoon, and his sisters delighted in getting the place ready to live in by making sure the kitchen was organized and the bathroom was set up and the living room was comfortable. His brothers simply moved things where their sisters told them to and looked on with envy.

Things moved along well at work for Frank over the next few months. His hard work and attention to detail got the attention of the owner, one Craig Minor.

Frank was sweating over getting a hoe sharp enough to shave one morning when Craig stuck his head out the door. "Frank, come into my office, please."

Frank stood just inside Craig's office door twisting his cap in his hands and asked, "Is everything okay, Boss?"

"Sure, sure! Everything's fine. I just want you to know that I'm giving you your own crew."

"Really? I'd like that, Mr. Minor!"

"I thought you might be pleased. Frank, you're the hardest worker I've ever seen. But you're also the smartest worker I have. I need a man like you to stick around. Keep up the good work." Craig leaned back in chair and put his hands behind his head. "Of course, I can't put any white men on your crew. That wouldn't be right, but you'll have the responsibility for all the other boys."

"Yessir, Mr. Minor."

And work out they did. Frank worked for Craig and steadily moved up the chain in responsibility over the next year. Eventually, Craig promoted him to Lead Foreman with three crews of his own under him. Frank answered to no one except Craig.

Frank was locking up the tools and machinery at the end of a long day when Craig leaned out the door and motioned for Frank to come into the office when he finished.

Again, Frank found himself standing in Craig's office, but instead of wringing his cap by the door, he was wringing his cap standing in front of Craig's desk. Craig's wife, Lisa, was in the office with them, sitting on a couch smoking a cigarette.

Craig asked, "Frank, do you like working for me?"

Frank's face went from nervous curiosity to outright fear. "Yessuh, I sho' do! You not about to fire me, are you, Boss?"

Craig laughed. "Fire you? Hell, no! I need you too much for that."

Frank visibly relaxed and tried to stop twisting his cap. He reached around and stuck it in his back pocket.

Craig leaned back in his chair. "Frank, Lisa and I have bought a business in Florida," he explained. "It comes with an estate. A large estate. I want you to maintain that estate for us."

Frank was confused. "You want me to move to Florida and maintain your place? Who's gonna run this for you up here?"

"No one. I'm selling off the assets and closing it down."

Frank was quiet while he thought this through. "So, if I don't go with you, I'm out of work?" He didn't like his options, but he needed to make sure he understood the situation. "Is that what you're saying, Mr. Minor?"

Craig frowned. "That's one way to look at it. But I was hoping you would accept the position." Craig pointed his finger directly at Frank. "I don't trust anyone but you to handle it. It's large, and I don't want to hire someone I don't know to keep it up."

Frank asked, "How much land we talking about, Boss?"

Lisa broke in. "Sixty-thousand acres. Most of it is—"

Frank interrupted. "Sixty-thousand acres?!" Then he stopped himself. "Sorry, Miss Lisa. I didn't mean to be rude. I's just shocked, that's all."

Lisa smiled. "That's okay, Frank. As I was saying, most of it is wild, so it's really just a position to keep an eye on things."

Frank looked down at his shoes and shrugged his shoulders slightly. "That's a mighty large piece of land to just keep an eye on," he egged-on. "That would be an all day and all night, all week-long job. I would need transportation into town, a place to stay. There are so many things I would need."

Craig drolled, "Uh-huh." He sat forward in his chair and interlaced his fingers, resting them on the desk. "Well, what do you think 'those things' would cost you? Say, $125 a week?"

Frank stood a little taller and chanced a momentary look directly into Craig's face. "Well, I was thinking, seeing as I would do such a good job for you and all, that $150 sounds a might bit closer. Seein's as I'm gonna have to move down there and buy new uniforms and—"

Craig held his hands up so Frank would stop talking. "Okay, okay!" Craig shook his head in disbelief. "$150 a week for a Negro. I never thought I would see the day. If I had known you were this good at negotiating, I would have let Lisa ask you. You sure you aren't part Jew?"

Frank smiled. "Nosir, Boss, I ain't part Jew. But I'm yo' man in Florida, yessiree!"

Craig was a little bigoted, but he treated Frank like a man. And working for him turned out to be a pretty good deal most of the time. He liked the outdoors, and when the Minors built their mansion, they put in lavish servants' quarters. He was glad to see that; he wouldn't have to live in a hut anymore. He was never invited to any of their parties, but that didn't bother him any. He and the maids got together sometimes and partied on their own, though he never found one he wanted to spend his life with. That didn't matter. The estate was his wife.

Chapter 9—Coquo et Comedo

verb [käk'-kwō ət kä'-mə-dō]

1. Prepare and eat.

Aaron Darveau

Craig's guests started trickling in around six o'clock, about an hour before the food was ready to serve. The first two to arrive were Warren and his wife, Riley. Warren was tall, darkly tanned, and handsome, with some grey starting to show at his temples. Riley was tall, also darkly tanned, and gorgeous with light blue eyes and sun-bleached blonde hair. They were dressed alike and looked as if they belonged on a yacht sailing somewhere around the Caribbean. They wore matching top siders, pressed shorts, and polo shirts with some sailboat logo on the front left pocket. They were nice enough, if a bit aloof. They had an aristocratic civility about them combined with a cultured northeastern accent. Warren had a firm, but not overpowering, handshake that was obviously refined in boardrooms around the world. Riley had one of those soft, womanly handshakes that could mean either submissiveness or back stabber. Her face was a mask of porcelain, so it was hard to determine which without knowing her any better.

Aaron was finishing his introductions with Warren and Riley when Craig turned his head to one side as if listening for something and announced, "Here come Bill and Glen." A few seconds later, a large 4x4 Dodge Power Wagon with a 12" lift kit and buckshot mudders came roaring up the private drive. Waylon Jennings's voice crooned loudly through the rolled down windows and over the rumbling of the glass packs. Aaron was looking forward to meeting these two. Country music and a four-wheel drive pickup truck could only mean good ol' boys, and it'd been a long time since he'd hung out with that type of crowd.

Aaron caught a glimpse of Warren tilting his head back. If Aaron didn't know any better, he would have sworn he saw him sniff the air. His face crinkled into a frown, he scoffed and turned around, muttering, "Stoned and drunk again." Then a little louder, "Craig, you shall bail them out should they encounter members of the law enforcement community again tonight." Aaron thought it was possible Warren knew them all too well.

Bill and Glen climbed out of the truck, and it was immediately obvious to Aaron they were brothers. It also wasn't hard to conclude they started early with the cocktails. They were staggering and slapping their cowboy hats on the legs of their frazzled jeans over some trivial, macho brag only they knew about. They could have passed for a couple of drunken sailors if not for the long hair and the doobie they were sharing.

They caught up with Aaron at the smoker, and introduced themselves. Aaron found them to be quite the riot, doing funny handshakes and laughing. When they found out Aaron was from Louisiana, they roared in unison, "Cooooon Aaaaaass!" The way they dragged the two words out made Aaron laugh.

He countered with, "That's *Mr.* Coon Ass to you."

Bill addressed Glen, his face screwed up into mock seriousness, and mimicked Warren, "Cocky runt, isn't he?"

Glen replied, "Yeah, but I like him anyway." He shouted at Karen across the pool, "You can keep him, Princess." She responded with the universal sign of contempt, a well-formed flipping of the bird that pulled even more laughter out of them. Glen looked at Aaron with a playful smirk. "Do my eyes deceive me, or did our princess just give me the finger?"

While Aaron nodded in the affirmative, Bill added, still in Warren-speak, "There's no doubt about it. She most certainly did, Glenford. How rude! No pudding for her tonight."

Craig surprised Aaron when he scolded them. "Show some respect, guys."

Bill looked at Glen. "His house, his rules."

Glen responded, "Yeah, I know. Let's find the beer." They went off, exploring the various coolers around the pool in search of their redneck nectar.

Nobody knew James was there until Lisa screamed, "James, get out of that smoker!" He dropped the lid and turned around to confront his accuser with the look of a child who had just been caught being naughty. He was short and muscular with a large, walrus mustache that nearly covered his entire mouth. His foray into Lisa's domain foiled, he went over and introduced himself to Aaron.

Aaron turned back toward the kitchen window to check and see if Lisa was watching. He whispered lowly, "Come back by in a few minutes. I'm in charge of the basting this afternoon. I'll get you a chunk to gnaw on."

James laughed. "No worries. If I didn't stick my fingers in it when I first got here, she'd think I was sick or something. It's a game with us."

He turned and kissed Karen on the cheek and asked how she was doing. Aaron wasn't quite sure he liked the kiss; it lasted a little longer than what he considered polite. He wasn't sure how he knew it, but these two had a romantic history with each other.

Aaron thought everyone who was going to show up had shown up when Summer and Autumn, twin sisters, decided to make an appearance. Aaron thought they were both beautiful in a country-club sort of way, with soft, chocolate brown eyes and craftily tangled blonde curls. He'd seen women like this before, and the phrase *High Maintenance* came to mind. He guessed they felt like slumming, because they immediately attached themselves to Bill and Glen. Aaron sneaked glances at them whenever he thought Karen wasn't paying attention.

A few others came in and introduced themselves to Aaron, but didn't spend more than a minute or two talking with him. Aaron was left with the impression they didn't want to spend any more time with him than was polite, not out of rudeness, but out of uneasy respect. He was confused by this, but welcomed it. Their unease made him feel the same way.

Most everyone mingled with each other while Craig joined a few men whose names Aaron couldn't remember under the gazebo for cigars. Aaron caught them looking over in his direction a few times and talking. He assumed the conversation was private so he stayed with Karen until dinner was served, leaving her side only to tweak the dampers on the smoker to maintain the temperature. He caught various bits and pieces of everyone's conversations before dinner and they mostly centered on him; if he was feeling uncomfortable before, it only got worse.

"The hunt was nice last month."

"…seems a little young."

"You were, too, once."

"…never that young."

"Yes, you were."

"How's the boat coming?"

"…see in him?"

"Oh…think he's cute."

"…chose Craig."

"…ran into a Fector at the…"

"…problem with the bilge."

"Lisa would have bit you."

"…worth it…try out Aaron."

"Karen…bite you."

Around 7:30 dinner was served. Everyone filed out of the rear foyer to the backyard and gathered at the picnic table Maria and her temporary help had set up on the patio. Craig, a gracious host, ensured everyone had plenty on their plates before he filled his own while Lisa refreshed everyone's drinks. Once Craig took his position at the head of the table, everyone stopped talking.

Craig made a toast, "To our old friends and our lost friends!" then looking at Aaron, continued, "And to our new friends!"

Everybody cheered, "Hear, hear!"

Karen made sure she and Aaron sat next to Emma and Ricardo, good friends of hers and the Minors. Ricardo was one of the men Aaron saw under the gazebo with Craig smoking cigars. He had one now, and it reminded Aaron of the kind his dad smoked—Cuban seed if his nose wasn't lying to him. Ricardo was of average build, the same height as Aaron, but about twenty pounds heavier. He was of Latin origin and the type who would make a jealous boyfriend leave a room with his date—just to ensure she didn't lay eyes on any unwanted competition. He spoke with an educated cadence tempered by a slight, southern United States accent. Emma was short and petite and wore a pair of white sandals below a flowery skirt and sheer white blouse. Chestnut hair and green eyes finished the portrait of this lady. She had a sophisticated poise and didn't mind smiling affectionately when she greeted everyone.

While dinner was underway, Ricardo leaned over and gave Karen a big, fatherly hug. "It's good to see you, Princess."

She returned the hug. "It's good to see you, too, Ricardo. You don't get down here enough."

"I know. Work keeps me busy." He leaned forward a bit and asked, "Is this Aaron?"

"Yes," she beamed. "Aaron, this is Ricardo and his wife, Emma."

Swallowing a not quite completely chewed mouthful of food, Aaron tried his best to be mannerly. "Nice to meet you."

Aaron didn't get the hug treatment. He instead got a handshake that left him thinking he'd latched onto a piece of angle iron. Ricardo didn't squeeze, but there was no give in his grip. He smiled at Aaron and asked, "So you're the one our little princess has chosen, huh?"

Aaron chuckled, looked at Karen and replied, "Actually, I chose her. It took me five tries before she finally said yes."

Ricardo raised one eyebrow and said in all seriousness, "If that's what helps you sleep at night, feel free to believe it."

Craig Minor

Craig found the conversation at dinner engaging. Mostly, everyone was catching up with the news in each other's lives. This was a close-knit group of people comfortable with spending a couple of days each month together, and it was easy to see they cared for each other. Craig was surprised James was behaving himself considering Karen had rejected his overture as mate. The conversations died down about the same time everyone finished eating.

Everyone offered their congratulations and thanks to Lisa for dinner before they moved into the courtyard to sit around the pool for dessert. The conversations started up again, only now, the boy was bombarded with questions about his past. What did he like to do for fun? How did Karen and he meet? It was the usual get-to-know-you questions.

Craig had his doubts if Aaron had the breeding to do what was necessary. Karen's intuition said he did, and the Gift was rarely, if ever, wrong, but Aaron came from a blue collar family, not "landed gentry" like Craig. Craig had a proper upbringing, born in Richmond, Virginia in 1929, the oldest of five boys and three girls. He considered it his calling to lead the way for his younger siblings into society, showing them how to make it in the world.

He also considered himself the consummate Southern Gentleman. He did, after all, grow up on an old plantation with many servants, all of them "Negroes" as he liked to say. He didn't figure they would amount to much, so he considered it his duty to keep them employed. Take Frank for example. He would still be working some dead-end job in Virginia if Craig hadn't lifted him out of that life. Some people these days considered that attitude racist, but he didn't look at it that way. Those folks simply hadn't been raised around Negroes as he had.

Craig had a business degree. Sure, he'd failed in a few different ventures before he found this wholesaling company, but his father was there to bail him out. That's what family connections are for!

Aaron had none of that. Granted, they both had military service, but Craig had been an officer. He also served during wartime, whereas the boy had not. Admittedly, Craig's time was spent in Japan, far away from the enemy, but he wanted to fight. It was only because his father pulled some strings that he didn't get to experience the glory of fighting the enemy.

Aaron was scraping the cake crumbs off of his dessert saucer when the subject of his time in the Navy came up. Glen asked, "How much longer you got 'til you get out?"

Aaron picked up his napkin and wiped his mouth before answering. "About two months. I've been thinking of re-enlisting becau—"

He abruptly stopped talking because Glen's amusing demeanor unexpectedly broke into anger with an outburst that shattered the pleasant evening. "Re-enlisting? You're gonna fuckin' stay in the fuckin' Navy?!"

Karen stood up and flashed a dark look at Glen. "He's *my* choice so button it, Glen!" she yelled with indignation.

Glen jumped to his feet too, waving his hands in the air. "Princess," he yelled, "I'm just curious why you brought home a fuckin' sailor, that's all. How's he gonna—"

She heatedly interrupted him, but Craig didn't catch what she said. He was watching Aaron. The boy looked on in confusion while a blood vessel pulsed quite visibly in his forehead; he didn't appreciate the way Glen was talking to him or his girlfriend. *Good. I thought that might raise that temper of his.*

Then he saw the boy take a deep breath and grab his side, as if a knife had been sunk into his stomach. Craig was surprised he didn't cry out in pain. *Boy's got spunk, I'll grant him that.* The pain must have faded because he stood up, took a deep breath, and looked over toward Karen's bedroom. *Probably wondering if he can make the bathroom.* He regained some of his composure, but then he doubled over. Everyone forgot the fiery exchange between Karen and Glen when they saw Aaron fall to his knees.

Craig slashed off the ensuing argument by standing up. "Good job, Glen. It worked. You and Bill go get the crate."

Karen snapped her head in Craig's direction. "What do you mean '*it worked?*'"

"Lisa doped his meat with a little *Lupum lues*," he confessed. "Combined with Glen's badgering, it raised his blood pressure just enough to force the *renovatio* early. It's not the *plenilunium* in case you've forgotten. I didn't want him transforming later this week in the middle of a Navy base when the moon *did* fully show itself."

Karen snapped, "A little warning would have been nice."

"We didn't make the decision until a couple of hours ago. You two were practically tied at the hip so I couldn't get you the word." He raised his hands in surrender, and a little, crooked grin crossed his face. "Sorry! I didn't expect you to defend him so ruthlessly."

The boy was on his hands and knees now and deep in the throes of his *renovatio*. Craig remembered his first change, and not with fondness. He knew what the boy was going through. Right now, he probably thought he was dying.

Well, Karen, you wanted him, you got him. You better be able to control him, or we'll have a real mess on our hands. A wildling running uncontrolled around my villa is not on the menu tonight. Karen insisted she would be able to keep Aaron under control, but Craig wasn't so sure. He didn't think Aaron was wrapped around her finger as tightly as she thought he was.

She rushed to the boy's side and scrambled around in front of him. She held his face between her hands. She had the *look*, the look of a *renovatio* being held back, but he smelled something else. *Victory? It's a little early to celebrate. Love, maybe? Surely not, but she didn't defend him like a she-wolf for nothing.*

She cooed, "Aaron, don't fight it. It'll be over soon. You wanted me. This is what you wanted, remember?"

Aaron struggled to look up at her. His voice shook. "What are you talking about? What's happening?" Then he looked up and over at Craig, pleading for answers, for help, for an end to the pain. The fire of Craig's own *renovatio* caressed him, wanted to be free, but he held it in check, pulled it under control. He looked around the table—everyone had the *look*. Their eyes were all dark blue, reflecting their *lupus* heritage.

Craig watched as Karen turned the boy's face back to hers. "If you want me, you have to endure this just a little longer. Just a little longer. Just look into my eyes. Know I'm here. Know I chose you. Just keep thinking about me."

Aaron Darveau

Aaron descended into madness because it was the only place he could hide from the pain, the unbearable pain.

When he was twelve years old, during the temper tantrum that sparked his entrance into Tai Chi training, he slammed his hand down on his family's stove. It landed on one of the electric burners, the one his mother had just taken the boiling water off of. Every nerve from his hand to his shoulder told him his arm was on fire. Only now, it wasn't just his arm—it

74

was every nerve in his body. His skin was on fire, and it all originated from the scars Karen left on his back from their first night together. As suddenly as the first cramp hit, the fire coalesced into millions of mini-fires covering his entire body. His clothes rubbed against him like alcohol and sand paper on an open wound. He ripped them off to escape the pain, not caring if he destroyed them or not. He had to get them off, and he had to do it now. Every hair on his body turned into a red-hot needle and pierced his skin. His vision was foggy, and if not for Karen's face right in front of him, he would have wished for death. Instead, he held her face in his heart and remembered the last time he held her in a lover's embrace, and wondered if that was the last time he would do so. As he was consumed by the fire, coldness rose from his chest. It spread throughout his body, dousing the fire.

Madame Jajine

Madame Jajine was cleaning up candle wax from her last appointment of the day when the vision hit. It was strong, stronger than any to have hit her in quite a few years. It was a relief in a way—she was afraid she might have been losing her mojo. She sat down on the couch. "Luna, this is a good one, girl. Take notes!" She reached over to the end table and grabbed a charm, a chicken claw, from behind Joey's picture. The charm possessed no supernatural properties. She needed it to scratch herself, to draw a little blood—not much, just enough to smear on the mirror set up on the TV tray. When the entire surface was covered, she stared at it. "Let's see what voodoo we can stir up dis evening. *Moutre m!* Show me what be goin' on!"

The bloody face of the mirror swirled around like liquid peppermint candy then slowly faded to a clear picture. "Oh, there's that nice boy, Aaron, who visited here all those years ago. Look at him, surrounded by all his new friends. It took him long enough, didn't it, Luna?" She continued to watch Aaron perform his first *renovatio*. She adjusted the mirror some, permitting a view of his front. She was looking for something. "Ah! He's wearing it, Luna! Good boy, Aaron. Good boy. You'll be fine if you've been wearing your necklace this long."

She adjusted the mirror again by waving her hand over it, looking for someone in particular. "Hello, Craig, you old *con lungyet.*" She knew Craig couldn't hear her but talked to him anyway. "You're a history buff. Do you know what Marcus Cicero said? No? Well, he said dat only a war waged for revenge or defense is just. Welcome to my pit of justice, you old sonuvabitch!"

Aaron Darveau

The coldness reminded Aaron of his dream, how it would spread out through his body when he was changing into the not-hellhound. He reached up to touch his hippy necklace, but he couldn't find purchase. He looked for his hands. He had grown paws! Black paws! *I'm not dreaming, so what is this?* He looked up to Karen, but instead saw his backyard in Louisiana. *Maybe I am dreaming. Or I've been beamed back to Louisiana.* He saw his rake lying on the ground. He saw the large, black dog rushing him.

Finally! It's time to finish this once and for all.

Aaron was its equal. He had the claws, the strength, the teeth. No, he was more than its equal because he still had a soul. The hellhound hadn't won it yet. They clashed.

They reared up trying to find a tooth-hold on each other's throats, and a woman's voice broke through the growling. "Fight it, Aaron, fight it! Don't let it win!" New strength flowed into him from the voice.

The voice was familiar—*Jajine?*—but he was too busy to spend time thinking about it. Aaron found his teeth around one of the hellhound's ears. He bit down as hard as he could and pulled. The hellhound let out a shriek and backed off half a step before lunging back into him, grabbing Aaron's right shoulder with its jaw. The pain shot through Aaron's arm like the time he burned his hand. He was paralyzed. The hellhound stood still with Aaron's shoulder between its teeth, growling, tempting Aaron to worsen the damage by trying to shake free.

Aaron's confidence swiftly eroded. The pain was too much for him to endure. Better to let go. But if he gave up, he would lose possession of his soul—he was already slipping back into the madness. The only way to attack was to leave part of himself in the hellhound's mouth, to rip himself away from its jaws. But he would bleed out. He could think of no way to win! Suddenly, he pictured himself standing on the bridge of the Enterprise. Jajine was sitting at Uhura's station, dressed in the red mini-skirt, earpiece sticking out of her ear.

She mocked him, "Captain Kirk doesn't believe in no-win scenarios, boy. Why do you?"

Instantly, he knew what he had to do. He changed the rules of engagement. He twisted his body so it pushed up against the hellhound's. It lost its grip. The snap of tendons tearing and flesh ripping told him he was hurt, but he channeled his Chi and converted the pain to energy, boosting his strength and his speed. Aaron mounted the hellhound from the side and sank his teeth into the nape of its neck. He hung on with his jaw as he willed his front right leg over the hellhound's back, forcing it to find purchase, to hold on. His claws dug deep into the black dog's side.

The hellhound couldn't find anything to bite, and it couldn't shake its attacker free; Aaron was completely behind and above it. The more the hellhound struggled, the deeper Aaron's fangs sank into it. Finally, the hellhound's spinal column brushed against Aaron's fangs, and he shook his head back and forth, separating the animal's head from its body. The cursed beast gave one final shriek of pain as it collapsed.

Aaron had won. After all of these years of waiting to fight it, he had won. He had fought evil incarnate and won. He knew his soul would never again be in danger. If he could have grabbed it like a trophy, he would have held it above his head in victory.

Aaron again pictured himself back on the bridge of the Enterprise. Jajine was still there, but dressed as he remembered her, gypsy fashion. "Jajine! How? Why? You saved me. That *was* you!"

"I didn't save you, boy. You saved yourself. I just gave you the tools. I can't stay long, so I have to be quick."

"What just happened?" He took a couple of steps toward her.

"Something miraculous. Something they never saw coming—a future without *them* in it." She started disappearing, as if a *Star Trek* transporter had her. "I have to go now. Trust your instincts, Aaron. They're good instincts. I'm proud of you, boy!"

"Wait, I've—" but he found himself looking at Karen's face.

I am Aaron.

Everyone around the pool is gawking at me in disbelief, eyes wide and mouths dangling open. All my senses are on high alert. Smells are sharp. Vision is—it looks like it is daytime, but the colors are funny, muted maybe. The pool lights are on. They're on a timer, so it's definitely night time. My hearing—my God, I hear everyone's hearts beating! Wait, I hear one more, somewhere, faster, smaller—afraid. I smell its fear. Wait! How do I know it's fear? I don't know. I just do. It's a sickly-sweet smell. I also smell it from the women here. Why would they be afraid of me? Craig is oozing something else. It smells like anger, but that isn't quite right. It's mixed with something else.

Jealousy, maybe.

Insects are buzzing around my ears. Why won't they go away?! I can't shake them away! They must be huge to make such a racket! Where are they? They're over by the pool! By the pool! Good God, what's happened?

The water lapping along the edge of the pool is as loud as Daytona Beach on a stormy day. He curiously steps over and peers into the water. A reflection of a wolf stares back at him. He's not scared, but he is surprised, and yells out, "**Ah!**"

That wasn't a yell! That was a howl!

Bill and Glen are pushing a dolly with a crate on it. Are they going to Edgar Allen Poe me, bury me alive? My lips curl up and a growl escapes my throat. I relax when I realize they're not. Suddenly, I hear the smaller heartbeat within and I no longer think about what I saw in the pool.

This is much more interesting.

Glen opens the side of the crate and I see what's afraid, what possesses the rapidly beating heart. It is a deer. Its attention lands on me as soon as it's freed from its cage and bolts, heading for the open fields out behind Craig's estate. I smell the urine it releases as it runs and my heartbeat jumps up.

It is scared.

It knows it is prey.

It knows I am a predator.

My mouth starts salivating, so I lick my lips. The fur on my snout rubs against my tongue.

Craig utters a single word, "Eat."

I don't need his permission. I'm already running after it.

Part II - Renovatio
noun [re-nə-vä'-tē-ō]
1. Rebirth.

Chapter 10—Suscitatio
noun [sə-se-tā'-tē-ō]
1. Awakening.

Aaron Darveau, April 24, 1983

The woman next to Aaron stirred in her sleep. They were spooned together with his normal morning glory pressing against her in a satisfyingly erotic way. She stirred again, but this time was more deliberate with her motion, rubbing her hips against him. He forced himself awake and discovered they were in the middle of a field. It must have rained because the ground was damp. It wasn't uncomfortable, though. Quite the contrary—it was if he was reborn! He was full of energy, and his skin tingled like an electrical shock was running all over it. He wasn't sure where they were. He only knew he was content and didn't want to get up. In fact, he wanted to do something else.

He gently nibbled the nape of the woman's neck, and she responded by turning over and facing him. They made love in the field with an urgency he didn't recall feeling before. They craved, not each other, but the sensation of that one simple act representing life itself. He didn't know where they got their stamina from. Their responses to each other were animalistic.

He rolled off the woman, slaked, and his memories from last night, though dim, slowly awoke. He knew something astounding happened but wasn't sure what. Confusion and darkness ruled. They untangled from each other and lay back in the grass. The woman searched his face for something; she was familiar, but he couldn't put a name to her. He sat up and stretched, adoring the brilliant colors everywhere, the smell of damp grass and a hundred other things, and the echoes of a world freshly awakened.

Memories of last night began to crowd his consciousness, but they were jumbled, out of order, and some appeared missing altogether. Then, just as if someone turned on a light switch, in a flash, everything from last night crashed through the darkness. What he remembered drove him from one emotion to the next while he put it all in perspective.

He laughed at the craziness of it.

He panicked at the horrifying nature of it.

He giggled at the impossibility of it.

Then he thought about all the movies he'd seen and books he'd read. *Mythology had to be founded on something other than imagination, but this is too fantastic to take seriously.* He stood up and wandered in circles while the possibilities screamed through his brain. His emotions kept changing from moment to moment as more and more information slid into place. If Spock were here, he would be trying to convince him of the insanity of it, but the evidence was overwhelming; there were too many memories to the contrary.

Running through a field.

Chasing a deer.

Catching it.

Offering the kill to Craig and Lisa.

Eating his fill.

Sharing with Karen, then everyone else.

Relaxing.

Chasing each other and counting coup on Bill and Glen.

Growling at James.

Coupling with Karen.

Howling at the moon or at nothing in particular.

Lying down to sleep next to Karen.

He still refused to believe it. Like a keystone is used to hold an arch up, there had to be something else to these memories, something to tie them all together and produce a conclusion other than the one staring him in the face. He again pulled each memory from last night into the light and savagely examined it as if it were new.

All of his memories appeared intact. His conclusion was sound.

He looked up from his internal investigation and caught a whiff of something, something familiar. He had questions needing answers, but the smell was…distracting; it drew him. He followed the smell to where it was strongest and found his hippy necklace. The leather thong was broken, so he tied the loose ends together and slipped it around his neck. When the fang dropped against his chest, it was just as cold as ever.

"I'm a werewolf, huh?" he asked, directing his attention to Karen. It was a rhetorical question. He knew he should have been horrified, but he felt detached—like he was looking at someone else.

The look on her face supported his conclusions. She sat up and folded her legs beneath her. Her hands rested on her thighs while she looked up at him through tears of joy. She tucked her chin and slightly twisted her head to the side. Her lips formed that simple little grin with that small gap between her front teeth that always melted his heart. Sitting there as she was, naked, she looked like a nymph from some of the more adult fairy tales he'd read. "We prefer the term *Lupus sapiens*." The way she said it lilted in his ears. "Or simply the Race, but you can use werewolf if you want. That's what humans call us, anyway."

Hearing the words spoken caused Aaron to doubt his sanity again. Coming to the conclusion through logic was one thing. Having it confirmed by another party jolted his emotions. He quickly grabbed the fang hanging at his chest and watched the morning light twinkle and burst from between his fingertips. *I thought werewolves were supposed to be allergic to silver.*

"How do you feel?" She must have seen the absurdity on his face because she sounded sincere.

"I'm not sure," he puzzled out in measured tones. "Part of me believes it, accepts it. Another part wants to scream in panic. And another part is worried." He looked down and took stock of himself for the first time since waking up. "And I feel really naked."

She stood up and took him by the hand. "Let's get back to the house. I usually make sure I wake up near some clothing. Last night was a riot, though." She shook her head and a tiny giggle escaped her lips, but it turned into a laugh as she looked down at her naked body. "I didn't really plan to wake up in the field like this."

They strolled hand in hand for a few minutes, as naked as Adam and Eve, when a nervy shudder brought him to an abrupt stop. "Did I kill anyone last night?" He was certain he didn't, but he wanted confirmation.

"No," she comforted with a fond smile, grabbing his hand with both of hers.

Relief. "You knew this would happen?" he asked, narrowing his eyes.

She emphatically nodded her head.

"How?" he asked, his eyes darkening as they narrowed even further.

Her hands slipped out of his, and she circled around behind him to lightly run her fingertips over the small scars on his back, the scars *she* made that first night they shared together, the scars where the fire originated from during his change last night.

Am I cursed now? "I thought werewolves had to bite you?" he asked.

"Myth, though if its claws are in you, its teeth probably are, too," she held, giggling.

He didn't find it amusing. He put his hand on his chest, and his breathing started coming in shorter and faster bursts.

"Aaron, it's okay," Karen assured him with soothingly firm persistence. "You're safe, but you need to calm down. If your blood pressure gets too high, you might change again, or you might pass out."

Aaron pulled Chi from his surroundings and used it to anchor himself to the ground, to that moment. This centered him, and his breathing slowed. His apprehension shriveled down to a cold pit in his stomach.

Karen smiled. "That's better!" she exclaimed. "Your control is amazing! I knew I made the right choice. I knew *you* were the right choice. Everyone said I was being foolish. They said to think of the Race, to pick someone who had more experience, to—"

"Slow down, slow down." He held his hands up and stepped back from her, as if she might transfer some other—disease—to him. "What do you mean by *right choice*? What are you talking about?" His panic level started rising again, the detachment from a few minutes ago was fading, getting closer to home; he kept looking for a door to run through, to get away, but he was in the middle of a field. He didn't know which way safety lay.

She followed him and grabbed his hands in hers. He didn't resist but didn't encourage it, either. "I'll try to explain. You remember that night you had a flat tire? With your friends?" she asked.

Curious, but doubtful, he nodded his head. "Yes. What about it?"

"That was us. You were trespassing on private land, our hunting grounds. Here, actually." She spread her arms out and twirled in a circle, indicating everything as far as the eye could see. She stopped and pointed. "Two miles over that hill is where you had your flat tire. We were watching you. We didn't know what you were doing back there. The road is so long and so isolated that people rarely drive down it. We were curious."

"We were lost," he cried defensively.

"We suspected that but didn't know for sure. So we watched the three of you. I studied *you*, though. Something about how you moved piqued my interest." She stepped up to him and slowly ran her fingers down his chest. "You had such confidence in yourself. You knew something was wrong, but you kept a level head. You kept your friends under control too, kept them from panicking."

Aaron snapped at her, "Holy Fuck! That was *you*? For your information, we didn't panic until you attacked!" Aaron remembered that night all too well. He had, for the most part, tried to forget it. He'd experienced a few close calls before—like the time his boat turned over in the Ouachita River and he got tangled up in that trotline—but in his estimation that night on the dirt road was the closest he had ever come to actually dying.

"We didn't attack! Or at least not all of us." She started leading them back. "Let's keep walking and I'll explain what really happened."

Chapter 11—Luto Via
noun [Lü-tō()(v)(w)ē'-ə]
1. Dirt Road.

Karen Argali, January 28, 1983

Craig twisted his head and peered over his shoulder, ears at attention, and nose dilated to catch the breeze. The wildlings were playing in the field, but Karen could tell something was bothering him. He nuzzled Lisa to follow him as they loped off over the hill.

Karen and the other *frenatus* surrounded the wildlings. If something warranted Craig's attention, it was up to the *frenatus* to keep them corralled until the *all clear* was sounded. Unfortunately, there were only four of them tonight to control eighteen wildlings. Unbridled *Lupis sapiens* are hard to control when their curiosity is aroused.

The smell of human drifted over the hill, and a few of the wildlings got a whiff. They raised their snouts, sniffing, and then howled, letting out a *vagor*, signaling to their prey it was now being hunted. Karen growled and snipped at the ones within range, exerting her influence, but she couldn't get them to stop from running over the hill. Bill, Glen, and Summer attempted to get in front, but the wildlings simply ran around them. They were in full bloodlust now. Hopefully, Craig could redirect them. Killing humans wasn't outlawed, but without more information on the situation, the *frenatus* needed to keep them corralled.

The gentle vibration of a pack of wildlings in full sprint abruptly ceased in response to Craig's *vagor*. By the time Karen and the other *frenatus* made it over the hill, Craig and Lisa had stopped them, but it was a losing battle. Karen and the rest showed up in time to keep them from stampeding again.

Craig led everyone to a small copse of trees bordering a large field across the road from where the three humans were trespassing. They were replacing a flat tire. Karen managed to pick up bits and pieces of their conversation and realized they weren't hunters looking for the Race. That was good—for the Lamp of Truth to break the arrangement now, after so many years, would be a disaster. These were just men, possibly lost, and not an immediate danger.

One of them caught Karen's attention, though. He was the shortest one, but the other two deferred to him. He knew something wasn't right, that they were in danger, but wasn't letting it panic his friends. He worked quickly on the tire while his friends stared nervously into the woods. Yes, he definitely knew something was wrong, knew they had to leave immediately. He was worried, but he didn't let it cloud his decisions. He maintained control of himself. The other two were terrified, but covered it up with false bravado. They were unconsciously depending on the leader to keep them safe. That was interesting—a natural leader, his life in danger, showing no fear. Scared yes, but refusing to let it overwhelm his mind.

Karen let her *Mulieres intuitionem*, the Gift all females of the Race shared, tell her about this leader. What it told her was beyond belief. This man had come out of nowhere, not even *lupus*, and her intuition told her he could very well be her king, her *Lupus Rex*. She studied the other two—they were just meat—and then the leader again. There was no doubt. She whispered to Lisa, and it came out as a series of growls and whines only *lupis* could understand. "*Lupus Rex*," she communicated. "**The short one.**"

Lisa's ears relaxed, her pupils dilated, and her lips closed.

Karen objected with a low snarl. "**I'm not crazy, Lisa! Look for yourself.**"

Lisa studied the short one for a few moments before closing her eyes. When she opened them, they were hazy white, pupils just a shadow in the middle, showing she was deep in her *Mulieres intuitionem*. They slowly cleared up and her ears twitched in understanding. "**Yes, but there's a complication. He's already spoken for. I don't know by whom, though. She's mercurial—**"

Indifferent, Karen boasted, "**A mate? I'll deal with that later.**"

"**Be sensible, Karen. If you *veneno* him and he doesn't work out, you risk us all. You can't infect him until you know for sure! You know how long it takes to learn to *frenis*. Are you willing to spend the time to teach him?**"

Karen sighed. "**You're right. But I think he could be the one, Lisa. I thought James was, but I've always had reservations. He's too greedy. This one is unsullied. I can control him.**"

"**The next blue moon is only seven months away. He has to be able to *frenis* during the *caeruleo lunaris* to take the oath. What makes you think he can learn by then?**"

"**He doesn't need to know. In fact, it might be better if he couldn't—**"

"**You can't choose someone as *Lupus Rex* if he can't *frenis*!**" Lisa growled. "**The conclave won't sit still for it**."

"**You could help me convince them**," Karen suggested, slinking slowly to the ground in submission. "**Show them how powerful he could be if given the opportunity**."

Karen watched as Lisa's eyes turned hazy white again. "**Perhaps. He is powerful. I can see it, but I still don't like it. It's your prerogative, obviously, but I do wish you would reconsider. He might not even take to being** *lupus*."

"**Let me worry about that. Let me spend some time with him. I'll be more certain then**."

Karen turned to Craig. "**Don't kill—**" but realized she was talking to empty air. Craig was gone! She searched the surrounding area until she picked up his scent. He and the other *frenatus* had taken the wildings with them to set up an ambush from the other side of the road. She let loose a *vagor*, "**Craig, stop!**"

Craig howled back, "**Why?**"

"**One of them is my** *Lupus Rex*! **Don't kill them!**"

Craig hesitated briefly, muttering, "**That damned intuition of hers**." Then louder, "**I don't know if I can!**"

Before Karen had a chance to answer him, he growled loudly to the wildings. "**Come back!**" It was too late, though. They were on the attack, taking advantage of the momentary lessening of his control.

Karen watched the three humans. The two who were terrified stood rigid, unable to move out of pure fear. The leader yelled at them to get into the car. That broke their paralysis. One slid into the back seat from the driver's side while the leader slid behind the steering wheel. The third one was so scared he dared not go to the other side. He could hear the wildings approaching. "*Leave him behind and save yourself*," she thought to the leader.

Then she saw something amazing. The leader, knowing death was coming, stepped out of the car and let his friend in. It looked like stupidity, but she knew it wasn't; he didn't move with uncertainty or carelessness. His actions seemed well-defined and skillful. They were timed perfectly. He unconsciously knew what to do to ensure the survival of his friends. Yes, this was a *Lupus Rex*, unaware of his power or his abilities. Or his destiny....

She watched him slip easily into the car and speed away. He wasn't making much headway, but it was enough to outrun the pack.

Chapter 12—Sequentia: Suscitatio

noun [sē-kwən'-shə:()sə-se-tā'-tē-ō]
1. Continuation: Awakening.

Aaron Darveau, April 24, 1983

Aaron listened to her story in dreadful fascination. He always believed he was in danger that night, and her story confirmed it. He didn't like the idea of not being at the top of the food chain anymore. *Actually, I think I graduated to that position last night.*

"See, there are two castes," Karen remarked. "One caste is able to maintain control of their emotions and make conscious choices while changed. We call it the ability to *Frenis*. Those who can *frenis*, we call *Frenatus*. The other caste is composed of nothing more than animals; those who have not yet learned to *frenis* or those who probably never will. We call them *defrenatus* or wildlings. The wildlings are the ones who attacked. We tried to hold them back, but they were restless. When I realized they were about to rush you, I ruined the attack on you and your friends with that first *vagor*. If I hadn't, you would never have escaped."

Aaron tried to wrap his head around the idea of werewolves having a caste system. *I thought they were all animals.*

"I watched you handle the situation," Karen said. "Your friends were frozen in their tracks, and you took charge. Your swift decisions gave your friends time to get in the car, knowing it was too dangerous outside of it. You knew you had to leave immediately, but you waited for them."

"I didn't feel like a leader." Aaron shrugged his shoulders and lowered his head. "I was trying to get the hell out of there, and they weren't moving fast enough for my liking."

"Well, you are…a natural leader, I mean," she praised, squeezing his hand. "Aaron, you're able to maintain control in a deadly situation. And you have compassion for those under you. Believe it or not, we look for people like you. But you got away."

"Wait—how did you find me?" he asked suspiciously. "It couldn't have been blind luck you ran into me in the Trail Boss."

"No, I searched for you," she confessed sheepishly. "It took weeks to find you, driving around Orlando, trying to pick up your scent. When I finally found you, I followed you for weeks more. Aaron, I went to the Trail Boss that night because I knew you would be there. I just needed to see you, watch you for a few minutes. See if you were what we were looking for."

"Why? How? How would being close to me tell you anything?"

"Women's intuition. Once I was convinced we could trust you—" she lowered her voice to a near whisper, "—you were safe."

He snapped his head around, the muscles in his jaw working back and forth. He stiffly opened his mouth and asked, "What do you mean by *safe*?" He was afraid of the answer, but wanted to hear her say it anyway.

"If you posed a threat, you would have died that night."

Aaron's mouth formed a straight line and found itself desperately in need of spit. He looked at her with a new understanding of exactly what he had stumbled into. *Tread lightly. This is what Jajine warned me about.* "You took a big risk on intuition," he spoke evenly and with as little inflection as possible.

"It's rarely wrong. Females of the Race have strong intuition. It isn't always precise, though. That's why I had to spend some time with you."

"Once you knew you were safe, why didn't you leave?" Aaron paused long enough to stoop over and pick up a stick. He didn't intend to strike her with it...he just needed something to hold onto. "Why couldn't you have just left me alone?"

"Once I saw you through a woman's eyes, I knew you were my choice," she burst out as if out of breath. "The first time you stood next to me, your scent, it overpowered me."

She shivered with excitement, a response he'd seen before on so many nights. He threw the stick out into the field as if he were throwing away those images in his head.

"I almost ran out of the bar in fear," she confessed. "I'd never been overcome like that except after my first few *innovationes*, my first few changes. But I couldn't be with you. You were human." Her eyes welled up with tears. "I was so conflicted that night. I kept saying *no* to you, hoping you would just leave. But I also wanted you to keep coming back. Then you threatened not to. I told myself I wanted more time to think. What I *really* wanted was you, so I said *yes*. Once you held me in your arms, I didn't want anyone else." She took a moment to look Aaron straight in the eyes. "I chose you."

Aaron had visited a few *I Love You, Sailor, Buy Me A Drink* bars during his time in the Navy. The stories he'd been told in them weren't quite as elaborate as this, but he still wasn't convinced. Something didn't make sense. "Chose me for what?" he asked coldly. "You kept referring to something called *Lupus Rex*. What is that?"

"Before I can answer that, I need to tell you a bit of our history first." Her forehead creased between her raised eyebrows. "Are you willing to listen to that?"

"Do I have a choice?"

"Yes. But if you choose to leave, you won't know what you're missing."

Aaron raised his hands. "What are you waiting for? Impress me then."

Chapter 13—Lupus sapiens

noun [lü'-pəs()sā'-pē-ənz]
1. Wise wolf.

Karen Argali

"Okay, let's see," she muttered. "Where to start?"

"Why not with the basics?" Aaron suggested. "How many of us are there? How are we organized?" He realized with surprise he now counted himself in with them.

She nodded her head. "There are tens of thousands of us scattered around the world," she began, "and we're organized into packs. We call it a *grex*—which is Latin for pack. By the way, most everything having to do with the Race has a Latin word or phrase for it. We've been around awhile.

"Anyway, each *grex* is pretty close to what most people think of when they think of a wolf pack. They function in much the same way. They usually consist of a single, extended family. But they might also consist of numerous families or just friends with close family ties."

Aaron asked, "Last night, was that our *grex*?"

"Most of them were, yes," she confirmed.

"So not everyone is related," he concluded.

Karen bobbed her head back and forth, somewhere between nodding and shaking. "Yes and no," she countered. "We're related in that we're the same strain of *lupus*. We are not related in that we are not all blood related like you think of brothers and sisters being related—like Summer and Autumn and Bill and Glen."

"I think I understand." Aaron rubbed his chin. "So because you scratched me, we're related as it applies to the pack, the *grex*, right?"

"Sorta. We're more related at the clan level, but I'll get to that in a minute. A *grex* is led by an Alpha male and Alpha female. Other than that, there's no common or set formula for how they're organized. Some are large, covering vast swaths of territories. Some are small, hunting in minor towns away from the influence of modern civilization."

Aaron stopped her. "If I didn't like this *grex* for some reason, could I quit and go join another one?"

"Yes. It's uncommon, but it happens. Sometimes people rub each other the wrong way." She giggled. "Why, you ready to quit the *grex* already?"

"Huh? No. No, I hung out with a motorcycle club in Virginia Beach for a bit in my younger days. They had a few different chapters around the area. Sometimes if two members butted heads, one would transfer."

She raised her shoulders and tilted her head slightly. "It's sometimes easier than the alternative."

"Easier than what?"

"I'll get to that later, too—where was I?"

"You were talking about *grex* sizes."

"Oh, yeah, the *grex*. Six to ten *grexes* form a *Familia*, or family. Families are not typically treated as individual organizations; a *grex* will typically shift allegiances from one family to the next depending on the circumstances, so the notion of a family head is vague and titular at best. At any given time, a family of like-minded *grexes* may elect a single Alpha to speak for them on Race matters, but that is about as far as their authority goes."

Aaron slowly shook his head, lost. "I need an example."

She thought for a moment. "About a year ago, a few *grexes* were upset that another, larger *grex* was moving into their area. They picked one of the Alphas as their spokesman and sent him to speak on their behalf."

"This is starting to sound more like a Godfather movie than a horror show."

"Not quite, but there are strong similarities. Anyway, ten or so *Familiæ* form a Clan under the leadership of a *Dux Lupus*, roughly equivalent to a Duke in feudal societies. In fact, that's where the title comes from. The twelve *Dux Lupis* form what is known as the Conclave. This Conclave is led by *Lupus Rex*, the King, and *Lupa Reginam*, the Queen."

Aaron reasoned, "Yes, definitely like the Godfather."

"I'm reluctant to agree outright, but it's probably closer to that than anything else. You have your Godfather at the top, his captains, wiseguys, all that, all the way down to the soldiers on the street."

"You seem to know a lot about how the mob is organized. Is there anything else I should know about you?" His eyes grinned at her no matter how hard he tried to remain stern.

She was silent for the next few steps, causing Aaron to expect some other bizarre revelation, but she only said, "Nothing of importance."

Aaron decided to drop the subject. "How do you keep from being seen by the public in general?" he asked. "Any type of criminal organization usually has the FBI or someone investigating them."

"We aren't criminals," Karen emphasized with stern conviction. "We have a set of laws we abide by. These laws keep us hidden."

Aaron raised his hands up and to the side. "It just seems fantastic to me that I'm not seeing werewolf stories all over the evening news."

"Up until about five hundred years ago, you might have. We weren't quite as organized as we are now."

"What happened?" he asked.

"Lysistrata happened."

"What?"

"Not what, who," Karen noted. "She was the woman who changed everything." She sighed deeply. "The Race was almost dead. We were constantly fighting amongst ourselves, and the Church was crusading against us. It took its toll. Lysistrata was tired of seeing everyone she knew and loved die in what she considered senseless slaughters. Eventually she codified a Pact and forced the men to accept it."

"Whoa!" Aaron exclaimed. "How did she do that?"

"She convinced the women of the Race to stop bearing children until they did. It took a generation, but the men finally came around."

Aaron was silent for a few minutes. "So, what's this Pact?" he finally asked.

"It's a series of laws all *lupis* must live by.

"The First Law states no *lupus* can kill another *lupus* without permission of the Conclave. The two exceptions are self-defense and if a *lupus* is *Utlagatus*—that's Latin for outlaw. Outlaws can be killed on sight.

"The Second Law states no *lupus* can perform an act that draws the ire of Homo sapiens. In other words, don't piss off the humans.

"The Third Law states *Lupa Reginam*, the Queen, can only serve a period of ten blue moons, or about twenty-seven years, and must then name a *Postpartor* or successor."

Aaron asked, "What's a blue moon?"

"About every two and half years or so, a season has four full moons instead of three. The third one is called a blue moon."

"So about twenty-five years. Okay, go on."

"The Fourth Law, what some consider the most important, states *Lupus Rex*, the King, is to be chosen by the incoming *Lupa Reginam*. Instead of *Lupus Rex* choosing a new wife, he is removed from power along with the *Lupa Reginam* in favor of a younger, fresher generation."

"Wow!" Aaron stopped in the middle of the field and stared at Karen.

"The King just steps down?"

Karen laughed. "Now you know why it took a generation to force this down their throats. Laws Three and Four might not sound overly burdensome today, but when they were proposed, they were radical. You have to understand, for centuries we warred, jockeying back and forth for position with the strongest or luckiest coming out on top. Now it was all gone with those two laws. Those laws' intention was to prevent the possibility of a power-hungry and perhaps unstable Alpha taking control of the Race and plunging us back into warfare."

Aaron was confused. "What keeps the Queens from picking a nut job as King?"

"Females of the Race have strong maternal instincts, stronger than human women. Remember when I told you about the females' intuition? It's so strong that it borders on precognition. We call it *Mulieres intuitionem*, which interestingly enough translates directly to Women's Intuition. We usually just call it the Gift. *Mulieres intuitionem* is a mouthful."

Aaron cast an understanding expression at Karen. "So because of this Gift and their maternal instincts, it was assumed their decisions would be best for the Race. By instinct, the Queen would be forced to select the best candidate."

"Yep. And as the females would become the dominant bloodline, leadership of the Race no longer derived from the most powerful warrior. It may have flowed from *Lupus Rex*, but it was derived from *Lupa Reginam*."

"A matriarchy-patriarchy." Aaron nodded his head in understanding. "Like a real wolf pack."

"Yes. And like a wolf pack, *Lupus Rex* rules at the convenience of *Lupa Reginam*. Her decision to select the next Rex couldn't be taken lightly though. Not only would this male be King, he would also be her mate. For her bloodline to survive, she had to know he would be strong enough to rule and compassionate enough to protect not just her children, but the Race as a whole. The females hoped this would prevent the males from going to war over position."

Aaron dwelled on that. "How do you enforce this? It sounds all neat and tidy, but surely there are those who do things they aren't supposed to."

"True. And that's where the Fifth Law comes in. It states all laws are binding, whether they are known or not. The punishment for breaking the Pact, regardless of the infraction, is the same—shunning. Only clan heads and *Lupus Rex* can shun someone, though. *Grex* Alphas cannot; they have to petition their clan head if they want one of their *grex* mates shunned. A shunned *lupus* is known as *Lupus solitarius*. They don't survive long without a pack, so this seemed adequate punishment."

Aaron raised his brows. "Why not?"

"All members of the pack protect each other. We're a family, remember? There are those who would do us harm."

Aaron wasn't sure he liked the sound of that, but there were a million other questions he wanted answered. "What if shunning doesn't work?"

"Then he or she could be declared *Utlagatus*. Only *Lupus Rex* can declare someone *Utlagatus*. A *lupus* can also be declared outlaw for doing something treasonous to the Race not specifically covered in the Pact."

Aaron raised his eyebrows in appreciation. "Lysistrata had some balls."

Karen turned to him and smiled. "Yes, she did. Without her, we wouldn't be here today."

"What happened to her?"

Karen grimaced. "When she presented the Pact to *Lupus Rex*, he put her to the stake and burned her alive for defying his will. It did no good, though. She'd already made copies and distributed them to various women, including each of the Dukes' wives, the *Ducissa Lupas*. *Lupus Rex* ordered all women who had read the Pact put to the stake as well."

Aaron was shocked. "Their Gift didn't see that coming?"

"It did, but the Race was as good as dead already. It was in its death throes. They figured they had ten years before they were all killed anyway if things continued as they were—some sooner than that. This was the only way they saw to save it."

"What did the church have to say about this?" he asked with a chuckle. "I thought they had the patent on stake-burnings?"

"Interestingly, they sat back and watched. If we wanted to kill ourselves off, they didn't feel an overriding need to get in the way."

Aaron slowly shook his head in disbelief. "And the males went along with it? Incredible."

"No, they fought it tooth and nail. For an entire generation, no *lupis* were born. Some warlords enslaved us and treated us as breeding stock, but it took too many resources to keep us under constant guard. Creating *lupis* was easy, but not all of them could easily *frenis*. Rogue *lupis* pillaging the countryside only brought the wrath of the humans upon us again.

94

Eventually, they saw the light. They didn't have a choice; the Race was all but dead."

"I'm surprised some of the women didn't cozy up to the leadership. Surely not all of them agreed to this."

"Most certainly. The ones who did volunteer their 'services' and ended up pregnant were found dead within a few months, usually poisoned."

"Didn't the King try to reason with the women?"

"Not really," she grimaced. "He was eventually assassinated by Lysistrata's father, *Dux Lupus* of Clan *Acer Dens*. He adopted the Pact."

"Yeah, I can see that. He probably wasn't too happy about his daughter being burned alive."

"No." She was silent for a few more minutes. "In the end, things worked out, just as Lysistrata's Gift showed her they would. The Pact was a sea change in how members of the Race interacted with each other and how they survived in a world of men. In much the same way the United States of America drafted and ratified their own Constitution, the *Lupus sapiens* race drafted and ratified their own Pact. It's stood for centuries."

"Amazing," he whispered. "Werewolves writing a Constitution." He ran his fingers through his hair. "How hard was it to implement?"

"Pretty easily once the decision was made. The larger and stronger clans, led by the strongest warriors at the time, took this as an opportunity to band together and wipe out the smaller and weaker clans. The twelve clans currently forming the Conclave are all that remain.

"Since then, every tenth blue moon sees the ascendency of a new *Lupa Reginam* and her chosen *Lupus Rex*. Although tradition usually has *Lupa Reginam* passing from mother to daughter, it's not law. Some don't have daughters. Some daughters are too nuts to serve, and others have too weak of a Gift to be effective. It really isn't a hereditary position."

Aaron had a sudden flash of insight. "Craig's *Lupus Rex*."

"That's right. How did you know?"

"I'm not sure. I just do. And Lisa's *Lupa Reginam*."

"Again, correct. And there's something else." Karen stopped in the middle of the field and gently grabbed Aaron's hands. "Lisa didn't have any daughters," she revealed, "only sons, so she's picked me as her *Postpartor*. Aaron, I'm next in line as *Lupa Reginam*."

Chapter 14—Sequentia: Suscitatio
noun [sē-kwən'-shə:()sə-se-tā'-tē-ō]
1. Continuation: Awakening.

Aaron Darveau

Aaron stood there for close to a minute thinking over what she just said. "So this is what you meant when you said you *chose* me." Realization finally dawned on Aaron. "This whole damned thing is a marriage proposal. You're asking me to marry you!"

Karen smiled brightly and nodded her head. Aaron backed off a step and stared at her in stunned silence while the ramifications of that filtered through his mind. Then it hit him what she had actually done to him.

"Wait a minute," Aaron looked at the ground and held his hand up as a barrier between them while he slowly pieced together what he wanted to say. "You said I was the right choice?"

"Yes. Last—"

"There was never any doubt?" Aaron asked firmly.

"No."

He dropped his hand and looked her dead in the eyes. "Would I have still been the right choice in a week, two weeks, a month, six months?"

She saw where this was going and looked down at her hands. "Yes."

Aaron's voice sizzled like cold grease on a hot frying pan. "But you decided to curse me anyway! On our first night together! Leaving me no other options! You couldn't get down on one knee and ask me? You had to mark your fucking territory?" *Why would she do something like this to me?* His hands shook, his head suddenly felt feverish. The scars on his back tingled. He yelled, "Karen, people in love are supposed to trust each other! How am I supposed to ever trust you again?" The veins on his forehead stood out in stark contrast to the rest of his face, forming the letter "Y" as if his body was also asking the question.

Aaron sensed a shift in her demeanor. She went from loving and caring to distressed and concerned.

She tried to hug him but he stepped back from her. "Aaron, I know I screwed up," she cried. "I should have told you. I should have given you the choice, but I thought this is what you wanted. You said you wanted me!"

"Yeah, I do want you, Karen!" he exclaimed. "Or did! But I also wanted a say in the matter. You've left me with no choice."

Aaron pulled up every ounce of Chi and massaged it into a shield to hold back the feelings of betrayal. Now was not the time to lose control. He didn't have time for that. Through sheer force of will, he made himself concentrate on the sounds and smells around him. He pictured himself doing his forms. It helped—his breathing slowed, but his hands wouldn't stop shaking. He recognized the anger he worked so hard to keep contained. Anger was one of the worst of the emotions to experience; it led to thinking about revenge. Revenge led people to do things they regretted. *And I'm beginning to regret ever having met her, because it's led me here. And where's here? Namely, I'm a fucking monster.*

If it hadn't been for Jajine, he would probably be a mass of quivering jelly right now. Her warning kept coming back to him. Everything she said to him rang in his head as clearly as a crystal bell. *"Evil is coming for you, Aaron."* Well, it most certainly has, and it was wearing Karen's face. *She's a damned succubus, is what she is, and she is not going to let me go.* He saw the predator standing before him. For all intents and purposes, she still had her claws buried in his back.

WWKD? Gather as much as information as possible first. Then make the best decision possible based on that information.

After a few minutes, he looked back at her. She was studying him, waiting for him to say something. He wasn't sure there was anything left to say, so he curled his mouth up in derision, shook his head, and wandered off, not so much in turmoil as in anger, without knowing which direction the house was.

Chapter 15—Karen Argali

Karen knew she screwed up. Wildlings usually wake up dazed and confused, malleable. They're easy to control. But he bridled on his first *renovatio*! He took control of the change, kept his sanity, didn't turn into a wildling. She'd never seen or even heard of that happening. If she would have had any inkling he would be able to do that, she would have told him what to expect, started the process of earning his trust again a little sooner. It usually takes some time, years even, before new *lupis* accept their condition and begin to trust their *grex* mates. Karen expected a wildling, not a *frenator*. *Everyone* expected that. For him to have that kind of control, that kind of self-discipline and confidence, there was little chance of manipulating him later. She needed to work fast to link their wills together, intertwine them so they worked toward the same goals. Right now, he was maturing without her. As he grew into the role of *Lupus Rex*, she would slowly be relegated to nothing more than breeding stock.

She grew up in a life like that in Little Italy, Buffalo, New York—at a time when she was just another woman in a man's world. Her father was a member of the Magaddino crime family, running booze over the Canadian border into the States. Prohibition was long gone, but the profits from bringing in certain products kept the line active. She was six years old when her brothers and her dad were killed in a turf fight spurred on by several attempts on the life of the family head, Stefano Magaddino. At that time in America, most women didn't take care of themselves. To some in the mafia, that concept was even worse; the women were almost considered a man's property.

Her mother, Constance, was a woman whose life wasn't complete without a man around the house, so a few months later she married back into the only thing she knew—the mafia. Peter DiMalli, her new husband, was not quite as high ranking as her first husband had been, or as intelligent. He was also a mean drunk, as evidenced by the bruises her mother often tried to cover up with makeup and large sunglasses. Constance left a few times, but she always came back, unable to function on her own.

When Karen was fourteen, DiMalli tried to rape her. It was only his drunkenness that prevented him from completing the deed. After he rolled off of her and passed out, she caved his skull in with an iron. Although it was a clear case of self-defense, she still feared for her life; DiMalli was a made-man.

She left home and hitched rides west where she eventually fell in with some hippies. She travelled back and forth across the country with them for a few years until she ended up back in Buffalo. She was nineteen and tired of the constant anti-war marches and protests that weren't making the slightest difference to the direction the country was headed. She was also homesick.

Upon her return, she found her mother had married another man, Alphonse "Big Al" Moretti. In her estimation, Big Al didn't sufficiently describe this tub of lard. Moretti must have been DiMalli's protégé because he beat her mother frequently too whenever he was liquored up.

Whenever Constance was not at home, Moretti made advances on Karen. He wasn't forceful with her, but she knew it was only a matter of time. She started looking for her own place to live, but before she could find one, Moretti beat and raped her. She didn't move back in with her mother when she got out of the hospital, choosing instead to stay with some friends.

The mafia war escalated when Magaddino was killed in '74, and Karen knew the fight would eventually spread to her mom's house. Not wanting to see her mother end up as collateral damage in a war she had no control over, and knowing her mother would never voluntarily leave Moretti, she decided to take matters into her own hands. One night, when her mother was not home, she went to Moretti under the guise of wanting to have sex with him. She drugged his drink and then torched the house in classic mafia fashion, burning him alive. She went to get her mother, who was waiting tables at a local bar, but couldn't convince her to leave town. In fact, she went into a near-panic state of mind when Karen told her about Moretti. That's when Karen knew her mother was too far gone. She'd be married in a couple of more months to a man who wanted nothing more out of her than her ability to keep his prick fat and happy.

Crushed, Karen went back on the road. She ended up in Florida a few months later, pan-handling on the beaches for food money, her dignity left behind her in tatters all the way down the East Coast. The best thing about being at such a low point in one's life is it can only get better.

If Lisa and Craig hadn't been visiting the beach that day in 1975 and seen her panhandling, she wouldn't be where she was now, ready to take over a race of werewolves where the women have all of the power, not the men. She was not about to let Aaron ruin this for her. She had to get him under control.

Unfortunately, it could all still backfire. He might not need her as much as she hoped he would by now. She did everything she could over the last month to make him fall in love with her. It worked, too; he *was* in love with her. She could smell it on him. But if he decided to let her go emotionally, then he would have the upper hand. She bet the future of the Race on everything she knew up to last night. But things were different now. It was a real possibility she could lose him. He was strong.

Although that was her biggest worry, something else nagged at her. He didn't have any silver burns on his chest from that stupid hippy necklace of his. He wore it all night. When they changed back, she had to take it off of him before she could lie up against him. It was possible his immunity was natural—that happened sometimes—but it was usually passed from *lupus* to *lupus* during the *veneno*. And although it was highly unlikely he had help, it was not something she could ignore. It was too coincidental that a silver canine fang would be worn by someone who managed to *frenis* during their first *renovatio*. *"Some crazy fortune teller in New Orleans,"* he said. Craig needed to be alerted. If some witch was using magic charms to create silver-immune *frenatus*, she needed to be stopped.

Chapter 16—Sequentia: Suscitatio

noun [sē-kwən'-shə:()sə-se-tā'-tē-ō]
1. Continuation: Awakening.

Aaron Darveau

Aaron's sense of smell was more acute and more precise since awakening in the field. He found the house by following his nose. He'd relished in the vibrancy of the different scents around him while talking with Karen, but he hadn't realized just how sensitive it was until he began his trek back. He followed the smell of barbeque and smoke in the direction it was strongest.

He was also impressed with the sheer size and scope of Craig's estate; it took him nearly an hour to make it back to the house. Craig had sixty thousand acres, one hundred square miles, with a couple of large ponds that bordered on being lakes, a non-trivial number of smaller ponds, prairies, and a stand of timber reminiscent of Aaron's home in northern Louisiana. The meat wholesaling business paid well

As he came upon the back patio, he stormed straight through the backyard, into the courtyard, past the pool, and into Karen's bedroom. He dressed, packed, and then sat on the bed for what seemed an eternity, with everything that happened over the last couple of hours running through his head. Eventually, the frenzied excitement started to wear off, and the morning stretched out into day. The idea of being a werewolf was starting to sound silly, and he wasn't even ready to think about being *Lupus Rex*. As much as the idea appealed to him on some primitive level—who wouldn't want to be the King Werewolf?—the memories of his reading in Jajine's apartment kept coming back to him.

He was certain this was the evil she was referring to all those years ago—or at least the anti-good. Perhaps it was a matter of perspective—they did what was necessary to survive. *Is a she-wolf evil if she kills a human to protect her young? Depends on whether you're the human or the wolf.* From what he'd seen so far, and it hadn't been much, they didn't seem evil.

Aaron muttered to the empty room, "Yeah, but when you infect someone off the street, and tell him this is his new destiny, that is certainly anti-social. And that's putting it mildly."

He let out a long, drawn out sigh and stood up. He took a moment to look at the bed he and Karen had shared so many times over the last month. *Just yesterday I was worried about screwing things up. If I'd known what was in store for me then, would I have done anything differently? Hell, this was written a month ago. Yesterday wouldn't have made a single bit of difference.*

Suddenly, the timing of this whole situation sprang into his mind. He'd been coming around for practically a full month now. She infected him, spent a month getting him to fall in love with her, and then sprung the trap—all between two full moons. *Bitch!* The scars on his back started tingling again.

He scowled as he grabbed his overnight bag and headed to the bathroom. He stared at himself in the mirror for a few minutes, grappling with the thought that the woman he spent the last month with, the woman he fell in love with, was not who she had led him to believe she was. He scooped up his toothbrush, toothpaste, razor, and deodorant and put them all in his bag. He didn't bother looking for yesterday's clothes; they were in tatters, if his memory of the events by the pool were accurate. *Damn, those were my best pair of boots too.*

He was almost to the front door when Craig emerged into the foyer. He had a fatherly look on his face, gentle and open. "How are you feeling, Aaron?"

In a fit of rage harkening back to his childhood, Aaron yelled, "This is total bullshit, Craig! No one bothered to ask me if I wanted this!"

Craig stopped dead in his tracks, taken aback by this outburst.

Like a crack of thunder, Aaron commanded, "You will not fuck with my life again!" He didn't know where the conviction he could order Craig around came from, but it surged from him as naturally as the Mississippi River surged after a springtime rain.

Abruptly, the last fifteen hours hurtled out of the sky onto his shoulders. He stood there while his life flashed through his mind's eye. His life as he knew it was coming to an end. The woman he loved had forever altered its course without as much as a *fuck you*. He couldn't see anything past that moment because an insurmountable black wall stood in his way. He may not have planned much for the future, but he knew there was something beyond what he currently knew and experienced every day. However, this was overwhelmingly too much to grasp onto. He had no center to hold himself inside of. The adrenaline blast of the last few hours finally trickled down to nothing, and he found himself falling to the floor. His head hit something hard, and the world turned black.

Chapter 17—Craig Minor

Craig was trying to make sense of the last fifteen hours. Somehow, the boy managed to *frenis* last night during his first *renovatio*. After the boy—now their new *frenator*—chased the deer out through the rear foyer, Lisa ordered the men to run with him to keep him busy while she huddled the women together to consult their *Mulieres intuitionem*. Craig wasn't part of the circle, but as *Lupus Rex* he was the only man the circle was open to so he could take the discussion from the women's Gift into consideration as he made his decisions.

What the women saw was inconclusive. Aaron was powerful, obviously, but that was the only thing they could agree on. The best composite image they could put together showed him, if left to his own devices, tightly binding the Race to his will, and his will alone. He completely changed the formula by exhibiting a willpower not tied to *Lupa Reginam*. It harkened back to pre-Pact anarchy, a time when the wills of *Lupus Rex* and *Lupa Reginam* were not the same.

Autumn decreed, "If his and Karen's wills are not the same, he must die."

Karen leaped to her feet and shouted, "No!" She threw a hard look at them. "I can still control him. He loves me. Give me time. Give *him* time. With a *Lupus Rex* this powerful, I need more time to tie our wills together."

Summer spoke up. "But Karen, even you can't see the future in any detail anymore. As soon as he bridled, your intuition was as useless as ours." She looked around at all the other women present before addressing Karen again. "What would you have us do?"

Karen sat down. She looked reasonable and more like an equal, less intimidating. "Listen, I know you're all scared. But he is just one *lupus*. We're aware of him. He's not a maniac. He's practically living here now. Craig, Lisa, and I can keep an eye on him. Let us teach him. Once he understands his place, he'll come around."

Lisa took that moment to interject on Karen's behalf. "I have to agree with Karen on that, at least. He is a great kid. He's kind, and he's inquisitive. I've never seen the temper he says he has, but I can't imagine it being any worse than Craig's. If Karen can manage to control him, he will be a *Lupus Rex* for the history books."

No one but Riley was willing to make a suggestion, but she detailed what they were all thinking, "We'll give you until the next *plenilunium*. If he isn't tied to you by then, Craig will declare him outlaw. We won't even bother with shunning."

Karen scoffed. "One month? We'll be bound tomorrow morning. Now, let's go join the hunt!" Everyone performed a *renovatio* and joined Aaron and the rest of the men.

Craig left the meeting hoping Karen was right. He liked Aaron. He would hate to shun him. But when Craig encountered him in the foyer as he was leaving, Craig realized just how much Karen, Lisa, and he had underestimated the newest member of their pack. The boy was so irate that if he had been a wildling he would probably have performed an uncontrolled *renovatio* right then and attacked.

Craig was staggered at the boy's dominance; when Aaron rebuked him, Craig instinctively took him as *Lupus Rex*. He found himself, for just a moment, fighting to keep from looking at the floor in submission. Even then, Craig thought they might still come to blows.

Then Aaron fainted and fell to the floor.

Craig blinked and with a start, rushed to his side. "Lisa! Come help me!" he yelled over his shoulder.

Karen rushed into the foyer, tying her bathrobe's sash, while Lisa followed closely on her heels, wiping her hands on her apron.

"What happened?" Karen asked, kneeling down next to Aaron.

Craig mumbled, "He popped."

Lisa abruptly stopped wiping her hands, leaving her apron hanging in the air and entwined within her fingers. She arched her eyebrows at Karen. "Again?"

"No," Karen told them, shaking her head. "This is the first."

Craig's voice peaked as he questioned Karen. "He's made it this far without popping?"

Karen reached down and clutched her *Lupus Rex's* hand. "He's resilient."

Craig checked Aaron's head and found a small bump on the side, but no bleeding, and his breathing and pulse were steady. Once he satisfied himself Aaron hadn't hurt himself by falling to the stone floor, he said, "Help me get him to bed."

When they were done, it was Craig's turn to be livid. While Lisa tended to Aaron, Craig pulled Karen out to the patio. "Dammit, Karen!" he yelled.

"You need to clean this up, and pronto. You said you could control him. Well, get control." Everyone knew the dangers of a pissed off *frenatus* who didn't understand his place. Putting that kind of power in someone's untrained hands was akin giving a hand grenade to a two year old. They didn't understand what they were truly capable of. "Neither one of us wants to see him declared *Lupus solitarius*. You know what would happen to him out there without us. You might be the incoming *Lupa Reginam*, but you are still a member of my *grex*. I'm Alpha and I'm *Lupus Rex*. You're putting the whole fucking Race in danger."

Craig knew he was treating Karen like a child, but he believed that was the only way to treat some people when you wanted things done. He was also secretly ashamed of his behavior in front of Aaron. If the boy had known what he was genuinely capable of, there was a real possibility one of them would be dead right now; two Alphas don't live under the same roof for long.

Karen rolled her hands into and out of fists, and her face blushed. "Craig, I know what I have to do, probably better than you do, so can it!"

They both stopped for a couple of deep breaths.

"Craig, look—he's extremely strong-willed. I'll admit I miscalculated. We all did. I should have trusted him more in the beginning. He was angrier with me than he was terrified of his condition."

"Oh, don't I know it," Craig mocked. "Our encounter in the foyer was—interesting—to say the least."

Karen grabbed a length of hair and twisted it as she paced around the patio. "I don't know where he gets his self-esteem from. It's like...it's like he's been ruling the Race his whole life. His instincts tell him he's *Lupus Rex*—yes, that's what I sensed in him this morning—but his emotions were in a jumble; it was hard to separate them. He doesn't know what those feelings are because he's never actually experienced them before now."

Craig was miffed. "Well, I've got news for him. I'm *Lupus Rex*, not him! Don't get any ideas. Ascension isn't for a few months yet."

Karen eyes flashed contempt as she gave him a sideways glance. "Don't worry, we aren't deposing you yet." Then she walked to the edge of patio and put her hands in her robe's pockets. "This is the man I saw on the side of the road fixing that flat. Nothing fazes him for long. I wouldn't be surprised if he woke up in there and started ordering you around."

Craig considered what she said, but mostly how she said it. She may be fighting it, but she was already bending to Aaron's will. She wasn't angry with him. She was more disappointed she failed, sorry she let *him* down. Maybe she really did love him. In either case, if Aaron didn't need a shoulder to cry on when he first woke up, she'd already lost control of him. He rubbed both hands over the stubble on his chin. "Karen, I think we need to take a different approach. Let me give it a try. When he wakes up, let me show him what the possibilities are. Right now, he's only seen us and those from last night. And of all of us, the one he loved proved to be a conniving bitch. He hasn't had the chance to think things through."

Karen's eyes welled up in tears, but before they overflowed onto her cheek, she rubbed them dry with the back of her hand. She turned away from Craig and stared out at the fields beyond the patio. A few moments later, she turned back, her eyes white as she used her Gift. She whispered, as if in a dream, "You may be right. He doesn't know who we are. He doesn't know who he is now. Yes, I see it. *Astutia*. Get him back here Wednesday. Let him see the *grex*. Right now, I see that as our best option. If he doesn't come around then, I won't stop you if you want to shun him. The Race will be in danger otherwise; we don't have the month Riley gave us."

She came out of her trance. "There's something else," she confessed. "Did you notice that charm of his?"

"His necklace? I noticed he didn't rip it off." He shrugged his shoulders. "That happens sometimes. Why?"

"It's silver, and it didn't burn him."

"He's immune to silver?" he asked confusedly. "I didn't think there were any silver immune *lupis* in your and Lisa's line."

"There's not as far as I know." She shook her head. "I think he might have had help, some witch in New Orleans maybe."

Craig unexpectedly shuddered. "Are you sure? A witch? Do you think the two are related? Why didn't you say something last night to the *lupas*?"

"For one thing," she exclaimed, "I didn't want to make them any more nervous than they already were! They were ready to declare him *utlagatus* on the spot. I needed time. It could be coincidence—"

"We don't have time for 'It could be coincidence!'" Craig shouted, his voice rising in pitch at the mere rumor of a witch being involved. His Southern Gentleman façade was rapidly disintegrating as his wildling from so many years ago tried to reawaken within him. "There's a reason we kill them whenever we can! You know witchcraft interferes with your Gift. If we can't rely on it, we don't know if what you see is uncertain, misleading, or downright fucking wrong." He stopped for a breath and regained a bit of his composure, ashamed of himself for losing control like he did. "Karen, the entire power structure of the Race could be in jeopardy!" He ran his hands over his stubble again, and that one, simple act calmed him down enough to pull his *lupus* under control. "I suggest you ascertain whether your suspicions are correct or not," he commanded with renewed dignity. "Otherwise, you and every other female are useless to me."

Chapter 18—Astutia

noun [ə-stü'-shə]

1. Clever Persuasion. 2. Diplomacy.

Aaron Darveau

Aaron woke up in Karen's bed. Lisa was sitting next to him, leaning over and adjusting something cool on his forehead. Her scent brought back one of last night's memories; she and Craig were sitting on a small knoll, and the wind blew their scents to him. They were tightly mingled with each other but easy to separate. He realized Craig was *Lupus Rex* and Lisa was *Lupa Reginam*, though he didn't know their titles then. He just knew they were in charge. That's why he offered his kill to Craig first last night. Both smells were majestic, but one was confident and the other supportive. She was the confident one. That confused him for a moment until he remembered his history lesson. The *Lupa Reginam* picks the ruler; she, alone, determines the future of the Race, for good or bad.

He tried to sit up, and flashing lights flooded the room. Lisa must have seen his distress because he slipped back onto his pillow, guided by the gentle pressure she exerted on his chest. "Just lay there for a bit. You bonked your head on something when you fainted. The doorknob I think."

Aaron couldn't recall ever having fainted before. He'd almost been knocked out a few times during Tai Chi bouts, though. "I fainted? How long was I out?"

"A couple of hours. It's almost twelve o'clock. Don't worry about it. It was from exhaustion instead of a head injury. Most first timers do a lot worse than you did. They usually go catatonic in the middle of the field the next morning. We call it popping. You lasted a good three hours." She smiled in a motherly way at him. Aaron was reassured, if not a bit embarrassed.

"I still don't know what to make of all of this," he gently protested because his head still hurt. "You could have asked me if this is what I wanted. Hell, y'all could have warned me at the very least."

"You're right, of course," she acknowledged while she adjusted the compress, "although no one but Karen was in on the decision. Craig and I both agree she acted hastily." She had a sad smile on her face. "But in her defense, her intuition overrode her manners and her self-control. If she had been in a less, um, compromising condition that first night you spent together, she might have worked up to it. As it turns out, she didn't take the time to think things through. Instinct took over."

Aaron's memories of their first night together flickered to the front of his mind. *Neither one of us were doing much thinking.* He mentally shook his head in disgust. The woman he spent the morning with was not the woman he fell in love with over the last month. "So, what do I do now? I'm stuck with this the rest of my life, right?" The fretfulness rose again, but he pulled it under control with a deep breath. He looked over at the door. Craig stood there, leaning against the jamb with his arms crossed. "I'm feeling really conflicted right now," he told them both. "I love her, of course. Or did. But part of me is downright pissed off at her, too. Dammit, I don't know anything about being this *Lupus Rex* character she expects out of me." Aaron reached up and took the towel from his forehead. He slowly sat up, waiting for the lights to hit, but his vision remained clear. Lisa shifted some toward the foot of the bed, and he turned and put his feet on the floor. He felt a bump on the left side of his head. It wasn't big, but it let him know it was there.

Craig reminded him, "You did say you wanted her. If you want her, this is the only way you can have her."

Aaron's face got hot and he snapped, "That's a trap and you know it. I can't have her the way I should have her—the way a man and woman should have each other." Aaron looked at both of them in turn, then said with a bit more respect, "Who are you people, that you can just dictate what I do with my life? Even if I did decide to take her up on her offer, I'd have to marry her, right?"

"Obviously," Craig answered with a little laugh. "Why? Is that a problem?"

"I can't trust her. And besides, I'm not sure she loves me." Aaron looked down at his hands and found them empty, so he rubbed his palms on his jeans.

Lisa smiled. "Craig and I didn't love each other when I picked him," she divulged. "In fact, he was a wildling. I worked with him for nearly a year before he was able to *frenis*. We were in love when we married but not when he was chosen. Who's to say Karen wouldn't learn to love you the way you expect and deserve, given enough time?"

Aaron dwelled on that for a moment but still couldn't think clearly about it. "I don't know," he finally burst out. "I thought I wanted her, but now I'm not sure. Not really."

Craig extended an olive branch. "Can I make a suggestion?" he asked. "Yes? Before you make any rash decisions, think it over, son. We'll all still be here. We're not going anywhere." He then hesitated and rubbed his chin. Aaron knew he was going to suggest something he didn't like. "You know, you don't have to accept. We would be disappointed, but you can turn it down. Leadership is not for everybody."

Aaron wasn't sure if Craig was trying some psychological, reverse logic bullshit or not. In either case, it didn't matter. He asked, "If I do turn her down, would I be shunned for defying the will of *Lupa Reginam*?"

The look on Craig's face might as well have spoken the words—he would be *Lupus solitarius*.

Lisa shot Craig an unkind look before she assured Aaron, "That's an option, of course, but we're hoping you'll change your mind." She then shined a smile toward him. "We like seeing you around here." She play-poked him in the ribs and then put her hand on his knee, not in a sensual way, but with comfort and support. "Aaron, it's a given. Karen has certainly made a mess of things. James was first in line as her choice—mind you, she hadn't chosen yet—but everyone was expecting it. They were engaged a couple of years back. Did she tell you that?"

Aaron shook his head. "No, she didn't. I suspected they had some history, though. What's his role in all of this?"

"He's *Dux Lupus* for Clan *Gloriosi*," she explained. Then she pointed her head at him. "Your clan. His wife died in a car accident a few years ago. He hasn't remarried yet."

"Oh. *Gloriosi*?"

"Yes. It's Latin for Glorious."

"Sounds presumptuous," he snorted.

She laughed a bit. "Yes, I suppose it does," she agreed, nodding her head, "but when you're living in the Middle Ages, you probably need all the encouragement you can get."

"Yeah, probably," he conceded.

"Anyway, she's made her bed. Yours, too, by the looks of it. She's going to have to sleep in it. You two are going to have to work it out. I wish I had an answer for you, but I don't."

Aaron had the feeling Karen was being sneaky and listening right outside the door. "Where is she, anyway?"

"Oh, probably out walking the grounds, trying to clear her head. From what she told Craig, you really let her have it. She's probably trying to figure out how to smooth things over with you." She laughed lightly, and Aaron saw a twinkle in her eyes that let him know he had every right to feel the way he did. Then she stood and straightened her apron. She leaned over and gave him a hug before moving toward the door. She looked over her shoulder. "Late lunch in half an hour."

Aaron listened to Lisa's footsteps echo out of earshot. It seemed to take a long time, and he realized his sense of hearing had greatly improved, too. "When did you turn into a werewolf?" he asked Craig.

Craig rubbed his stubbly chin, thinking back. "It was 1957. I owned a fishing boat out of Virginia Beach. I wanted to learn every aspect of the business, so I signed onto my own boat as deckhand. During a particularly rough storm, one of the other deckhands, Derek Mills, got swept toward the edge of the deck. He was in danger of being washed overboard. I managed to grab him by his jacket shoulder, wrapping my hand within the folds of the material. But he's kicking and screaming and scrambling for anything to get a handhold or foothold on."

Aaron nodded his head. "I can imagine! I've been in some rough weather, myself."

"I'm sure you have," Craig stated. "Anyway, the only thing I can grab onto to keep both of us from falling over the side is the safety cable lining the deck. So there I am, holding Derek with one hand and the safety cable with the other. And Derek is hanging over the side, still screaming and struggling, and I'm yelling for him to climb up my arm and onto the deck." Craig got quiet and dark rings formed around his eyes. "When Derek reached up to find purchase, his hand was hairy and had long fingers with talons on the ends of them. His eyes were a dark blue where they were supposed to be brown, and his face was menacing looking. He ripped through my jacket sleeve, leaving deep gouges in my upper arm." Craig rolled his sleeve up to show the old scars. "Here is what Derek left me."

Aaron looked at the scars and thought about the ones on his back. They weren't as bad as Craig's, but they were visible. "I'd have freaked out right then and there. I'm not sure I could have held onto his ass."

"Unfortunately, that is what happened," Craig groaned with a gloomy sigh. "I 'freaked out' as you call it, and I lost my grip."

"Sorry, Craig. I didn't mean to make light of it. I know what it's like to lose a shipmate."

"Yes, well, a couple of days later, we made shore. My scratches were completely healed up. The doctors were impressed," he smirked. "First night back, a man visits me and explains my new 'situation.' I, of course, laughed him off, but the memory of seeing Derek's claws raking across my upper arm still haunted me. I decided to trust he was telling the truth and showed up at his place the day before the full moon. The rest, they say, is history."

Aaron slowly nodded his head. "So, it was an accident for you."

"Yes." The silence stretched out until Craig asked, "Feel good enough to get up? I've got something I want to show you."

Aaron stood up, and when his vision didn't cloud over, he looked at him. "Sure."

Craig turned into the loggia. "Walk with me."

Chapter 19—Lisa Minor

Lisa listened to Craig and Aaron talk for a few minutes before they went down into the basement. She remembered those days well, that part of their lives before she and Craig moved from Virginia Beach to Florida. Growing up in Grand Rapids, Michigan, she had never run into a Southern Gentlemen, so Craig's baritone accent captivated her when they first met. The only accents she had ever heard, outside of a movie theater, were Michigander, her father's German, and her maternal grandparents' Dutch. He was a real-life version of Rhett Butler from *Gone with the Wind*. Unfortunately, a Southern accent on an educated and cultured man doesn't guarantee intelligence as she found out.

It was her Gift that helped him build his lawn care business in Virginia Beach. It was her father who convinced the previous owner of Sun State Meat, Poultry, and Fish to sell his business to Craig for the rock-bottom price he did. And it was her Gift, again, that kept the company afloat in spite of Craig's unique ability to turn gold into straw. She wonders if Craig would've amounted to anything if she hadn't met him that day in Virginia.

As the daughter of William Stoddard, *Lupus Rex* at that time, she had certain advantages growing up. The one she liked the most was the travel. William ascended in 1932, and he and his wife, Dorothy, and their family started traveling around the world, visiting the different clans and getting acquainted with the Race in general. It was during one of those trips William made the decision to go on the offensive against the Fectors. They had tried to kill him and his family while visiting Germany, and he didn't appreciate their zeal in pursuit of their foolish belief that *Lupis sapiens* were a race of evil demons.

Lisa didn't remember the details of her father's plan, but she did remember it was a couple of years in the making, constantly running from one safe house to the next, staying one step ahead of the enemy. Whenever she started to make friends, they had to move again. Then one morning her mother came in and said it was all over. Her father had beaten the Fectors, and they wouldn't be a problem any longer.

She was her parents' only daughter to be born *lupa*, her older siblings being human and refusing the infection until much later in life. She learned to *frenis* when she was fourteen. When her mother named her *Postpartor* on her eighteenth birthday, her Gift suddenly showed a stormy future. It upset her to the point she asked her mother a few days later to pick someone else.

Her mother told her, "All new *Postpartors* see that until they've met their *Lupus Rex*. Be patient, dear."

When she met Craig during a hunt in '57, her intuition immediately went off, telling her he was her *Lupus Rex*. The stormy visions finally disappeared. Lisa decided right then to move to Virginia Beach because she needed to include herself in Craig's life; she couldn't do that from Michigan. Over the next couple of weeks, she showed up at his place of business and at the restaurants and the clubs where he would relax with his friends, trying her best to get him to recognize her.

Lisa told her mother during one of their nightly phone calls, "I am just about out of options here, Mother. My intuition says it's him, but he won't ask me out. How am I supposed to marry him if we can't even go on our first date?"

Dorothy laughed into the phone. "Lisa, he's a man," she teased softly. "They like to think they are in control, and this tends to cloud their judgment. Ask him out yourself."

"Mother!" Lisa exclaimed. "I can't do that! What would people think?"

"Who cares? I asked your father out first."

"No! You didn't! How scandalous, Mother!" Lisa was a bit embarrassed by the whole conversation, but her curiosity overrode her manners. "What did Grandma say?"

"The same thing I just told you, dear," Dorothy divulged with wicked delight. "It seems this is a common occurrence between *Postpartors* and their selection. Now go ask that boy out before some other hussy gets to him first."

"Moth-ther," she giggled loudly into the phone, "I am not a hussy!"

But she took her mother's advice and asked him, right in front of his friends, in the middle of his favorite club. It turned out to be quite outrageous—his friends stared with wide eyes and knowing grins on their faces—but she found she liked the feeling of taking the lead. Craig took the lead himself after that, asking her out every couple of nights. A couple of months later, he arranged for a special evening at their favorite restaurant.

After they finished eating, he got down on one knee. "Lisa, would you do me the honor of becoming my wife?"

She knew this was coming and already had her answer prepared. "Yes, I will, Craig. But not until you learn to *frenis*."

Craig slowly dropped his hands to his knee and pulled his head back slightly. He furrowed his brows and asked, "What has that got to do with us getting married?" he asked with a small squeak. "I'll learn in time."

"I know you will." She turned in her seat toward him and rested her hands on her thighs. "But there's something about me you don't know."

He slowly stood up and sat down in his chair again. "Okay, now I'm curious. Please tell me."

"My last name is not Hoeke. It's Stoddard."

"Stoddard?" Craig's brows went from furrowed to raised, and his eyes opened wide. "As in *Lupus Rex* William Stoddard?" he asked.

She smiled. "Yes, he's my father. My mother chose me as her *Postpartor*. I'm to be the next *Lupa Reginam*, Craig, and I've chosen you as my *Lupus Rex*. But you have to learn to *frenis* before we can ascend."

Lisa chuckled to herself as that memory flashed through her mind. *Oh, was he pissed when he found out their relationship was not all his doing. He came around, though. So will Aaron.*

For the next several months she worked with Craig, teaching him how to control his passions. She was just about ready to give up on him, but in early 1958, Craig finally learned how to do it. She smiled to herself as the memories of that long and passionate celebration the following weekend came flowing back.

Lisa called Michigan and informed her dad Craig had learned to *frenis*. He moved down to Virginia Beach so he could teach Craig what it took to be *Lupus Rex*. Lisa was sure she could have handled it, but men like to think they're in control.

Her dad spent a couple of months working with Craig and introducing him to various Clan heads. When he judged Craig able to handle the role Lisa laid out of for him, a date was set, and they were married.

Eight months later in 1959, they ascended.

Chapter 20—Historiae Nostrae

noun [his-t(ə-)rā()näs-trā]
1. Our history or past.

Aaron Darveau

Aaron followed Craig out into the loggia and turned left toward the back of the courtyard. The smells of last night's activities hung in the air. They were so thick he might as well have been slogging through wet cotton. It was like a pack of dogs had gotten into a case of barbeque sauce. They followed the loggia down and stopped before the statue of Diana. Craig had a serious look on his face, one Aaron hadn't seen before, and it demanded his attention.

"Aaron," Craig began, "only three people alive today have seen what I am about to show you: Lisa, Karen, and me. Even James doesn't know about this, though I'm sure he knows it's around here somewhere." He placed his hand on Aaron's shoulder. "I'm only showing you because we're on the fast track here."

Aaron's curiosity jumped up like a kid on Christmas morning, but he suppressed the urge to ask what it was.

Craig addressed Aaron formally. "I need your word you won't divulge anything you see here this morning."

"Why?" Aaron asked, shifting his feet.

"It's for Conclave eyes only. I don't want a stream of *lupis* running through here," he explained. "Nothing I'm about to show you is really a secret, but the existence of it is."

"I'm not sure I understand," Aaron pondered. "It's a secret about something that isn't a secret?"

"Um, think of a museum," Craig offered. "The displays are for all to see, but not everybody has permission to touch them. That is what I'm about to show you—a museum, of sorts. I just haven't made it completely available to everybody."

"Okaaay…," Aaron trailed off, "I'll keep my mouth shut."

Craig reached behind Diana's head and fumbled around for a moment until a click ricocheted out from the corner. The alcove split down the center, and the two halves silently swung back about eighteen inches, enough to completely push the pedestal into the walls and reveal an opening in the floor large enough for a man to fit through. Stairs were visible inside the opening. Aaron wondered what happened to the men who built this if they weren't on the list of "those alive who know about it."

Craig led the way into the basement. Aaron couldn't see much past him as he followed, but he could see it was brightly lit beyond. He followed as soon as Craig's head cleared the floor, stepping gingerly onto the top step. The hole looked small until he started his descent. Once on the stairs, it was easy to navigate them; they were wooden, sturdy, and wide. Hand railings were mounted on both sides, worn smooth from what looked like long-term use. The stairs went down approximately ten feet to a platform. On the left side of the platform, another set went down another ten feet. They did that two more times until they emerged into a large, man-made cavern, about fifty feet by fifty feet with fifteen foot ceilings held in place with large stanchions. There was another, larger set of stairs in the opposite, diagonal corner. The room's décor did not match what was up top. This was strictly a basement.

Arranged into aisles and spaced within the columns were various racks, chests of drawers, bookcases, sea chests, wardrobes, and tables. The tables were piled high with something, but it was impossible to determine what as they had canvas sheets spread out over them. The place had a slight musty smell, but it wasn't overpowering. Aaron suspected he wouldn't have smelled it at all if not for his newly-sharpened *lupus* senses. Along the ceiling were five rows of fluorescent lights running the entire length of the basement. He saw an air conditioning unit mounted in the far left corner and saw the ducts running cross ways to the lights, ending every ten feet in vents. The unit must have kept the dampness out of the air. Aaron followed Craig as he maneuvered his way around a couple of tables and made his way up the center aisle.

Aaron tried to stare at everything at once and asked, "What is all of this?"

Craig turned his head to him. "Your history. Or part of it, anyway. As *Lupus Rex,* it is my responsibility to maintain the history of the Race. It is important to know where we came from."

True, Aaron thought. *Those who don't know history are bound to repeat it.*

They reached a table near the other end of the room, and Craig pulled the canvas sheet from it. The entire table was heaped high with numerous books—all neatly arranged into stacks. The table itself was a large, wooden model about four feet long and three feet wide. A large, leather, office chair sat at one end. Aaron took a few minutes to scan the books, and he saw the ones near the far end of the table were older than the ones near the chair. A vast majority of them appeared to be leather-bound. He'd heard of leather-bound books, but he figured they were rare. These looked rare *and* old. They leather-bound ones were decorated with carvings depicting symbols and words from various languages. Toward the front of the table, where the chair was, the books were actually spiral-bound notebooks of the type found in school supply stores. One was open and had a pen lying next to it. Moving from the front of the table to the back was like stepping back in time.

Aaron commented, "Doesn't seem like a lot considering how long you've, I mean we've, been around."

"You're right. This isn't everything," Craig admitted. "This is just the stuff I've managed to collect in my lifetime. There are other caches hidden around the world, a couple dozen or so. They are mostly in Europe as that's where the Race's history more or less starts."

One lifetime? Aaron spent a few minutes taking in everything he could see from where he was standing. The racks were filled with pole arms, axes, and ancient slug throwers. Some artwork hung in various places, though it was hard to see any details from a distance. Everything else was either in drawers or chests or under the canvas sheets.

"Where do you get the money for all of this?" He stepped over to one of the racks and pulled down a spear. He wasn't an antique dealer, but he could tell this was high quality; it was old but well-maintained. The head was obviously hand-made from a piece of metal the size of his palm, but it was shiny. The shaft had been whittled from a long piece of oak and then sanded to a glass-like smoothness. There were symbols from some ancient culture painted all along its length.

"Why, investments, of course," Craig remarked in a casual tone, as if the idea should have been easy to figure out. "The Race has been around for a long time, Aaron. It's amazing what we were able to accomplish once we stopped fighting amongst ourselves. All *frenatus* have access to resources, a small trust fund if you will. We don't have to work for a living, but the majority of us do. The trust fund only supplies the bare necessities to live— enough for a modest apartment, a car, food, etc. As our population doesn't expand that much, the pie slices don't get much smaller as time goes on."

Aaron carefully replaced the spear in the rack. "What do you mean we don't expand that much?"

"We limit how many people we infect," Craig dryly said.

"What about births?" Aaron asked. "Is the infection passed from generation to generation?"

Craig shook his head. "Not all of the time. Both parents have to be infected and then there's only about a twenty-five percent chance of the infection being passed on." He took a deep breath. "Don't ask me why that is. I'm not a scientist—something about recessive gene traits." He held his hands out to his side in surrender. "You'd have to talk with Ricardo about that."

"So what happens to the children not born with the infection?" Aaron asked.

"Typically, they're raised within their immediate family, but we don't usually infect them until they come of age and ask for it." Craig grinned mischievously. "Sometimes though, an infected child may have a hard time controlling their anger and become a danger to their non-*lupus* siblings. When that happens, the parents usually choose to send one or the other to live with a foster family within the Race."

Aaron tugged his earlobe. "How do you keep the kids from spreading the secret?" he asked.

"If they learn the secret, we homeschool them until we feel confident they can keep their mouths shut."

"Hmph. What about the shunned ones, the *Lupis solitarius*? Don't they infect people? I'd think they'd contribute to the growth, if for no other reason than the fact they can't *frenis*."

Craig's face darkened. "The Fectors usually get them before they can do much damage." He abruptly shut his mouth, as if he had spoken too much already.

"Fectors," Aaron blurted out. "I've heard that word in whispered conversation before. Who are they?"

Craig looked thoughtful for a moment, as if deciding whether he wanted to change the subject or not. "We usually hold off on telling new *lupis* about the Fectors until later. But with your *frenis* last night and Karen's decision to choose you, I think we need to skip the normal training methods." He crossed his arms and leaned back onto the edge of the table and took a deep breath. "The Fectors are a fanatical religious group leftover from the crusades who spend their entire lives in single-minded pursuit of us. They used to consist mainly of warrior monks from the various Catholic military orders, but the last few generations have seen them replace their ranks with murderers from other religions, too."

Aaron guessed, "You mean, Templars?"

"No, not Templars, but I'm sure a few of them made it into the order as well. They call themselves the *Lucerna Veritatis*, the Lamp of Truth. We call them *interfectores*, killers, or simply Fectors. They call us howlers, like it's some sort of insult. They aren't very organized, but swarm like locusts if in pursuit of a known *lupus*." He paused briefly and looked Aaron in the eye. "We survive because we stay hidden and don't kill indiscriminately."

Aaron thought, *Okay, I've got bad guys who want to kill me. That's just wonderful.*

"Thankfully," Craig said, "they are more interested in *Lupis solitarius* than they are in the clans. Easier prey, I guess. We've managed for the most part to convince them we aren't the monsters they think we are, but there are a few cliques that have stepped off the reservation and do things their own way. They'll try to catch any *lupus* they know of unaware. We don't run into them that much these days, at least not since we went on our own 'crusade' about fifty years ago, back in the thirties."

"What happened?" Aaron asked.

"William Stoddard." He looked up the ceiling, using his eyes to point to where the kitchen was. "He was Lisa's dad and also *Lupus Rex* at the time. He waged war on them. But it was not all out—we only went after the fanatics. The rest of the Fectors were caught totally unprepared. When the dust settled, he made a gentlemen's agreement with them; they don't come after the clans, we don't go after them. Under other circumstances, they wouldn't have agreed to it."

"What changed their minds that time?" Aaron asked.

"It was the Order's soldiers who had most of the weapons." Then he laughed. "*That* was who Stoddard targeted. The rest of their organization was mostly staff and logistics. William, in one bloody night, managed to do what untold generations could not—he killed untold hundreds of Fectors."

"How do we know they aren't rebuilding, these Fectors?" Aaron asked. "If I was in their shoes, I would be." Aaron suddenly saw in his mind's eye secret training facilities set up like large karate dojos with thousands of priests practicing how to kill werewolves.

"We really *don't* know," Craig admitted. "There are a couple in the

Conclave who believe they are rebuilding." He got a look on his face like he had just tasted a glass of sour milk. "The majority doesn't believe it, though. They've lived too long chasing tame deer around their estates. They've gotten fat and content." He closed a nearby book and moved it into the stack. He spent a few moments shifting things around, organizing them. Aaron could tell he was organizing his thoughts; he'd seen him do similar things on other occasions.

When the books were all neatly stacked—and suspiciously close to their original positions—he scrutinized Aaron, judging him. "You said you would be rebuilding if you were them. Why?"

Aaron looked at Craig with wide eyes and exclaimed, "To have your life's work brought down in shambles around your feet? What other choice would you have? I feel a little bit of what they went through right now. Everything I knew is gone. I have to find some way to rebuild. I suspect they have a fifty year head start on me."

Craig nodded his head and murmured. "Perhaps Karen saw something in you even I missed. You even think like *Lupus Rex.*" Then a little louder. "And I don't think they're sitting around since the Calamity either."

"The Calamity?"

"Oh, sorry." Craig offered. "That's what the Fectors call it, what Stoddard did to them."

The silence between them stretched out as what Craig said sank into Aaron. He broke the silence by pointing at the table of books they were standing next to. "What's all of this?"

"Here—" Craig turned his attention to the table "—is where I record our history as I live it. I get reports from various clans, and I include it in my chronology. Each clan also maintains their own cache of records in secure locations, so I don't have to record every little minutia. However, I do record enough of the information, so the next *Lupus Rex* will have a smooth transition." He looked back up to Aaron. "That's why I brought you here. As I said earlier, this is probably one of the most important functions of *Lupus Rex*—ensuring our history is not forgotten."

Aaron sighed. "I'm not much of a writer. I tried keeping a diary when I was younger, but I could never get into the habit."

"You'll be boss," Craig reminded Aaron with a smirk and slight scoff. "Assign someone to handle it for you. Autumn is a magazine editor. She would love to do it."

"A magazine editor?" Aaron asked incredulously. "I wouldn't have expected that. Neither one of them strike me as particularly bright."

Craig laughed at that. "Don't let their behavior fool you. Both of those girls have minds as sharp as pins."

"So, what's their story?" Aaron asked. "They don't seem like the werewolf type, if you get my drift."

Craig rubbed his chin. "Well, I believe they are about twenty-one years old. I know they're Florida natives, but they went to Yale University."

"Yale? No shit?"

"Correct. Their parents are quite well off, but they didn't have to fork out one red cent. The girls got full-ride scholarships. Their father, Cornelius, is Alpha for a small pack in Bradenton. And both are natural-born *lupas*, too."

"Wait." Aaron did some mental calculations. "They have to be older than twenty-one then if they went to college."

"I believe they graduated from high school when they were fifteen or sixteen and started college shortly after that. They've lived here in Orlando for the last year."

Aaron snapped his fingers with glee. Something finally made sense. "And they joined your pack because it was convenient. Karen said that sometimes happens."

"Correct. Anyway, you two could sit down a couple of hours a week— you dictate and she writes. There's nothing secret in the Archives. At least, I feel that way. All *lupis* should have access to their history."

"Nothing is secret?" Aaron asked with sarcasm. "Everybody has secrets they want to keep, Craig."

"True." Craig displayed a wry smile and nodded his head. "I do keep a personal journal. That will be yours to read when I die. Not everyone keeps one, though. And of course I keep this cache secret. But if someone is interested in reading up on their history, I'll pull out the appropriate book for them. They can read it right there in my kitchen."

Craig sighed and looked around the room. "Still, so much is lost. For centuries, the stories were only handed down from generation to generation through oral traditions—stories and songs. One of our greatest Rexes, Octavio son of Hildebrandt, knew these stories would eventually disappear, so he set to recording them. I don't have them here, but I have visited the archive. If you've ever read Shakespeare, you have an idea what it's like to read them. He was one of the early Rexes following the adoption of the Pact. Although he managed to get quite a few of the stories recorded, the smaller clans were wiped out before he had a chance to finish."

Aaron cocked his head to side in confusion. "Karen mentioned there was some strife once the Pact was adopted, but she didn't mention wholesale slaughter on that kind of scale. Why didn't he order those smaller clans be saved? I thought the Conclave could only approve killing another *lupus*."

Craig laughed. "*Lupus Rex* is King, not dictator," he replied. "The strongest members of the Conclave wanted the smaller clans wiped out, less competition. The writings from that time period make for fascinating reading and are a good treatise on political maneuvering."

Aaron looked around at the museum. This was just one cache. Dozens more were scattered everywhere around the world with no way to access them other than by going there. "How do you find anything down here?"

Craig chuckled at that. "Yeah. It can be a pain in the ass, no question about it, but—" He stepped over to another table and lifted the canvas off one corner, revealing a large, recipe box full of index cards. "I keep a list of everything I have here. You have to know my method, but as I am the one who built it, it's easy for me. The other caches, not so much," he conceded with a wry grin. "They each have their own method. Usually, I just send out a request to the *custodes*, the keepers, the ones who watch over the caches, and they send back what they can find. It's not the most efficient way, but it does get the job done."

Aaron thumbed through the index cards. "Have you ever thought of building a central location where it would be easier to find everything—a private library for the Race? You could set up a reference section, a card catalog even; organize it by date and subject and Rex. Something like that would sure make it easier to find things."

Craig shook his head. "We've thought about it, but I'm afraid of putting all our eggs in one basket. However, we do have one cache in the Scottish Highlands attempting to use one of those new-fangled copying machines to make duplicates of some of the older books, the ones falling apart and in danger of being lost. It's slow going. Some of the books are far too large for the copier to handle. And the copies only come out in black and white." He pulled one of the older looking books from a stack and gently opened it. "Some of these have drawings, and they are all in color." He thumbed through a couple of the pages and the smell of old paper flooded the area around them. "We lose the depth and character of the originals. Still, the alternative is losing them altogether; I'm not willing to take that risk. If this works out, we might have full, readable copies at every cache. The technology just doesn't exist today to make computerized copies of everything. We're estimating that by the mid-1990s we'll have more efficient ways of storing and searching the information." Craig pulled the canvas sheet back over the catalog. "In the meantime, we're experimenting, seeing what works and what doesn't."

Craig was about to leave Aaron there to look through everything, when Aaron suddenly burst out, "How did you do it, Craig?"

Craig slightly twisted his neck to the side and squinted one eye. "Do what?" he asked.

"Get used to be being a werewolf!" Aaron exclaimed. "You were my age when you were turned, yet you seem so comfortable with the thought. You weren't brought up *lupus*, but you act like you were. It's like the Race is all you know! You say you consider the Race's history to be your most important job. How did that happen? You had dreams that didn't involve the Race, and yet you still look at it as if it was your life's calling."

Craig chuckled under his breath. "I'll admit, it took a while. I suspect the changes wrought on the body by the virus also affect the way we think. Hell, I don't know. All I know is that I think like a *lupus*. I can't remember thinking like anything else." He put his hand on Aaron's shoulder. "Give it time, Son. You're unique. You're a *frenator* who hasn't had the time to come to grips with everything yet. It's been less than a day." Craig dropped his hand with a slight smile. "Hell, boy, you may come around faster than anyone I've ever known!"

Aaron felt a wave of dizziness descend, but he quickly pulled it under control. "Maybe. Right now, I can't see it."

"Like I said, give it time," Craig advised with a rare tenderness. "Listen, I'm going up to get something to eat. Browse around down here if you want. Read some books if that takes your fancy. I'll tell Lisa to keep the food warm for you. Come up when you're ready. Just cover the table before you leave though."

Aaron offered his thanks and spent the next hour strolling along the different aisles, looking at the different artifacts Craig had acquired.

A few tapestries showed different battles of *Lupis sapiens* in mortal conflict with Homo sapiens. The humans were winning. Weapons galore of every type imaginable were in the racks, from simple slings to fully automatic weapons. It wasn't an arsenal—these were museum pieces. Books, clothing, maps, pieces of worked stone, statues, small carvings; all of these pieces were somehow related to *Lupis sapiens*. Aaron realized this was his new history.

He would have stayed longer, but his stomach complained about the lack of attention. *This could all be mine someday*, he thought. *Well, not really mine, but I would have access to it*. He knew Craig would certainly turn it all over to the *custodes*, and it would be scattered around the world, protected and categorized.

Aaron sat down and ate a late lunch of leftover barbeque with Craig and Lisa; everyone else was already gone for the day, and Karen was nowhere to be seen.

Aaron got into Lil' Red and broke every speed limit on the way to the base. Seeing the museum made him feel small. This was bigger than he was, a whole lot bigger. A whole civilization existed completely hidden from the modern world, coexisting alongside it. He was part of it now, for good or bad.

He changed into his gym clothes and ran around the base. He tried to get back to his center by doing Tai Chi. Nothing worked. He finally gave up and went to the Petty Officer's club on base and drank himself silly on 3.2 percent alcohol beers.

Chapter 21—Tiro
Noun [tir-ō]
1. Recruit

Mrs. Goetz, 1928

A howl pierced the walls of Mrs. Goetz's kitchen, and she froze, her chopping knife suspended one inch above her vegetable-covered cutting board. She'd heard the howl before but never this loudly and never in the daytime. She wasn't sure how long she stood there with her knife gripped tightly in her hand. She slowly crept over to the window and saw John fall out from the burning, hay lift door. She cried out, "John, No!" and then dropped her knife on the floor, grabbed a blanket off of the settee in the foyer, and ran outside. The barn was a raging inferno, but she was able to beat her way over to John just in time to smother the flames before they fully engulfed him.

John Billings, 1928

The nurse pulled the thermometer out of John's mouth while he picked at a scab under his pajamas. "Stop scratching, John, or it'll get infected again," she warned. He had severe burns over most of his body, and they weren't all healed yet. Thanks to Mrs. Goetz, John had lived, but he had to learn how to take care of himself all over again, because hot and cold didn't register on those spots any longer. He pulled his hand back up, casting an embarrassing look across the room at his mother, and then laid back into his pillow.

That night, long after Mrs. Goetz had picked up his mother to take her home and the doctors had gone home and the nurses had begun their pinochle game, a priest snuck into his room. John was surprised because once it appeared he was no longer going to die, they stopped visiting him. He guessed others needed the prayers more than he did. He welcomed the company though, even if it was a priest. He rarely slept anymore these days because the nightmares were too intense.

John waited until the priest shut the door before greeting him; visiting hours were over, and the nurses had sensitive ears. John's raspy, fire-burned voice cut through the darkness. "Can I help you, Father?"

"Yes, you can," the priest admitted. "I apologize for sneaking in like this, but I needed to talk with you without prying eyes and ears around. My name is Father Matthew." He pulled a chair up close to the bed. When he turned the nightstand light on, he recoiled at the sight of John's burned face but recovered his composure just as quickly. He got right to the point of his visit. "I'm interested in the events that brought you here. What did you see in the woods? And why did you burn a barn down around yourself?"

John's memory screamed back to that morning. It no longer sent chills up his back to think about it, but he didn't like to dwell on it either. "To kill a monster," he claimed, deadpan. He figured that answered both of the Father's questions.

The priest held him with a steely gaze. "Can you describe this monster?"

"Yessir, I can." John sat up in his bed. For the last couple of months people would look at him like he was crazy whenever he told the story. The only people who believed him were his mother and Mrs. Goetz. Mrs. Goetz believed it because she'd heard the howls and his mother only because the other two did. But they were worried the doctors would put him in a home for the insane, so they convinced him to change his tale. The official story now was Hale Hopstein was chasing him again, John threw jars of moonshine at him, and Hale was smoking. Boom.

Father Matthew though, seemed to want the truth, so John spoke rapidly, "It looked half man and half wolf. It was taller than me, and I'm not short. It was fast, and it was smart."

"Did it scratch you?" the priest asked with a shakey voice.

"No," John confirmed, "it never got close enough."

"Good." Father Matthew sighed. "I believe you had an encounter with a howler."

John scrunched his eyebrows. "Howler?"

Father Matthew appeared to relax now that the truth was out. "Yes, that's what we call them." He sat hard against the back his chair. "They're actually known by the scientific name, *Lupus sapiens*. Wise Wolf. Wolf Man. Lycanthrope. Werewolf. Take your pick. In the end though, they're evil of the worst kind. I work for an organization dedicated to eradicating them. We call ourselves, *Lucerna Veritatis*, The Lamp of Truth."

"There's more of 'em?" John swallowed and snuck a glance at the window and then the door.

"Unfortunately, yes." Father Matthew looked grim. "And we're severely outnumbered. Every time we get close, they disappear into the woods, so to speak. It's rare we get to speak with a survivor with their soul unscathed."

John's eyes suddenly welled up with tears, but he couldn't feel them roll down his face. The scarring was too bad. "Mr. Goetz sacrificed his life for me," John cried through viscous sobs. "He threw himself into its jaws to give me time to escape."

Father Matthew stood up and made the sign of the cross. "John, how would you like to continue what you started, killing howlers?"

"I don't know nuthin' 'bout fightin'." His country roots seeped back into his speech patterns. "I'm good at runnin'. And now Mr. Goetz is dead 'cause of it. If'n I knew how to fight, I mighta saved him."

Father Matthew made the sign of the cross again. "Mr. Goetz made the ultimate sacrifice," he preached solemnly. "He was a good man. An honorable man. And it sounds like he loved you as a son. I'm sure he's watching us now, waiting on your answer, just as I am." When one was not forthcoming, he continued his spiel. "As far as the running, sometimes that's the only way to win, John. We're looking for people who'll think. Trapping that howler in the barn and burning it down around him tells me you know how to do that. As for everything else, we'll teach you what you need to know."

The priest must have seen the answer he was looking for on John's face, for he placed a rumpled social card on the nightstand. "Call that number when you're ready to begin." He then slipped out of the room just as quietly as he had entered it.

Chapter 22—Lucerna Veritatis

Noun: lü-ser'-nə()ver-i-tā'-tis

1. Lamp of Truth.

John Billings, October 1933

Father John Billings, now *Lucerna Veritatis* Postulant John Billings, stood within the Chapel of the Convent of the Order. He had come far from that burning barn in Pennsylvania. Far indeed. Now he was about to be ordained into an ancient order of warriors who swore to defeat *Lupis sapiens*, that evil race of chimera, bred by Satan himself.

Other than him, three other men were present. In front of the altar was The Superior; on his flanks were two monks. One held the Papal banner of white and yellow, the other a black banner with a dagger and red cross above a skull and crossbones. The word INRI was prominent with the Latin words *Iustum, Necar, Reges, Impious* imprinted below it. These words gave the Order the permission to exterminate or annihilate all *Lupis sapiens* and any who would harbor them.

Postulant John knelt upon the floor, centered on a red cross made from inlaid marble. In his left hand, he held a black cross. In his right hand, he held the blade of a silver dagger, the bane of howlers everywhere, with the point on his chest. The Superior held the hilt and began administering the oath[1]....

When John was done reciting the oath, he opened his mouth to receive the Blessed Sacrament from The Superior. He then pressed the tip of the silver dagger into the skin on his bare chest, over his heart, and wrote his name in the Order's journal with blood drawn with the dagger.

The Superior commanded, "You will now rise to your feet, and I will instruct you in the rite necessary to make yourself known to any member of the Society of *Lucerna Veritatis* belonging to this rank.

"In the first place, you, as a Brother *Lucerna Veritatis*, will with another, mutually make the ordinary sign of the cross as any ordinary Roman Catholic would...."

What followed was a lengthy instruction on how a challenger would swipe his fingers across his crucifix and how the respondent would answer.

With the instruction complete, The Superior asked, "What name shall all *Lucerna Veritatis* know you by?"

Only one answer came to mind for that question. "Ignacio," Father

John Billings revealed, "Latin for fire."

The Superior commanded, "Rise, Father Ignacio, and join your brethren."

Father Ignacio, February 1935

"What do you mean, 'It is not here,' Brother Elijah?!" Father Ignacio asked the monk who was standing before him delivering the bad news. They had chased William Stoddard across the country for months, from one safe house to the next. They finally cornered it here, outside of Denver. Or at least everything indicated they had.

Brother Elijah replied, "We've searched the entire area, including the cabin. We were closer this time than ever before. The coals in the oven are still warm, and there are dirty dishes in the sink." He reached into a leather messenger bag he was carrying and pulled out a sheaf of papers. "And we found this on the kitchen table, too. It's in Dutch, I think."

Father Ignacio looked through the papers. *Definitely Dutch.* It would take weeks to get it back and forth from someone who could translate it, and for all he knew it was in Dutch *and* coded. The howlers were quite adept at being sneaky. "Brother Elijah, how did the howler know we were coming?"

"I don't know, Father," Brother Elijah stammered with downcast eyes.

"You've been watching it for the last week. Did you get too close possibly?"

Brother Elijah looked up. "We, we," he faltered, "we've done exactly as you've taught us, Father. Get no closer than one mile and never permit less than two levels of separation between them and anyone we talk to."

Father Ignacio nodded his head and sighed. "Perhaps it was one of their witches then," he conjectured. "I didn't think they were accurate enough to alert them like this, but maybe their queen bitch is particularly strong."

Brother Elijah's shoulders relaxed. "Perhaps," he readily agreed. "What's our next move?"

Father Ignacio turned to walk off. "We wait," he ordered. "They'll show their faces soon enough." Then he stopped and asked, "How's the interrogation going on the one we captured?"

Brother Elijah tensed up again. "Not good. He, I mean it, died."

"Very well. Tell Brother Marcus we'll need another one. I don't care where he gets it from."

"Yes, Sir."

130

Chapter 23—Concoquo

verb [kän'-kō-kwō]
1. Assimilate through hardship.

Aaron Darveau, April 27, 1983

Aaron's phone rang around six o'clock that following Wednesday evening. It was Glen. "Hey, Aaron! Tonight's the full moon, man. You comin' or we gonna see you on TV tomorrow?"

"I thought Saturday night was."

"No, Craig slipped you a mickey to force it early. The way you were able to *frenis* your first time, I have no doubt you could perform a *renovatio* this evening all by your lonesome, but why take a chance? Come on out, man, it's gonna be a blast!"

Aaron had been staying on the base, away from Karen. He was trying to decide if he wanted anything to do with her anymore or not, but the seething anger that flooded through him on Sunday had subsided to a trickle, and he was able to think clearly on the matter. "On my way."

"Great!" Glen exclaimed. "See you soon. Get here before dark. And, man, you need to get a calendar or you really will find yourself on TV. It's *Viam Lupus*, dude."

"*Viam Lupus?*" Aaron asked.

"The Way of the Wolf, man!"

After changing into his civilian clothes, spending ten minutes hiking across the base to where Lil' Red was parked, and fighting rush hour traffic like they were in a Roman gladiatorial ring, it took Aaron close to two hours to get there. He arrived with no time to spare because as soon as he crossed into the foyer, the *renovatio* hit him. The black dog rushed him as the fiery madness consumed him, and then, like before, the coldness spread from his chest, quenching his burning body. He brushed the black dog to the side with a simple Tai Chi redirection. It turned to look at him over its shoulder as it slunk off, deciding today was not a good day to challenge him. The pain left Aaron's body while the madness diminished to an annoying buzzing in his ears. It seemed to take a lifetime, forcing one foot in front of its partner and ripping his sand-paper encrusted clothes off, but in reality, it was over by the time he crossed the length of the foyer, fifteen feet. He looked back at his ripped and shredded clothing lying in his wake. *Damn! That was my favorite shirt, too.*

He trotted into the courtyard and crossed over to Karen's room. She kept a large, full-sized mirror in there, and he wanted to see what he looked like. All he had a chance to see the last time was a flash of his face before he was interrupted by the start of the chase. He wasn't missing the opportunity again. He hurried in, unconsciously avoiding the door and then the boots on the floor, to find Karen lying on the bed with her nose resting on her front—paws, claws, hands, whatever they were—listening to Duran Duran sing *Hungry Like the Wolf*. They looked like human hands, but her fingers were elongated with sharp talons protruding from them. Her ears stood at attention, pointed forward, alerted to him coming across the courtyard. He stopped short and looked at her. Her face was strongly lupine mixed with her human features. She had large eyes and whiskers, and a short snout lined with lethal looking teeth and fangs.

He didn't know what to say; he wasn't sure he wanted to say anything to her right then, but that song made him chuckle quietly to himself. He relaxed some even though his feelings for her were still intermingled with some of the more negative ones—deception being the strongest. He could almost understand her infecting him that first night, instinct is a powerful motivator, but they'd been living together for nearly a month, and she never once said anything to him, never tried to prepare him for what was coming. She let him think everything was wonderful. That's what he was most upset about—she didn't think enough about him to let him in on that one little secret.

Even after all of that, he was still constantly thinking about her, her smell, her touch, her—everything. He may have been disappointed, but he still loved her. Maybe Lisa was right. Maybe that would be enough.

Standing there, he appreciated her beauty. She was an exquisite creature with a shiny, sable coat, and dark blue eyes. The eyes brought back memories of his first *renovatio*. Everybody had dark blue eyes except for Ricardo and Warren. Ricardo's were red and Warren's were pale blue. She raised her head and pulled her lips back into a snarl. His new *lupus* sight saw a smile, though.

My, what large teeth you have! Then he asked her aloud, "**How are you doing?**" What left his mouth was a series of grunts and growls and whines arranged in a rhythm he understood.

She lithely jumped off the bed and nuzzled him. "**Fine, now that you're here**," she rumbled. He nuzzled her back.

After getting reacquainted, he hurried in front of the mirror. He certainly looked lupine, similar to Karen, but masculine. He stood up to his full height, a solid seven feet tall. He had the ability to walk upright, but the ability to run on all fours was evident as well. His arms were longer in comparison to a human and muscular like his legs; it was a chaser's physique. His coat was dark chocolate, darkening even further to black around his snout, feet and hands, the tips of his ears, and the end of his tail. He took a few minutes to inspect his hands.

They were certainly human-like, five digits each, including an opposable thumb. They also looked like dog's paws. The palms were padded like a dog's, but the 'toes' extended out into long fingers. The nails were about an inch long, with a strong, wide base tapering to a knife point.

Karen offered, **"We call them culas instead of hands."**

"Culas?"

"Yes, it's short for the Latin word *manicula*, which isn't quite right, either." She pointed to some raised bulges at the base of his talons. **"Those are *fel saccula*. The closest translation for that is venom sac. It's not really venom, though that's what we call it. When *lupis* wish to infect a human, this is where the infection comes from."** She squeezed one of the sacs, and a clear, viscous liquid oozed out along his talon. **"So, between *manicula* and *saccula*, it's been mangled through the years into cula. They aren't quite paws, and they aren't quite hands, and they aren't quite venom sacs."**

Aaron examined the sacs with a renewed interest. **"So this isn't some supernatural curse?"**

"No. It's a virus."

If it's a virus, can it be cured? **"Is this how you infected me?"** he asked.

"Yes," she rumbled and whined softly.

"But you weren't *lupus* then," Aaron rumbled.

"*Lupa*. Females are *lupa*. Males are *lupus*. Plural is *lupis*, though sometimes it might be *lupus* depending on the circumstances. You'll get the hang of it.

"Anyway, with enough practice, you'll be able to change different parts of your body whenever you want to. That's what I did; I changed my fingers. When you strike someone, the pressure of the blow is transferred from your talons to the sacs, causing them to release the venom. That's how it gets into the bloodstream."

133

The subject of her infecting him without his permission hung in the air. He turned back to the mirror and continued his self-inspection. His eyes were dark blue, and when he stared into them, he recognized himself. If he stared long enough, he no longer saw the wolf, his *lupus*; he saw his human face. He didn't know if that was wishful thinking or imagination. In either case, it helped center him as he knew who was looking back at him.

They trotted out of the bedroom toward the back of the courtyard where he picked up a familiar sound and smell—deer on the hoof. Neurons in his brain slapped together, releasing that special chemical, serotonin, which tells the owner it likes something. Right then it was telling him he liked chasing deer!

He yelped with excitement, "**Come on, hurry up!**"

They dropped to all fours and ran the rest of the way. His body was amazing—agile, strong, and vigorous.

Karen spotted the rest of the *grex* first. "**This way, Aaron!**" she yipped with delight as she took off in their direction.

He followed her and caught up easily enough. Although they were only loping, their stride was easily five yards long.

Aaron saw about twenty *lupis* here, about the same number as last time. Karen whimpered harshly, "**These are your *grex* mates, Aaron. Except for James over there. The *grex* tries to get together during the *plenilunium* to hunt together.**"

Aaron sensed the majority of them were wildlings. The madness was overwhelming their minds, and they were on the hunt without regard to anything around them. The *frenatus* worked to keep them under control as the chase resumed a more structured design.

Lupis sapiens are more efficient than a wolf pack when it comes to teamwork during the hunt. They have the intelligence of man and the cunning and instinctive mentality of the wolf. This was Aaron's first time on a structured hunt, and he was not aware of how the *grex* hunted. However, he'd seen enough television shows as a kid to know they were employing the same techniques as would wild wolf packs.

That night, they used the classic drive method; about one third of the *grex* chased the deer while the rest lay in hiding, waiting for the prey to be chased into their grasp. As the newest member of the *grex*, Aaron was allowed to chase. He was happy with that decision; he wasn't sure he could have sat still while the chasers toyed with their food, running it one way across the estate and back. He loved the forced breeze through his coat and the sensation of the ground as his feet and culas dug into it, propelling him ever farther forward. He also got a taste of why dogs like to hang their heads out of car windows; the smells were incredible as they were pushed against the receptors in his nose without any effort on his part. He did think they were cheating though, turning a deer loose on the estate and chasing it. He supposed that was better than chasing cars down the street.

Alas, the time came when Karen turned their quarry toward the ambush. Aaron watched as *Lupus Rex* made the kill. It was swift, clean, and quite practiced. He leapt out from behind a brush pile and grabbed the deer by its neck in mid-flight, sinking his culas and teeth into it. When he landed, the deer's neck was broken, the windpipe was crushed, and the arteries were severed. The deer never knew what hit it.

There obviously wasn't enough meat to sate everyone's appetite. The kill was mostly symbolic, a history lesson to keep everyone grounded.

As with wolf packs, all members have a rank; *Lupus Rex* and *Lupa Reginam* each took the first share. Aaron was next as their *Princeps Lupus*, then James, their *Dux Lupus*. Karen would have partaken after Aaron, but he took the liver and shared it with Karen, to the approval of all present. Next came Autumn and Summer followed by Bill and Glen. Aaron was surprised to see the ladies ranked higher than the boys. The carcass was then turned over to the wildlings; if they didn't get a share, the *frenatus* would have had a hard time controlling them the rest of the night. The wildlings had their own hierarchy which did not appear to be a concern of the *frenatus*.

A momentary rush of pleasure roared through Aaron's brain when he tasted the deer's blood. It was similar to the feeling he would get from drinking a large glass of water after working in the yard. It was thirst quenching. He looked at everyone present, and they all had a satisfied look on their face.

When everyone had their share, they all relaxed in the middle of the field, basking in the moonlight. Karen cuddled up next to Aaron while the others paired up—Craig and Lisa, Bill and Summer, and Glen and Autumn. James went back toward the house. The wildlings were running around the field, howling and mock fighting each other. The *frenatus* all watched them with a humorous enjoyment. Although the wildlings were a step away from a bloodlust rage, here amongst their *grex* mates, they were little more than children; children with bad tempers, but they were children nonetheless. They did need watching out for, but with strong leadership they knew their place in the hierarchy.

Around midnight, Karen stood up to stretch. Aaron lay there admiring her, and she swiftly leaned over and nipped him on his tail.

He sat up quickly. **"What the hell, Karen?"**

"Don't like it," she snarled playfully, **"stop me!"** She did it again, only this time, she turned and ran a few yards, stopped, and then looked back at him with a large grin on her face. Aaron knew this game. He jumped up and ran after her. He wasn't sure if he actually caught her or she let him catch her, but he bumped her with his nose then ran off. The rest joined in, including the wildlings. For the next hour or so, they played a game of tag, never tiring. The quarries never got too far from the hunter. However, when the hunter got too close to someone, by unspoken agreement, everyone spread out simultaneously, and then closed back in, teasing the hunter. This was practice for a group attack, and it was viciously effective.

The first time Aaron was tagged, he tripped, fell over, and then lay there for a minute, laughing at his clumsiness. Everyone came back to laugh with him and he dropped his ruse, tagging one. The wildlings fell for it every time—the *frenatus*, never again.

The game of tag stopped when James returned and issued a challenge. **"Bill, you think you're ready to take on your clan Alpha?"** Everyone gathered into a circle in restrained excitement.

Bill jumped up with a large grin on face. **"You come into my *grex* talking shit? You gonna get your ass kicked, old man!"**

Glen laughed at him. **"Bro, you ain't gonna kick nobody's ass sittin' there jawin' about it!"**

James laughed. **"Bring it on, Honky-Tonk!"**

James and Bill circled each other a few times with feints thrown by both to test weaknesses and to check for any openings worth exploiting. Aaron wasn't sure which one would win in a true fight; James had the weight advantage while Bill, the speed. In the end, James won by pinning Bill to the ground with a gentle bite to the neck. Bill got up, and James howled for a moment in triumph.

James looked over at Aaron. **"I think it's time to begin your training, Aaron,"** he goaded. **"Give it your best shot."**

Every head turned his way and all were quiet, even the wildlings. Craig took a special interest and moved closer to the action.

As someone who had studied Tai Chi since age twelve, Aaron wasn't sure this would be a fair fight. He wasn't feeling cocky, but he just watched James and knew it wouldn't be a contest. Seeing James and Bill wrestle reminded him of his first match with Master Chen. Master Chen, obviously, mopped the floor with him every time Aaron rushed in. He told his class a story after his "demonstrations" with Aaron.

"Once, two great and powerful Tai Chi Masters found themselves in the same town. As this town was too small for two masters, the local warlord told them they were to fight to the death. The winner would get to stay in town. As the two masters approached each other, the townsfolk were excitedly hushed; who would win this fight? The masters each relaxed into their defensive stances, touching the backside of their right wrists together at chest level, left arms protecting their lower left mid sections. They held this stance for three days. Finally, one spoke, 'You are indeed the supreme ultimate. Let us share a pot of tea.' At which point, the other one said, 'You are mistaken, Master. You are the supreme ultimate! I would be happy to share that pot of tea with you, though.' They both stood and bowed to each other, wrapping their left hands around their right fists—the universal sign of the Warrior-Scholar."

The moral of the story is never initiate combat, and let your opponent show you how to defend. At this point, most students ask who won. Sifus just smile and continue on with the lesson, never answering in words. In time, the students learn they both won; nobody wins a fight. Just because you can fight, doesn't mean you should.

However, in a wolf pack, winning is everything.

As Aaron and James slowly circled each other, James took Aaron's refusal to probe as a weakness and rushed in using the same technique he used on Bill. He attacked from all fours, leaping at the last moment in an attempt to land on Aaron. Using Tai Chi, Aaron simply lowered his body to the ground, too late for James to adjust his approach. As he ran over Aaron's head, Aaron lifted up and used his nose to goose James in the belly. He applied no more force than what it would take to lift a pillow. James landed, sprawled on his back after doing a complete head-flip. Before he was back on his feet, Aaron was already within his circle with his teeth on James's neck. James surrendered on the spot. The rest of the *grex* sat in unbelieving silence.

Karen displayed pride in her stance—chest out, head high, and tail swishing back and forth—while Craig had a neutral yet interested gaze.

They both had seen Aaron doing his Tai Chi forms in the backyard, but neither of them truly considered it a martial art—until now.

Not to be shown up by a rookie, James again challenged Aaron, this time trying a different tactic, but still using weight and ferociousness to overwhelm him. James came in upright, as a human would. Aaron stood still and did nothing more than place his right cula out in front of himself, waist high, palm up, fingers straight. James's stomach came into contact with Aaron's talons and his forward momentum abruptly stopped; the alternative was to be impaled. Aaron raised his left cula to James's face, and pushed him to the ground by taking a single step forward, keeping his talons in James's midsection, and exerting a slight downward pressure. James tripped himself to the ground as his feet were in position to move forward, not backward. Aaron didn't need to force the submission. He stepped back and allowed James to rise in defeat.

James's anger hit Aaron's nose; it was bitter and made him want to sneeze. James was *Dux Lupus*, but Aaron was to be *Lupus Rex*. Even though he'd not made up his mind yet, he still had a position to maintain.

Finally, James decided it was time to stop this and went on the attack for real, out for blood. He used his culas to try to gut Aaron. Aaron grabbed his arm, lifted it up, and kicked his legs out from under him, throwing him on his back. He gawked up and found Aaron's right cula under his chin, wrapped around his throat, his heartbeat pounding his artery against Aaron's talons.

Aaron growled, "**Do you yield, or shall I find out what a clan head tastes like?**"

James yelped, "**I yield!**" Aaron let him stand.

Aaron sensed some unease from the *grex* and outrage from James. *Did I miscalculate? Should James have won this? Perhaps I can save the moment. Even visiting masters never embarrassed Master Chen by defeating him in his own studio.*

Aaron spoke to the *grex*. "**Do not let what you saw here burden you. I have spent years training in hand to hand combat. *Lupus Rex* and Karen can vouch for that, but James was not aware of it. I feel I have cheated and betrayed my *Dux Lupus* by not warning him. I now ask his forgiveness.**"

Aaron prostrated himself in front of James. He knew he was taking a risk, but he needed to make sure James didn't lose the respect of this *grex*. By submitting to James's authority, willingly and without coercion, it told everyone present Aaron had honor. It was a dangerous gambit, though. James could kill him with one swipe. The question James had to answer was what he wanted more—revenge or honor? For James, it was a win-win situation. He wouldn't lose honor by taking revenge—Aaron had submitted himself to him—but his honor would go up if he showed compassion to an honorable adversary. He hoped James was smart enough to conclude Aaron would make a better live ally than dead adversary. Today anyway.

James looked down on Aaron, raised his cula in the air, and then gently placed it on Aaron's shoulder. **"You fought honorably, Aaron. You did not betray me, therefore no forgiveness is necessary."**

The *grex* tilted their heads back and howled.

Karen Argali

Karen was stunned at what just happened. Aaron managed to ingratiate himself to the *grex* while at the same time saving James's honor. He was already pulling the Race to his will, and he had only been *lupus* four days. She looked over to Craig and watched him walk off, James following closely on his heels.

Everyone settled down and Aaron issued the challenge. **"Who's next?"** he asked.

Bill jumped into the middle of the circle. **"Dude, you have *got* to show me that move you pulled on James when he rushed you the first time. That was bad ass! The way he went flying? Shit, I've never seen that before."**

After a couple of hours of showing different ways of avoiding the most obvious attacks, Glen spoke up. **"Time for hide and seek!"**

Bill approved. **"Hell, yeah!"** He looked at Autumn and Summer. **"Come on, girls!"**

The girls agreed wholeheartedly, and the four of them ran off together toward the stand of trees to the southwest leaving Aaron alone with Karen in the middle field.

Aaron looked at Karen. **"Hide and Seek? How hard is it to play hide and seek with an intelligent creature with the ears, eyes, and nose of a wolf?"**

"Not hard at all," she whimpered with a grin that only a lupus could produce. **"Depends on what you're hiding and who's doing the seeking."**

Aaron laughed lightly and muttered, **"I was wondering how I was**

going to get you alone.”

Karen awoke alone in the field to find Aaron had already left for the day. She was upset until she made her way back to her room where she found a note he left for her on her bed.

Karen,

Sorry I left you in the field, but you looked too peaceful to wake up. I have to be back at the base by 0800. I'll see you this evening.

Aaron

She smiled. *Maybe he's coming around after all.*

Chapter 24—Illustro

verb [i'-ləs-ˌtrō]
1. Enlighten.

Aaron Darveau, April 30 to May 15, 1983

Aaron was granted leave, military vacation, for the next two weeks. His division officer approved his request easily enough; Aaron had quite a bit of it saved up, and he was due to get out of the Navy in a month and half anyway. He and Karen spent the time out at Craig's estate getting acclimated to their new situation, and Karen seemed to be giving him all the time he needed to come to terms with his new condition.

On the weekends, Craig and Lisa hosted parties to introduce Aaron to the *grexes* in the local family. Everyone sat around eating, drinking, swimming, and visiting with each other. As the time rolled by, he became more and more comfortable with the idea of being *Lupus sapiens*, and the whole picture of him becoming *Lupus Rex* no longer struck him as fantastic as it did at first.

He didn't spend all of his time at the estate, though. He, Kyle, Bill, and Glen spent a few days crawling through junkyards in the area, trying to find parts for Lil' Red's restoration. It turned out Glen infected Kyle a couple of years before Aaron met him at the car show, and was working with him on how to *frenis* all this time. Bill, Glen, and Kyle had been friends for quite some time and called themselves *The Three Wolfketeers*. After a couple of days of Aaron hanging out with them, Glen started calling the four of them *The Four Wolfketeers*. Bill made some wisecrack about not forgetting the little people when he ascended. Aaron wasn't sure he liked the sound of that, but didn't pursue the subject any further.

What time he did spend at the estate was spent in Craig's basement reading through the Archives. Aaron had always been curious so this didn't seem like work to him.

He took the family TV apart once to see if he could find all the little people inside. He couldn't find them, which was frustrating, because after getting his ass whipped he really wanted something to show for it.

He kissed the girl across the street when he was five because it looked nice on television. Although not unpleasant, he didn't know what the big deal was.

He tried smoking one of his Dad's cigars. He liked it so much he snuck more of them over the years.

He tried jumping his bicycle across a gully. He liked that, too. Until he landed.

He jumped off the roof with a homemade kite strapped to his arms. Like the gully adventure, it was fun until he landed.

He really couldn't remember all the laughable episodes of his childhood. However, one thing he did know was if he needed to find an answer to something, it was not going to be found in the USS Enterprise's databanks listed under "Unknown Energy Sources." Finding a trove of information on something unknown to the modern world seized his imagination.

The first thing he realized was he needed to take a correspondence course on Latin. Quite a bit of the Archives were written in that dead language. Luckily, Craig wasn't well-versed in it either; he had a well-thumbed copy of a Latin to English dictionary sitting there on the table next to the history transcripts with hand-written notes stuffed inside with various phrases already translated.

The second thing he found, and was happy when he did, was that the Race didn't kill humans at random. They tried to keep things contained. *Lupis sapiens* were carnivores of the highest order, but they were not murderers and didn't appear to consider humans food. What Karen told him about the Race was correct—assuming the records were accurate.

The wildlings were a different matter. Everything the human race publicly knew about werewolves was based on rampages wrought by the wildlings. After the Pact, things settled down. The *frenatus* kept them under control. The occasional problem came up, and stories of werewolves running around London and other major cities throughout the world remained isolated. In time, the knowledge of werewolves turned into myths, and the myths turned into stories, and the stories turned into movies. The humans all but forgot about *Lupus sapiens* and stopped hunting them. That didn't apply to the Fectors, though. They hunted the *lupus* relentlessly until about sixty years ago during Stoddard's reign.

Studying about the Lamp of Truth led him to research the *Lupis solitarius*. Aaron wasn't sure he liked the whole *Lupus solitarius* bit, but he could find no records where any *lupus* had actually been shunned. Of course, history is written by the victors and *Lupis solitarius* are not the victors. It was either never recorded, erased from the records, or Craig didn't have those records here. One other possibility is it never happened, and it was something to scare new *lupis* into behaving.

All in all though, he didn't think being *Lupus Rex* would be a bad arrangement. Experience was not something required, either. When a *lupa's* intuition—and that barely described it as it was the closest thing to ESP he ever heard of—pointed to a *Lupus Rex*, that man became *Lupus Rex* and ruled with an even hand. From what he could glean from the records, that intuition was never wrong.

Another thing he couldn't find was any record of anyone being able to *frenis* when they performed their first *renovatio*. Supposedly, the more confident someone is, the faster one learns to *frenis*. He suspected his ability to *frenis* his first time wasn't due strictly to willpower; Jajine probably had a hand in it. He reached up and touched his necklace. He assumed she understood how it worked. Her voice bounced around in his head. *"Trust your instincts."* He decided he would keep that secret to himself for now. *No one has to know about her or the black dog. If they believe it is willpower, let them think I'm some sort of Tai Chi Master or something.*

As he got closer to the most recent records, he found out *Lupis sapiens* weren't that different from humans. Karen told him it was a virus; he just had a hard time visualizing it. But if what he read in the records was correct, *Lupis sapiens* really were created by a virus. It facilitates certain changes in the body's chemistry and DNA, extraordinary changes to be sure, but at the most basic level *Lupis sapiens* really were human.

"I've been reading about the virus," Aaron told Craig one evening, "but there's quite a bit of medical terminology I don't understand. Exactly what is it we're dealing with here?"

Craig scratched his chin. "Ricardo could help you much better than I can if you are truly interested. He does some of the research in Shreveport. Do you require detailed information?"

Aaron shook his head. "Probably not. I did good in shop class while in school, but not so much in biology. Just give me your impressions."

"Okay. About fifty years ago, a group of Nazi scientists—"

"Nazis?" Aaron exclaimed.

"Yes." Craig frowned. Aaron knew he didn't like being interrupted. "They were looking for a way to produce a super soldier. You've probably read about that in other books. Anyway, they did quite a bit of research on *Lupis sapiens*. What they found out was it wasn't some sort of supernatural curse. See, Aaron, we aren't evil. We're just perceived that way. Hell, for centuries we even thought that way ourselves, that we were touched by evil. But we knew we were still human too. After all, we didn't kill wantonly when changed, only when threatened. Anyone would fight back if attacked. We just happened to be better at it. The Nazis wanted to tap that source of savagery."

"I'm surprised y'all went along with them," Aaron put forth accusingly. "I've read they weren't too nice to their test subjects."

Craig's face darkened. "We didn't go along with them. We lost quite a few members of the Race during those 'experiments.'"

"Sorry."

"Think nothing of it," Craig allowed. "You didn't know. Anyway, these scientists discovered a virus flowing within the bloodstreams of *Lupis sapiens*. After World War II ended, the research disappeared and it was thought all of their work was lost. Then about twenty years ago, it was found in one of the caches in South America. We've been studying the work since, but it's slow going. What we have discovered is it isn't a virus so much as it's a parasite. Actually, it's a combination of the two. During a *renovatio* the virus feeds off of the chemicals in the brain that control emotion. The brain becomes polluted with the excrement of the virus. These impurities block the signals that permit us to direct our own thoughts, blocking higher brain functions. The *frenatus* are the ones who are able to push through those roadblocks set up by the impurities."

Aaron stated, "Sounds straightforward enough. Develop a vaccine. They did it with polio."

Craig shook his head. "That would prevent humans from becoming infected. It wouldn't cure us."

Aaron thought, *If the humans got their hands on a vaccine, they could vaccinate everyone and eventually* Lupis sapiens *would just die out without so much as a whimper.* "So, what is the end game here? Are we looking for a cure or not?"

"Not so much a cure, but a way to control it," Craig explained. "Finding out about the virus helped us understand our history better. For centuries, no one understood why certain people were able to *frenis* and others couldn't. Now we know. It takes years to learn to do it, though." He smiled. "Present company excluded, of course. Unfortunately, we still don't understand *how* it is done. How do you teach someone to play tennis? Practice, practice, practice. The more we practice, the better we get at it. Some of us have the ability to change whenever we want, in whole or in part. And some have no control at all, spontaneously transforming when under stress. The one thing we can't do is prevent it from happening on a full moon—something about a buildup of the impurities. The information is sketchy in that regard. But imagine if you will, having all of the benefits of being a member of the Race but not having to perform a *renovatio*."

Understanding dawned on Aaron. "I see your point." Aaron did feel stronger and healthier, and in hindsight, it struck him it all started the morning after his first *renovatio*. Just this morning, he took his hay fever tablet and realized it had been days since he last sneezed. His senses were amazing too, even his hearing. He used to suffer from high frequency hearing loss in both ears—something left over from his many concerts in high school—but the ringing was gone now. He wasn't a superman, but he *was* acting like a finely tuned machine. "Do we get sick, diseases and such?"

Craig shook his head. "No. If we infect someone who has a debilitating physical disease—muscular sclerosis or cerebral palsy for instance—it doesn't cure it, but it doesn't get any worse. However, there are no recorded instances where any *lupus* has ever contracted those diseases, either. The *lupus* virus is the ultimate vaccination—other than the nasty side effect of being a wildling."

Aaron was impressed. "Yes, that would be something, wouldn't it? Have you thought of approaching a less—militaristic—organization? I'm sure there're some here in the U.S. who would love to work on this."

"No." Craig shook his head emphatically. "After what happened in Nazi Germany, we're not willing to take that risk."

Aaron asked, "What happens when we have to go to the doctor, like for a car accident or something, and they run blood tests? Has the virus ever been found?"

"Not that I'm aware of," Craig touted. "It's rare we ever end up in a hospital, though. We're pretty tough and heal quickly."

So we don't get sick, and we heal up quickly. Yes, this would be a boon for mankind if we could control the renovatio.

"So, what's the success rate on those who know how to *frenis* and those who don't?"

"Only about one-fourth ever learn how to *frenis*."

Aaron did some rapid mental calculations—one-fourth of the Race was the number of *lupis* in the ruling class, the *frenatus*, according to the Archives. He wondered if was by design or merely coincidence. "Are there any *Frenatus* who are not leaders in the Race?"

"Not really, no. *Frenatus* can think," Craig boasted. "Just like humans can think and therefore rule over animals, *Frenatus* rule over the wildlings."

Aaron sat back and chewed on that. *It's a virus and not a curse. And after 50 years of research they still don't know how to control it?*

After Aaron read all he could understand on the medical research, he moved on to the Pact. *Lupus Rex* could only be removed by breaking the Pact or, obviously, by death. By accepting the role as *Lupus Rex*, he took an oath to uphold and enforce it. If he broke any part of it, any member of the Conclave had the right to bring charges against him. In such situations, the Conclave would act as the jury with the *Lupa Reginam* acting as judge. She also had final say. Being found guilty resulted in being declared *Lupus solitarius*. No *Lupus Rex* had been brought up on charges in over 200 years though, and none had been removed from the position since the Pact was adopted.

Interestingly, no rules were documented for bringing charges against *Lupa Reginam*. That nagged him for a few days—it almost sounded like *Lupus Rex* was a kept man and *Lupa Reginam* had all the power. He was sure he was missing something but he couldn't put his finger on it. Craig didn't act subservient to Lisa. They were like any other old married couple. Like his parents were to a certain extent, they were a team. Perhaps that is what he and Karen would turn into. Aaron admitted to himself there were probably worse fates than spending his life with Karen.

Next, he found a chart detailing the different clans. He scanned down the list and when he got to Ricardo and Warren, he thought back to his first *renovatio* and the different eye colors he saw. His curiosity got the better of him and he searched the Archives for anything on eye color. He couldn't find a thing so he went back to studying the chart. He admired the colorful artwork that went into drawing it and noticed the clan names and glyphs were in different colors. Warren's and Ricardo's clan crests were in their respective eye color. Each clan crest was a different color. *It must be the infection.*

Clan Name	Area Controlled	Dux Ducissa	Eye Color
Acer Dens	Germany	Walther & Freja Brinkerhoff	Yellow
Celeriter	Spain	Juan & Josefina Campos	Pale Red
Sans Peur	British Isles	Tàmhas & Maisie Hamilton	White
Os Ruptor	East Europe	Mieszko & Alicja Mozdzierz	Dark Green
Ambrosius	West Asia	Modest & Natasha Petrov	Brown
Gloriosi	North America	James Gondolfin	Dark Blue
Venatio	North America	Ricardo & Emma Paige	Red
Luna Amator	NE U.S.A.	Warren & Riley Freeman	Pale Blue
Pulsante Ungue	China/East Asia	Bao-Heng Lim	Grey
Tonitrua	South America	Antonio & Paulita Speddada	Pale Green
Pilo Crasso	Australia	Esmond & Dolly Heath	Orange
Mors Atra	Africa	Chidike & Afua Afolayan	Black

Aaron thought the list might be incomplete because Craig's name wasn't listed. Then he remembered Craig was *Lupus Rex* and a *grex* Alpha; he pulled double duty, just not as a *Dux*. In all, five clans were in Europe and Western Asia, three in North and Central America, one covering China and Eastern Asia, one in Africa, one in Australia, and one in South America—it was the largest, numbering almost three thousand. The Chinese clan rarely made Conclave meetings. They respected *Lupus Rex*, but they had their own way of doing things.

The politics were fairly easy to navigate through. James had final say on clan matters, even over *Lupus Rex* unless it was a Pact violation. He was a member of a different *grex*, but tried to perform his *renovatio* with all of the *grexes* in the clan to keep up on current events. Warren and Ricardo were both friendly to Craig, so they tried to visit a couple of times a year during their hunts.

He was reading about the Ascension Ceremony when he decided to look up when the next blue moon was. What he saw took him slightly by surprise. In a little over three months, on August 23, 1983, Karen expected him to ascend as *Lupus Rex* for a race of werewolves.

He had to admit that maybe she was right. His last two changes went smoothly. Then something occurred to him as he was thinking about all of this. He was no longer thinking of it as something thrust upon him. He was thinking of it as he did during all of his Navy training—he was preparing for what lay ahead. He was surprised when he realized that.

He still didn't think Craig, Lisa, and Karen were telling him everything, though. He felt they were holding something back, something he couldn't quite nail down. It wasn't that he suspected they were telling him outright lies, but something less Machiavellian. It was little things like sentences being cut off too early or incomplete descriptions of events they related to him. Their questions seemed *too* innocent.

For instance, over dinner one evening, Craig asked, "Aaron, you've been spending quite a bit of time in the Archives. Any ideas where your silver resistance might have come from?"

Aaron shrugged his shoulders. "I'm not sure," he admitted. "The Archives only mention a few dozen *lupis* with the resistance that I can find so far, and most of them are all virus-related. It's suspected that if one goes back far enough, a relation will be found. I'm having a hard time with the Latin, though. I seem to spend more time translating than actually reading."

Lisa smiled. "You seem to be taking your studies seriously. You know you don't have to spend all of your free time digging through those dusty tomes, right?"

Aaron nodded his head. "Yeah, I know, but it's helping me come to terms with all this."

Karen then said, "Hey, let's all go to the beach tomorrow!" Thus, the subject of the silver resistance died.

Another time, Karen asked, "So are you ever going to tell me about that crazy fortune teller from New Orleans, the one who gave you that necklace?"

Aaron looked shocked. "You remember that?" he asked.

Karen giggled and crinkled up her nose. He'd learned she did that when she was nervous. "Sure!" she exclaimed. "I'm just curious, that's all."

Aaron took a deep breath. He saw Craig and Lisa staring at him, waiting on an answer. "Well, I don't remember much. New Orleans is full of fortune tellers during Mardi Gras, so it could have been any one of them. It's just a stupid hippy necklace. Why are y'all so curious about it?"

All three of them laughed easily, too easily.

"It's just a strange coincidence, that's all," Lisa offered up for the three of them. "A silver-immune *lupus* ending up with a silver wolf fang charm? Of course, we're curious!"

Aaron shifted nervously in his seat and then Craig changed the subject.

Aaron chalked it up to the fact he was still a new *Lupus sapiens*. Even the Navy didn't expect new sailors to know everything when they got to their first ship. The first few months were spent just teaching them the basics about how to find the mess deck, their berthing compartment, and their duty station. New sailors thought they were drinking from a fire hose, but in the grand scheme they were only spoon fed.

Jajine's voice still reverberated in his head, though. *"Trust your instincts, Aaron. You have good instincts."* Would his instincts permit him to be a good *Lupus Rex*? He didn't seem to think this is what she had in mind. She seemed to think he would be facing some kind of evil. So far, he hadn't found it.

As the end of that blissful hiatus from Navy life rolled to a stop, Aaron found himself sitting on the back porch swing with Karen. The porch and swing were made from cedar and they were the two blatantly anachronistic indulgences Craig allowed himself as far as the outward appearance of his house was concerned. Craig was a little pompous when it came to his villa so the cedar porch seemed out of place. Craig said his Grandmother had one, and it was a source of pleasant memories from his childhood. It ran the entire length of the rear left side of his house, about three quarters of the total length. There were two cedar steps on the left as you stepped onto the rear patio from the back foyer. The steps rose onto the porch, and the swing hung at the far end overlooking a small koi pond.

Aaron found it interesting Craig would put an Asian decoration on his Greco-Roman villa; turns out koi ponds were popular in Rome during the time of the Christian expansion in Europe. He overheard Craig bragging to Ricardo about how this koi pond was an exact duplicate of Emperor Charlemagne's of the Holy Roman Empire.

Aaron enjoyed watching the koi swim around during feeding time. As he threw another fish food pellet into the water, Karen got up and paced in front of him. She had been restless all afternoon. She had the scent of anticipation, as if she were waiting for a long-lost friend to show up at the door.

"What's bothering you, Sugar?" he asked. He already knew what was bothering her, but he learned she liked to express herself. She liked to think she had control of the situation.

She sighed, not wanting to expose the subject to daylight, but pulling back the curtains nonetheless. "Aaron, have you given any thought to our future?"

"What about it?"

"*Lupus Rex!*" she exclaimed.

"Oh, right. You need a decision now?" He knew which of her buttons to press and how hard. As hard as he just pressed that one, she deserved a smile so he twitched the corner of his mouth.

She realized he was purposefully agitating her and sat back down on the swing with him. She smiled back, hopefully. "It would be nice, yes."

"Get down on one knee and ask me nicely this time."

She looked at him like he had lost his mind, but she slowly moved around in front of him and knelt down on one knee. "Aaron, would you please marry me, be my king, my *Lupus Rex?*"

"Yes. But I want a big wedding with a limo and lots of bridesmaids. Oh, and a vacation to Florida and—" He didn't get a chance to finish because Karen covered his mouth with hers.

Lisa Minor

Lisa stepped out onto the patio just in time to overhear the conversation between Karen and Aaron. At first she was glad Aaron was finally coming around, but then she frowned. *I think he has her wrapped around his finger instead. He thinks he's finally accepted things, but I'm not so sure. If he had, he wouldn't be putting Karen through the wringer right now. It's time for a wake-up call.*

Chapter 25—Inperium

noun [in-pir'-ē-əm]
1. Authority. 2. Commandment.

Aaron Darveau, May 16, 1983

Aaron had just knocked off for the day and was back in his barracks changing into his civilian clothes. Ever since he'd made up his mind to become *Lupus Rex*, he walked around as if a weight had been lifted from his shoulders. He still planned to continue his studies at Craig's, but he finally knew his place in all of this craziness.

Of course, that meant he couldn't re-enlist. Being a werewolf was not a skill the Navy would be happy to find out he had acquired, especially if he practiced that new skill onboard a nuclear powered vessel. He would have to find a job. *How do I look for a job? I'll stop the career office here on base next week. They should know what I need to do.*

His phone rang as he finished zipping up his jeans. It was Craig. "Oh, thank God you're there," he spoke breathlessly. "I need your help."

Aaron had never heard Craig so worked up before. "What's going on?" Aaron asked.

"Family business," Craig groaned. "Can you come out? I'll explain when you get here."

Family business could only mean it was Race-related. "Sure, I was on my way anyway. Be there shortly."

Craig sighed appreciatively over the connection. "Thanks, Aaron. See you soon."

When Aaron got to Craig's, he saw that most of his *grex* was there in addition to some from other *grexes;* the majority of all present consisted of wildlings. He'd met a few of them, but he couldn't remember all of their names. He worked his way through the crowd up to the house, and the ones milling around outside quieted down and looked at him, expecting him to say something. He had no clue what to say; he didn't know what the problem was. Something told him this wasn't going to be over soon, though. He wondered what in the world would bring different *grexes* together when the moon wasn't full.

He strutted in like he owned the place; this attitude only came easily because he'd spent so much time there. A wave of silence spread out from him to the other end of the courtyard. "Where's Craig?" he asked to no one in particular.

Lisa appeared at his side as if by magic. "He's in his office waiting for you."

Aaron looked back at a sea of expectant faces but asked her, "What's going on?"

They all started talking to him at once in a deafening roar. "Talk some sense into him, Aaron. Don't leave him for the Fectors." "He's one of us!" "He broke the Pact. My sister broke the Pact and she was shunned. He should be too!" "We can send him away; tell the Fectors we took care of it." "Yeah, that might work." "They're too fast to judge. That makes four this year!"

Aaron knew he wasn't getting an answer this way so he yelled, "Slow down! I don't know what's going on, all right? Let me talk to Craig." He hurried down the loggia to Craig's office. The door was slightly ajar, so he stepped in without knocking.

After Aaron shut the door behind him, he looked at Craig questioningly. "What the hell was that all about?"

Craig looked up from his newspaper and stated matter-of-factly, "Kyle performed a *renovatio* and attacked a woman this afternoon, his girlfriend, Sally."

"Kyle?" *Oh, shit, Kyle, what have you done?* "What does this have to do with me? James is *Dux Lupus*."

"James is in Texas on family business. I'm the only member of the Conclave around. The wildlings are raising all manner of Holy Hell because they're afraid I'm going to declare him *Lupus solitarius*."

"Are you?" Aaron asked.

"Yes. No choice. That's why I need you here. You're their next Rex. With both of us here, it will help drive home the message."

"Is this really necessary? I mean, is Sally okay?"

"Sally's fine other than some scratches and a couple of broken ribs. She managed to make it to her car before Kyle could squeeze his fat ass out of the front door."

"Shit. Did he hurt anyone else?"

"No. Luckily, Bill and Glen were driving by when it happened and corralled him. A couple of years ago another wildling got loose. We weren't so lucky—he killed four people." Craig's voice betrayed no emotion, and he stared over Aaron's shoulder into nothingness. "Anyway, long story short, she went to the police, and now they're sniffing around. It won't be long before the trail leads here."

So this is what happens when a wildling gets loose on the town. He looked at Craig. "Are we going to adopt her?"

"I'm not sure we have that option. She may not want to come here. She's terrified. So now we have Kyle who has fucked up, and we'll have another wildling running around downtown Orlando during the next *plenilunium.*"

Aaron pleaded with Craig, "We need to send someone to her, tell her what's going on. She'll be a sitting duck for the Fectors, if what y'all've told me is true. And so will Kyle if we cut him loose. Let me talk to her. I know her."

Craig came to his feet in an instant. This was not the Craig Aaron knew. There was no doubt in his mind the man facing him was *Lupus Rex.* "We're not here to talk about Sally, Aaron. I'll handle her. We're talking about Kyle. He broke the Pact: *Don't bring down the ire of the humans.* He's done that. The law is the law. If I let him go, what do I do about the next one or the one after that? We've survived for centuries by observing the Pact. I'll not have another crusade launched against the Race because of some drunk who likes to beat up women. This is a tough decision but one that needs to be made." Then he dropped a bomb. "I want *you* to inform him of it." He indicated who *him* was by nodding his head toward his door.

"Me?" Aaron took a step backward and bumped into the bookcase.

"Yes, it's time to exert your authority." He returned to his chair and started reading the newspaper again.

Aaron stood there silently, hopelessly searching Craig's face for a shred of humanity. After a few moments, Craig impatiently looked back up at him. "You still here?"

"Craig, I can't go out there and send a man to his death. I'm not *Lupus Rex* yet. I don't have that authority. And even if I did have it, I'm not sure I have it in me to kill someone, especially a friend. Surely there's another way to handle this."

Craig put his paper down and looked Aaron straight in the eyes. "You aren't killing him. You're shunning him. And authority is taken, not given. You aren't in the Navy any longer."

"But the Fectors! You, yourself, said they usually take out any *Lupus solitarius* they find. He's one of us. We need to protect him. At least give him a fair trial."

"He's admitted to attacking that girl," Craig growled. "Case closed!"

"No, it's not—"

Craig stood up again and spoke in a booming voice, one that carried with it the authority of a drill instructor. "Are you *Lupus solitarius* or are you *Princeps Lupus*? The first one, you only have to worry about yourself. The second one, you have to worry about everyone else. Make up your mind right now."

Aaron didn't like his choices. He liked implied ultimatums even less.

He turned on his heel and stalked out into the loggia. The conversations were heating up again as he made it into the middle of the crowd. He took a moment to check the smells, to ensure there weren't any humans in attendance; there weren't. He jumped onto the table and asked everyone to be quiet. No one paid him any heed. He presumed they could smell his uncertainty because when he yelled the next time, they still ignored him. A couple of guys were close to coming to blows in one of the far corners, and he smelled everything from fear and anger to woe and confusion. The situation was ungluing at a rapid pace. *So much for familial harmony.*

Aaron looked back to Craig's office door, hoping to see some support magically appear, but *Lupus Rex* remained stubbornly absent. If someone didn't take charge, everyone here would perform a *renovatio,* and it wouldn't be long before they were running all over north Orlando. The situation was that dire. He never stood at the heart of a wildling feeding frenzy, but he'd seen a school of sharks in a feeding frenzy off the coast of Jamaica once. His mind's eye winced at the image of land sharks running across the lawn, eating everything in their path.

He rapidly strode back into Craig's office. "You do realize it's getting pretty bad out there, right?"

Craig never looked up from his paper. "Then you better do something about it."

Disgusted with Craig, he ran back to the courtyard and jumped onto the table again. He knew what needed to be done to bring this under control, but he wondered if it was even possible for him to do it. He'd seen Karen do it a couple of times, but the odds of him making a complete fool of himself were high. He remembered something his dad told him. "*Only bet on sure things.*" He was about to let his dad down because he was betting his life he could do it.

He sat down and took his last pair of boots off. He'd only done this twice, and this time he wouldn't have the patronage of the *Plenilunium* to help him.

He called the black dog, *"Here, little puppy dog. Come over here and get a belly rub. You aren't so big and bad. You're just a little puddle maker, a little shit eater. What can you do to hurt me?"*

Unexpectedly, the fire consumed him, and the madness pushed into his mind. The black dog came running, ready to pick up where it left off. Aaron again brushed it aside with a Tai Chi redirection. It was over just as fast as it started.

Aaron's *vagor* split the heavens, compelled attention, and foretold of retribution to any and all who refused to take heed. His howl tapered off, and the courtyard fell silent. His silhouette reflected back at him in the eyes of those around him. He was the howling Aspect of Preeminence, charismatic yet feared, ears at attention, tail high, hackles reaching for the sky, fangs exposed, and his dominance irreproachable. An area miraculously appeared in front of his table, his throne, in anticipation of *Lupus Rex's* next royal decree.

He searched for Kyle and sensed him on the other side of the pool; his scent was undeniable—fear, sorrow, pain, remorse, acceptance. Aaron commanded, ***"Show yourself!"*** with a short, low snarl. Kyle acknowledged Aaron's sovereignty, slowly slinking over and shrinking before him, looking at the stone slabs below. *Why did he have to go and attack Sally? Now I'm forced to make a decision I don't want to make.*

Even though Aaron had accepted Karen's proposal and seemed outwardly comfortable with it, he suspected Craig knew he wasn't ready for the job, that Aaron still harbored some resentment against her, and through association, against Craig and the whole *Lupus sapiens* race. Aaron wasn't angry with Kyle. He simply took his anger out on him. Perhaps that is what Craig intended. Aaron needed someone other than Karen to direct his anger at, and Kyle made the perfect patsy.

Aaron endured Kyle's groveling while he decided what to do next. He released Kyle from his gaze and scanned his audience. Each person he made eye contact with offered themselves to him by dropping their gaze in submission. Aaron continued this until all were subordinate to his will. The riot was crushed. There would be no wildling stampede tonight.

He placed Kyle back under scrutiny and rumbled, "**Kyle, you have** broken the Pact. I consider you a good friend, but the protection of the Race outweighs my personal feelings. I declare you *Lupus solitarius*." He turned to Lisa and saw Karen, Frank, and Maria standing next to her. *Frank and Maria are lupus, too? Of course they are. I remember them from the hunts.* Lisa's expression bore approval, but Karen had a haughty, "*I told you so,*" look. He detected a scent from Craig's office; it was relief mixed with a twinge of sorrow and surprise, like jumping onto a dusty, feather bed. Aaron wasn't sure how he knew it, but Lisa was behind this and not Craig. "**Lisa, please see that *Lupus Rex* is informed of my decision and all appropriate steps taken to confirm this order.**"

He didn't wait for a response. He jumped off the table leaving his tattered clothes behind him. He landed on his human feet, grabbed his boots, and stamped out to Lil' Red. Everyone parted before him like he was Moses and they were the Red Sea. Aaron's bare feet slapping on the stone and Kyle's sobbing filled the courtyard.

He decided to spend the night at the base. He had already learned to keep a spare set of clothes in the trunk. *Lupis* may not mind him running around naked, but the Navy base's personnel wouldn't appreciate it.

Two days later Aaron found a manila envelope on his bunk. He detected the scent of his roommate and the scent of someone he didn't know on it. His roommate's scent made sense; he must have put it there. The unknown scent, it was of leather and wood and oiled iron. Aaron opened it up, curious as to the personal nature of the delivery. It contained a single newspaper clipping about a gruesome double murder, beheadings, down on Orange Blossom Trail. A wave of dizziness poured through him as he studied the victims' pictures. It was Kyle and Sally. He filed that scent away for future reference. He looked at the date on the newspaper clipping. Yesterday. That meant they were killed the same night Aaron shunned Kyle.

Attached to the clipping was a handwritten note that simply asked, "*Do you know who you are sleeping with?*"

He didn't know who sent it, but he strongly suspected the Fectors. He couldn't figure out why, though.

Aaron immediately drove out to Craig's estate.

Part III—*Sui Deceptio*

noun [sü'-ī()di-sep'-tē-ō]

1. Self deception.

Chapter 26—*Illustratio*

noun [il'-lus-ˌträ-tē-ō]

1. Enlightenment

Aaron Darveau, May 18, 1983

Craig, Lisa, and Karen were enjoying the sunset from the patio and sipping on coconut margaritas when Aaron stormed out to them. He demanded their attention by blocking their view of the fields out behind the villa. He got right to the point. "Hey, y'all, how did the Fectors know to go after Kyle so quickly after he was shunned? There's no way they could have known."

Craig refused to make eye contact with Aaron. He took the straw in his drink and swirled it around in the liquid concoction before taking a sip. "They must have gotten lucky."

Aaron was agitated at the lack of respect he was receiving. "Lucky? We lose one of our own, and we chalk it up to luck?"

Lisa and Karen were watching the exchange between the two of them with interest. This time Craig did turn his head toward him. "We've had this conversation already, Aaron. The needs of the Race outweigh the needs of the individual."

Aaron had a sudden flash from the last Star Trek movie. Spock sacrificed his life, stating, "*The needs of the many outweigh the needs of the few, or the one.*" That may be a truism, but Aaron was sure Spock didn't mean it was something imposed on someone else. He shot back, "You don't seem too broken up about it." He turned to Karen. "Sugar, we spent time with them. You and Sally seemed like you were friends. These weren't faceless strangers. You support this?"

Karen hung her head for a few seconds before raising it back up and meeting his gaze. "Yes, I do. It was necessary, Aaron."

Aaron stared at her and quickly saw the same woman who tricked him into this *Lupus Rex* thing, that woman from the morning after his first *renovatio*. The stranger. *Oh, she's good. She about had me convinced that woman didn't exist. Well, there she is, the succubus unmasked.*

Aaron took a calming, deep breath and caught a whiff of something emanating from all three of them. They were hiding something they were ashamed of. But it was also something they wanted, something they were addicted to. *Strongly* addicted to. Strong enough to kill for and to keep secret. His instincts screamed at him that this was that one little thing he could never put his finger on they were hiding from him.

"Tell me about the Fectors again, Craig. You said they usually only go after *Lupis solitarius*, right? How do they know when someone is *Lupus solitarius*?"

Lisa and Karen suddenly tensed up and stopped breathing as they waited on Craig's answer.

Craig watched his own hand as he set his drink on the table. "Sit down, Aaron. I think it's time you learn how we do things around here."

"Just answer the goddamned question, Craig!" Aaron growled at him. "Did you tell them?"

Craig's voice dripped with contempt as he leaned forward in his chair. "All right, you little punk. Yes, I did tell them!"

"Craig, why would you go and do that?" Aaron asked incredulously.

"Remember when I told you about William Stoddard?"

"Stoddard," Aaron repeated. "Yeah, Lisa's dad, the one you said forced the truce with them, right?"

"That's right. Only it wasn't as cut and dried as I first presented it. The terms of the truce were that they leave the clans alone, and we let them know when we have a *Lupus solitarius*. Effectively, we police ourselves and let the Fectors handle the punishment."

Chapter 27—Father Ignacio

November 1935, Italy

Father Ignacio turned over in his bunk to frown at his stateroom door, wondering who was in the passageway making such a noise at this hour. He took a deep breath to yell at whoever was out there when a young voice called out to him. "Father Ignacio?"

Sigh. "Yes, what is it?"

"Father Ignacio, the Captain sends his compliments and asks that you please report to the port quarterdeck."

His ears perked up in the lonely silence. The squeaking and banging of a ship underway was gone. The stale, lingering smell of puke was still prevalent though, evidence of his first time at sea in over two years. "Have we made port?"

"Yes, Father," the small voiced echoed from the passageway.

Father Ignacio sat up in his bunk and bumped his head on the one above him. *After two months, you'd think I would remember not to do that.* He fumbled for the switch next to the bunk, turning his stateroom from a dark mystery into a dimly lit metal prison. He rubbed his eyes. "Thank you, my son. I'll be there shortly."

"I'm to wait and ensure you find your way, Father."

"Give me a couple of minutes then." Father Ignacio was not a morning person, but when his stocking-clad feet touched the cold, steel deck, his morning fogginess evaporated. His wafer-thin cotton socks did little to keep the wintry chill away from the soles of his feet. He dressed quickly, washed the sleep out of his eyes with icy-cold water, and stepped into the passageway.

The owner of the young voice belonged to a boy who couldn't have been more than fifteen and wore the insignia of a ship's steward. He looked like he recently rolled out of his bunk too—his black hair was hastily combed, and his jacket was buttoned one off, the left side hanging lower than the right. He nervously averted his eyes when he looked up at Father Ignacio. The Father was accustomed to that. The scars on his face tended to bring out the pity in people—or self-blessings for thanks they didn't have to endure what he had—whenever they met him for the first time.

The Father handed over his leather satchel and suitcase, but held onto his sword. It was encased in a long and narrow wooden box with leather straps and brass buckles; not everyone understood the need for a Catholic priest to carry a sword in the open so he transported it incognito. He held his arm up, pointing it down the passageway. "Lead the way."

Two priests were waiting for him at the busy quarterdeck. It just started snowing, and a fine dusting of the white powder lay upon all of the flat surfaces. Sailors were taking turns scurrying up and down the slippery gangplank carrying various boxes, bags, and all the other supplies necessary to keep a ship running. One of the priests was short and squat, built like a barrel, and the other was of average height and thin. Both had dark hair and brown eyes, and like the boy they nervously averted their gaze when Father Ignacio stepped onto the quarterdeck. They were far older than he was, but they were of his Order; they gave the "sign," a small twist of their fingers as they reached for their crucifix. Father Ignacio made the countersign, a small wipe on his.

The barrel-shaped one stepped forward and spoke with a distinctly German accent. "Father Ignacio, I presume?"

"Yes."

"I'm Father Ezekiel, and das is Father Jeffrey. Velcome to Italy."

Father Ignacio addressed them both. "Thank you for meeting me. Shall we go?"

"Ja." Father Ezekiel took the leather satchel from the steward while Father Jeffrey took the suitcase. They slipped and skidded to their car, dodging sailors and port workers who were trying to get the ship resupplied.

The heavy military presence on the pier was hard to miss and ignore; uniformed soldiers were marching back and forth while a few roamed around on the lookout for anything out of the ordinary. The priests had to present papers showing they were on official Vatican business before they were allowed off the pier and again before they were allowed to leave the port. Soon, they were on the road south toward Vatican City.

Father Ignacio asked, "I don't suppose you can tell me what this is about? I was trying to put my monastery back together after William Stoddard killed nearly everyone assigned there. And then I get summoned here."

Father Jeffrey spoke in a patently British accent. "I'm afraid we don't have any information, old boy. We weren't even aware you were coming to Italy. The Superior personally asked us to pick you up. The bloke woke us up himself, if you can believe it."

Father Ignacio whispered, "I wonder what's going on."

"I say, you'll find out soon enough."

They were quiet as they pulled up to a military checkpoint on the road where they had to present their papers again. They pulled out and Father Ignacio asked, "I heard some news on the ship. Mussolini has turned his nose up at the League of Nations and attacked Abyssinia?"

"Yes, he did," Father Jeffrey sputtered out in amazement. "That's why the military is being so tenacious. It's made for quite the scandal in the Vatican, I can assure you."

"Why is that?" Father Ignacio asked.

"With the Holy See's implicit approval of the ongoing attacks in Ethiopia, Mussolini has decided to stretch his muscles even further. There are some who are wondering if his Holiness shouldn't have denounced the attacks. Now it is feared it may be too late."

Father Ignacio chuckled. "We have a saying where I grew up. 'You don't crap in your own backyard.'"

"Jolly good, old boy! We have similar banalities in England. 'When surrounded by wolves, learn to howl.'"

Father Ignacio couldn't suppress the smile tugging at his face. *That's awfully close to our oath.*

They had to stop and show their credentials two more times by the time they arrived at Vatican City.

They pulled up to the Order's curia and Father Ezekiel drove into an underground parking lot. He let his two passengers out. "Father, I'll have your belongings delivered to your room." He then turned the car around and drove back the way they had come.

Father Ignacio followed Father Jeffrey up a series of old, stone stairs leading from the garage into the curia. This was a different path than he remembered taking during his induction into the Order two years ago. The smell was the same though…centuries of dampness mixed with foot-worn stone. They came out at the top into a long hallway with tapestries hanging along the walls and suits of medieval armor standing between them. A long, blood-red rug stretched the entire length of the hallway, ending at a set of carved oaken doors. Father Ignacio wanted to view the tapestries, but Father Jeffrey was walking with a purpose that left little time to study them.

What he did see showed they were depictions of battles between man and *Lupus sapiens*.

They walked into a large open area at the end of the hallway. A desk with no one sitting at it stood next to the door along with a small uncomfortable looking couch. "Well, old boy," Father Jeffrey looked around them, "this is The Superior's antechamber. Wait here and his assistant will be out for you shortly."

"Thank you, Father."

"You're welcome! I'm terribly sorry I can't sit with you while you wait, but I have other duties to attend to. Cheerio!"

Father Ignacio watched Father Jeffrey disappear through a door behind one of the tapestries back down the hallway they just passed through.

He sat there for about thirty minutes before a nun mysteriously appeared, as if out of thin air. "The Superior will see you now."

Father Ignacio stood up, straightened his cassock, and hurried into The Superior's office—seemingly all at the same time. Being summoned by The Superior meant something of high importance was happening. Father Ignacio did not plan on keeping him waiting any longer than necessary.

The Superior's office was large and well-appointed with thick carpet, a large, floor-level fireplace alive with a crackling fire, and two large windows holding back the snowy city beyond. The walls and trim were somber and appeared to be constructed from mahogany. A large wooden desk, cherry perhaps, with two plush, leather chairs arranged in front of it sat between the two windows. Scores of pieces of paper littered the desk.

The Superior stood behind the desk while a man with eerily familiar blue eyes stood by one of the chairs. The Superior appeared to have aged ten years since Father Ignacio had last seen him. His hair was silver, wrinkles grew around his eyes, and his jowls sagged. *It's only been two years!* The man with the familiar blue eyes was dressed in a grey, civilian business suit and appeared to be middle-aged; greying hair flew back from his temples. The Superior had a dour look on his face while the other man appeared disinterested.

The Superior offered graciously, "Welcome, Father Ignacio." He held out his hand, and Father Ignacio kissed the ring of office. "Please have a seat."

"Thank you, Your Eminence." They all sat down, but Father Ignacio did not relax. He sat on the edge of his chair, back straight and hands clasped on his lap. He gave The Superior his undivided attention.

The Superior stated, "I'm going to get right to the point, Father. I need you to pay very close attention to what I am about to tell you."

"Yes, Your Eminence." He straightened his back even more and leaned forward.

"The man sitting across from you is William Stoddard."

Father Ignacio listened as intently as he could to The Superior, but the words didn't quite register with him at first. The Superior might as well have proclaimed himself Jesus Christ for as much sense as they made. *William Stoddard? That man just destroyed my monastery. The eyes!*

"William Stoddard!" Father Ignacio exclaimed as he sprang from his chair and reflexively reached for his sword—then remembered with dread it was still with his baggage in the car. He stared wide-eyed at one and then the other while shouting, "Your Eminence! This—"

The Superior followed him to his feet and ordered, "Control yourself, Father!"

William Stoddard remained seated at apparent ease.

Father Ignacio considered attacking with his bare hands but knew Stoddard would kill him in an instant. Something wasn't right with this whole scenario. "But, Your Emi—"

"You will obey!"

Father Ignacio stared at The Superior with wide eyes and tasted the coppery taint of his own blood as he bit his tongue. He couldn't believe what he was being forced to do! The Superior might as well have been consorting with Satan. The man who received his oath was consorting with William Stoddard, Satan's leader among the howlers. Stoddard wasn't the Anti-Christ, but he was next in line; he was *Lupus Rex*.

The Superior ordered firmly, "Father, be seated and hear me out."

Father Ignacio sat down again and didn't say anything.

"Thank you." The Superior pulled a handkerchief out of his sleeve and patted his forehead. "Father, William Stoddard is my guest. He's here under a flag of truce. He approached us." He then sat back down in his chair.

Father Ignacio narrowed his eyes in suspicion. "Why?"

The Superior sighed. "Because we are out of options."

"I don't understand."

"Your monastery wasn't the only one sacked." He picked up a handful of the pieces of paper lying on his desk. "I've been receiving reports from

163

our commanders all around the world over the last couple of months. Just about every one of our monasteries has been sacked." He let the paper flutter back down.

Father Ignacio saw The Superior's office turn on its side in a bout of vertigo. *Every one of them?* "What? How?"

The Superior's voice was littered with defeatist tones. "It doesn't matter. What does matter is it happened."

Father Ignacio sat in stunned silence. If what The Superior said was true, *Lupus sapiens*, in an example of coordination the Lamp of Truth didn't think they possessed, attacked every monastery around the world at about the same time. *That means our martial capabilities have been reduced by as much as eighty percent. We're open to attack! Wrong, we're in danger of being exterminated! How did this happen?*

He turned to Stoddard and asked through clenched teeth, "Why not finish us off?"

William Stoddard sat up, cleared his throat. "As a race, we aren't murderers. We—"

Father Ignacio yelled out, "Bullshit! Your history is replete with instances where you wiped out entire villages. I, personally, saw one of your ilk kill the man who practically raised me."

William raised his hand, appealing for calm. "I said 'as a race.' Every population has sociopaths, those who can't get along with everyone else. We're no different." He took the time to examine his fingernails while he spoke. "But that doesn't matter at this point. I have an offer I think you should take."

Father Ignacio asked, "What's this offer?"

William sat back in his chair and rested his hands in his lap. "Do you know what *Lupis solitarius* are?"

"Yes. Those that have been shunned for violating some internal law you have."

William raised his eyebrows. "Exactly. I would like to know how you know that, but I won't press the matter. Anyway, once a *lupus* is shunned, we have no further use for him. He is dead as far as the Race goes."

"So? Get to the point."

"If you agree to cease the attacks against the clans, I can assure you a steady supply of *Lupis solitarius*. We'll alert you when one is shunned. We don't want them running around anymore than you do. In addition, we will henceforth consider any *lupus* not in 'good standing' with the Race to be *Lupus solitarius*. These are usually *lupis* who have been infected but are not under the control of the Race. They're rare, but if they're wily enough to avoid us then they should make for good hunting on your part. You are free to hunt them and kill them as you please."

Father Ignacio looked at The Superior. "You agree with this?"

"We have no choice, Father."

Father Ignacio turned back to William, "Why would you do that?"

"Two reasons, really. One, it strengthens my position; I'll look like I've stopped the crusades. Two, it allows us to self-police; we kick out the troublemakers."

Father Ignacio swallowed a mouthful of sour spit. "And then we do your dirty work for you."

"Exactly!" William exclaimed, raising his arms to emphasize the point. "You've always been the bogeyman to the Race. That won't change."

"Wait." Father Ignacio turned back to The Superior. "Why am I here for this? It seems you've already made up your mind."

The Superior revealed an interesting tidbit of information that Father Ignacio had not heard. "You're the only remaining commander left in America. I'm placing you in charge of all American monasteries, or what's left of them anyway. Before I promote you though, I want your assurance you will abide by the truce."

Making direct eye contact with William Stoddard, Father Ignacio hissed, "I don't like this, Your Eminence." He then set his gaze on The Superior. "But I will obey if that is your command."

The Superior nodded and closed his eyes in obvious relief. "It is."

Father Ignacio glared at his nemesis. "Well, Stoddard, it appears you've won. So, how many howlers will you be placing on this new Altar of Peace?"

"I think sixty per year is sufficient. That's five per clan."

Father Ignacio scoffed and shook his head. "Not enough. We terminated five times that number before this…this calamity."

A particularly beastly and predatory smile formed on William's lips. A chill wormed up Father Ignacio's spine as The Superior's large office suddenly didn't seem large enough. William remarked, "Perhaps. But you no longer possess the ability to do that." A wide, genial smile quickly replaced the monstrous one. "However, your point is taken. I'm willing to negotiate that figure. If it's too large, I'll have a hard time keeping the deal secret. And you're still free to chase *any* of the *Lupis solitarius* you find without interference from the Race."

In that instant, the passion for hunting the beast that killed the man who taught Father Ignacio to be a man blazed into a fury toward the beast who would dictate the Order's movements.

Chapter 28—Lupus Solitarius

noun [lü'-pəs()sä-lə-ter'-rē-əs]
1. Lone Wolf.

Aaron Darveau, May 18, 1983

"Craig!" Aaron exclaimed, "the Fectors only have one punishment—death! I'm not a lawyer, but from what I've read in the Archives, shunning wasn't supposed to be an immediate death sentence. You've turned it into one."

"The alternative is constant warfare with the Fectors," Craig barked angrily. "Those bastards showed me what they could do back in '58. They caught me and three of my friends in a parking lot late one evening. Out of the four, they let me live with a warning. 'Stick with the truce, or we're mounting your head in our lodge.' Do you want that? Do you want to walk down the street, never knowing when one of them would come out of the darkness and slit your throat? Do you want to spend your life hiding in caves?"

Aaron was quiet while he chewed through everything Craig said. "No," he finally admitted. *It is an easy way to handle malcontents. Still, it doesn't sound right. If you know someone is going to die, you don't ignore it. You try to help, dammit! That's what separates us from the animals.*

Aaron asked, "How many are typically shunned each year?" He was secretly praying it was a small, trivial number.

"The arrangement is we supply two hundred *lupis* per year to them."

"Two hundred? Two hun—" *Is discipline that bad in the ranks? That's...200 times 27 years...that's over 5,000 lupis!* "What if no one violates the Pact?"

Craig's face betrayed no emotion. "We find a violation," he said.

The wind was sucked out of Aaron. He remembered something his father made him read when he was in high school. His parents weren't liberal by any stretch, and they believed everyone should think for themselves and not rely on others to do it for them. His father exposed him to many different schools of thought, hoping Aaron would learn to objectively view the world around him and make his own decisions. One book on his reading list was a collection of Martin Luther King, Jr.'s writings and speeches. Buried amongst the insolence against ostensible injustices were two sentences that had stuck with Aaron since he first read them. He studied those words, printed on the page, until he could recite them verbatim. They contained one potent ideal that summed up Aaron's explosive realization of what he had to do. *"He who passively accepts evil is as much involved in it as he who helps to perpetrate it. He who accepts evil without protesting against it is really cooperating with it."*

"That's not an arrangement, Craig," Aaron spit out. "That's outright murder. You can't send someone to their death because you want the easy life."

"Bullshit, I can't! I'm *Lupus Rex!*"

"You want me to sacrifice innocent people to keep the peace? You want me to sit still while two hundred people are cut down in cold blood, every year, because you don't want a fight?" He turned to each in turn. "You can all three go fuck yourselves. I don't know who or what you think I am, but I am not a murderer. I'm out of here. You can shove this *Lupus Rex* promotion up your asses."

Karen's eyes welled up in tears, layering an untold number of years onto her lovely face. "I beg you, Aaron, don't do this. I love you."

"You love me?" Aaron scoffed. "You don't know what love is! If you did, you'd know I wouldn't betray everything I believed in, not for you, not for anyone."

If her face had truly been as cold as it suddenly appeared, those tears would have froze on her face. Aaron saw in his mind's eye that if he ever ran into her in an alley somewhere, she would try to kill him on the spot. He had never seen that look before in his life. Her eyes were empty and completely devoid of any soul. A biting chill skittered up Aaron's back, but it wasn't fear causing it. He finally recognized what he'd been sleeping with for the last couple of months. These were not good people even if they weren't eating babies and sacrificing virgins to some Cthuloid monster. Jajine was wrong. These people were evil as far as he was concerned. He was ashamed of himself for not seeing it before now.

Craig stood up and faced him. "Aaron, I can see you're never going to accept this role. You want out?"

"I'm already out," Aaron spat at him. "I just haven't let the door hit me in the ass yet."

Craig stood there and pursed his lips. Aaron had seen that expression before. Craig was making a decision, and Aaron knew what that decision would be.

Aaron made it easy for him to decide. "I suggest you wait until I've left

Florida before you alert the Fectors. This serves two purposes. One, you don't want the messy death or even the disappearance of a sailor who is stationed at the Navy's nuclear power training center all over the news, especially one who's so close to being discharged. All my friends know I hang out here so this will be the cops' first stop."

Craig nodded his head. He knew that's exactly what would happen. "You're right. What was the second reason?"

Aaron laughed contemptuously, "It gives me a chance get the fuck outta Dodge!"

Again, Craig nodded his head. "I'll give you until the twelfth then, your last day in the Navy if I remember correctly." Craig stood motionless and a dispassionate expression washed over his face. "Well, that's that then."

Lisa reluctantly turned away from Aaron while Karen stood up and stiffly strode to the edge of the patio. They both gazed out across the fields.

Lightning struck. Craig's hand lashed out, his cula, and struck Aaron across the chest from upper left to lower right followed by his other cula from upper right to lower left. Aaron fell to his knees in pain, confused and dazed, while Craig stood over him, visibly holding his *lupus* at bay.

Aaron looked down at his chest and watched the gouges start healing. He understood that now every *Lupus sapiens* in the world would know his status simply by seeing the crossed cula marks on his chest.

Craig turned his back on him. "Get the fuck out of my house."

Craig listened to Aaron stumble out of the house and into the front yard. He remembered his own introduction to the agreement so many years ago. It was shortly after Lisa announced Craig was her chosen and William moved to Virginia Beach to teach him the ropes.

Craig, himself, had those same doubts. It was too much to take in. Sending two hundred people a year to their deaths? He told William and Lisa he needed a few days to think about it. Well, William wasn't going to wait that long. He taught Craig a lesson in power politics that night when he arranged for that Fector attack, for the death of his three closest friends. Craig knew he didn't have a choice then, and the very next day told William he'd abide by the truce. He wondered through the years if Lisa knew, but was afraid the answer would be *yes*. He never brought it up with her in all the years they'd been married.

He took a deep breath. "He's right. He's pretty much untouchable until he's out of the Navy. We'll give him until the twelfth. We won't alert Father Ignacio until then."

Lisa shook her head. "I don't understand it." She stared off into apparent nothingness with hazy white eyes. "I still see him as *Lupus Rex* if we wait that long. And Karen isn't in the picture. You should have killed him. I know it's inexplicable, but he still ascends."

Karen shrieked nightmarishly, "I don't see anything at all, Lisa!"

Craig rubbed his face with both hands. *Who am I fooling? If I had the brass balls that Aaron has, he wouldn't have left this house alive.* "My order still stands. We wait. He's *Lupus solitarius*. He can't hurt us. You both need to have your intuition tuned up."

He turned to Karen. "Shall I call James, or do you want to? You need to pick your *Lupus Rex.*"

Aaron performed his Navy duties as required for the next few days. Craig said he would give him a month before alerting the Fectors, but Aaron didn't really trust him. Anyone who would willingly send two hundred people a year to their deaths could not be trusted to keep their word. So, he sat on the base, out of sight of everyone, waiting on his discharge date to arrive.

When he wasn't at the office, he was at the Petty Officer's club. Alcohol remained his friend throughout and asked nothing in return; it would listen to him lament about how Karen had gotten him to fall in love with her before springing her trap, and about how he had sent a man and a woman to their deaths.

He was at the club drinking beer and listening to Merle Haggard wail from the jukebox when the full moon, his Harsh Mistress of the Night, decided to show her ugly face. He sat there at his table while his mind flashed Red Alert, warning him about what was coming. He had a beer-induced, spurious belief he wouldn't need to perform a *renovatio* if he wished it hard enough, so when the cramps hit, he was totally unprepared. He ran out of the club and saw a grove of trees across the street. He made it barely in time to remove his clothes before the transformation. *I'm going to have to learn to plan these outings a little more carefully.* The drunk he was working on disappeared after a few minutes. His *lupus* metabolism dealt with the alcohol substantially faster than his human system did. *Well, that's one way to get rid of a hangover.*

He hid out there in the grove until the urge to feed overwhelmed his discretion. He left to find a hunting ground.

Moving through the base and across town was as effortless as breathing. Millennia of social and cultural evolution had produced a predator capable of sneaking and hiding within feet of a target without being seen. This same ability allowed him to use the shadows and available cover to his advantage, staying out of sight of humans while he ran for the safety of a small forest five miles away.

He set to hunting once he was within his natural habitat. He let the surrounding hints of prey come to him and was rewarded with the sounds and the smell of a wild boar a few hundred yards deep in the stand.

He fed well that night, not having to share his kill with anyone.

He spent the remainder of the night enjoying running through the stand, chasing whatever animals crossed his path. The natural high he rode because of the blood pumping through his body, powering his muscles, and the symphony of sounds and smells that only a *lupus* could make sense of made him wonder why he turned down *Lupus Rex*. Then he saw Kyle's face in his mind's eye. *I'm not a murderer, that's why.*

He made his way back to the grove. He didn't intend to awaken five miles from the base, naked and without a ride.

Chapter 29—Venator

noun [və-nā'-tər]

1. A hunter.

Aaron Darveau, June 10, 1983

"That's it, Petty Officer Darveau." The Orlando Navy base's personnel officer, Lieutenant O'Malley, put Aaron's signed discharge papers into a large folder. "You are a free man."

Aaron asked, "But I'm okay in the barracks until Monday at 0800 though, right?"

"Correct. Sunday is officially your last day, but the Navy doesn't sign paperwork on weekends." He grinned. "At least, *I* don't sign paperwork on the weekends." He handed Aaron a stack of papers. "These are your copies. DD-214, discharge evaluation, medical file, final paycheck. Anything else I can do for you?"

"No, Sir. I think that's it."

"You headed back to Louisiana?"

"Yes, Sir," Aaron lied. He hadn't actually decided yet, but he didn't know how to say that without getting into too many details. He didn't like lying, but it was just easier this way. *Will the rest of my life be filled with lies to hide who and what I am?*

Lieutenant O'Malley locked the drawers on his desk and stood up to indicate they were done. "Drive safely."

"Aye, aye, Sir. Thank you."

He glanced at his watch as he rushed out of the personnel office. The coroner's office had finally released the bodies, and heads, of Kyle and Sally for burial after full autopsies and a thorough police investigation had been performed. When people get their heads lopped off, it isn't something that gets buried on page twenty of the newspaper. The results weren't surprising—they died due to decapitation. The newspapers and the television stations reported on the story for several weeks. Everything from drug dealers to the mob to Middle Eastern radicals was blamed. The answer was much more sinister than any of those though—*Lucerna Veritatis*. Aaron knew his worldview had shifted because he was observing events such as this with a new illumination. The killer, of course, was never found.

Aaron was surprised his name didn't come up during the investigation. He was a friend of Kyle's, and they had visited more than a couple of different car shops in the area together. He wondered just how deeply the Race and the Fectors were involved with the local police jurisdictions.

Attending the funeral was hard. It may not have been his fault they were killed, but his self-imposed morals forced him to bear responsibility. It was his decree that removed the protection of their *grex* which allowed the Fectors to get close enough to kill them. He stuffed them into those pine coffins as surely as if he had swung the blade. But he needed the closure a funeral would provide, so he put on his Navy Dress Whites and went to it.

He was afraid he'd already missed it because when he took his seat he saw no more than half a dozen people, including the priest, and three of them were manning the doors. Undertakers probably. He saw no one from the Race in attendance which didn't surprise him. As far as they were concerned, Kyle was dead to them before he got his head chopped off. He was *Lupus solitarius*.

Aaron sat there listening to the priest give his benediction and wondered if this was what was in store for him. *I will not go down easily. They better bring everyone they have because I'll make it my life's mission to kill them all if they fuck with me.* He wondered where that attitude came from. Was that the *lupus* talking?

Everyone filed past the closed coffins to give their final farewells when the priest indicated the service was finished. There would be no graveside service; Kyle and Sally were indigents and would be buried on the county's dime.

Aaron had just helped a sweet old lady with a walker maneuver through the front doorway when the priest who performed the service stopped him. He was tall, close to six and a half feet, and although he had a slight stoop, Aaron could tell he kept himself in shape. He had large, calloused hands and silvery hair and eyebrows on a large, square head. "Are you Aaron Darveau?" His voice had a touch of roughness to it as if he might be a smoker.

"Yes, why?"

"I'm Father Thomas Elliot. Kyle Tillman asked me to give you something. Would you mind coming to my office?"

"Kyle asked you to give *me* something?" Aaron asked, his eyebrows jumping up in astonishment. "What is it?"

"It isn't much. Just a small wooden box." Father Thomas turned and started down the hallway. His office was Spartan except for a German cuckoo clock hanging on the wall next to the window behind an old desk.

The pendulum was swinging in a steady rhythm behind the three winding weights hanging beneath it. *Tick, tock, tick, tock* were the only sounds in the office other than those made by their movements. The chair behind the desk was old and worn, the leather cracked and numerous snaps missing. It looked more comfortable than the two chairs in front of the desk, however. Aaron sat in one of them. Father Thomas sank into the comfortable one, and it gave a strong squeak. The greying priest opened one of the drawers on the right side of his desk and pulled out a small wooden box about six inches by six inches square and three inches deep. He held it in his hands, rubbing it some, as if dusting it. Aaron guessed the box meant something to him.

"Mr. Darveau, Kyle was my nephew. I became the father figure in his life after his father left him and his mother alone—oh, I guess when he was about seven. We did the things fathers and sons should do together."

Aaron thought of his own dad and all of the things they did together— fishing, hunting, camping. He suddenly missed both of his parents terribly.

Father Thomas's voice brought Aaron back to the present. "One of the things we did together was woodworking. I have a shop in my backyard. He'd come over a few days a week, and we'd work some small project." He lifted the box up out of his lap high enough for Aaron to see it. "This was the first project he crafted on his own. I know it meant a great deal to him.

"Anyway, a couple of weeks ago, he came to my house late one night. His mother, my sister, died a few years ago so I was the only family he could go to when he had a problem. He said he'd gotten into some trouble with some guys and thought they might try to rough him up. He usually hung out with a rough crowd, so I gave him my standard lecture on choosing his friends more carefully." He took a deep breath and Aaron's *lupus* ears picked up a distinct flutter in his lungs, as if he were holding back a sob. "Sadly, a father figure is not the same as a dad. He said that if anything were to happen to him, he was to make sure I gave this box and all its contents to Aaron Darveau. He said I could find you at the Navy base. I saw you in your uniform and thought it might be you.

"I'm not sure what trouble he got into, Mr. Darveau, but I didn't expect him to get killed over it. Do you have any idea what happened?"

"No, Sir, I don't," Aaron lied. Again. "In fact, I didn't know him that well. I considered him a friend, but we've only known each other a few months." *Then I shunned him.* "Certainly not long enough, I would think, for

174

him to feel he had to leave me something."

"Hmm," Father Thomas grunted out with a crooked grin. "Well, you must have thought more of him than that to take the time to attend his funeral."

Aaron didn't have an answer for that.

"Anyway, here it is." Father Thomas handed the box across his desk while Aaron stood up to take it from him.

Aaron sat down again and admired the craftsmanship that went into the cherrywood finish. It was a fine piece of work. He slowly lifted the top and saw a folded piece of paper lying in it. He took the paper out and saw a set of keys attached to a Mustang key ring. His heart skipped a beat, but he held himself under control as he unfolded the paper. It was a handwritten letter from Kyle, written in his conversational tone.

Aaron,

If this letter finds you, it means I'm dead. I've lost the protection of the grex, so I know it was them Fectors who done got me. I don't blame you for what you went and did. You didn't have no choice. Everybody heard you and Craig arguing about a lowly wildling. You may not know it, but you made a lot of friends in the family over that. You were the first high-ranking frenatus to ever care for us I ever heard of. I hope things work out for you.

Oh, one more thing. Inside this box, you'll find the keys to my Mustang. I know you'll take good care of her. I hope you know now I ain't mad at you.

Kyle

Aaron had a hard time refolding the letter because his eyes were blurry with tears. He rubbed them and put the letter back into the box, but not before taking the keys out.

Father Thomas made the sign of the cross and then smiled when he saw the keys in Aaron's hand. He pulled the title for the car out of the top drawer of his desk. "I guess he thought more of you than you thought he did. The car's out back when you want to pick it up. Let's get the title turned over to you. I've backdated it to the day before he died so the State doesn't come after it."

Aaron asked, "You're a notary?"

"Yes. It helps with marriage licenses and the like. Saves my parishioners a few dollars here and there." Father Thomas forged Kyle's signature right next to Aaron's and then notarized it. It was Aaron's now.

"Thanks. I don't know what to say, Father. He was a good guy, and I liked him. But I didn't think, I'd have never guessed—" He had no words for his surprise at this turn of events. He stood up and shook Father Thomas's hand. "Thanks again. I'll be back in a day or two to pick up the car. Do you mind holding onto to it a bit longer?"

Father Thomas shook his head. "No problem."

Aaron put the keys back into the box and with a fright asked, "Wait! How did you know Kyle was giving me his car? Did you read the letter?"

Father Thomas's heartbeat boomed across the desk. "Yes," he whispered quietly. "You aren't messed up with the same guys as Kyle, are you?"

Aaron looked down at the floor and listened to the *tick, tock, tick, tock* of the cuckoo clock. "Yes, I'm involved. Against my will, though. I lied a minute ago, you know. I do know what happened to Kyle, and they're coming after me too." Then, with more grit in his voice, he growled, "They're going to find me a much harder target to deal with."

"That's what I thought." Father Thomas drew an uneasy breath. "Are you—are you *lupus*, too?"

Aaron quickly raised his head and stared at Father Thomas. "You know about that?"

"Not much." He shook his head. "I just know they exist."

Aaron broke down, crying in heavy sobs. "Father, I killed them. It was all my fault. They would still be alive if I hadn't done what I did. God will never forgive me for this."

Father Thomas made the sign of the cross again. "God forgives everyone, Son, even if we don't think we deserve it. Please, sit down. I'm a good listener."

Aaron sat down and told him everything, from Jajine to Karen to Kyle. Father Thomas sat there silently and watched Aaron erupt in a sobbing, cathartic release, finally able to tell someone of the life-altering changes he'd experienced over the last couple of months.

"Aaron, it sounds to me like you did everything in your power, short of sacrificing your own life, to protect Kyle and Sally. If you hadn't done it, then this Craig guy would have. And they would still be dead. What more could you have done?"

Aaron was leaning forward out of his chair, his elbows on his knees, and his forehead in his hands. "I don't know." He sniffled and Father Thomas handed him a tissue. Aaron wiped his nose. "Something. Anything other than what I did."

Father Thomas leaned back in the squeaky chair and formed a steeple with his fingers. "Perhaps, now that you're no longer protected by the Race, you should seek out some allies. Perhaps this is a blessing in disguise, Aaron. You're free to act now, to protect those who can't protect themselves. To protect those like Kyle and Sally."

Aaron chewed on that thought. *Is that possible? Could I prevent another Kyle?* He remembered something from the last Star Trek movie. Spock said to Kirk, *"He is intelligent, but not experienced. His pattern indicates two-dimensional thinking."*

"I'm a Navy electrician, not a special forces operative," he argued. "I'd love to help them out, but I wouldn't know where to start. Nothing would please me more than to drag down their whole temple, Prime Directive be damned."

Father Thomas squinted his eyes slightly. "Well, I don't know what a *prime directive* is, but you do have options. Although I hate to have you consorting with voodoo priestesses, this Jajine lady sounds like a staunch ally. And you have me, of course. But there is one other option.

"I heard something a few months back about a motorcycle gang in Miami. They call themselves *Viam Lupus*. Supposedly this gang is composed of shunned *lupis* as you just described. I brushed it off, but after hearing you relate to me what you know about *Lupus solitarius*, I believe you might find an ally there, as well.

"Son, you aren't as alone as you think you are."

Chapter 30—Father Thomas

Father Thomas sat back in his squeaky chair and relaxed. He stared through the window, watching Aaron's car disappear down the street. Although he didn't originally join the priesthood to minister to people, he found he rather enjoyed it since his retirement from the *Lucerna Veritatis*. It was a major change from his life as a warrior, fighting for God under the direction of the Pope.

He reached down on the left side of his desk and pulled an old, time-beaten picture album out from the bottom drawer. Inscribed across the front in faded, gold letters was *Thomas Elliot, February 2, 1927, San Francisco,* and inside were pictures of his life, from his birth on forward. He only had a few pictures from the first fifteen years or so, personal cameras being a rare and expensive toy, but he had managed to scrape together shots of his two older brothers and his two younger sisters, along with some of his father's woodworking shop. All of the boys spent time there learning their father's trade.

He spent a few minutes reminiscing over the picture of his older brothers as they were getting on the bus for boot camp. He chuckled lightly to himself as he remembered how dismayed he was at the time because he was too young to go with them. Hank, his oldest brother, ended up dying in the Pacific fighting the Japanese during World War II.

Letters would arrive every few weeks, and his father would read them aloud to the family in the living room, taking the time to pronounce each word carefully so as not to miss anything his sons had to say. Thomas lived for those letters, praying his brothers would return home safely, and lighting a candle for them at church when he had the opportunity, while hoping the war wouldn't end too soon so he would get his chance to enlist. His wish came true the day he turned seventeen, though the Army assigned him to Europe and not the Pacific as he had hoped. The scandal with the Sullivan brothers, five brothers who all died together at sea, prompted changes to where and how family members were stationed. With both of his brothers in the Pacific, the Army was not taking any chances.

The war was progressing quite well for Allied Forces by this time, and they were making the hard push toward Berlin. To counter this threat, the Nazis developed a plan they called "Operation *Werwolf*." It was a resistance force trained to operate behind enemy lines as the Allies made their way to

Berlin. The Allies, in turn, developed their *own* counter to the German's counter. They developed "Sweeper Squads," and they assigned Thomas to one. Sweeper squads followed Allied Forces by a day or two into towns recently liberated from Nazi occupation, going door to door hunting for Nazi holdouts, or werewolves as the Allies nicknamed them.

He gently ran his fingers over the picture of his squad. There were six of them when it was taken. Nicky was from New York. He was the runt of the litter, but made up for it in attitude; he wasn't afraid of anyone. Billy was from Texas. He came off as dimwitted, but that was all an act. He had a degree in geology and a mind like a steel trap. Standing next to Billy was himself, the lucky one. Sandy was next from New Jersey. Sandy didn't talk much, and he was a crack snap-shooter. He could bring his rifle up from attention and shoot the hair off of a gnat's butt at two hundred yards—without aiming it seemed. Sergeant Alawitz was from the Bronx. He was all gruff and blood, but he cared about his men. He wouldn't hesitate to put his boot up someone's ass if they needed it, though. Lastly, there was Lieutenant Brost from Illinois. He was a good officer in Thomas's opinion, and like Alawitz, he cared about his men. Brost insisted George Patton hung the moon and threatened to fight anyone who didn't agree with him. If there had been bubblegum cards with Patton on them at the time, he would have had the entire collection. He also had a habit of quoting and paraphrasing Patton.

Father Thomas remembered one of his first missions with the squad. They entered a small hamlet on the Meuse River in France. Allied Forces left a couple of days earlier, so it was their turn at the enemy. Nicky, being the newest member of the squad, was the one who had to knock on the doors while the rest of the squad took up covering positions. Nicky had only banged on the door three times when it swung open and two rather belligerent "French Whores"—a common Allied phrase for female Nazi sympathizers—came running out, yelling and cursing at him. Brost was the only one who could speak French, which at times seemed no more than enough to ask for beer, food, and which way was north, but he clearly understood what they were saying. They wanted the Americans to go away. Brost ordered Billy to keep an eye on the two "ladies" in the street while the rest of the squad searched the house.

The downstairs was clear, but they found a large steamer trunk sitting in the middle of one of the upstairs bedrooms. They carefully opened it up, and a Nazi officer sprang out shooting in all directions. They killed him. They found a second trunk in another bedroom covered with a large blanket and a couple of boxes stacked haphazardly on top of it. They mechanically shot that trunk full of holes before they opened it up—to find a freshly-dead Nazi officer inside it as well.

Killing the Nazis didn't bother Thomas. That was his job. It was what happened to the women afterward that still gave him nightmares. He still heard their screams as they tried to escape the townsfolk's vigilante justice.

But it was another house, in another little town, that cast the mold for the rest of his life.

The squad was making their way through another little town when a shot rang out. They all scrambled for cover. It took close to five minutes of crawling around—an eternity when under fire—and sticking their heads up when they thought they were in the clear, and a few lucky misses before they figured out what was truly cover and what wasn't.

Billy never found cover. He took a bullet a half-inch below his helmet, spraying his brains all over the street. The grey and red slimly, sloppy mess still laid there, a stark reminder that what they did was just as dangerous as any other combat job in the Army.

Alawitz belly-crawled along a stone wall lining the church's courtyard. It wasn't quite four feet tall, so standing or running next to it, even crouched over, left you exposed. He stopped where Brost and Thomas were hunkered down. "Lieutenant, he's in the bell tower and got the whole damned square under his sights."

Brost asked, "Where's Nicky, dammit?! I need to call in some air support."

"Ah, the damned radio's shot to hell, Sir," Alawitz reported. "It saved his life, but we're on our own right now."

Brost accepted Alawitz's report with a dour look before scanning the area around them. His gaze fell upon a two story house across the street. It was in better shape than most of the other houses in the immediate vicinity. "Are you sure he's in the tower?"

"Positive." Alawitz took his helmet off and held it up with a stick, just above the stone wall. A shot rang out at the same time a bullet richocheted off of the helmet, spinning it on the stick. "That's him, all right. We aren't going to get any closer to the church than we are right now while the sun's up."

Brost pointed to the two-story house. "Sergeant, I want a man in one of those second story windows covering the north road for any enemy reinforcements. Nightfall, he's our covering fire while we get into better positions. Tomorrow morning at six sharp, I want him peppering that tower. Force the bastard to keep his head down while we rush the doors and make him die for his country."

Alawitz pointed at Thomas. "Elliot, get your ass up there and don't get it shot off. And don't let anyone see you. Total surprise. You read me?"

Thomas examined the house and what it would take to get over there. He was going to spend an hour belly-crawling across the dusty sidewalks until he could stand up and run. It didn't matter, though. It was five hours until nightfall.

"Got it, Sarge. I'll be there."

It took Thomas over two hours to actually make it upstairs. The back door and windows were locked when he got there, and he didn't want to make any noise breaking in. He spent twenty minutes trying to get inside, first trying to jimmy the lock and then trying to carve out the door jamb with his army-issue knife, without much success. The rear half of the backyard was a blackened cinder, and the charred odor was so noxious it made his eyes water. Then he decided to check the windows once again and found time had rusted and partially loosened one of the latches. He finished the loosening part of the job with his knife. Most of the town was deserted because of the recent heavy fighting, but he checked the first floor anyway once he crawled through the window, steering clear of the west side as much as possible so as not to give away his position to anyone in the bell tower who might be watching. It was empty, as he expected. If anyone was there, they would have surely heard him trying to open the door and come to investigate. Or shoot him.

He slowly made his way up the creaky stairs to the second floor to clear it, staying away from the west side again as well. Satisfied there was no one upstairs, he crawled through the hallway until he got to the room overlooking the north road and the church courtyard to the west. It smelled like his little sisters' room back home. Girly. Luckily the door was open because when he crawled in, the steeple was clearly visible through the broken west window. If he would have had to open the door, the movement could have been seen from the bell tower. He crawled along the floor, keeping his head low enough to avoid line of sight to where the suspected sniper was positioned. *If I can't see him, he can't see me.* He sat against the west wall, the wall with the church on the other side of it, with its window on his right, eating a cold supper of cheese and crackers. He watched out of the north window until nightfall, with his loaded M1 Garand rifle across his lap and his last ten clips of .30-06 next to him, eighty rounds.

All hell broke loose at sunset. Nicky screamed in abject terror as he pulled his trigger as fast as he could. Five loud retorts in rapid succession confirmed the danger he was in even before his scream was cut short.

Thomas had never heard anyone scream like that before.

He stuck his head up over the north window sill to see if he could make out what just happened. The sky was darkening to a deep blue, but there was still enough ambient light to see by. He didn't see anything, so he grabbed his mirror and held it up in the lower corner of west window. He couldn't see anything there either. He pulled his rifle up and set it on the sill of the window, leaving no more than an inch of his barrel hanging out. He knelt further back inside the darkened hole in the wall. He knew he needed to keep his head down, but if his squad was engaged with the enemy, he needed to be ready.

Suddenly, something caught his attention in front of the church. The sun was going down behind it, lengthening the shadows, but he saw something run across the courtyard, fast, and jump the stone wall. Lieutenant Brost gave out a loud and short horrific scream before the silence thundered down again.

Then just as suddenly as it had turned quiet, one of his squad—he didn't know which one—started shooting in rapid succession. Sergeant Alawitz bellowed, "Elliot, kill it! Kill it!" as he ran out into the middle of the street.

Something—Thomas didn't know what, but it made his blood run cold through his veins—was chasing Alawitz. It was human shaped, but long-legged and tall, agile and precise. Sandy ran out into the street, too, but froze in his tracks at the sight of the monster. It leapt into the air and landed on Alawitz, turning his prayer that someone shoot *it* into a garbled and bubbly shriek, ripping him to shreds with fingers that looked like short, curved bayonets.

Sandy jumped into action when Alawitz went down. He raised his rifle but wasn't fast enough. The monster swiftly closed the distance to Sandy and flayed him open with those deadly claws while his shots went wild.

Thomas fired in rapid succession until his rifle ejected its empty ammunition clip with a loud and distinctive "ping!" *Eight rounds gone already?* His first four shots swung the monster's shoulders around each time he hit. The last four hit dirt. Still, the monster stayed up. Thomas automatically reached down for another full clip and inserted it into his rifle's magazine, never letting his target leave his crosshairs. The monster glared up at the window, directly into Thomas's eyes and howled. Thomas was suddenly glad he was already hiding because every hair on his body, from his ears on down, stood up straight. He fought the impulsive need to pull away from the window and hide further. The monster jumped out of the street, toward the house Thomas was in. He couldn't see it any more, but a crash from downstairs told him it was now in the house with him.

The tinkling and clinking of shattering glass shook Thomas out of his fear-induced inaction. He scrambled back from the window and slid a scruffy-looking bed between him and the door and then threw a small piece of wooden furniture, a combination nightstand/bookshelf, on top of it. He reached down for the empty clip his rifle had just ejected and held onto it, taking up a position of safety behind the barricade. A shadow appeared in the hallway leading to the bedroom as soon as he took a bead on the doorway. *It's upstairs already?*

There was still a bit of light coming in from the west window, so he was able to see the soundless shadow dash across the opening. It was too fast to hope for scoring a hit, but he fired twice anyway and then threw the empty clip into the air. He continued watching the doorway as the clip flew up and then tumbled down. The distinctive "ping" of an empty rifle filled the room when the clip bounced on the floor. Experienced German combatants didn't usually fall for the ruse. Whatever was outside the room did though, and came rushing in.

Thomas Elliot, Corporal, United States Army, stared into the face of evil, but he smelled his squad mates' guts. His training took over, but something told him not to go for the body shot as he had from the window. The muzzle seemingly responded to his misgivings on its own at the last possible instant and raised itself six inches. He squeezed the trigger, and half of the monster's head vanished in a red mist.

He stayed in position behind his barricade for a few more minutes, scraping together enough courage to walk around it. He finally took a couple of deep breaths, willed his hands to stop shaking, and rushed out from behind the bed, rifle at his shoulder and ready to fire. What he saw confused him. The body on the floor was not a monster, but human. And naked. It was missing part of its head, but he didn't see any other bullet wounds. It had a tattoo of a wolf's head overlaid on a swastika on the left side of its chest. *Couldn't heal up from a headshot, could you, you sonuvabitch?*

Thomas stayed in the room with his rifle pointed at the body until the sun shined into the east window.

Thomas didn't have a working radio, so he couldn't call for reinforcements. He found a man with a somewhat serviceable bicycle and asked him to deliver a hand-written message to his commanding officer. He had a hard time conveying exactly what he wanted; the man only replied to him in French. However, when Thomas produced two chocolate bars, the man's command of the English language took a sudden turn for the better. Thomas watched the man ride off with his chocolate bars and wondered if he would have to make the hike back himself anyway.

A convoy of jeeps showed up later that evening to find Thomas had laid his squad out in the church courtyard and covered them with their ponchos. He had their dog tags in his pocket.

He had left the monster upstairs where he had killed it.

The adrenaline rush Thomas had been running on since noon the previous day had completely wore off. He sat in a feverish haze while a whole parade of officers inspected the bodies of his squad. They pulled the body from the house out into the street and inspected it, too. They nodded their heads and looked at each other grimly when they saw the tattoo. They asked him some questions. They showed him a picture of the monster and asked if that was what he had seen. He nodded his head.

His company commander, Captain Hershaw, came up to him, and Thomas forced himself to stand up. "At ease, Corporal," Captain Hershaw ordered, "and remain seated." Captain Hershaw paced back and forth for a few moments, folding and squeezing his lower lip, before he appeared to make a decision and sat down on the edge of the sidewalk, resting his arms on his knees. "Corporal, things are about to move fast for you," he revealed. "I'm upgrading your security clearance because what I'm about to tell you is secret. You're to talk to no one else about this without permission. Understood?"

"Yes, Sir," Thomas replied, squinting his eyes at the Captain. Thomas was a bit taken aback the captain was sitting down next to him, but he was too tired to sit up straighter.

"As you know," Captain Hershaw began, "your squad has been part of the Army's counter to Operation *Werwolf*." He took his hat off and ran his fingernails back and forth over his buzzed scalp. "Well, up until a few months ago, we all thought it was nothing more than as advertised, a resistance force." He turned his head and looked directly at Thomas. "As you've seen, Operation *Werwolf* is much more than that."

Thomas felt his anger rising, but there just wasn't enough adrenaline to fuel it. Still, he managed to ask, "So the Army let my entire squad die?"

Captain Hershaw hung his head. "We didn't know how much of what we were told was true. It's really quite fantastic if you think about it. Werewolves? Who the hell would have thought they really existed?"

Thomas slowly shook his head. "When I came downstairs this morning, I still wasn't sure what I'd seen was real or not." Then he turned and looked at the row of ponchos. A slender breeze stirred up and fetched for him the smell of death. "That was until I saw their bodies. Nothing human could have done that." He handed his squad's dog tags over. "They're real, all right, Captain," he insisted.

Captain Hershaw took the time to stare at each tag as if trying to burn its image into his memories. When he got to Brost's tag, he whispered loudly, as if he was afraid someone other than Thomas would hear him. "Brost and I grew up on the same block. Our mothers used to play cards every Tuesday night." He turned the tag over in his hands a few times. "I wish I could have seen it." He raised his head and looked at the window to the room where Thomas killed the werewolf. "All I've got are pictures."

It was Thomas's turn to look the captain in the eye. "I wish it was something I'd never seen, Sir, but I did, and I'll never forget it either. Trust me; you do not want to see one face to face."

The captain softly shook his head in consideration. "Maybe you're right."

With a sudden burst of energy, Thomas asked, "Sir, how did the Army find out about them?"

Captain Hershaw revealed, "There's a group of priests who call themselves the 'Lamp of Truth.' They may be men of God, but they damn

185

sure know how to hunt these monsters down. And they're highly adept at killing them. Turns out they have millennia of experience, because werewolves are not something invented by the Nazis. Anyway, these priests came to the Allies a few months ago and warned us what the Nazis were up to. We didn't believe them, but there was too much evidence to dismiss them as crazy. So we started listening for certain words in our communications. You were the first to survive an encounter with one."

Captain Hershaw put the dog tags into his shirt pocket and then sat there in silence for a few minutes. Suddenly, he stood up, and Thomas followed him. "Grieving time's over, Corporal. I'm promoting you to Sergeant, effective immediately, and reassigning you to a special platoon they're forming to hunt and kill these damned things. Gather your gear. You leave within the hour."

"Yes, Sir!" Thomas shot out.

Thomas intended to join the Lamp of Truth after the war, but to his chagrin, they only took priests. He wasn't willing to give up on this chosen path so he entered seminary school, much to the approval of his parents. If he had to be a priest to kill these howlers, then a priest he would become. He received special permission to read and study the books on the history of the Race and the Lamp of Truth; his experiences in the war earned him his own key to a small room in the main library where these books were stored.

He was ordained in 1959, immediately inducted into the Lamp of Truth, and then assigned to the Orlando Monastery. Again, his experience hunting and killing howlers benefitted him. He was put in command of a three-man team known as a cloister. He and his cloister were responsible for killing over one hundred howlers in the American southeast during the next couple of decades.

Father Thomas closed his picture album and reflected on how much easier it was to kill howlers than it was during the war; now they knew most of the information about the howler before they engaged it. A monk would show up at the door with an intelligence packet containing a picture of the howler in human form, its address, and other pertinent information like silver allergy, combat experience, etc. Father Thomas and his cloister would then go out and kill it. Yes indeed, it was much easier to kill them now.

Now they just walked up to your door.

Chapter 31—Præda

noun [prā'-də]

1. Prey.

Aaron Darveau, June 10, 1983

Aaron didn't realize how cold it was in the church until he walked outside and stood under the Florida sun. He found that strange in a noir-humor sort of way; every funeral he had ever been to, it was either raining, cold, or both.

He opened up the door to Lil' Red and suddenly his hackles jumped up. He detected a scent, and his memory brought up that haunting memory from a couple of weeks ago—wood, leather, and oiled iron. He instantly stood up a little straighter and scanned the area, straining to find the source of his angst, but could find nothing that would trigger his reaction in the parking lot or on the sidewalk. He should have been more discreet in his examination of the surrounding area, but his surprise was total.

Good way to get yourself killed! Next time, play dumb and keep your head down.

Once he was done scolding himself, he used his *lupus* senses. He should be able to determine where the smell was coming from if he let the breeze carry the surrounding scents to him.

There it was…to his left…across the street maybe? He shrugged his shoulders and got into Lil' Red. He was sure whoever was carrying that scent was observing him, and he didn't want to give away he detected anything more than that. They were hunting him, and he knew it was only a matter of time before they attacked. *So much for Craig's word. First day off the base since my shunning, and they're already hot on my ass.* He put the key in the ignition and started the engine, all the while peeking through the windshield across the street, trying to catch a glimpse of his pursuer. Again, he saw nothing out of the ordinary. He pulled Lil' Red's gear shifter into drive and drove onto the street while keeping his senses on high alert. He lost the scent about one block from the church.

The ride back to the base was uneventful. He kept trying to catch sight of anyone out of the ordinary, but if anyone was following him, he couldn't see them. He *did* notice a large, black Ford pickup truck about halfway into the trip that appeared to be following him. He kept his attention on it, trying to see if he could see who was driving, but it hung back too far. He turned down the street to the base's main entrance and it kept going, so he wasn't sure if it was following him or not. It was probably just his paranoid mind.

His dad told him once, *"Never chase your opponent. Both of your paths will cross one day and when they do, deal with him then."* That sounded a lot like what he had learned in Tai Chi. He decided to take that advice and let the truck go on its way.

Saturday turned out to be a typical Florida summer day, warm and sunny. His friend, Rick, didn't have to work, so Aaron got him to help pick up Kyle's car and ferry Lil' Red to a used car dealer.

After Father Thomas, Rick, and he made small talk for a few minutes, Father Thomas handed Aaron an envelope. "Here's where you will most likely find the location of *Viam Lupus*—you know—if you happen to find yourself in Miami. Ask for Jose Suarez. Tell him you want to see his ugly sister. And I wouldn't mention me if I were you. If they find out a priest sent you, they'll probably think you're working for these Fectors you told me about."

"Thanks, Father." *Viam Lupus—Where did I hear that name before?*

Rick followed Aaron to the used car dealer. Aaron only got about two thirds of what Lil' Red was probably worth, but he didn't complain. He wouldn't have received a single dollar if two people hadn't died for it.

With that out of the way, they drove around for a few hours, enjoying the day. Devil Car, as he had christened his new Mustang, was what his dad called a "tire squaller." It would squeal the tires whenever he punched the accelerator. Aaron just happened to push a little too hard each and every time he came off of a red light, and when the tires chirped, he secretly complimented Kyle for his mechanical know-how. He *publicly* appreciated Rick's jealousy, though.

The day wasn't as carefree as Aaron had wished it would be, though. Several times during the ride, Aaron noticed an eerily familiar black pick-up traveling in the same direction as well as the scent of his stalker from the funeral home. Those two events convinced him beyond a shadow of a doubt he was being hunted. He decided it was time to confront them and put an end to this. He experienced a fleeting fantasy that if he could just talk to these people, let them know he wasn't a threat, perhaps they would leave him alone. He didn't think there would be much of a chance of that happening, so he decided he was going to pick the place where they would meet. It would be on his terms, not theirs. He wasn't going to let them catch him unaware in a bathroom at some fast food joint.

He dropped Rick off at his barracks and then went to his own room to think about how to control the upcoming encounter. He pulled the newspaper clipping off of his desk and knew exactly where to lead them—Kyle's place. It was proper he should meet his stalkers there. He spent the next few hours meditating and doing his Tai Chi forms, preparing himself for what lay ahead. A couple of hours after dark, he climbed into Devil Car and left.

Kyle lived in a trailer, or *had*, near the outskirts of town on a two-acre lot situated next to a junkyard. His job was security, keeping people on the public side of the junkyard's fence where they belonged. The junkyard was about the size of an entire city block and had a tall, twelve-foot fence with aluminum slats run through the chain links to prevent people from seeing inside. Aaron pulled into the gravel driveway around midnight and turned off the engine. He patrolled around the fence, on the lookout for anyone who might be waiting and to get a feel for the lay of the land. He spent a few more minutes searching around the field; the grass and weeds were overgrown to about mid-thigh and would be easy for a stalker, *lupus* or human, to hide in it. Satisfied he was alone, he took off his clothes and put them in the trunk. Then, he leaned against the front left fender of Devil Car to wait on someone to show up. *If it's the cops, I'm going to have a hard time explaining why I'm naked, in possession of a dead man's car, parked in front of said dead man's house, at one o'clock in the morning.*

He waited, spending his time studying where life used to exist—Kyle's trailer. It was old and rusty, and most of the windows had duct taped boards of some type in their place. There was police tape across the door and two chalk outlines of headless bodies, mostly washed away, in front of it on the patio. He scanned the dark field, searching for his would-be assassins. He reached into the car and checked his watch. He'd been waiting for an hour, and he was still alone.

He opened the trunk to get his clothes when he picked up that haunting scent again. He let the evening breeze bring the smell to him while he stood there behind Devil Car. He saw no need to let them know he detected them. The smell was coming from in front of him, around the corner from the front gate. He picked up the scent and sounds of one man sitting there. *I guess my opinion of Craig was correct. He alerted them early—lying bastard.* He continued to stand there while keeping his attention on that corner. His heart was racing and his senses sharpened up as the thought raced through his mind at warp speed that perhaps this was a bad idea.

He wanted more information on this guy, but he didn't want to give away he knew someone was there. He closed the trunk of Devil Car and then walked around and leaned against the driver's door. He still couldn't see anything, but he did get an accurate picture of his stalker's intentions from the combination of smells and tiny sounds carried on the breeze— crunching grass, someone leaning against a chain link fence, and the brush of metal rubbing against leather. The smells also brought back a memory— the nights he chased deer with his pack, he picked up a scent from those who were lying in wait—anticipation and an over-abundance of confidence. He smelled the same thing right then. Someone was around that corner, and they hoped Aaron would step into their trap.

Aaron's concentration on the corner was broken by a *crunch, crunch, crunch* of someone slowly sneaking through the grass on his left, out in the field. Two sides covered. Then from behind him—someone was at the end of the driveway. Three sides covered by attackers with a tall fence on his right. It wasn't the most tactically safe place to be. *Yes, this was a bad idea. Well, I'm here. Let's see what we see.* He needed an advantage. He knew what that advantage was, but he also knew where it would end if he played that card. *WWKD?* He would use every advantage at his disposal.

Part of him was thinking he could just run them off, but another part of him laughed at the audacity of that thought. *You came out here on purpose. You knew they were tracking you. You led them here. Did you really think tonight was going to end without a fight?*

No, I didn't. Okay, I've lured them here. Now I need a plan.

He reached into the car window and started the engine and turned the music up loud enough to drown out any sounds he might make. He crossed his fingers as he taunted the black dog, and it came running like a heroin addict being offered free product. About the time he started congratulating himself for a flawless *renovatio*, he remembered something his preacher said years ago. "*Pride comes before the fall.*"

This time the black dog came at him from the side. Aaron wasn't prepared for that, and the dog got in one good blow before he was able to reorient himself and send it on its way. It was enough to delay him and shake him of his cheerful confidence. His *renovatio* wasn't as smooth as it was last time, but it still worked. That's all he was concerned about; he'd work on technique later.

Dogs started barking on the other side of the fence. They must have recognized the car when he first pulled up because it used to be Kyle's. They would be familiar with its sound. But now something else was out there, and they didn't like it one bit. He wasn't surprised they didn't bark at the stalker around the corner, though. He remembered when he was buying parts for Lil' Red back home—the owner's dogs were trained to sit and wait on any miscreants to come over the fence before unleashing Hell. Perhaps these were trained the same way.

Now to pick his first target—of the three, the one near the end of the driveway was the most nervous—he kept shifting around, making noise. He couldn't sit still. Aaron crept along the side of the car and over to the fence, keeping low to the ground, facing toward the street. The dogs came to the fence and he scared them off with a low snarl. They ran back into the yard but didn't give up their incessant yapping. Maybe that would work to his advantage; it was more noise to cover his approach. The area around the fence was unkempt with a lot of overgrown brush and grass along it to hide in, and it was still damp from the four o'clock, fifteen minute Florida rain shower. He was able to move without making a sound. He instinctively placed a paw and then a cula silently onto the ground, tested for stability, and only then placed his full weight on it. Aaron slowly came upon the end of the fence and saw his quarry, Stalker Three, hiding down next to the culvert where the driveway came off the road. He wasn't looking in Aaron's direction. He was concentrating on where the music was coming from. It was a long stride from the fence to the ditch, and Aaron wasn't sure he could make the distance without being spotted. He decided to turn the corner and work his way further down the fence, paralleling the ditch, to get behind his target. Once in the ditch, he should be able to sneak up—the street lights were mostly out, which gave him a large assortment of shadows to hide in.

He made it about fifty feet down the fence line when he saw Stalker Three stand up to get a better look up the driveway. He was being impatient. He still wasn't looking in Aaron's direction, so Aaron belly-crawled to the ditch. The grass along the side of the ditch was tall, perfect predator cover. He scrunched back down as he prowled up the ditch to his prey.

Aaron stuck his nose in Stalker Three's ear, growled, and was rewarded with the smell of loosening bowels. Stalker Three slowly turned around, wide-eyed, his face the same color as the priest's collar he wore, staring into Aaron's snarling face. He looked down at the crossed cula marks on Aaron's chest, and Aaron sensed disbelief.

Stalker Three took a deep breath, and swallowed a lump that magically appeared in his throat. "You should be ripping me to shreds right now!" he exclaimed. "Why haven't you ripped me to shreds yet? Unless you're not a.... you're not a wildling! Solitaires are always wildlings! You can't be a solitaire. We only go after the wildlings—whoever heard of a *frenator* being shunned? She lied to us! That bitch! Oh God oh God oh God—"

Aaron's world turned into a buzz of madness and a sheet of crimson rage. He considered letting Stalker Three go, but his *lupus* growled in anger, **"He's here hunting me! He wanted to kill me! He killed Kyle and Sally. They didn't fucking deserve to have their fucking heads fucking cut off."** He turned his *lupus* loose, and it was over with one snap of his jaw—the wet crunch of Stalker Three's neck vibrated through Aaron's teeth and into his skull.

A momentary rush of pleasure short-circuited his brain as he licked the blood off of his lips and snout. It was much stronger than when he tasted that deer's and pig's blood. He experimented with pot in high school, and the sensation was similar but stronger. And addicting. Each time his tongue touched it another wave burst through and ruined his concentration. *Human blood is so much better! Does it do this all the time?*

He wanted more! Then Jajine yelled at him, *"Not those instincts, Aaron! Get back to work!"* It was enough to bring him back to reality. Part of him was horrified he stepped that close to the edge of his humanity.

He examined Stalker Three's equipment. He had a rifle, a sword, a crossbow with silver tipped bolts, and a long machete. But that smell, that haunting smell of wood, leather, and oiled iron, was heavy here. That was what Fector equipment smelled like. He suspected it might have been one person, but it appeared that was their smell in general—their equipment.

The Fector was dressed in something similar to ninja outfits he'd seen on television, the difference being this one had a priest's collar. The shoes were designed for stealth, the pant legs were tucked in, the gloves had high-tech grips on the palms, and the head and face were covered except for the eyes.

One down. Two to go.

Aaron lifted his nose into the air and sampled the scents in the area. No one else was around other than the other two stalkers. He sneaked across the driveway to the ditch on the other side, following it until he was well behind Stalker Two, before crawling into the field. His hearing was slightly deadened by the loud music, but his smell and sight were still good. A random breeze brought the smell of old grease and dead cars to his nose as he circled around behind his target. Stalker Two was sneaking up toward Devil Car, about seventy-five yards in front of Aaron. He wasn't sure if it was his imagination or not, but he swore he smelled the blood, that sweet candy, pulsing through Stalker Two's veins.

Aaron tensed up to start his run then held himself in place as he caught movement coming from the top of the trailer and against the still backdrop of the junkyard. He scrunched down further into the grass. A new one, Stalker Four, was lying in ambush with a hunting rifle and a large pair of goggles. Aaron had heard of night vision goggles, but he'd never seen any. Stalker Four had the area around Stalker Two covered.

Aaron needed to take care of that sniper first so he sat there and observed him for a few minutes looking for weaknesses. He needed to adjust his plan to take the extra stalker into account, but he needed information on him first. He watched the sniper and noted the conservation of his movements roughly matched the sounds made by Stalker One from earlier. A slight, momentary breeze brought his scent to Aaron. The smells were similar to Stalker One, as well. This was not a fourth stalker. This *was* Stalker One; he had changed position. Aaron decided to continue his circle through the field until he was on the other side, behind the trailer and on its opposite end from where Stalker One was sitting.

Silence thundered across the area. Stalker Two had turned off Devil Car's engine and with it, the music. That hurt the stalkers more than it hurt Aaron, because he could now hear footsteps coming toward the end of the trailer where he was hiding. Stalker One was trying to be quiet, but overly optimistic to think he could move around on a sheet metal roof without Aaron hearing it. Stalker One peered over the edge, and Aaron leaped up, grabbed him by the shoulders using both culas, and pulled him down, using his fangs to rip out his throat in the process. The rifle went off with a loud crack when it hit the ground. It served as an exclamation point to the pleasure flooding Aaron's brain that was triggered by the blood gushing across his tongue.

Two down, one to go.

Stalker Two immediately jumped into action and came running in his direction. Aaron jumped the fence into the junkyard—and right into the middle of three barking Rottweilers. A single snarl from Aaron put them at bay, but they continued to bark and cry out at him, giving away his position. Stalker Two was getting closer. The alpha looked unnervingly similar to the black dog from his dreams. Instead of killing them, he decided he could use them.

Aaron let loose a *vagor* and established his dominance as he had at Kyle's shunning. He may not be *Lupus Rex*, but he had the conviction. He was *Fortitudo Incarnatum*, Strength Incarnate, the *Big Dog They Did Not Want to Fuck With*. He leaned forward on his front legs, stuck his tail out straight, raised his hackles, and made eye contact. Combined with his snarl and a low guttural growl, the alpha stepped back like someone had punched it in the head. It whined, urinated, and looked for a place to hide through squinted eyes. Aaron relaxed his lips, loosening his domineering hold, and it shrank before him, wagging its partially tucked tail. The other two took their former alpha's lead and came up to him in puppy-dog fashion, tails tucked in, bouncing on their front legs. Aaron took off into the middle of the junkyard with his three new friends behind him.

They lay in wait for Stalker Two to come around the corner, down the only path to their ambush site. Aaron positioned Elwood, the alpha he just named, on the hood of some old pickup truck, Jake, dog two, on the roof of a large sedan, and Penguin the Nun, dog three, at ground level between two piles of crushed cars. Stalker Two would pass the dogs in that order. Aaron sat in the shadows at the end of the path, within eyesight of all three dogs to keep them under control.

They knew Stalker Two was coming as soon as he climbed over the clinking fence. All of their ears stood up, and they turned their heads in his direction. The stalker tried to move silently, but the crunch of his boots on the gravel sounded like sledgehammers on concrete to their ears. He crept around the corner into their gauntlet and stopped when he saw Elwood. He slowly started moving down the path again when he saw that Elwood wouldn't accost him. He came upon Jake, acting just like Elwood. Stalker Two turned around to check his rear and saw Elwood was following behind him. The confusion Aaron sensed from Stalker Two was profound. He continued warily past Jake, taking the time to look up ahead, trying to glean what was in store. His heartbeat jumped up as he reached into his pocket and brought out a flashlight, and as he watched Jake jump off the sedan and fall in beside Elwood, he saw through the ruse. His heartbeat raced as he dropped his flashlight and raised his rifle.

Aaron let loose a serious of snarls and yips. The three dogs heard, **"Tear him apart."**

Aaron watched the dogs finish off Stalker Two. He sat back and avoided the human blood because he was afraid he might begin to like it too much if he gave into the temptation of tasting it for pleasure alone. They crowded around Aaron when they were finished, and Aaron nuzzled each one. They had done a good job this evening.

He collected the other corpses and put them with Stalker Two and let the dogs destroy them as well. Perhaps that would be enough to keep interested, yet unilluminated, parties off his trail; he hoped they would think these three men were trespassing and the dogs got them—assuming no one looked out by the road or behind the trailer.

Aaron was preparing to jump the fence one last time when he spotted a slip of paper on the ground. It was too fresh to have been there too long, so it must have fallen out of one of his stalkers' pockets. He picked it up and saw it was a picture Karen took of Aaron when they visited the Florida Keys. Aaron brought it to his nose and smelled deeply. In between Karen's sweet smell and the smell of the Fectors, there was something else, something distant but still intimate. The scent of revenge. He remembered Stalker Three's words. *"The bitch." Must have been talking about Karen.*

He changed back into human form, washed off with a water hose he found next to the trailer, got dressed, and left. He only made it a couple of blocks from the junkyard before he had to pull over to the side of the road and puke. He wasn't sure if it was because he just killed three people, liked the taste of their blood too much, or because he'd finally accepted the fact Karen truly wanted him dead. He decided it was a little of all three—and probably a few other things he couldn't think of right then.

He stumbled back from the side of the road to Devil Car and leaned on the trunk for support. He turned around to face the road behind him, and loneliness attacked him as he looked at the pockmarks of shadow scattered along that stretch of concrete. Each shadow reminded him of a death he was responsible for, and he looked on in horror as he counted more shadows than number of dead. The shadows were not only telling him of his past but of his future, too. A lively breeze carried the ticklish smells of grass and trees to his nose, but there was also an undercurrent of death lingering to remind him of what he had caused and what he still had to do.

His eyes picked up a faint movement before his ears heard anything. Something was on the road and running toward him in a straight line, passing into and out of the shadows, leaving him with the surreal impression it was turning invisible, then visible, and then invisible again. He stood up from the trunk when he saw it was a large black dog. He had almost convinced himself he was in his dream again until he saw he was still on the side of the road, not in his childhood backyard. His adrenaline spiked momentarily as he prepared to fight, but then it dropped back down when he saw the dog was running up to him in a submissive way, like Aaron was a long lost friend, and it had finally found him. It scurried up to him, and he saw it was Elwood, the alpha from the junkyard. He had scratches all over him like he had squeezed out through a fence.

Aaron asked, "What do you want?" His teeth were gritty, and the back of his throat was still scratchy and sour with the aftertaste of his vomit.

Elwood set his butt on the ground and nervously scooted a little closer to Aaron, tongue hanging out of his open mouth, tail wagging. Aaron knew Elwood was waiting for him to show him some affection.

"Well, if you're going to go with me, there're some ground rules. First, no pissing or shitting in my car. Drooling's out, too. You got that?"

Elwood answered with a little, "Ruff," as if he understood.

"Second, I don't like dealing with malfunctioning animals. The first time you bite me or one of my friends, you're road kill."

Again, as if he understood, he gave a little, "Ruff," then rolled over on his back, exposing his stomach to Aaron. Animals don't expose their vulnerable parts to predators unless they trust them not to take a bite. Aaron knelt down beside him and rubbed his belly while he inspected the scratches. They weren't too bad, but tomorrow he'd need to find some first aid ointment. A chill ran up his back as he saw the new scratches on Elwood's chest were eerily similar to his own; they were crossed.

Aaron rummaged around in the trunk and found an old towel to put on the passenger seat. "All right, get in. And don't bleed all over the place."

Elwood leaped in and sat there like he'd been riding next to Aaron for years. He looked up at Aaron, mouth open and tongue hanging out to the side.

Aaron glanced back down the road to see if Jake and Penguin had followed him, too, but he didn't see them. "Did you go and leave your buddies behind, you traitor?"

Elwood gave a little whine and then sneezed.

"Well, we better go check on them. Don't want them stuck in the fence." Aaron got into Devil Car, turned around, and drove back toward the junkyard. The other two dogs barked when he got within range, but they were lonely barks, not cries for help. "They're okay. You're lucky." Aaron reached over and scratched his ears.

Aaron didn't feel good about stealing another man's dog, but he knew this wasn't another man's dog anymore. Elwood became his the instant he established himself as the new Alpha.

Chapter 32—Forma

noun [fŏrm'-ə]

1. Form, shape, fashion, plan, mold.

Aaron Darveau, June 12, 1983

Aaron had a hard time getting to sleep once he returned to the base. He couldn't shake the notion Karen tried to have him killed. Knowing they would call the Fectors and finding out they actually did it was two different things. He'd broken up with girlfriends before, and a few had broken up with him, but none of them tried to have him killed. Of course, none of them turned him into a werewolf before, either. *Well, there was that crazy bitch, Sheila, who slashed my tires once.*

Once he did fall asleep though, he slept straight through the day until nearly dark. Aaron's roommate had already left the base for the evening so Aaron was alone other than Elwood, who was sleeping on the foot of his bunk. Aaron snuck him in and out of the back door to do his business because animals weren't allowed in the barracks. The scratches on Elwood's chest were scabbed over and looked okay, but Aaron washed him down in the shower anyway and ended up with as much water on himself as on Elwood. After he dried the dog off, he dug around in his medicine cabinet for some first aid ointment. Elwood must have thought he'd died and gone to heaven. He rolled over onto his back while Aaron rubbed it into his belly and chest. He let Aaron do that as much as he wanted to.

While Elwood snoozed on an old towel, Aaron contemplated his situation. He considered heading back to Louisiana, but there wasn't anything there for him since his parents were killed—their old house on a couple acres of land would be hard to live at permanently without them around. And hanging around Orlando would certainly be too dangerous. He didn't like his options. He knew he was going to have to face Karen and her friends—*Hell, they used to be my friends!*—to resolve this. The way he saw it, he had three choices.

The first one was waiting on them to attack. This scenario gave them all the advantages and left him with none. Tai Chi might have stated he should let his opponent show him how to defend, but that was when you were already facing each other. His dad's words of wisdom about chasing someone didn't apply if you were being chased. Depending on the Fectors to cross the street in broad daylight, giving him time to prepare and react, was too much to hope for. He mentally scratched Option One off of his list.

The second option was to confront them. He suspected if he waited somewhere long enough, like what happened last night at Kyle's, they would show themselves. But he killed three of them. They wouldn't send just three the next time they met. They might all decide to come. He remembered Craig's words about them swarming when going after a known target. He knew he had the stealth and the reactions to handle several of them, but he didn't know how many they would bring to the party. That was important information he didn't have. He removed Option Two from his list.

That left Option Three—cutting the head off of the snake. Were Craig and company the head of the snake? Or was Karen acting alone? They were certainly in charge of directing the Fectors, or it appeared that way. If Karen and company were dead, would the Fectors cease chasing him? *Probably not. I just killed three of them. Something tells me the truce included not killing any Fectors.* Option Three didn't seem feasible based on his lack of knowledge. He was getting a bellyache again. He hated mysteries.

He stared at himself in the mirror. WWKD? *Shields up, fire photon torpedoes. But where to aim them?* He needed information so he picked up the phone and dialed Bill.

Bill's cheerful voice echoed in the phone. "How do!"

"Bill, this is Aaron. Don't hang up—"

"Man, I'm not supposed to be talking to you. Are you trying to get me in trouble?" Aaron could picture Bill sneaking a look out of his window to see if Craig was walking up the driveway or not.

"They aren't bugging your phone, man. Keep cool."

"Yeah, probably not. Still, you're shunned. Who did you piss off?"

"Karen and Craig and Lisa."

"Holy shit! A trifecta! What did you do, piss in their Cheerios? Never mind; I don't want to know."

"You don't want to know what happened, why I was shunned?"

Bill's voice suddenly dropped to a loud whisper. "No. It just happens. Nobody asks why."

"I turned down Karen, refused to be her *Lupus Rex*."

"You did what? Who would turn down being *Lupus Rex*? You're nuts, man. She's a fox. Why would you do that?"

Aaron was starting to think everyone was in the dark. He decided drop a hook in the water and see what would bite. Unfortunately, he only had one piece of bait. "Because of Kyle. Y'all had him killed, man. I don't want any part of that."

"What do you mean, 'we had him killed?' I didn't have anybody killed."

"Craig ordered it."

"You're full of shit, man. The Fectors got him." He tried to sound convincing, but Aaron could tell he knew better even if he didn't want to believe it.

"Exactly. Craig ordered the Fectors to get him. He told me."

"Bullshit!"

"I know it sounds crazy, but they almost got me, too. And they all smelled like Karen had been rubbing against them all day long."

"What are you talking about, they almost got you? Who almost got you?"

"Last night. Three Fectors at Kyle's place. I found evidence Karen sent them after me."

"I don't believe it. Why would Karen and Craig work with Fectors?"

"It's not just them, it's the whole damned Conclave, I think. What I do know is they have to shun two hundred *lupis* every year, send them to the slaughter like sheep. If they do that, the clans are left alone."

"Bullshit," was all Bill had to say, but there was doubt in his voice. His certainty was weakening.

"Then you tell me how the Fectors know when someone's been shunned, Bill." Bill didn't answer. Aaron could hear Bill's heartbeat rate go up, even over the phone connection. "Bill? How do they know?"

"Aaron, man, this is too wild. Why are you trying to stir up shit like this? You say you got away? Then leave. Run. Hide out."

"I didn't get away from them. I had to kill them."

"You killed three Fectors? Shit." Bill laughed mockingly. "They ain't gonna forget about you, dude."

"I know. They'll follow me." Aaron let that settle. "Bill, you really want to see me dead?"

"You're shunned, Aaron. You're on your own. You pissed off Craig. You knew what you were getting into."

"No, I didn't! Karen infected me without my permission because she wanted me as *Lupus Rex*. She didn't give me a choice. She's a real bitch."

"Yeah, well, most women are, man."

"So, where does that leave me? She infects me. I turn her down. I get shunned. Then she sends the Fectors out after me. What are my choices at this point?"

"I don't know. But I know what'll happen if you keep trying to get in touch with any of your old *grex* mates. You'll be declared outlaw and have the whole damned Race after your ass. I wish I could help you, man, but you're on your own. And you know I can't lie to them if they ask if I've been in contact with you."

"I can't believe you are going to sit there and let them send innocent people to their deaths. I thought more of you than that."

Bill yelled into the phone, "Don't put this shit on me, Aaron! I didn't have anything to do with it!"

"You're cooperating just by not doing anything about it."

"If what you say is true, then you've put my life in danger, too. Goddamnit, Aaron!"

The phone connection went dead as Bill hung up on him.

Chapter 33—Bill and Glen Benson

Spring 1977

The day after their escape through the woods, Bill and Glen were in Howie's shop repairing Bertha's front differential. It turned out the u-joint wasn't the only thing broken. The linkage the u-joint connected to on the differential was cracked. They had to replace it, so they scoured junkyards in the neighboring vicinity looking for a replacement. They were also trying to keep a low profile. If someone was out trying to kill them, they might try again.

Glen, being the mechanic of the two, was under the front end of Bertha while Bill was handing tools back and forth. Bill examined Glen's arms while they worked. "Those scratches on your arms are almost healed up. What gives, dude?"

"I don't know. Something weird, no doubt." He rolled out from under Bertha and sat up, resting his forearms on his knees. "I've been thinking about what we saw. We might have been a little stoned, but we weren't on PCP or any other hallucinogen. What we saw was real. I think it was a werewolf, dude."

Bill had been thinking about it, too. He'd just been too afraid to say it out loud. It seemed too ridiculous to take seriously now that it was over and done with. Still…. "Yeah, I have to agree with you."

"Do you think I'm one now?"

"I don't know. I thought they had to bite you."

"Same here. But with my scratches healing up lickety-split, I wonder if the claws do the trick, too."

"I guess we wait until the full moon next month to know for sure."

Glen sighed. "We won't have to wait that long. The next one is tomorrow night. I already checked."

"Tomorrow? What was that yesterday then? La'Man's Halloween costume? I thought werewolves could only change on a full moon?"

"Don't fuckin' ask me, man." Glen stood up and went over to the shop door and looked out. "Maybe he's some kind of special werewolf, can change whenever the fuck he wants. Shit, I don't know."

Bill went over and stood next to Glen, looking at the house. "We need to tell Howie that Daffodil is busted. We'll need to find another field somewhere."

"Yeah. He's gonna be pissed."

"Yeah, well that's nothing compared to the brick he's gonna shit when he sees you change into a werewolf."

They both turned their heads to each other and realized they were no longer talking about it as an "if." They both knew it was *going* to happen.

Howie didn't believe a word they said. He accused them both of lying to cover up the fact they got took by La'Man. The only proof lay in the woods in the form of three headless bodies, two broken spears, and the claw marks on Glen that looked weeks old.

"I've heard some tall tales in my life, but this one is new. If you boys think you can pull some cockamamie bullshit story like this past me, you are dead wrong."

Glen stood up, "Howie, we ain't lying. Why would we make up something like that? If we were found out, then yes, we'd defend ourselves. Why would we need to come up with the werewolf angle?"

Howie shook his head. "I don't have a clue. Maybe you boys have been sampling your product too much."

Bill jumped into the conversation, "Well, we'll find out come tomorrow night."

Bill and Glen were taking the werewolf angle seriously. Both of them feared what might happen when Glen turned so they came up with some precautions. They wrapped a towing chain around Glen's waist twice and then around a sturdy tree twice and then padlocked the whole thing together so it wouldn't come off. They left enough slack for him to sit down in a chair they left next to the tree—just in case nothing happened.

Howie came out to check on the boys and laughed at them when he saw what they had done. "You shitheads really think this is real, don't you?"

Bill objected defensively, "If you saw what we saw, you'd be worried, too."

Glen settled into his chair and Howie and Bill put their chairs out, too, but a good fifteen feet away. Howie antagonized them. "I think this is one of the most ridiculous things I've seen, but I'm willing to let you boys hang yourselves. Show me a werewolf."

Shortly after dark, Glen doubled over with a cramp.

Bill asked, "You okay, Glen?"

Howie sat there laughing. "Ha, ha. Very funny!"

Glen snapped his head up and glared at Howie.

Bill stared slack-jawed and Howie stopped laughing when they saw the change in Glen's eyes. They were dark blue and insanity burned there, something animalistic and primitive. Glen cried out in pain again. This time, the cry was more guttural than before.

Carol, Betty, and a few of the kids came out on the back porch. Carol yelled, "Everything okay out here?"

Howie yelled, "Get back in the house and lock the doors. Now!"

Howie and Bill watched Glen as he changed. Hair sprouted all over his body, his limbs extended, his head and face became lupine, talons grew from his fingers and toes. His clothes ripped themselves to shreds under the lengthening and expansion of his new werewolf form. Through it all though, his cries of pain grew at an alarming rate until they turned to anger. Finally, about five seconds later, the crying stopped. Howie and Bill stood there by their chairs, well out of reach of…Glen…and stared.

Bill whooped, jumped up in the air, and slapped his cowboy hat on his leg. "We told you! Didn't we fuckin' tell you?"

Suddenly, Bill and Howie found themselves scrambling a bit more out of reach as Glen lurched for the both of them. He was pulled up short by the chains. He tossed and turned and screamed and yanked and pulled and bit and clawed at the chains and the tree but they both held. This went on for about five minutes before he settled down and glowered at them. The chair was destroyed in the ensuing escape attempt, but it didn't matter. Glen wasn't sitting down. He continued to stand there next to the tree, never taking his eyes off of them.

Howie whispered lowly, more to himself than Bill, "Whoa. What the fuck, man?"

Bill whispered back to him, "We told you, dude. Glen's a fucking werewolf."

Howie's face was as white as his t-shirt. "He looks like he wants to eat us."

"Well, yeah! The three that chased us looked like they wanted to eat us, too. These sumbitches are at the top of the food pyramid, Howie."

They were both taken by surprise when Glen howled and again tried to make his escape. Howie and Bill were frozen in place as the sound reached down into their subconscious and told them they were about to be eaten.

They watched in horror each time Glen backed up against the tree and made a run for them. The chains made a loud twanging sound each time they were stretched to their limit. Again, Glen settled down after about five minutes. He stood there and glared at them.

Howie murmered, "This ain't funny no more. This is really giving me the creeps."

Bill agreed. "So, now what?"

"Hell, I don't know. Y'all seemed to have it figured out. What next?"

"I guess we wait here until morning."

"Yeah. I'm gonna go get the shotgun and move everyone into the cellar. Your moms are gonna freak out, but I ain't taking any chances in case Glen gets loose. You got it covered until I get back?"

"Yeah." Bill reached down next to his chair and picked up his camera. "I'm gonna take some pictures."

The first time Bill snapped a picture the flash sent Glen into a worse frenzy than before. At one point, Bill had serious concerns the padlock would give and break. He categorically ruled pictures weren't important.

Glen tried numerous times to get loose throughout the night, but the chains continued to hold. Each time he tried, he howled first, and each time Howie and Bill found themselves feeling like prey. Finally, around fifteen minutes before sunrise, Glen laid down and fell asleep. Howie and Bill watched him change back into a human, his hair sloughing off of him and disintegrating within seconds of hitting the ground.

Bill let Glen sleep for an hour, and when he was convinced he didn't have a werewolf disguised as a human, he unlocked the chains. "Glen, you awake?" He reached down and shook his brother's shoulder. "Glen, wake up, bro."

Glen stirred slightly and his eyelids fluttered. Shortly, he was fully awake, sitting up, rubbing his eyes, and scratching his head. "What happened? Did it work?" He shivered and realized he was naked. He tried to cover up his privates and yelled, "Where the fuck are my clothes, bro?!"

"Dude!" Bill exclaimed. "You were the big, bad wolf last night!" He reached down for a paper bag. "Here, I got these out of your closet."

Glen grabbed the bag. "Thanks. So I turned? I don't remember anything." He tilted his head to the side a moment. "Wait, I remember feeling like I was on fire and then you shaking my shoulder just now. That's it."

They were quiet while Glen got dressed. "What do I do now?" he asked as he sat in one of the chairs.

"Man, I don't know."

"Where's Howie?" Glen looked around for him.

"Sittin' in the house." Bill turned and pointed his head that way. "He's kinda freaked out about it. His hands ain't stopped shaking since you changed last night, and he's drank so much coffee he's taking a piss every fifteen minutes."

"Yeah, I reckon." Glen studied the area by the tree. Claw marks scored it in numerous spots, his clothes were shredded and scattered all around, and the chair they left by the tree was kindling. "I guess the chains held."

"Yeah, but there were a few times I didn't think they would. You really wanted to take a bite out of me."

"Dude, I'm sorry. I don't remember anything."

"Don't worry about it, bro. We're cool." He started pacing in a slow circle. "There's something we need to consider, though."

"Yeah, are there any more of them?" Glen answered for the both of them.

"Exactly. If there are, they know we're probably the ones who killed those other three. They were there to kill us."

"Yeah. They might be looking for us now."

They both looked up at the house, their home. In their minds' eyes they saw their brothers and sisters and parents in there, ripped to shreds by the talons of a werewolf.

Bill suggested what they were both thinking. "If it was the Lordy gang, they'll kill everyone in there to get to us."

Glen nodded his head. "I know."

Bill sighed. "I've always hated Florida. They'll never expect us to head that way."

Bill and Glen packed and drove down to Florida that day. They told Howie they were leaving, but not where they were headed. They weren't trying to hide out from him, just making sure he didn't have anything anyone could beat out of him. It was for his protection, the protection of their family, and their protection. Tearfully, they hugged their mothers goodbye and left.

The boys didn't have a high maintenance lifestyle. They had been in the pot growing and supplying business for a couple of years and had quite a bit of cash saved up. They drove around Florida for close to a year, staying out of sight, and keeping a low profile. They camped when they had to, met up with some of their more trustworthy contacts, but mostly stayed in long term hotels for a couple of weeks at a time. They found a place out of the way and chained Glen to another tree on nights with a full moon. Each time he turned he was as ferocious as the last time. Bill would sit back with his shotgun and hope the chains continued to hold. He wasn't sure he could kill his brother if he ever got free.

They called home every week or so to check on the family. True to form, Lordy and his gang came to the house looking for them. They scared Carol, Betty, and the kids, and they roughed up Howie, but left without any information. Howie was forced to give up two of his fields in *payment* for killing three of his men. Howie never let on he knew about the werewolves.

Spring 1978 found they boys in a secluded stand of trees about an hour or so north of Orlando. It smelled of old swamp—damp leaves, mud, and rank, stale water. They did their normal thing, tracking around the area a couple of hundred yards out from a nice, sturdy tree to make sure there weren't any people around. Bill went through the ritual of chaining Glen to the tree, setting up his chair a good twenty-five feet away, and then sitting guard in it with his shotgun across his knees. Glen gave his normal howl as soon as he changed, but Bill was long familiar with it so it didn't send him into a panic anymore.

This time though, a couple of more howls called out from the distance. Glen stopped his thrashing and directed his attention toward the howls, ears raised and tilted forward. He raised his snout into the air and howled again, this time a little differently. The howls in the distance returned the call.

Bill didn't panic, but he did stand up and faced the direction the howls came from. He hissed, "You need to stop, Glen! They might find us!"

Glen glared at him with the same bloodlust he always did. Bill realized it was useless to try and reason with him. He had hoped that he might be able to eventually get through to Glen the Werewolf, but after a year of trying, he had about given up on that tactic.

Glen and the unseen werewolves continued to communicate, first one and then the others. That went on for a few minutes until Glen renewed his thrashing about, trying to free himself. Bill didn't think he was trying to get free to kill and eat him but because he wanted to go join the others. Bill flashed his light into woods, and a set of glowing yellowish-white eyes reflected back at him. Then another set and then another set.

Bill raised the shotgun to his shoulder and yelled, "Any mother fucker tries to hurt me or my brother here is gonna get a face full of buckshot! Now get the fuck outta here!"

Something rustled behind Bill, and before he knew it, his gun was snatched from his hands, and he was thrown to the ground. He stared up into the face of another snarling werewolf. It stood above him with one foot on his chest, not enough to crush him, but enough to immobilize him. Glen launched into another bloodlust tantrum, growling and thrashing and trying to get free. Bill was sure Glen was angry with this other werewolf, but didn't understand why; all Glen ever tried to do was get to him and kill him.

Bill thought it was the end for him when three more werewolves prowled out of the woods. They snuffled and growled and whined and snarled at each other in some form of language instead of attacking though. These werewolves didn't strike him as being as bloodthirsty as the ones he and Glen had run into before. Or even as bloodthirsty as Glen. One of the new ones, the one the others all seemed to defer to, turned to Glen, growled, and backhanded him, striking him across the side of the head. Glen immediately stopped his thrashing and looked at the ground in front of his attacker.

Bill tried to sit up, but the claws from the foot pinning him to the ground reminded him he was in no position to demand anything. Still, that was his brother over there. He yelled, "Quit it you sumbitch! You're hurting him!"

All four of the other werewolves turned their heads and stared at Bill. The other three joined the one pinning him and stood there observing him.

Bill muttered, "Well, this is it then. Y'all gonna eat me now? Well, let me tell you, you wouldn't like me. I'm a Georgia boy. We're tough as gristle and leave a bitter aftertaste."

The four werewolves all conversed for a few minutes, glancing down at Bill with dark looks from time to time and snarling at him, before they seemed to make some decision. Bill saw one of them do something quite surprising—it reached down for the shotgun, unloaded it, and set it in his chair. The werewolf that had him pinned released him and sprang back two steps. All four of them were snarling at him, but they didn't seem like they were going to attack.

Bill stood up. "Not gonna eat me after all, huh? Good choice." Bill wasn't sure if it was a good choice on their part or his.

Then one of them walked over to Glen and grabbed the lock holding him to the tree. The werewolf turned its head to Bill.

Bill asked, "You want me to unlock Glen? Are you nuts? He'll try to kill me!"

One of the werewolves next to Bill took one menacing step toward him, growled, and stuck its hand out, palm up. He'd seen Glen's hands numerous times, just never this close before. Bill spent as little time as possible looking at the "hand" because it was not natural looking, and the mere sight of it gave him the willies.

"Okay, okay! Hold your horses, dude!" Bill reached into his pocket and pulled out the key. "Here." He cautiously reached out and dropped it into the werewolf's hand.

The werewolf loped over to Glen and unlocked him from the tree. Then three of the werewolves, along with Glen, loped off into the woods. The fourth one stayed there, watching Bill with curious eyes.

Bill took the opportunity to examine this one in detail. It was about the same size as Glen, but female instead. The face had feminine features, too. If Bill had to guess, the woman behind that face was probably a looker. The eyes had an intelligence behind them, not like what he saw in Glen's eyes. He chanced a question. "So, Sugar, what's your sign? You come here often?"

He was rewarded with a menacing snarl.

"All right, all right, I get the message. Just stand here and keep my mouth shut." He gazed longingly over at his chair. "Listen, I want to sit down. I am not going for my—"

The werewolf leaped over to his chair and snatched up his shotgun, throwing it out into the woods. Then it moved away from the chair and continued to watch him.

Bill sat in the chair until dawn, not daring to fall asleep. Watching a werewolf all night was not a new skill to him, so he didn't have any trouble staying awake. The sky was just starting to lighten up and the temperature starting to fall to a pre-morning low when the werewolf gave a small yip and disappeared into the woods. If Bill hadn't known better, he would have sworn it was telling him good bye.

He stood up and yelled, "What about Glen? How do I find him?" When he didn't get a response, he yelled. "I'll just wait here then!"

Bill waited for about an hour before he went and found his shotgun. No one—or no werewolf—showed up to take it from him, so he put that, his chair, and the chains into Bertha. He pulled out a map and thought that if there were people in the area, he might find them by following the road he was on. It looped around a couple of miles, so there might be houses along it.

He muttered to himself, "Yeah, and what do I do when I find one? 'Excuse me, Sir, do you know where there're some werewolves hanging out?' I might end up in the loony bin. Or shot. Or eaten. Alive." He shuddered.

Bill resolved to follow the road anyway. He had to find Glen. He made it about half-way around according to the map when he ran upon a well-maintained dirt road and followed it, passing through a few open, rusty gates, until it ended at a large, stone house that reminded him of something out of *Ben Hur*—except for the cars parked in front. He figured cars meant people, so he pulled in behind the last one in line.

He climbed down from the cab and headed for the house, still uncertain as to how to ask about werewolves, when a good looking woman with long black hair walked out of the front door. "Good morning, Bill. I'm Karen. Glen's waiting for you inside. Come on in." She flashed a gorgeous smile at him.

Bill continued to walk toward the house but slowed his pace somewhat. "Is he okay?"

"He's fine!" She winked at him. "Come on in, I won't bite." Bill made a mental note that she didn't say she *didn't* bite.

Bill smiled and followed Karen through the front doorway into a large, arched foyer that led into a huge courtyard. He gawked as he took it all in, yet remained cautious until he saw Glen sitting at a table next to a swimming pool. He started to rush over but pulled himself up short; he glanced around, checking to see if anyone would stop him. He saw an older man and woman sitting with Glen, and they were watching Bill with big smiles on their faces.

Glen stood up and yelled, "Bill! Holy Shit! Last night was fuckin' awesome, dude!"

Bill ran the last couple of steps and hugged his brother. "Man, I thought you bought the farm."

"No way! It was a blast! Let me introduce you to everyone." He turned to the people at the table. "This is Craig and Lisa, and that fox behind you is Karen. Bill, they're all werewolves, just like me! They're the ones who met us last night. And they didn't try to eat us. In my book, that means they're the good guys!"

Craig stood up, chuckling. "Bill, it is indeed a pleasure to meet you," he stated. "To add to your brother's enthusiastic introductions, I am Craig Minor." He pointed to the older lady next to him as she stood up. "This is my wife, Lisa. And the young lady behind you is Karen Argali, whom I believe you have already met. You just missed James by about fifteen minutes. He was the fourth member at our unintentional rendezvous last night."

"Um, howdy. I'm Bill Benson, Glen's brother." Bill stepped forward and shook each of their hands, and when he got to Karen, he studied her face and recognized something there in the wolf he saw last night. "Was that you standing guard over me?"

Karen smiled and nodded her head.

"Thanks for not eating me."

She winked at him. "You're welcome. I probably wouldn't have liked it anyway. Georgia boys are supposed to be tough as gristle and leave a bitter aftertaste, right?"

Bill laughed along with everyone else, and he immediately relaxed. He told Glen, "I should've known you'd come out of this smelling like roses."

While Karen went up and stood next to Glen, Craig asked, "Would you care for some breakfast? We're having ham, eggs, toast, and juice."

Lisa added, "If you don't like what you see here, I can make something else. Pancakes perhaps?"

The sight of the spread currently on the table made Bill's stomach rumble and his mouth salivate. Werewolves vanished from his mind. "No, Ma'am. What you have here looks great. Thanks!" He pulled up a chair next to Glen while everyone else sat down too. He dug into the meal, serving himself double portions. He had a crazy thought they might be trying to fatten him up for later. *I'll just have to do some extra pushups tonight.*

Lisa sat back and gave Bill an appraising look. "Bill, I have to say that your dedication to your brother is astounding. Surrounded by four werewolves, you stood your ground. Under normal circumstances, that little clearing would have been rank with the smell of fear. It was still there, don't get me wrong, but I also smelled courage in a far greater quantity. It's rare to find such qualities in today's world."

Bill was slightly embarrassed but not so much as to show good manners. He told her around the food in his mouth, "He's my brother. Courage ain't a factor. He'd do the same for me."

Lisa nodded her head. "I am certain he would."

Bill was swallowing his second mouthful of food when he paused briefly and then hurried up and finished. He exclaimed, "Glen, whoa, you remember what happened last night?"

Glen grinned widely and nodded his head. "I was wondering when that was gonna hit you."

"How?"

Glen turned his chair to Bill and talked at breakneck speed, never taking a breath between sentences. "Craig called it *frenising*, that's Latin for keeping your shit in one sock and it's rare for a werewolf to be able to do that but everyone last night could but not all werewolves can and the nasty monsters in the movies are the ones that can't."

Craig asked, "Glen tells me he was infected by a werewolf in Georgia? A gentleman by the name of La'Man?"

Bill laughed. "'Gentleman,' yeah. Backstabbing bast—sonuvagun is what he was. There were two others, too."

"And you two by yourselves killed three *lupis*?"

"*Lupis*?"

"My apologies. That's Latin slang for werewolves."

"Yeah. They weren't that tough. Scary as hell, though." He stopped eating and nervously looked around at everyone. With a mouth of half-eaten food, he asked, "Are we in any kind of trouble over that?"

Craig chuckled and gently slapped the table. "Absolutely not. You defended yourselves. Of course, their pack might not be happy with you. I can make a call on your behalf, help smooth things over with them if you wish."

Bill finished chewing his food and Glen answered for the both of them. "Man, that'd be great. Thanks. We might actually get to visit home again."

Bill added, "Yeah, thanks."

Craig smiled. "Consider it done!"

Lisa smiled and stood up. "I'm sure you boys have a lot to discuss. Craig, Karen, and I will be on the back patio enjoying the morning. Feel free to join us when you're done eating."

Bill finished eating his third helping, let out a deep, rumbling belch, and pushed back from the table. "These guys don't fuck around when it comes to breakfast. I love smoked ham. That was better than Mom's I think." He pulled the toothpick from his Swiss Army Knife and picked at a piece of ham stuck between his teeth. "And they don't seem that bad of a bunch either."

Glen stopped grinning. "Bill, they're great. Last night...I remember everything. I remember you standing up to four werewolves...by yourself! That is always going to be my first memory of being a werewolf. A *lupus*. Thanks, bro."

"Why the serious look, Glen."

"Bill, I want you to join me. Be a *lupus*, too. We can live right here together." He pointed to each of the different doors around the loggia. "Those are bedrooms. Each one is as large as our entire downstairs back home, and we would each get one. Craig said we could stay here until we get a place of our own."

"You want me to be a werewolf? Are you nuts?"

"Bill, I was able to maintain control last night," Glen insisted. He placed his hand on Bill's shoulder. "You know what that means? I don't need you to chain me up anymore! I can change and know who I am, know who you are. You can do the same thing."

A hollow, cold breeze rushed through Bill's stomach at the thought of Glen no longer needing him. "I don't know, Glen."

"Craig said that as much time as you've been around me, you would probably be able to *frenis* pretty quick, too, because you know what to expect. You wouldn't be freaked out as much."

"Would I have to be chained up like you?" Bill remembered all the times he chained Glen up, and Glen was not happy about it. Bill didn't think he would be too happy about it either.

"Craig said no. See, he's the pack leader. We take his lead. He says he knows how to keep wildlings under control. That's what I was before last night, a wildling."

213

"Yeah, I saw how he kept you under control. He bitch-slapped the shit out of you."

"It didn't hurt. Werewolves are tough."

"Shit, bro. This is too weird. We meet four more werewolves, and they live in this nice-assed house and want to give us a room and feed us and shit? You know what Howie says, 'TANSTAAFL—There Ain't No Such Thing As A Free Lunch.' What's their angle?"

"I asked them that last night. We're all a family. We have to watch out for each other. This is my family now, Bill."

"I'm your brother, Glen!"

"And you'll always be that. But people move on. I belong here, and I want you here too."

"What would Howie say? Both of us? Hell, he freaked out when just one of us was a werewolf."

"You want to know what Howie would say? The same thing he always says. 'You're brothers. You need to watch out for each other.'" Glen refilled his glass of juice and downed it in one gulp. "I'll be on the back porch." He stood up and put one hand on his brother's shoulder again. "Bro, I need you on this. I'll do it without you if it comes to that, but it's really gonna suck."

Bill watched Glen walk out back. He sat at the table for a few more minutes before he got up and wandered over to the pool. He took his boots and socks off, rolled up his jeans, and sat down on the edge, dipping his feet into the water; he'd had his boots on twenty-four hours straight, and his feet were a little raw. The cool water was refreshing and cleared his mind.

The idea of losing Glen to another 'family' really hit home with him. He felt lonely just thinking about it. Bill was the older of the two, though only by one month, but they both naturally assumed he had all the answers. This time, it was Glen with all the answers. It was a strange feeling to see his *kid* brother making the transition from follower to leader.

He knew Howie's opinion had no bearing on the matter. Bill was the one who had to make it. Sure, Glen could change him anyway, but Glen wasn't that way. Craig and the others didn't seem that way either from what little he had seen of them.

He put his socks and boots back on and went out to the porch. "All right, bro, make me a werewolf. You still need me to watch out after your sorry ass."

Craig stood up. "Excellent news!"

Bill pointed a crooked grin at Craig. "Well, we'll see. I hope you don't regret letting us into your house. We're mostly house broken, but I can't guarantee we won't have the occasional accident."

Everyone laughed, stood up, and gave Bill big hugs.

Glen stepped back after his hug. "Thanks, man. We're gonna have a blast." He raised his hands, confused at what the next step was. "How do I do this?"

Craig looked embarrassed. "Unfortunately, you won't be able to right now. In time, you'll learn to control the change with more precision, but you currently don't possess the necessary skills. Bill, with your permission, however, I can perform the deed."

Bill clapped his hands together and put them on his hips. "Sure. Let's get it over with."

"Please remove your shirt and turn around." Bill took his shirt off, slightly embarrassed to do so in front of Karen and Lisa. Craig warned, "This might sting a bit."

If Bill had been a betting man, he would have bet Bertha that Craig raked a hot fire poker across his back. He tried to suppress a scream, but he let one out anyway. "Owwww, shit, man! You said sting, not burn like hell." He wondered how Glen managed to suppress the pain a year ago.

Glen put his hand on Bill's shoulder. "You all right, man?"

"My apologies, Bill," Craig offered. "That was the venom that passes the infection into your system. The pain will pass shortly."

True to his word, the pain disappeared completely before he had a chance to put his shirt back on. "So when do I become a werewolf? On the next full moon?"

"Yes," Lisa confirmed. "But you are a member of our pack now. Anything we can do to help you is yours for the asking." She and Karen gave Bill and Glen big hugs again. Craig shook their hands.

The first few weeks the boys spent on the estate were nice. Lisa liked to cook, so she always left something for them in the fridge to eat when she, Craig, and Karen left for the week on business. There were plenty of ponds and a few small lakes on the estate containing large bass and catfish, so the boys never ran out of things to do. The groundskeeper, Frank—also a werewolf—knew all of the nooks and crannies around there, so he was able to point the boys to the best fishing holes. They both liked Frank and found him to be a wealth of information about the Race in general and about how things worked there at the estate. Still, they weren't sure how far they would be able to push Craig's hospitality. Glen fried some catfish for a celebration supper on the evening after Bill's first *renovatio*, and it was then they brought it up with Craig.

"We've had all the fun we can handle," Glen began. "Y'all have been great, but we really need to start earning our own way. Our cash is going to run out eventually, and we can't hide out here for the rest of our lives."

Craig's response was mixed with surprise and admiration. "Already? I figured it would take you gentlemen about two months, not one."

"We've been working since we were fifteen," Bill explained. "We're just not used to this sitting around and playing all of the time."

Craig chuckled. "I understand. I truly do. It's good to see your father instilled a work ethic in you. A man has to find his own way in the world. But I have to ask, what are you qualified to do? You're too young to have too much experience, I think."

Glen spoke up first. "I'm pretty good at fixing things, engines and stuff. I'm thinking I might want to find a shop somewhere around here."

Bill murmered, and not without a bit of embarrassment, "The only thing I've ever been good at is being an outlaw."

Everyone laughed good-naturedly at Bill's comment, but Craig spoke up first. "Well, I'm sure you could find yourself a position with one of the local gangs, but I would prefer you found something more respectable. If you get caught by members of the law enforcement establishment, as all outlaws eventually do, they will follow your trail back here. As you can imagine, we don't need that kind of publicity.

"As for Glen, yes, I believe I know someone in Jacksonville, a member of the Race. He owns a marina and sells yachts to the rich and famous. I'm sure he has a position available in his repair shop. Would that satisfy your requirements?"

Glen smiled hugely. "Damned straight it would!"

"Excellent." Craig gently wiped the corners of his mouth with his napkin. "We'll make a call tomorrow and arrange a trip up there together for a personal introduction." Then his chin tensed up, and he said thoughtfully, "You, Bill, are going to be the interesting one." He placed his napkin on the table. "You used to grow cannabis, I believe, yes?"

Bill nodded his head with a shy grin. "Yeah, cannabis. Actually it was a hybrid of…" and then he lapsed into a detailed disquisition on the various intricacies of cross breeding different variants to achieve certain desired traits. Craig, Lisa, and Karen sat there through it all in stunned silence, their food cold because they had forgotten to eat it while Bill was lecturing.

Lisa enthusiastically broke the silence. "You need to talk to Frank!" she exclaimed. "He's been trying for years to cross breed some roses. He hasn't had much luck. He could probably learn a thing or two from you."

Bill's face turned a shade of shy pink. "Um, thanks, but we've already been talking about it. He was real close and would probably have figured it out eventually, but look for those blue roses you've been wanting next year."

Lisa's face brightened with delight.

Craig's Southern Gentleman veneer peeled back a trace, "You learned all this plant husbandry from growing pot?"

"Kinda. Actually, that and learning how to keep weeds and other trash plants from growing in our fields. Howie had the green thumb. I picked up quite a bit from him."

Glen piped in. "Yeah, Bill here's a wizard when it comes to making things grow. Our moms started taking his advice on how to keep our garden looking green from the time he was twelve."

Craig asked, "Your moms?"

Glen blurted between mouthfuls of food, "Yeah, we have different moms. Howie's our dad, though."

Craig raised his eyebrows. "Both of your mothers lived with your father at the same time?"

"Yeah," they both said in unison.

Craig's veneer peeled back a bit more. "You were raised on a commune?"

Both boys laughed and looked at each other with a private *here we go again* look. Bill explained, "I guess you could call it that, if living on a commune means working your asses off to keep each other fed. It wasn't all flower power and shit, though. Our dad just loved two women, and they both loved him. We aren't Mormon or anything like that. We're just folks."

Lisa and Karen sat there with wide eyes and closed mouths, holding their comments in check.

Craig deduced, "So you're half-brothers. Interesting. I would never have guessed it from looking at the two of you. You look like twins.

"In either case, I believe we can find you employment with any number of greenhouses in the area. They are always looking for someone with the proverbial green thumb."

Over the next six months, Bill and Glen learned about *Lupus sapiens* and the Pact. They also learned the differences between *frenatus* and *defrenatus*. One of the problems with being a wildling was stressful situations tended to bring out the animal. When that happened, a human or multiple humans usually died. Craig expressed his surprise on numerous occasions that Glen never had an episode during the whole year the boys were on the run.

Bill mimicked Marlin Perkins from *Mutual of Omaha's Wild Kingdom*, "Watch as we tame the wild beast with a small application of Howie Wowie."

While Glen laughed beer out through his nose, Craig said in a bored and monotone voice, "I suppose that's one way to do it."

A *grex* meeting was called during the boys' fourth month with the pack. The rest of the pack was already there when Bill and Glen roared up Craig's driveway in Bertha. James, the clan head, was there, too.

James stood up on a small pedestal and spoke to everyone. "Ken Wyman has violated the Pact. Last night, he got into a bar fight at the Sundowner on Orange Blossom Trail. He performed a *renovatio* and killed two people. He is currently at large somewhere in town. We don't know if he is currently *lupus* or human. In either case, we have to find him and get him back here."

Karen asked, "Is *Lucerna Veritatis* chasing him, too?"

"Probably." Craig turned to everyone else then. "Which means we have to keep our eyes open for them ourselves. We don't want a run-in with them."

A member of the *grex* that neither Bill nor Glen were familiar with asked, "Why don't you just shun him now and let them have him?"

Lisa answered, "We don't want to take the chance they're dragging their feet. We need to keep him from killing more humans. We don't need him showing up on the 11 o'clock news."

Another member they didn't know asked, "What do we do when we find him? Kill him?"

Bill and Glen stared wide-eyed at each other when that question was asked.

"No," James answered. "Only the Conclave can issue a kill order. We're to bring him back here. I'll deal with him. But if he attacks you when you try to bring him in, you are allowed to defend yourselves. The goal is to get him off the streets."

The pack hunted Ken Wyman over the next three days. He killed two more people before Frank discovered he was hiding out on the estate when he, himself, wasn't hunting. Craig and James tried to corral him, but he had turned full wildling and could not change back to human. He was in a constant state of bloodlust and attacked. They had no choice but to kill him.

"Just like hunting wild hogs," Glen remarked. "They always return to their lair after rootin' around all night."

"Yeah," Bill agreed. "I'm surprised we didn't think of it ourselves. You know, I never considered myself part animal until now." Bill thought about the wildling in him. "I hope I learn to *frenis* soon. I don't want to get caught up in the same shit Ken did."

Glen grinned. "Fuck that, dude, you'll be fine. Besides, do you realize what this means? We got a lair!"

Bill didn't return the smile. "Yeah. Cool."

Craig showed the boys a newspaper article from the *Orlando Sentinel* the next morning at breakfast. Buried back on page fourteen they read:

November 6, 1978

Officials at the Central Florida Zoo were investigating Friday the specifics on how a lion escaped its enclosure and was allowed to roam free for four days, killing four people in downtown Orlando.

The zoo's big cat wrangler, Harris Ottoman, said a female African lion walked through an opening in the rear of her enclosure. "We're lucky the rest of her pride didn't follow her."

The 10-year-old lion had to be put down as is the law when a wild animal attacks a human.

Two months later, Bill woke up from a night hunt with the realization he remembered everything that happened the night before. He had made conscious decisions. He had learned to *frenis*. He was now *frenatus*. He and Glen celebrated with the largest torpedo they could roll.

Bill and Glen continued to visit Craig's estate every other weekend or so to go fishing, in addition to their monthly visits during the full moon. A few months after Bill learned to *frenis*, Craig caught them before they took off across the estate and called them into his office.

He got right to the point. "I've done some checking and it turns out La'Man and his two compatriots were doing a little mercenary work on the side. The pack is not connected with this Lordy Gang you were referring to. In fact, no one else in their pack is associated with the Lordy Gang either. Officially."

Glen scratched behind his ear. "What do you mean? La'Man always said that was who he represented."

"He was an independent contractor, doing things for the highest bidder. He may have simply implied such a connection to lend credence to his position with you."

Bill frowned and started popping his knuckles in rapid succession, a nervous habit his moms repeatedly tried to break him of. "If it wasn't the Lordy Gang who tried to kill us, then who the fuck was it?"

Glen shouted, "Yeah, it had to be him! He shook down our family!"

Craig explained. "Oh, it was the Lordy Gang who tried to have you killed. There is no doubt about that if my sources are to be trusted. But they didn't want to get their hands dirty. They hired La'Man to find out where your field was, kill you, and return with the information."

Bill and Glen shared a shy grin. This was interesting information. Bill asked, "Wait, the Lordy Gang is a bunch of humans?"

"Correct."

Bill and Glen shouted in unison, "Road Trip!"

Craig grinned cruelly. "I thought you would find that information useful," he acknowledged with a smirk. "Do I have to remind you that you are not allowed to do anything that brings down the ire of the humans? Doing so would be a pact violation, leaving you subject to being declared *Lupus solitarius*."

"We got it, Chief!" Glen shouted over his shoulder. "We're just going to visit our parents. That's all."

Craig shouted to an empty doorway, "Have a safe journey!"

Howie pulled his head out from under the hood of the family station wagon, wiping his greasy hands on a rag as the boys roared up into the yard, honking Bertha's horn. He smiled and hugged them both as soon as their boots hit dirt. "Sure is good to see you, boys! How you been?"

"Hangin' in there. You know," Bill answered for the both of them.

The rest of the Benson family stampeded across the porch and down the steps. "Bill! Glen! They're here! They're here!"

The boys spent the next hour and a half getting two years' worth of kisses and hugs.

Howie stood over the campfire, poking at the dying embers with a long stick. The smell of burning oak was pungent. "So, let me get this straight. You are both werewolves now. You can control your change. And you've joined a pack of other werewolves."

Bill nodded his head. Glen took a toke off of his doobie and sat back against a large rock.

Howie asked, "So you could turn into one right now if you wanted? Bullshit."

Bill didn't say anything. He simply stood up and performed a partial *renovatio*; he didn't want to ruin his clothes. He extended his arms, released his culas, and fully transformed his head.

Standing before Howie was a horrific chimera out of some deep and dark nightmare. He stumbled back and fell on his butt, dropping his stick and kicking up leaves and dirt as he tried to scramble away from the monster standing in front of him.

Glen laughed darkly. "That shit even looks creepy to me, bro. Stop it before you give the old man a fuckin' heart attack."

Bill changed back to human.

Howie stood up and yelled, "Don't ever pull that shit again! You fuckin' hear me? I'll fuckin' blow your goddamned head clean fuckin' off, son or not!"

Chastised, Bill hung his head. "Sorry, Howie. I didn't think it would be that scary if you knew it was me."

"Yeah, well—" Howie settled down some. "Just—just give me a bit of fuckin' warning next time, okay?"

Bill plopped down next to Glen. "You're right. You're right. I got cocky."

Howie sat back down and pulled a rolled doobie out of his shirt pocket. It took him three or four tries to get it lighted because his hands were shaking so much. After taking a deep toke and blowing the smoke out, he asked, "So what are y'all doing back home? Sounds like you got a decent gig down there."

Acid dripped from Glen's voice. "We're going after Lordy. He tried to have us killed."

Bill added. "And he put his hands on our moms. That fucker signed his death warrant when he did that."

Howie raised his eyebrows in disbelief. "You two are going to take out the Lordy Gang?"

Glen answered, "Naw. We're just goin' after Lordy, and we're gonna let it be known that if whoever takes his place ever fucks with the Bensons again, they're gonna get the same treatment."

Bill saw that version of his brother more and more these days.

Glen the Man assured Howie, "Dad, we're here to fix what we fucked up."

Howie nodded his head. "Good." He stood up and pulled an army-issue field knife out from under his shirt. The boys knew it wasn't Howie's because it didn't have a pot plant carved in the handle. He threw it at a tree and it sank two inches into the wood with a loud *ka-chunk*, quivering back and forth. "And when you do, I want you to plant that in his fuckin' skull."

The Lordy Gang came into existence when a group of friends from the Korean War returned home in 1953. They started out as a motorcycle club, but were enticed by the easy money of muling drugs under contract for a much larger gang out of Miami called the Miami Boys. The president of the club, Bob Lordy, didn't like the hard stuff, but didn't turn down the offer to protect a shipment if it came his way.

The Miami Boys and the Lordy Gang eventually came to blows, as happens anytime two or more people are involved with drugs, money, and guns. The Lordy Gang found themselves out-maneuvered, substantially outgunned, and in debt to the Miami Boys with no way to pay up.

Enter the Bensons.

Bob Lordy and Howie knew each other from the war. When Lordy started his club he wanted Howie with him, but Howie didn't want anything to do with any kind of organized group. It smacked too much like government to him. After Korea, he just wanted to be left alone. Lordy knew Howie and his boys, Bill and Glen, maintained a well-organized pot growing business to the north of Atlanta. The way he saw it, if he could take over the fields, he could cut the Miami Boys in for some of the action and get them off his club's back. There was just one problem—other than Howie being his friend. Those Bensons were sneaky bastards. Lordy and his boys had tried in the past to follow them around but couldn't maintain a tail on them. Then he had a meeting with La'Man.

Lordy didn't really like blacks. He didn't trust them. But business is business and La'Man had the relationship with the Bensons. La'Man had been supplying him with the Bensons' Howie Wowie for years. Like all pushers, La'Man was an easy sucker for cash.

Lordy believed he had sold his soul to the devil when he hired La'Man to kill Bill and Glen and lead him to their field, but he also knew he didn't have much choice. What Bob Lordy didn't expect was that Bill and Glen would take after their father so damned much; they may not have been in the Army, but they still fought like demons on the battlefield. They left La'Man pig speared four feet up in a tree, for God's sake, and left the rest of his crew headless in the woods. Lordy wasn't sure if that was a message or not, but it certainly got his attention. He was going to have to get serious with those boys himself. Unfortunately, they escaped Georgia for parts unknown. The cops never did find out who did it, and Lordy didn't feel obliged to tell them.

Lordy was getting desperate by this time. Without the payment that was due the Miami Boys in a couple of weeks, he and his whole gang would be shot dead in the streets if they so much as showed their faces. Lordy had no choice but to go to Howie himself and take the fields from him by force, so he and his gang *visited* the Bensons late one night. He slapped Howie, Carol, and Betty around in front of the children and left Howie with the not-so-subtle hint of burning their house down around their ears if he didn't cooperate. Howie gave up the location to Daffodil and Unicorn. One was already compromised, and the other one was in a fallow phase, so it wasn't much of a loss. He didn't feel an overriding need to divulge the existence of his other half-dozen fields.

Before he left, Lordy took his army issue field knife and cut a lock of hair from Carol and Betty. Then he stuck the knife in the mantle above the

Bensons' fireplace as a reminder of his visit.

Bill and Glen spent the next several weeks watching Lordy, finding out when he was alone, what his schedule was, looking for an opportune time to make their move. It was hard to do this during the day; there were too many people around who might see them. However, at night they could change to *lupis* and prowl at their leisure. They were hunters of the highest order, and hiding in shadows and moving silently was what nature intended them to do. They found they liked it.

Lordy had a paranoid mind; his schedule changed quite a bit, and he rarely took the same route to wherever he was going. However, he only frequented about a dozen or so different locations. One of them was the apartment of a cute little blonde woman he visited either on Tuesday or Sunday nights. He may have visited her on other nights, but these were the only two nights they witnessed him going there. The boys knew when he was going to see her because he wouldn't wear his floppy, jungle hat, and none of his compatriots would make the ride with him. If he left his house without that hat, he was headed to Irene's.

Luckily for them, her apartment was on the first floor. They decided to take him there, inside the apartment. Outside was out of the question—the front of the apartment was too well-lighted. Irene wouldn't be a problem, but they didn't want to kill her because she was an innocent in this. The apartment did have a rear, sliding-glass door that opened up into some woods about fifty feet away, but she kept it locked. It wasn't going to be easy to get into the apartment without making a ruckus. That was their only concern.

Glen asked, "Do you think we could lure him out the back and into the woods?"

Bill sounded doubtful. "I don't know. He's pretty fuckin' paranoid."

Glen concluded, "Could be why he's still alive after all of these years."

More to himself than Glen, Bill asked, "What would get you out there?"

Glen smiled. "If I was a gang leader without my gang? Not a fuckin' thing." He tried to imagine himself as Lordy. "If someone was coming in the front door and I knew a pistol wouldn't stop them, I'd head to the woods."

Bill shot that idea down. "Dude, if we're gonna scare him out the back, we might as well bust in the door and take him then."

Glen nodded his head in agreement.

Bill suddenly brightened, "Bro! You solved it for the most part."

"How?"

Bill explained. "Me in front, you in the back. I knock on the door. If he opens it, I change and attack. If he runs out the back, you're waiting there for him. In either case, we've got him boxed in."

Glen brightened this time. "Just like our hunts where we herd the prey. Way to go, bro!" Then he got thoughtful again. "What about Irene? She's probably gonna scream bloody murder."

"We just gotta be quick. No fiddle-fartin' around."

Glen worked the problem out in his head. "You forgot one minor detail. We'll have to leave an extra set of clothes in the woods."

"Yeah, good point," Bill admitted.

On the nights Lordy was visiting Irene, he didn't leave until morning. They would have all night. They didn't want to knock on the door too late—that would certainly raise too much suspicion—but they had to wait late enough that the area would mostly be devoid of human life. Lordy and Irene typically finished having sex around eleven o'clock. The snoring commenced about five minutes later. Those five minutes were their window of opportunity.

Bill knocked on Irene's front door, listening for what was going on inside. His *lupus* senses were marvelous. The smell of reefer was rife even through the door, and he could hear everything going on inside the apartment.

"Bobby, wake up!" Irene griped. "Someone's at the door."

Lordy's soft snore broke in half and he asked, "Wha—?"

"Someone's at the door!"

"Well, go answer it. It's your fuckin' door, not mine."

Bill knocked a few more times. *Knock! Knock! Knock! Knock! Knock!*

Irene complained, "Nobody knocks on a door this late at night around here."

"Fuck!" Lordy bellowed. He rolled out of the bed and it released an appreciative squeak. "This place better be burning to the ground, or someone's gettin' their ass kicked." The echoes of clothes rustling and a zipper running closed reached Bill's ears, and the thuds of Lordy's bare feet stomping up the hallway reverberated like clubs on a barrel. That was Bill's cue.

He took a quick look around the area and didn't see anyone. The door to the apartment flew open and Lordy yelled, "Wha—?" just as Bill finished performing his *renovatio*.

Robert Edward Lordy, President of the Lordy Motorcycle Club, slowly moved his gaze from Bill's chest up into the lupine snarl of something out of a nightmare. Bill raised his black lips in a snarl, showing off white fangs dripping with saliva.

Lordy wet his pants and opened his mouth to scream, but he had no air in his lungs, and he was too frozen to take a breath. Bill didn't waste time; he lunged forward and snatched Lordy by the throat, picking him up like he was a rag doll.

Irene called from down the hall, "Bobby, everything okay?"

Bill needed to get out the back quickly before Irene decided she should come down the hallway. He ran across the living room to the back door, without dropping Lordy, who was now clawing at Bill's arm with fear and panic as his crushed windpipe prevented air from making that oh so short of a trip into his lungs. Bill released some of the pressure, allowing Lordy to breathe, but not enough to drop him; he wanted Lordy alive to see what was coming. Bill's talons scratched the locking mechanism of the door when he released the catch.

Glen was already *lupus* when Bill stepped out into the backyard. They both loped to the woods where Glen handed the knife to Bill. Bill set Lordy down just enough for his feet to rest on the ground, allowing him to ease his grip on Lordy's neck a bit more so he wouldn't pass out. Recognition instantly dawned on Lordy's face, and his eyes widened even further in panic as he watched his own knife slip deep into his forehead. He was dead before Bill threw him back toward the building.

They were deep into the woods before Irene came into the living room to investigate the rummaging around she heard. Her screams wailed from the open sliding glass door as they found their clothes.

They went straight to their room as soon as they got home. Through unspoken agreement, they both knew they would never do something like that again. It wasn't that Craig would be upset with them. They were allowed quite a bit of leeway as long as the Pact wasn't violated. It was just that there's a fine line between murder and killing, and in their estimation they tiptoed along it that night. They knew they would forever have to keep the beast on a tight leash and away from that line.

The Atlanta Constitution, May 3, 1979, Page 4

A west Atlanta man was found brutally murdered last night by his girlfriend behind her home. Robert Edward Lordy was found with his own Army issue field knife embedded in his forehead.

Preliminary findings indicate a large man with uncut fingernails originally tried to strangle him. Mr. Lordy appears to have fought off that attack and was then stabbed in the head.

Atlanta police are asking for help in locating the murderer. Lt. Tony Womack said, "A 7' tall man with the strength to drive a knife into a man's skull should be easy to find."

Bill stared at the phone. The bell inside was still ringing from when he slammed the hand piece into the cradle, hanging up on Aaron. He yelled, "Fuck! Not again!"

He ran out to the garage to where Glen was working on Bertha. "Man, I got some weird-assed news just now."

Glen squinted up from the carburetor. "What?"

Bill told him what Aaron said on the phone. "I'm not gonna kill someone again, man. I ain't gonna fuckin' do it! Especially Aaron."

"Bill, what the fuck are we gonna do? If Craig finds out you done talked to Aaron, you know he's gonna shit a brick."

Bill shook his head lightly. "Honestly, I'm more afraid of Lisa finding out than I am Craig. She's the one with the balls in that family. Let's just keep our fuckin' mouths shut. We'll be okay."

Chapter 34—Sequentia: Forma

noun [sē-kwən'-shə:()fŏrm'-ə]
1. Continuation: Form, shape, fashion, plan, mold.

Aaron Darveau, June 12, 1983

Aaron didn't get the information he wanted out of Bill, but he did learn something interesting. The entire ruling class didn't know what was going on. They might control the Race, but only a few of them had influence with the Fectors. The rest were too afraid to ask too many questions it seemed. He wasn't getting any help from them right now. It was going to take one of them getting shunned before he had an ally.

Or a new head on the snake.

Then something Stalker Three said fluttered back into Aaron's memory. "*Whoever heard of a* frenator *being shunned?*"

Butterflies fluttered around in his stomach because he was so excited. He didn't catch it then, but things fell into place, made sense. *Does that mean they don't shun frenatus? What would they do if all of the wildlings could frenis? The whole purpose for having the frenatus, the ruling class, was to rule over the wildlings. How hard would it be to teach ten thousand wildlings to frenis? Would this be a better solution than a vaccine against the virus and letting the Race die off?* Aaron considered that near-fantasy, but he didn't dismiss it outright. He would have to think on it some more—when he wasn't running for his life.

Cutting off the head of the snake was beginning to look more and more like the only answer, but this snake had many heads. Aaron didn't think he could handle Craig, Lisa, Karen, and any other *lupis* who were at the estate at once. He needed to separate them.

Craig and Lisa usually left on Sunday nights for business trips leaving Karen alone with just the house staff—a minimum of one maid, possibly two. And Frank. Frank was usually out on the grounds at night keeping an eye on things. Aaron didn't think Frank would be a problem. He handled three Fectors easily enough. He wondered if he could handle Karen and maybe two additional *lupis*. Assuming he managed to kill all three, one of them was the incoming *Lupa Reginam*. He would never be able to live a normal life again—not that being a werewolf permitted that anyway. You don't kill Princess Diana and then sit down for a pint of ale.

Aaron was halfway to Craig's before he surprised himself by realizing he was actually going there to kill Karen.

Chapter 35—Non Evitabilis
noun [nän()e'-və-tə-bil-is]
1. Unavoidable

Aaron Darveau, June 12, 1983

Aaron pulled up to Craig's house. He cautiously got out of the car and took the time to survey the area, letting the breezes bring any scents and sounds to him. The woods were quiet tonight. He tried to remember if they were usually that quiet and decided that perhaps they were. He wasn't picking up any scents other than what was normal—old swamp, mud, and rank water. He did detect two other scents, and they came from the direction of the house—Karen's and Maria's. This was good news. Karen's scent was relaxed, confident, and expectant; she was waiting on someone to arrive. He needed to hurry before that someone got there. He told Elwood to wait in the car.

Aaron went up to the house and rang the doorbell. Karen opened the door and flashed those same cold, dead eyes he remembered from a month ago at him. "I was wondering how long it would take you to show up," she sneered at him.

Aaron was taken aback. He expected to do the surprising, not be surprised.

"You'll have to excuse me for not inviting you in," she sneered. "Craig doesn't really like *Lupus solitarius* sullying up his house. He doesn't believe they're housebroken."

Wounded by her tone, he responded as brutally as he could. "That's fine. As often as you go into heat, I don't want to find myself performing stud services this evening."

She turned red with rage. *Score one for Aaron.* "I know it was you who sent the Fectors and not Craig. I found the picture you gave them on their dead bodies. Why didn't you give me the time promised?"

She recovered quickly and laughed. Strangely, it reminded him of an ice cube dropping into a glass. "Why do you think? Haven't you figured it out yet? Damn, Aaron. I knew you were dense, but I didn't think you were slow, too. *Lupus sapiens* is a matriarchy. It has been for over five centuries. The men rule at our convenience. Anytime a male shows any kind of self-determination, he has to be gotten rid of. He's not only shunned, he's culled. And you are probably the most dangerous male to come along in generations."

"I'm dangerous? Why?" Aaron asked.

"Your will…it's…it's too strong," she reluctantly revealed, shaking her head. "You can't be controlled."

"Oh, you mean I won't murder to keep you in satin sheets and silk panties, right? Did you really think you could control me?"

"I should have known better," she snapped as she unconsciously reached up and checked the topmost button on her shirt, making sure it was fastened. "Lisa warned me about you."

"Then why didn't you leave me be? I guess your intuition was off a bit, wasn't it?"

"No, my intuition was correct. Is correct. You would make a great *Lupus Rex*. But your will has to be linked to mine. You want to do things your way. If you aren't willing to do things the way I need them done, then you're unacceptable."

"Your way would turn me into a murderer. I'm not a murderer, Karen!"

"Aaron, we're all murderers. You killed those three Fectors. They didn't stand a chance against you. You could have run, but you didn't. You chose to hunt them down and kill them. You sure didn't do it out of self-defense."

The facts as she recited them may have indicated as much, but Aaron knew the true answer was to be found much deeper. It was more complicated than that. He led the Fectors there. Yes, that was true. But that was so he would stand a fighting chance against them. If he had waited for them to come to him, they might have killed him in his sleep. That didn't matter, though. He was done talking. Karen might not have known it, but Aaron knew why he was here. He had to put a stop to this. It was time to bring the temple down. It was time to kill Karen.

"Then you should have had help here watching out for me. You know what I'm here to do." He performed a *renovatio*.

"Oh, I do. And I do…" she purred with a voice as thick as honey.

Aaron picked up the smell of wood, leather, and oiled iron all around him.

Aaron's *lupus* realized he was in a tight spot and wanted control. "***You really need to let me handle this***," it growled. This was the first time he could recall his new instinctive nature, his *lupus*, trying to save him, because he hadn't experienced this level of danger before. He turned control over to it. Although he was conscious of his actions, directed them, it still reminded him of his dreams with the black dog.

Aaron turns around as he hears the door slam behind him. He doesn't pay it any attention. He is concentrating on the dozen Fectors he senses around him, around the yard, hiding in the woods. He momentarily wonders why he didn't detect them earlier.

Shit! Why didn't I check the area around me more carefully? Rushing in without thinking is going to get me killed.

Aaron's confusion is interrupted by a sharp pain on the left side of his chest. He looks down and sees a hole. He then sees a few more holes appear in various parts of his body. He falls to the ground. He's dying. The holes bleed some and then stop as deformed bullets are extruded from his wounds. His ripped flesh seals up, and the pain is no more.

Brother Clarence

Brother Clarence had been looking forward to tonight for the past year, waiting for the opportunity to take down one of these howlers, one of Satan's Spawn, ever since he completed his training. He had finally been picked for a mission—they were going after one of the deadliest howlers the Lamp of Truth had faced in decades, possibly since William Stoddard, the architect of The Calamity. This one killed three from his Order last night. One of them, Brother Hank, had gone through training with him. Brother Hank had only been along as lookout, but the howler killed him too. Brother Clarence was looking for some payback.

He waited in the tree line and watched the howler get out of its car and stand there looking around the area for any danger. He and the rest of his brothers were told these new blankets would mask their scent, but they weren't taking any chances; they brought the whole monastery. He wasn't sure how the blankets worked, but they did appear to be doing their job. The howler went right up to the front door and knocked on it, never indicating they were detected.

The two howlers, the one they were hunting and the queen bitch, were arguing about something, but he couldn't make it out. Didn't matter. What did dogs usually argue about that mattered to men? Suddenly, the blue light flashed, signaling everyone to prepare themselves. He pulled his blanket off and took up position with his rifle. He was to make the first shot with a silver round. Everyone knew this howler might not be allergic to silver, but it didn't hurt to be prepared; the silver round was also blessed by Father Ignacio. But God worked in mysterious ways, and it was possible Brother

Clarence would miss. Everyone was waiting on him to make the first shot. Then they would follow up with their own blessed silver rounds. It was suggested everyone should fire at the same time, but they didn't have the means to coordinate that and were afraid someone would shoot too soon, ruining the ambush.

The howler turned as the door slammed and masked itself in Satan's clothing. That was his cue to shoot. Brother Clarence said a silent prayer and squeezed the trigger, but the bullet failed to find its mark. The howler had grown a couple of feet from the time he took his bead on its human head and the time he pulled the trigger. He chambered another round as a dozen more shots joined his, breaking the silence.

The howler dropped to the ground. Everyone watched it. This was too easy. Then it leapt back up and looked at Brother Clarence's hiding spot. *Impossible! Nothing could survive that many shots!* He squeezed the trigger again, and wooden shards sprayed from the door, from his shot and the shots from the others hiding in the woods. The howler wasn't standing on the door step anymore.

Brother Clarence's last thoughts were about his sister and parents back home. He hoped they would have a good harvest this year. He looked up after chambering another round and saw the howler swipe its right hand at him. *My, what big claws you have.*

Father Ignacio

The howler dropped to all fours and ran across the yard toward Brother Clarence. It was fast, and it was tough, and its recovery time was amazing. He waved his blue light in a circle signaling everyone to move to the open safety of the yard. You don't hunt howlers in the woods. In the open, he and his monks stood a chance. In the woods, they stood no chance at all. He'd been training the monasteries in North America for the last fifty years, and that was one rule you never broke.

He was too old to go on the hunting parties these days, but this was an important kill. He flew down with his own team from Chicago to personally lead the assault. This was the next *Lupus Rex*, shunned because it wouldn't abide by the truce, not that the truce mattered to the Order. Father Ignacio planned on breaking it himself following Aaron's Ascension; any truce made with Satan is no truce at all. It's surrender to heresy. Father Ignacio planned to do what he swore an oath to do, make nice with whomever or whatever was required so as to gather intelligence, and use it to prepare for war where he kills every *lupis* he can find. Those fifty years were surely needed to rebuild the Order after the Calamity too. Stoddard left it in shambles. Now it was almost time for the counter-offensive.

But he wasn't expecting Aaron Darveau to get shunned. That was something no one expected. It presented an opportune time to move his timetable up a year. Once Aaron was dealt with, Karen was next on his list. That stupid queen bitch invited them onto her property willingly. She was in for a nasty surprise.

Father Phillip, commander of the Chicago Monastery and currently second in command, ran up to him. "Father, what are your orders?"

"Prayer circle."

Research showed howlers had a hard time detecting a certain shade of blue light at night. Father Phillip relayed the command using his modified flashlight by flashing the beam in a specific pattern everyone was trained to pay attention to. His command was spread through the ranks, and he watched as the remaining monks, twelve of them, formed a large circle in the front yard, facing outward. Every second man dropped his rifle and pulled a sword. Every third man dropped his rifle and picked up a pig spear.

An ear splitting howl pierced the night air as they finished executing the maneuver, but Father Ignacio couldn't tell where it originated from. It seemed to come from all around them. The howl diminished in intensity and he shivered.

They were now the hunted.

Aaron Darveau

Aaron took a split second to look at the man he just killed. They were about the same age. He was dressed like the Fectors from last night, though. Smelled like them, too—dead. This made four men dead by Aaron's hands and his hands alone. He comforted himself by reliving the evil he saw in Karen's eyes, a look he was afraid would haunt him his entire life. He knew if he didn't finish what he started tonight, he would never have the opportunity again. He silently apologized to the man at his feet and then looked inward to his *lupus*. It knew what to do.

He unleashed it.

Aaron, though still directing its actions, felt like an outsider who was watching the events unfold. The *lupus* would make a suggestion and Aaron would do it. Right now, the *lupus* wanted to hunt, so Aaron howled. He instinctively knew prey always, *always*, relied on a fight or flight reaction. His

233

howl was one he knew would cause his prey to run in the opposite direction, to look for a hiding place. Unfortunately, he was hunting men trained to fight *lupis*. They wouldn't run. They would stand and fight. But they would know they were now the prey and that Aaron was the predator.

He examined the area, gauging his prey's location. They were all moving toward the front yard leaving none in his immediate vicinity. He crouched down behind a large bush and watched them form up. They were circling the wagons. Not all of them had rifles. Some had swords and some had long spears, pig spears from the looks of them. He'd seen pig spears before and knew he needed to stay away from them.

All chains have a weak link. Aaron let his senses work for him, telling him where the weak link was in the circle facing him. He found two. One of them originated with a tall man on the far side; he was old and weak. The closer one was right in front of where he was hiding, about twenty yards. *A trap?* He didn't know, but it was still his best bet. He leapt.

Father Ignacio

Father Ignacio recited a prayer, strengthening the resolve of his flock. The howler was certainly on the hunt. He had been hunting these evil beasts for fifty years, and he knew if they didn't run out and engage you right away, they were stalking you. He really preferred to know where they were located, and right now, he didn't.

The howler attacked as he finished his prayer. It leapt from where Brother Clarence died. He didn't expect that—the howler didn't move after making a kill. It didn't stalk around looking for further prey. It stayed at its last know location. This was just a puppy—a puppy with fangs that could rip a man's head off and talons that could rip through plywood, but a puppy nonetheless. This was good information.

He passed the word to Father Phillip with his flashlight. "Bear Witness."

Father Phillip returned a questioning gaze. *Bear Witness* meant they were to open their ranks and let the howler into the circle. There, they would surround it, perhaps long enough for a spear or two to find its mark. Experienced howlers never fell for the trap, but usually only experienced howlers were able to *frenis*. This one must be overconfident because it learned to *frenis* before it gained that experience.

Father Ignacio simply nodded his head and restated his command verbally, "Bear Witness, Father Phillip."

Father Phillip passed the command to the group, and he watched as the howler gutted two of his men while the rest of them opened the circle to allow it access. The monks on either side of the two casualties did as they were trained to do. They didn't attack, but instead stepped out of the circle to each side of the howler, feinting jabs at it. The howler in turn moved into the circle. The two men who risked their lives by leaving the circle then moved back in to close it.

Father Ignacio passed his command to Father Phillip, "Hail Mary, Full of Grace."

Aaron Darveau

Aaron dodged two attacks from Fectors who left the safety of the circle. He knew others were behind him, but his senses told him they weren't closing. He had a few seconds of reaction time, which would be plenty, but once he stepped back, the two Fectors moved in and closed the circle. Aaron was surrounded.

He asked his *lupus*, "*How did this happen?*"

His *lupus* grinned. "**What do you care?**" it asked. "**Now you have them where they want you!**" That line sounded awfully close to something Kirk would say.

Aaron sensed the weak spot that originated from the tall man across the circle disappear. It wasn't weak anymore. It was commanding. The Fectors with spears closed in on him, and they were smart about it too, because they didn't close in a staggered formation; they rushed in together. Aaron figured they either had extensive training, or they were using some sort of silent command structure. Or both. In either case, he needed to think rationally about the fight. He told his *lupus*, "*I'll take it from here.*" His *lupus* was good at killing, but Aaron had the advantage of Tai Chi; it gave him the ability to think strategically and tactically under stress. He knew he should have gotten out of this by leaping over and out of the circle, but that time had passed. It was time to fight, and it was kill or be killed.

Father Ignacio

The spear holders rushed the howler. Father Ignacio knew it would be dead shortly, because it had lost its chance to leap out of the circle. He said a silent prayer for the soul about to complete its descent into darkness. He normally prayed with his eyes closed, but he was a soldier too. He kept them open so as to better watch the battle unfold before him.

He was astonished. The howler moved in a fashion similar to an Asian marital artist. It ducked and pushed and deflected the spears, and each time it did, the infernal beast slipped along the spear's length and gutted the wielder. Three spear handlers lay dead at its feet! Under other circumstances he would have been impressed, but these were *his* men dying.

He considered ordering his men to shoot, ignoring any potential crossfire accidents, but the last spear handler scored a hit. Unfortunately, it wasn't a center-mass hit, a hit to the torso—it was only a leg. This did slow the cursed beast down though, and two men with swords came running up to finish the job.

Suddenly, Father Phillip cried out in pain, "Father, help me!"

Father Ignacio looked over at Father Phillip. He was lying on the ground with a large black dog standing over him, gnawing at his neck. Father Ignacio raised his sword and rushed over to the dog but was knocked down by one of the other brothers who was also rushing to Father Phillip's aid.

"God dammit, get the howler! I'll handle the dog!" He knew he would be paying penance this weekend for taking the Lord's name in vain. But that was later.

He scrambled to his feet and swung his sword at the dog. "In the name of the Father, I send you back to hell, Satan Spawn Familiar!"

It wasn't a solid strike, but the cursed familiar cried out in pain, releasing Father Phillip from its grasp. It didn't matter. He was already dead. The howler let loose another howl in response to its familiar's cry. Father Ignacio snapped around and watched his men falter as the *vagor* dug deep into their psyche, telling them to run and hide. He gave the order to fire the rifles, but the order turned to a gurgle as the black dog ripped his throat out. He had already told his men to concentrate on the howler, so none of them saw him go down under the familiar's fangs. Father Ignacio weakly reached for his dagger, the same one from his induction ceremony, but it was pinned underneath him, and he couldn't grasp the handle.

The last thing he saw as the familiar bit into his neck was the howler jerking the spear from the monk's hands, ripping it from its leg, and swinging it around in a circle.

Aaron Darveau

The black blur of Elwood jumped onto the tall man, taking him down to the ground. Aaron tore the spear from his leg and swung it in a circle, striking those nearest to him. His last howl sent the Fectors into disarray and gave him the precious time he needed to recover his bearings. His *lupus* begged to be turned loose, so he let it. He underestimated the Fectors and almost lost his life for the mistake. He hoped he wouldn't underestimate them again.

An intense euphoria engulfed him as he tasted the first blood of the evening. Jajine's voice was strangely absent from his thoughts.

Craig Minor, June 13, 1983

Craig pulled into his driveway and surveyed the landscape of death before him. The rancid smell of a dozen mutilated bodies overwhelmed his nose, and his confused stomach threatened to wash vomit up and over his tongue. Normally, *Lupis sapiens* would feel their bloodlust rise when around such carnage, but this was different. This wasn't a killing field; this was a charnel house. A dozen humans, Fectors, were lying dead around his yard. Injuries were hard to determine without examining each one, but a cursory glance showed they were violent. Primitive. *Lupus* did this. He was confused why the Fectors would be at his house, but he knew a Fector swarm when he saw one. *They stay away from here. They have* Lupis solitarius *to hunt.* Whoever they encountered here didn't appreciate their presence one little bit. He knew Karen had a temper, but he didn't think she, Maria, and Frank would be capable of this. If Karen did do it, she had to have had help. He couldn't tell who though; the smell of the dead was too overwhelming.

Frank underestimated the damage when he phoned earlier that morning. *"Mr. Minor, you need to come home. There's been an accident."*

"What is it, Frank?"

"I…it's family business, Boss. You need to come home now."

Well, Frank was wrong. This was no accident. This was a massacre.

Craig strode up to his front door. Lisa had a neutral expression on her face. She was good at hiding her emotions, even from him, but he'd learned when she had that look, she was in turmoil. She was holding back her *lupa*. He turned back to his front door and saw what killed these Fectors. His knees went weak, and the wildling from his past whined in fear.

Scratched across the door were the crossed cula marks of *Lupus solitarius*. That was a calling card he would never forget. He didn't need Lisa's intuition to know it would not be the last time he saw it either.

He quickly opened the door and met Frank coming out to meet them. He looked back at the front yard. "Frank, what the fuck happened here?"

Frank fidgeted a moment before answering. "Aaron showed up here last night, Boss."

Craig turned around to face him. "Aaron? Why?"

"I don't know. I just know when I got here early this morning, it was like this."

"Then how do you know he was here last night?"

"I met him as he was leaving."

Craig concentrated on the scents. *There it is, Aaron's scent. Oh, Karen, what have you done? You went behind my back and called the Fectors out yourself, didn't you?* "Aaron did this? By himself?"

"I think so," Frank hinted thoughtfully, looking around the yard. "He told me he did it, and there were no other *lupis* in the area, so I had no reason to doubt him. Mr. Minor, you need to go inside. Karen, she's—"

Craig didn't wait for Frank to finish his sentence. He rushed inside and pulled up short when he got to the courtyard. Maria's body floated face down in the pool, and her blood had reddened the water so much it was pink. As he rushed toward Karen's room, Lisa ran past him.

Aaron Darveau, June 12, 1983

Aaron surveyed the carnage scattered around his feet. Part of him was sad, but his *lupus* was in pure bloodlust. The blood drunk and the smell of dead humans kept the madness fueled. He understood how wildlings went crazy with the killing. It could be addicting if you didn't have the willpower to overcome it. It *was* addicting. Right now, he didn't want to overcome it. He had a job to do, and he needed the madness to help him.

He ran for the front door as fast as his wounded leg would allow, but it was latched and refused to yield to his grip. All the doors here at the estate were solid oak. He could probably break it in, but it would take time. He jumped onto the roof and ran over to the courtyard—it was open to the sky. He jumped down next to the pool, his partially lame leg giving slightly, and used his *lupus* senses to search for Karen and Maria. Maria was in human form standing before Karen's door.

"You should leave, Aaron. She doesn't want to talk to you."

"**Maria, I don't want to hurt you,**" he grumbled and snarled. "**You don't know what's going on here. Karen's working with the Fectors. She set them on me. This is between me and her.**"

"Karen working with Fectors? Impossible!"

"**Then why were they waiting outside for me? How'd they know I'd be here, Maria?**" The question suddenly sprang into his mind, "*How*

238

did Karen know I'd be here tonight? Her intuition must have told her this was my only move."

Maria hesitated, and her eyes misted over while she connected the dots.

Karen must have sensed her confusion, too, because she yelled from her room, **"He's lying to you, Maria. Kill him!"**

The wildling in Maria was too well trained to ignore an order from a *frenator*. Aaron saw her fear as she performed a *renovatio* and leapt at him. Aaron watched her fly through the air as if in slow motion. He knew at that point Karen had lost all sense of reality. Her rage was so great, she was willing to sacrifice one woman, one wildling, in a desperate bid to save herself. She knew Maria didn't stand a chance against him, but sent her to her death anyway. Aaron didn't even have to try to avoid her. He simply swung with his cula, leaving her throat a mangled, bloody piece of meat. She landed in the pool, dead before the first waves hit its edge.

Aaron yelled across the courtyard, toward Karen's room, **"Are you happy, Karen? Did you really think she could protect you?"**

"Of course not, you dickhead! But once she knew about the Fectors, she had to die. *You* killed her!"

Aaron knew immediately he had put Bill's life in jeopardy, too. **"So, who all knows about this little arrangement with the Fectors?"**

"The whole Conclave. And you, of course." She emerged from her room, strutting regally along the stone walkway toward Aaron. He admired her form; she was still a magnificent looking creature. Magnificent and deadly. **"The threat of *Lupus solitarius* wouldn't have any teeth if everyone knew the Fectors had been tamed. You should have run after the junkyard."** The tone of her voice turned acidic. **"You might have lived a few more days."**

"'Hell hath no fury like a woman scorned,' right, Lover?"

"Fuck you, Aaron! You had it all. You threw it away because you didn't want to kill someone? You're a predator. You're at the top of the food chain. Everyone else is just meat. Especially your witch in New Orleans."

"Witch? What do you—"

She leapt at him before he had a chance to finish his question. James had been fast during their wrestling matches a lifetime ago, but Karen was in a class by herself. What she lacked in training, she made up for in pure rage, agility, and cunning. A part of him was miserable it had come to this, but he would not be responsible for another senseless death when he could have prevented it. If what she said was true, they might be hunting Jajine right now. Craig might be in New Orleans *right now*. Deep down Aaron hoped Karen might have held some feelings in reserve for him. Her brutal attack removed all doubt. It made his decision to kill her easier to swallow.

He dodged to the right, and his wounded leg gave slightly. He barely got out of the way in time to avoid a deadly downward strike from her left cula. He raised his left arm to deflect it crossways and hopefully leave her with her back to him, but her lightning-fast strike made contact with his left shoulder blade, gouging a deep furrow before he could get his arm into position. He immediately turned to face her. She had already recovered and was rushing him again. He was unprepared for this rapid turnaround and stumbled onto his back. She was on him, left cula on his gut, talons digging into his flesh, and her right cula reaching for his throat. He reached up and grabbed her arms, pulled both feet up to his chest and kicked with everything he had. The wound in his thigh was close to being healed but still burned like fire. She flew away from him, crashing into one of the columns supporting the ceiling. He jumped to his feet and faced her. She climbed slowly to her feet, not winded but cautious, and licked his blood off her talons. Quite leisurely and languid, but with purpose, she circled him before moving in. Her eyes were a furnace burning with bloodlust and hate now. Karen was no longer home.

She moved into Aaron's circle, her culas working like a chainsaw. He deflected each in turn, right cula for left cula and left cula for right cula, stepping back with each blow. He was using a Tai Chi move called *Repulse Monkey*. It sounded strange, but it was effective at deflecting rapid-fire attacks.

He could find no opening in her defenses. She was savage and ruthless and animalistic. This type of attack was usually punctuated with holes, but not hers. She wasn't leaving anything for him to take advantage of. He knew if it wasn't for his training, he would be dead by now. Then he remembered what happened outside. The Fectors left an opening in the circle, and he willingly walked into it. He wondered if he could dupe her into something similar.

On her latest attack, he prepared a stance called *Play the Fiddle*. It was an old move, found in nearly all of the Tai Chi forms. His form, the Wu, had one that was particularly hard to predict. He took two steps backward and raised both hands up and to the outside of his protection zone. She took the bait and rushed into the opening, realizing too late it was a trap as Aaron brought both of his hands together into a position that resembled someone playing a fiddle. Her arm buckled with a wet-sounding crack, her elbow shattered and bent the wrong way.

Aaron ignored his lover's cry of pain. He turned to his left with her destroyed arm gripped in both of his culas. It was nothing more than a lever to drop her to his feet. His knee gouged into the back of her left shoulder, slamming her face and chest into the slate floor, breaking a fang off to skitter into the flower bed before disintegrating. He turned his *lupus* free when he saw the back of her neck within biting distance. It knew what to do.

He remembered the last time he killed an adversary like this. It was the hellhound from his dreams. Like then, he was fighting for his soul, for if he now refused to fight for the lives of all *lupis*, his soul was already lost.

He pulled away and howled in despair until his stomach cramped and his vision went dark from lack of oxygen. He changed back into human form and carried her human body to her bed.

Craig Minor, June 13, 1983

Lisa ran into Karen's bedroom and immediately cried out. Craig stood in the doorway while she performed a *renovatio* and howled in anguish. He stood there for a few minutes before he slowly staggered over and stood beside the bed. Karen was laid out neatly with her hands clasped on her chest. She was dressed in a blue skirt, a white blouse, and had a floral patterned scarf wrapped around her neck. Her feet were together and bare. Her head was at an odd angle so he slowly reached down and gently pulled her chin toward him—and scrambled to catch her head as it rolled off the pillow and onto the floor. Lisa renewed her howling as Craig picked it up and placed it back on the pillow. He wiped his hands on his shirt as if he had touched something forbidden.

He performed his own *renovatio* and howled with Lisa.

Frank Mason

Lisa and Craig howled for about five minutes before they settled down, but Frank decided to give them a bit more time before he delivered the next piece of bad news. He kept himself busy by cleaning up the mess Aaron left for him. "Mr. Minor, there's something else."

"What is it, Frank?"

"Aaron told me to tell you something, that you would understand the message. He said, 'Tell Craig the page has turned, a new chapter has begun.'" That was all he dared say. He'd worked for the Minors for over twenty years, since before he was infected, and in all that time, they never told him about the basement. He remembered the big hole the mansion had been built over, but they said they needed to put some pilings down deep. I guess they thought he was a moron to believe that.

Well, the secret was out now, and it did nothing more than add another item to the list of Frank's anxieties about different things he'd witnessed over the years. Things didn't quite seem to be on the up and up with Craig. There always seemed to be some poor schmuck getting shunned, and Craig didn't seem to care about it. Frank stayed away from the house as much as possible and humbly did his job. He even stopped running with the pack for the most part once he learned to *frenis*—not that Craig seemed to notice.

He went back outside. He didn't want to be around Craig and Lisa any more than necessary right now. He wasn't sure what the future held, but he knew things were about to change. Aaron was a genuinely nice, young man. For him to commit such an atrocity, well, something must have set him off. He suspected finding out Karen and the others were working with the Fectors might have done it. Frank was certainly upset when he found out about it. He made a point of not mentioning to Craig or Lisa that Aaron told him that piece of news. He liked his job and knew it would be hard to do it if he was dead.

Craig Minor

After Frank left the room, Craig put his arm around Lisa's shoulders and mumbled comfortingly, "We'll bury her out next to the big lake. She liked it out there. Now come with me. You need to go lie down for a spell."

Lisa stood up and let Craig lead her out of Karen's room. He took her to their bedroom and put her to bed. He'd never seen Lisa so malleable before. She was usually the strong one. They didn't have any daughters, so Karen was the closest thing they had to one. If losing a real child was worse, he was glad his boys were still alive. Perhaps he needed to make amends with them.

Right now though, he had Race business to attend to; he forced himself to concentrate on the task at hand. He put some clothes on and went to the Diana statue. He saw bloody, *lupus* cula prints all around the head, and he could smell Aaron in the blood. *Good, Karen landed at least one good blow.* He descended the stairs, following Aaron's scent, and ended up at the writing table.

He saw his last entry had a line leading from it to the bottom of the page, showing that page to be finished. At the top of the next page, he saw Aaron had written in his own blood, "Chapter Two: Rise of *Lupus solitarius.*"

He wasn't sure how long he stood there staring at that entry before he sensed Lisa standing beside him. She was nearly comatose, her eyes pearly white while her Gift surged through her.

She came out of it. "I still see him as *Lupus Rex!*" she exclaimed, her voice filled with anguish. "After all of this, he still rules! How can this be, Craig?" She looked to him for an answer.

He didn't have one, but he knew while he was alive, he would not allow what she had seen to come to pass. He went upstairs and faxed to all of the clan heads Aaron's new status as *Utlagatus.*

Buried on page twenty-three of the *Orlando Sentinel's* June 15th edition was a small article.

The Vatican reports that a missionary expedition to South America has gone missing and all personnel are presumed dead in the flash floods that have struck the region lately.

Father Ignacio, the head of the mission, was a longtime member of the Vatican's Ambassadorial Outreach Program. "He was a peaceful man of God and has surely earned his place at His side."

When asked if Father Ignacio would be up for Sainthood, the Vatican replied with, "No comment."

The mission's total personnel count was reported to be fourteen.

Part IV—Rise of Lupus Solitarius
noun [lü'-pəs()sä-lə-ter'-rē-əs]
1. Lone Wolf.

Chapter 36—Viam Lupus
noun [wē'-əm()lü'-pəs]
1. Way of the Wolf

Aaron Darveau, June 13, 1983

Things moved quickly for Aaron once he placed Karen in her room. After leaving Craig a message in the basement, talking with Frank, washing himself off with a water hose, and pulling yet *another* fresh set of clothes out of the trunk, he found Elwood already sitting in the car with his tongue hanging out of his mouth. They were far down the road when Aaron reached over to pet him and pulled back a bloody hand. Aaron went into a near panic, mainly because he was angry with himself for having entirely forgotten Elwood getting struck by that crazy priest in the ninja costume.

Luckily, the larger metropolitan areas of Florida host a large number of retirees. Retirees have pets, and these pets are family. When a family member gets sick after normal working hours, they require medical care just as if they got sick during the day. Aaron found an emergency pet clinic in the yellow pages and took Elwood in for some stitches.

The veterinarian inspected the cut in Elwood's hindquarter. "What happened to you, boy, hmm?"

Aaron answered for him. "We were down on Orange Blossom Trail, and a couple of gang members jumped out and tried to rob me."

"Gang members? Uh-huh. Well, that must have been a large knife they used." The vet didn't sound convinced, but he dropped the subject and got to work stitching Elwood back together.

Aaron found the men's restroom, took his shirt off, and spent a few minutes inspecting the wound Karen gave him. It was already healed but had left behind some light scarring. The bullet holes were completely missing as well as the pig spear wound on his thigh. It appeared damage done by mundane weapons would heal up completely while injuries from other *lupis* left small scars—like the crossed cula marks on his chest. At the time of his shunning, he wondered why that was. Then he remembered an entry in one of Craig's Archives; a *lupus* body treats further introductions of the venom as a bacterial infection. Just like severe acne leaves behind scars, this secondary venom infection does too. He wondered if plastic surgery could repair the scarring. *Yeah, and how do I explain to the doctor the reason for the rapid healing?*

About half an hour later, the vet came into the waiting room. "Well, ol' Elwood needed about ten stitches and he'll need pain and antibiotic meds three times a day for the next week. The cut wasn't too deep, but I still had to put him under. He should be awake in about another half hour. Just keep him settled, don't let him run around too much, and he'll be fine. And the poor dog needs to wear a big cone around his neck too, to keep him from scratching and gnawing at his wound. He'll probably need that about two weeks until the stitches are ready to come out. That'll be two hundred dollars." Aaron paid it and then he and Elwood got back on the road.

When Aaron started that new chapter in Craig's archive, he took a few minutes to skim the last few entries first. It turned out Karen wasn't spouting idle threats; Craig had people in New Orleans looking for Jajine. The Conclave was concerned that Jajine, who Craig referred to as a "witch," would teach other wildlings to *frenis*. One of the things that kept the wildlings in line was the idea the ruling class, the *frenatus*, protected them. If the wildlings didn't need the protection anymore, the *frenatus'* power would weaken. This was something they could not allow to happen.

He stewed on that long and hard after leaving the vet clinic. *Maybe my fantasy of teaching the entire Race to frenis ain't such a fantasy after all. Craig sure is taking it seriously.*

Aaron couldn't remember if he had ever mentioned Jajine's name or not. He looked into the backseat at Elwood. "The only thing I remember saying about her was she was 'a crazy, old fortune teller from New Orleans.' And they don't know if that fortune teller is male or female. You ever been to New Orleans, boy? No? Well, that's a fairly vague description to go on. You can't swing a dead cat in that town without hitting a fortune teller."

"Still, if Craig's actively searching for her, it's only going to be a matter of time before he finds her." He reached down and touched his hippy necklace. "We need to call her and warn her." He immediately pulled over to a pay phone. The first one he found was at a busy truck stop, and all of the phones inside were in use by truckers. There were two outside, but they weren't enclosed. The parking lot was full of trucks roaring by, and he had a hard time hearing the dial tone. He tried anyway and received an automated response from the phone company; her phone was disconnected and no longer in service. He became really worried then because if he couldn't contact her, he couldn't warn her. Then he remembered Father Thomas and called him.

"Hello. Father Thomas speaking."

"Father, it's Aaron. I've got a problem, and you're the only one I can trust right now."

"Aaron? Oh, yes, Aaron!" He yawned and asked, "What time is it?"

"Late. Early morning, actually. Sorry."

"That's okay. What's the matter?"

"Father, I need your help. You remember that fortune teller I told you about? Jajine?"

"Hmm, yes, the one who gave you the necklace?"

"Yeah. Well, the Race is searching for her. I let it slip once about her, but I'm not sure they know who she actually is. I can't contact her. Her phone's been disconnected. Is there anything you can do to warn her to get out of town? Call one of your churches in New Orleans or something to send someone over?"

"Why? What happened?"

Aaron hesitated, lightly clicking his teeth together. *I have to trust someone. If he can't be trusted, then I might as well slit my own wrists right now.* Even though he had cleaned the blood off of himself, he could still smell it, could still smell *her.*

He confessed, "Father, I killed Karen. I had no choice."

Didn't I? Could I have just run? Would that have been preferable than killing the woman I had loved at one time? No. But it doesn't matter anyway. It's over with. I have to live with that decision. And I now have to finish what I started. The silence stretched out on the phone. He finally broke it. "I also killed some Fectors. A lot of 'em. The *frenatus,* or at least the rulers, are working with them. They set an ambush for me."

He recounted the events of the junkyard and ended with his encounter with them at Craig's.

Father Thomas was silent for a few minutes. "Well, you certainly know how to make friends," he said. "You know you are going to have both groups chasing you now, right? You'll never be able to go home; you'll have to leave your entire life behind."

Aaron waited for an eighteen wheeler to rumble by. "Yeah, I know. And I don't want to put your life in any more danger than I already have. I know I have no right to ask you for help, but I really have no one else to turn to."

"I'll admit I'm having a hard time wrapping my brain around this whole situation. Fortune telling is against God's Law. Those powers come from Satan."

Aaron didn't even want to think about Good and Evil right then. His voice cut like a knife. "You're the one who reminded me she was an ally. I don't have a large abundance of them right now. I need to protect the ones I do have. Besides, is it God's Law I be killed because evil found me? Was it God's Law Kyle be killed? I didn't seek it out. I didn't seek *this* out. Jajine helped me. I don't know her reasons for helping me, but as far as I'm concerned, she has more Good in her than anybody else I've met. Maybe the Bible is wrong about Fortune Tellers."

"That's heresy," Father Thomas lectured curtly. "Consorting with the devil is a path that's hard to turn back from, Aaron."

"Perhaps. But I'll worry about my soul later. It's always easier to ask forgiveness than permission anyway, right?"

"That's sacrilegious." Father Thomas sighed on the other end of the connection. "But it's a truism nonetheless."

"So, you'll help me?"

"Aaron, I didn't say I wouldn't help. It's just—well, I'm going to have a hard time convincing the church to dedicate resources to saving her."

"Father, I don't have proof, but I feel strongly she is the key to bringing down the Race. Or at least transforming it. Preventing deaths like Kyle's."

"I believe you, Aaron. God help me, but I do." He again sighed into the phone. "Give me her address."

Aaron recited what little there was off of her worn and wrinkled business card and said he would call in the morning.

Before they hung up, Father Thomas asked, "Where are you now? What are your plans?"

"I'm going to look up this Jose character you told me about. I need support, and he's the only one I think I have a chance with right now. I'll be in touch."

Elwood's whine prompted Aaron to look at his watch. "Your stitches bothering you, boy? I guess it's time for your medicine." Aaron reached into the backseat to scratch Elwood's ears, and he showed his appreciation for the attention by licking Aaron's fingers.

They pulled over into a gas station parking lot, and Aaron reached into the glove compartment, pulling out Elwood's medicine. "Just two little pills, and then I'll walk you, okay?" Somehow, Elwood knew what Aaron was trying to do and kept trying to turn his snout away from him. "I know you don't like swallowing these things, but they'll make you feel better. Come on, Elwood, quit fidgeting! This isn't some improv theater show."

In the end, Elwood must have realized it was a lost cause because he let Aaron have his way with him. He was already sprawled out across the backseat and asleep by the time they got to Naples, Florida.

Knowing *lupis* had the ability to track from scent, Aaron didn't want to lead the Race directly to where he was heading. He decided to head to Miami via Naples and then east across Alligator Alley. He hoped the long distance would discourage any attempt to follow him.

The address Father Thomas gave him led to an old, abandoned construction site just outside of Miami devoid of any life other than a few bums. He couldn't detect the scent of *lupus* anywhere. He asked the "locals" if they knew of Jose Suarez or *Viam Lupus*, but all he got for his ten dollars in bribe money was a crowd of winos stinking of Mad Dog 20/20 all pointing in different directions. Frustrated, he got back into Devil Car and drove off.

How did Karen find me? She drove around until she picked up my scent. Perhaps I can do the same thing.

Two weeks later Aaron was wondering if Karen had lied to him about how she found him. He was beginning to wonder if there were even any *lupis* in Miami because he couldn't pick up their scent anywhere.

Every morning he called Father Thomas for an update on Jajine. The Father had called some friends in New Orleans, but it was hard to convince them—as he predicted. Unfortunately, neither one of them had good news to report. Father Thomas's friends couldn't find Jajine, and Aaron couldn't find Jose. Finally, near the end of the second week and only hours from when he would need to find a place to perform his *renovatio*, Aaron detected the familiar scent of *lupus*.

He followed the scent down a forgotten city street that could have been ripped from an old detective television show. Broken down cars lined its curbs, taped and boarded windows garlanded its storefronts, and old women pushed shopping carts containing everything they owned in the world along its grimy sidewalks. A ghostly presence of stale urine, spilled gasoline, and dead animals ruined the fresh smell of the Atlantic Ocean as it washed in from the shore. The scent he followed though, ended at an old apartment building where gang-style graffiti decorated the walls, big Harley's were parked outside, and Cubans milled about. He guessed they were Cubans; they certainly looked Latin to him. They all had big tattoos, leather vests, and long hair tied back in pony tails. They turned their heads and watched Aaron drive by their complex. Yes, the scent was definitely stronger there.

They were waiting for him in the main parking lot after he turned around and came back. Even though he was certain they could smell the *lupus* in him too, they didn't look too happy to see him. Elwood stood up in the front seat and growled.

"Settle down, Elwood, we have to talk to them. Besides, with your bum leg, you ain't in any shape to mix it up with them. Be brave on your own time." Elwood sat back down, but he kept his attention on the men in parking lot.

One of them raised his hand and yelled, "That's far enough, Yuma. What do you want?"

Aaron stopped the car and stepped out. "I'm looking for Jose Suarez."

"There's no Jose Suarez here, Yuma. Get back in your little car and leave."

"Well, can you point me to his ugly sister? I heard she was something you needed to see if you ever visited Miami." Aaron smelled the anger—and surprisingly, fear—from them soar as the tension wound itself tighter. Aaron experienced a faint, paranoid flash that perhaps Father Thomas set him up for his involvement in Kyle's shunning.

One of the men in the front stepped forward. "You have some cojones coming around here talking about my baby sister," he crowed harshly. "Who the fuck do you think you are?" Aaron could sense Jose wasn't just someone in the gang—he was the leader, the Alpha. He was tall and weighed at least two hundred fifty pounds. He might have been of Latin descent, but his skin was darker than the rest of his *grex*. His hair had large curls and was just long enough to fall half-way over his ears. His face was a chiseled block of granite with a wide, square jaw. His mouth was large, but his teeth were larger, making his lips look small.

"I'm Aaron Darveau. I need some help. I'm...I'm *Lupus solitarius*. I heard you were, too. Let me take my shirt off to prove it."

Jose took a couple of steps closer to Aaron. "You stink of *frenatus*. We usually kill your kind if they come sniffing around here, and I'm wondering if I shouldn't do it myself." As Alpha, Jose had to establish his dominance, but Aaron wasn't sure how much was act and how much wasn't. "Go ahead. Show us. Just do it slowly." Jose pointed his head at a couple of the other men, and they sauntered around to the sides of Devil Car so they could keep a close eye on what Aaron was doing. Aaron pretended to ignore them, but kept track of them. He wasn't here to fight, but that didn't mean it wouldn't happen anyway. Elwood's growl rumbled deeply from within his chest.

Aaron exposed his cula marks while he studied Jose. Aaron took an instant liking to him, but didn't know why. Something about him made Aaron think he could trust him.

Jose unwound when he saw the marks on Aaron's chest that proved his status. "Okay. You can come in."

Aaron asked, "Can my friend come in with me?"

"Friend?" He lifted a brow and looked over Aaron's shoulder at Elwood. "Sure. But if he bites anyone, we'll eat him."

Aaron wasn't sure if Jose was serious about that or not, but he didn't want to take any chances by leaving Elwood outside on his own, either. He whistled, and Elwood gingerly stepped out of the driver side door and limped toward him. Everyone snickered when they saw him limping, but got quiet when Aaron told him, "Don't forget the door, Elwood." Elwood stopped, turned, and nudged the door closed with his nose. Then he ran up to Aaron, keeping his left hind leg off the ground.

Aaron followed Jose into the first floor of the apartment building. He studied the patch on Jose's kutte; it was a wolf's head overlaid on the crossed cula marks of the *Lupus solitarius*. It had the Latin phrase *Viam Lupus* across the top—*The Way of the Wolf*. As soon as he saw it he remembered where he had heard that phrase before. Bill mentioned it when he invited Aaron out for his first official hunt with the *grex*. There was another phrase he wasn't familiar with across the bottom, though. He asked, "What does *Natus Ululare* mean?"

Jose chuckled. "The literal translation is 'Born to Howl,'" he revealed.

"Corny, I know, but that's what it was when I joined. Semantically, it means 'Created to Howl in Dominance.' Sorta."

Aaron took note Jose wasn't some ignorant, street thug. No one tosses around words like 'semantically' in everyday conversation. This was an educated man.

Cooking pork and vegetables flooded the hallway of the apartment building and made Aaron's stomach rumble. It was getting close to supper time, and neither Aaron nor Elwood had eaten yet. He was running low on cash and had been trying to eat on the cheap for the last few days.

Jose must have heard Aaron's stomach. "You hungry?"

Aaron smiled broadly. "Yes, I am!" he exclaimed. "It smells great, too."

Jose turned into one of the apartment doors off the main hallway. "Angelina, fix another plate," he yelled to someone inside. "We got company."

Aaron tripped over his own feet as soon as he stepped into the apartment, because he found himself staring at one of the most beautiful women he had ever seen. Karen was easy on the eyes, but this woman made her look like the girl next door. She was short, about five feet, three inches, trim, well-shaped curves in all the right places, coffee brown, almond shaped eyes and long, black hair hanging over the edges of her face, framing it in a shiny, black glow, before falling to her boisterous breasts. She had a dark complexion and was of obvious Latin descent, probably Cuban if she was from around this area. Aaron couldn't stop looking at her. *Get a hold of yourself, hoss. The last lupa you got mixed up with tried to kill you.*

She stared at Aaron down her nose, which should have been impossible as she was shorter than he was, in a rare exhibition of someone who had mastered the Art of Condescension. She asked, "Since when do you bring white boys home, Jose?"

"Just fix him something, Mama!" he pleaded with a flirtatious grin. "The man's hungry."

She scoffed back at him but forgot about the argument as soon as Elwood came through the door. Her face brightened and then flooded with pain when she saw him limping. "Oh, the poor puppy dog has a boo-boo!" She leaned over to pet him, and Aaron watched his killer dog lay down and turn over, revealing his belly to Angelina so she could scratch it. "Are you hungry, Sweetie?"

"Yes, I am!" Aaron exclaimed. Again.

"Not you, Yuma, your friend here."

Embarrassed, Aaron answered back less heartily, "Oh. Yeah, probably. His name's Elwood. He's usually a little more nervous around strangers than that, but you've found his happy spot." Angelina was rubbing the right side of his belly and Elwood was thoroughly enjoying it. His head was stretched all the way back—Aaron had removed the cone just that morning—and his right rear leg was jumping in rhythm to Angelina's strokes. Aaron made a peace offering. "Well, Elwood trusts you. That's good news. By the way, what does Yuma mean?"

Jose chuckled. "It means white boy, American, foreigner, whatever someone from Cuba wants it to mean. But, don't take it too harshly. It's like Gringo to the Mexicans."

"Hmph," Aaron grunted. "Well, I guess white boy is accurate no matter what language I'm called that in."

Jose sat down at the kitchen table, a wobbly, plastic and metal contraption. "Aaron," he announced, "meet my ugly sister, Angelina. Angelina, meet Aaron. He's *frenatus*."

Angelina stood up and stared off into the distance, her eyes a smoky white. "Yes, powerful he is. Danger, he brings here, too. That's all I can see. Send him on his way, Jose."

"Feed him first. Besides, your intuition isn't that strong."

She put her hands on her hips and snapped, "It's strong enough to see this."

Jose narrowed his eye lids at Aaron. "We'll see."

While Aaron was having his fill of pork stew and Elwood was eating some stale dog food mixed with scraps from the stew, Jose pulled out and lit a cigarette. "Okay, Aaron. Tell me what you want. A *frenatus* shows up with a sick dog, both of whom smell like they haven't bathed in days, and asks for help. This ought to be interesting."

Aaron didn't know where to start, but he didn't think Jose wanted too many details, so he just gave him the highlights. "I had a run-in with *Lupus Rex*, *Lupa Reginam*, and her *Postpartor*, and was shunned. I found out they were working with the Fectors. Soon after, the Fectors tried to kill me. So, in order to put a stop to it, I killed Karen, the Postpartor, and about a dozen of her Fector buddies." Aaron reached down and scratched Elwood's ears. "Elwood here got a couple himself."

Jose snubbed out his cigarette. "Craig's working with the Fectors?" he asked. "That's the craziest thing I've heard."

"It's true. They all told me, themselves."

"Why would they do that?" Jose asked.

"To keep the peace. The Race made some deal with them back in the thirties. Supposedly, if they shun two hundred *lupis* a year and let the Fectors have them, they'll leave the clans alone."

"Two hundred a year? That's bullshit. Someone would have noticed that many people disappearing."

"I've been thinking about that. If they were scattered around the world, amongst the different clans, that's only about sixteen or so *lupis* per clan per year. You could hide it that way."

Jose sat there and studied Aaron. "I'm beginning to agree with my sister. It's too dangerous to ride with you. Tonight's a full moon though. We have a place to hunt, and you're welcome to come with us if you want—you killed Fectors, and that's a grin. After that, you gotta leave."

Aaron wasn't happy to hear this. He'd really hoped this guy had more of a beef with the Race than he did. "Jose, I'm going on the offensive here. I don't know how I'm going to do it yet, but I've no choice. They're going to continue offering up untold thousands if I don't put a stop to it. You can help me, or you can stay down here and play "hide the salami" with your sister. Yes, I can smell it on both of you. I could care less, actually. But I'm not giving up." All during this small speech, Aaron's blood pressure kept rising, and the *lupus* in him stirred restlessly by the time he was done.

Jose regarded Aaron with amused surprise but didn't respond in any other way. He was hard to read. His scent and his confident manner showed him to be Alpha, but he wasn't willing to challenge Aaron's insubordination. He continued to sit there calmly until Aaron settled down. At that point, night time was close and everyone was ready to head out to their hunting grounds. "Follow us," he said.

Aaron followed the six of them for about forty-five minutes to a little campground on the edge of the Everglades. He took Elwood's water dish out of the trunk and put it on the backseat floor board, filled it up, and rolled down the windows. Elwood whined; he knew Aaron was leaving him there. Aaron scratched his ears. "You'll be okay. Stay here and watch the car. Besides, I don't think you want to run with *lupis* tonight. They might find you tastier than the local wildlife."

Elwood rested his snout on the rolled down window and sighed.

Viam Lupus left their motorcycles in the campground and hiked into the wilderness. Aaron was a little nervous at first, wandering around in unfamiliar territory, until he remembered something; he was top of the food chain here. He asked Jose, "Do you come to the same location each time? The guy at the front gate seemed to know you."

"No, we have four other ones we usually hit. The Fectors tend to take advantage of habits. We don't have the luxury of a closed environment like our previous *grexes* had. Still, we sometimes run into humans out here, even at night. We try to leave them alone, but every now and then one of them will take a potshot at us."

"What do you do then?"

"I try to keep a lid on things. Sometimes accidents happen, though. Until recently, I was the only one who could *frenis*. Angelina can *frenis* now too, so that'll help us in the long run."

Aaron was surprised at his admission, but pleased nonetheless. "You can *frenis*? I didn't know there were any *Lupis solitarius* who could."

"Yes. It took me less than two years to learn how," he bragged. "Angelina learned pretty quickly too, about the same amount of time."

This *grex* did things very similar to the way his old *grex* did, the major exception being they hunted gators and not captured deer. And all members got their fill.

They spent the next couple of hours relaxing in the moonlight. Everyone was dozing and even Aaron succumbed to the urge to relax. He tensed up when Angelina laid down next to him then relaxed when her cuddling warmth embraced him.

"**Do you have a mate?**" she murmured into his ear.

"**I did. Karen.**"

"**The woman you killed?**"

"**Yes.**"

"**Was it hard?**"

"**Yes.**"

"**Mmmmm. I like a hard man.**" She snuggled up even closer to him. Under other circumstances, he might have responded with more enthusiasm, but this was too similar to the time he and Karen made love during his second *renovatio*. Still, he didn't try to pull away.

"**Angelina, I don't think I would be good company tonight.**"

"**I understand—**"

Aaron sensed Jose almost too late as the Alpha leapt from where he was lounging to where Aaron was laying. Aaron rolled out of the way before he landed, and when they stood up and faced each other, Jose came at him with a snarl. **"That's my wife you're trying to fuck, *frenator*!"**

"Wife? I thought—" The smug grin on Angelina's face was enough to cut off Aaron's sentence. She really wanted Aaron gone and knew exactly what would make Jose angry enough to attack him. She might not be as subtle as Karen, but her methods were too close for comfort.

Jose lunged at him again. Aaron dodged him easily enough, but then Jose circled him like James did. *Where do they learn to fight like this? Is it instinctual or instinctive?* In either case, it was easy to counter. Once Jose thought Aaron wouldn't defend himself, he attacked...just like James did. Aaron stepped to the side, grabbed Jose's right arm with his left cula, stepped forward and behind him, and then grabbed Jose by the throat with his right cula. A little push sent Jose over Aaron's leg, where he unexpectedly found himself staring up from the ground into a salivating jaw full of bright white fangs.

"Jose, I'll end you right now unless you listen to me."

"What have you got to say, *frenator*, that hasn't already been said? You want the pack for some foolish suicide mission. That's easy to see. You kill me, and you also get my wife. I'll not be anything but Alpha."

"I don't want your pack." Then as if spitting out something foul-tasting, he growled loosely, **"And I damned sure don't want Angelina. I just want your help."**

Aaron released the pressure on Jose's neck, but didn't let him go. **"Don't you see what's happening here? We're doing exactly what the Race wants us to do. We'll never be able to defeat them, to truly be free, unless we work together, treat each other as family. This notion of family only works if we don't fight each other, don't kill each other off. Until then, the Race holds all of the cards; they have all of the advantages, and we have none."**

Jose stopped struggling. Aaron could tell he was listening. **"Jose, we have to stop the killing. The first step is to start treating each other like brothers and sisters. We're all a family. We have to start protecting each other."**

Aaron took a chance and released him, but stepped warily back in case

Jose took advantage of the situation.

Jose stood up, his eyes still angry, but he didn't launch another attack. He shot Angelina a menacing look. **"I'll deal with you later."**

Aaron smelled the confusion on the remaining four members of the *grex*. Their Alpha just lost a fight, but he was still alive. Jose strode into the woods alone, but not before he exerted his authority by snarling at them and forcing them to back down.

The next morning found Aaron sleeping in a tree. It wasn't that he didn't trust the *grex*, but he didn't want to give Angelina an easy out. He made it back to the parking lot and saw everyone was gone except for Jose, who mashed a cigarette out under his boot when he saw Aaron. "I sent them all home. We try to get out early in the morning in case any humans come stomping about."

"Makes sense. Thanks for waiting on me."

Jose nodded his head. "Hungry? On me."

"Sounds good. You know a good place around here?"

"Yeah, just up the road."

"Cool. Let me feed Elwood, and we'll be on our way. He's been in the car all evening—at least I hope he has been—and probably needs to take a crap, too."

Aaron followed Jose to a small diner about fifteen minutes toward town while Elwood sat in the backseat eating the last of the dog food. They chose a booth near the door out of earshot of the rest of the patrons. Aaron excused himself and made for the pay phone back near the restrooms to call Father Thomas.

"Father, any word?"

"Yes," he proclaimed, exuberantly, "she's safe! How are you?"

"That's great! I'm great! I finally found Jose. How is she?"

"She's fine, but from what I understand, she wasn't too cooperative at first. Catholic priests showing up at a voodoo witch's door don't exactly start things off on the right foot. Supposedly though, as soon as she heard your name, she packed what she needed and went along quietly. They've moved her to a safe location, but we aren't sure how long she'll be safe. There have been reports of increased *lupis* activity in the area. I'm catching a flight there later this morning to help with future arrangements and to defend her if need be."

"I guess that's my cue to head to New Orleans."

"We could certainly use your help. Write this number down." He recited a phone number to Aaron. "When you get here, we'll direct you to where we're holed up."

"Thank you, Father."

"How's it going with Jose?"

"I'm not sure. He's not what I was expecting, and I don't think he's ready to go against the Race just yet. And his sister isn't his sister; she's his wife. And *lupa*. And she doesn't like me at all—her intuition is sending up all kinds of alarms. He's going to take some convincing."

"Good luck and be safe. Call when you get to New Orleans. In the meantime, God be with you."

"Thank you, Father. I don't know how I can repay you."

Aaron sat down at the table and ordered up a three egg omelet with everything on it. He was anxious to get on the road but needed to finish his conversations with Jose first.

About half-way through breakfast, Jose admitted, "Aaron, what you said last night rings true. But I don't see how you can make it work. There are numerous *Lupis solitarius* around the country, hell, maybe the world, and they are all too afraid to band together. Anytime more than a dozen *lupis* stay in one spot too long, either the Race or the Fectors attack. *Viam Lupus*, at one time, had ten members. The Fectors were waiting for us at one of our *renovatio* locations and attacked before we had a chance to change." He hung his head. "The rest of us just ran." He muttered that last sentence as if he were ashamed.

"Why didn't you fight?"

"They were using silver. I was the only one immune to it, and I was more concerned about getting everyone out safe than I was about killing Fectors. No matter how many you kill, they come back stronger than before."

Jose wasn't quite the stereotypical, motorcycle gang leader Aaron was imagining he would find as he drove around Miami looking for him. He was intelligent, introspective, well spoken, and was truly concerned for his *grex*.

Aaron revealed, "I'm immune to silver, too. I understand it's rare."

"It is." He took a drink of his coffee. "So tell me, how long did it take for you to learn to *frenis*?"

"Actually…I did it on my first transformation."

"Bullshit. Nobody does it on their first time."

Aaron pulled out his necklace and was about to tell his story about Jajine when unreserved shock formed on Jose's face. He put his coffee down and stared at the necklace. "Where did you get that?"

"A fortune teller in New Orleans. Her name's Jajine. I'm not sure how, but this necklace sparked a series of dreams that…Well, I'm not sure what they did, but when the time came for my first *renovatio*, I was prepared. I'd had ten years of practice taming my inner beast." He chuckled under his breath. "At least, that's the only way I can think to describe it. Why, have you seen one like it?"

"You could say that." Jose pulled an exact duplicate out of his pocket. "Jajine is my mother."

"Holy shit!" *That explains why he looked so familiar to me, why I like this guy. Am I willing to push him? Kirk wouldn't hesitate. This could be the break I need.* Aaron confided, "You are going to be interested in what I have to say, Jose. That phone call I made when we first came in?" He pointed his thumb over his shoulder. "Well, I was checking on her. The Race knows about her, and they want her dead. They don't like the fact she's making *frenatus*. It's my fault they even found out about her I'm afraid, but she's safe right now. Father Thomas has managed to smuggle her to a safe house somewhere—"

"*Father* Thomas?! A Fector?"

"No, he isn't a Fector. He's a friend. I trust him."

"And this Father Thomas, he has my mother?"

"Yes. And she's safe, but he's not sure how long she'll remain that way. There's *lupis* in the area looking for her. I'll be leaving today to drive up to New Orleans to help."

Aaron saw a mixture of emotions run across Jose's face that finally ended with fear. By the time Aaron finished relating what he knew about the situation in New Orleans, Jose was standing up, paying the bill.

"Dammit, Aaron! I've been living down here in this hell-hole, hiding out for the last fifteen years specifically to keep her safe. I wasn't sure if the Fectors would go after her or not to get to me, so I cut off all contact. And you lead them right to her."

"Man, there are no Fectors involved. Just *lupis*."

Jose yelled, "Bullshit! Father Thomas is the name of the sonuvabitch who led an assault on us a few years back."

Aaron froze in shock. *Father Thomas is Lamp of Truth? He did seem to take the lupus angle all in stride.* He mentally shook his head. *No. Impossible.* "Jose, I don't believe he's a Fector. There are too many things going on that add up to him telling the truth. His nephew was *lupus* and got shunned. *I* shunned him. He wouldn't be helping me if I was the one responsible for Kyle's death. Father Thomas practically raised him."

"Fectors are sneaky bastards, Aaron. You can't trust them."

"Well, I trust him."

"Why? What makes you think you can trust him?"

"I don't know. It just feels right. That's all I have to go on. Your mother told me to trust my instincts. And right now, my instincts are telling me we can trust him."

"How did you find out about us?"

For the second time in as many minutes, Aaron froze up in shock. "Oh, fuck! He told me." Aaron fell back against the back of his chair and sighed.

Jose stood there and rubbed his forehead. "And now you've led them to us, too."

"No, I haven't. I didn't tell him where we were. The address he had for you was on the other side of town."

"Just something to get you in the area. They knew you'd track us down. They probably followed you."

Aaron took one last despairing look at his remaining omelet before he followed Jose out into the parking lot. Jose climbed onboard his motorcycle and asked, "Why are you trying to save her, my mother?"

Aaron was surprised at the question—until he realized Jose didn't know the whole story. "The short answer is she saved my life."

"Okay. I'll accept that for now, but only because you have the necklace, and I don't have the time to listen to the whole thing. I've got to get *Viam Lupus* ready for a road trip."

"Where are you going?"

Jose asked grimly, "You're shitting me, right?" He started his bike and raised his voice over the rumbling of the engine. "The Fectors have my mom, and *lupis* are hunting her. We're going to New Orleans with you."

Aaron had a hard time keeping up with Jose on the way back to his lair. Aaron knew something was wrong as soon as he turned the corner into the parking lot. Death reeked and poured through Devil Car's windows. Elwood whined with concern, so when Aaron got out of the car, he whistled. Elwood leapt out of the car window and followed at his master's heel. Aaron found the source of the smell once he stepped inside. The remaining members of the *grex* were all dead from multiple bullet wounds to their heads and chests. He had never seen silver wounds before, but read about them in Craig's Archives. These matched the description; the holes were burned around the edges. Jose came storming out of one of the back rooms, screaming, "Angelina!"

She came running in through the front doorway. "Here, Jose! I'm okay." Her thin frame shook as great sobs crashed through it.

They ran to each other and hugged, burying their faces in each other's neck. Neither of them spoke for a few minutes. Finally, he asked, "What happened?"

"They were here waiting for us. As soon as we walked through the door, they started shooting. I told you he was bad news!"

"It wasn't his fault." Jose lifted his eyes from Angelina's shoulder to look at Aaron. He could tell Jose wanted to blame him but couldn't. The fault lay with the Fectors. This is what happened to *Lupis solitarius*. If they hadn't shown up today, it might have been tomorrow or the day after, because that was the life they all led.

Aaron probed, "You couldn't smell them?"

She shook her head. "No. We should have, but we didn't."

Aaron exclaimed, "The same thing happened to me in Orlando! There were a dozen of them, and I didn't smell them at first either." His face tensed up. "Is that normal?"

"No, not if we're paying attention."

All three of them turned their heads to the tooth-shattering whine of police sirens coming through the doorway.

Jose exclaimed, "Bug out!" Then he and Angelina leapt into action, grabbing two overnight bags stashed in a closet by the front door. "They'll know to start looking for our bikes. Aaron, you have to drive."

Everyone climbed into Devil Car, leaving one Hell behind them and staring forward to the next one.

Miami Herald, June 25, 1983, Page 19

Shots rang out in Little Cuba again yesterday morning. Authorities believe this shooting is gang related. This is the fifth Miami-area shooting believed to be gang related in the past month alone.

Lt. Fisher of the Miami-Dade Gang Unit said four men were found dead in an apartment on 45th Ave. Automatic weapons, drugs, and drug paraphernalia were also found in the apartment. It is believed all victims were of the gang Viam Lupis and were killed by unknown assailants.

Miami Police were called in at 6:34 a.m. Friday morning on reports of shots being fired.

The area was blocked off for several hours as the Miami Police's Gang Unit investigated. Police are asking for anyone with information to please contact them.

Chapter 37—Confido
noun [kǝn-ˈfĭd-ō]
1. Confide.

Aaron Darveau, June 24, 1983

Aaron was eager to get to New Orleans, and it showed as he left Miami. "You might want to obey the speed limits," Jose recommended. "We don't know how close Craig's contacts are with the police. I'd prefer not to draw any attention to ourselves."

"You're right," Aaron conceded. He released the pressure on the gas pedal until the speedometer needle sat at 58, three over the speed limit. "The only thing going for us is they think I'm driving a different car. At least, I hope they do."

Jose sat up higher in his seat and threw an alarmed look at Aaron. "Did you steal this one?"

Aaron laughed. "Fuck no, I'm not that stupid. Kyle left me this car in his will."

"Kyle. The one you shunned? Father Thomas's nephew? Does Father Thomas know you have this car?"

Again, Aaron had the sinking feeling he may have misread Father Thomas. "Yeah."

"Well, at least only the Fectors know what we're driving," Jose bitterly shot at Aaron. "That's better than the police."

Aaron knew Jose was being sarcastic. The Fectors were much worse than the police. Unfortunately, Aaron couldn't fault that attitude even if he didn't agree with it.

Jose tried to get comfortable once they were cruising comfortably on the interstate. He lit a cigarette and took a couple of long drags off of it. "How did you meet my mom?" he asked. "What all did you talk about? I want to know everything, especially why the hell she gave you a necklace that's identical to mine."

Aaron told him everything he could remember, including everything that led him to being in Miami.

Jose chuckled. "You should have told her how young you thought she looked. It would have made her day."

"Actually, just using the word, 'Ma'am' was enough to make her day."

Jose laughed for a bit, but the tension in his face stayed there. "So, you were going to be *Lupus Rex* and told them to shove it up their asses. That takes balls, man."

"Not really." Aaron shook his head. "I thought I wanted it. I really did. But when Kyle got killed, I started doubting myself. And then I started asking questions. The answers I got back made me realize I didn't want anything to do with that. There's a line I won't cross. There's a line *nobody* should cross. There has to be another way to survive than to sell out our friends like that."

Jose didn't say anything, but he did sink a little further into the seat and rested his elbow on the top of door, hanging it out of the window. "You probably won't last long unless you're willing to do what needs doing."

"I have a problem with them sending innocent people to slaughter," Aaron stated curtly. "I don't have a problem doing what needs to be done." His recent experience with Karen and the Fectors remained unspoken.

"Yeah, maybe you don't."

No one talked until they passed West Palm Beach. Everyone was entombed in their own thoughts, trying to make sense of a world they weren't born into but would most likely die in.

Suddenly, Jose began his story. "They turned me when I was sixteen. They didn't do it on purpose, though. I was in Alexandria, Louisiana. I ran away from home after getting into a fight with Mom and Dad. Alex' was as far as my money got me." He reached into his shirt pocket for another cigarette and tapped it on the end on his lighter—packing the tobacco to one end—and then lit it. Aaron hadn't known Jose that long, but he recognized a well-practiced, nervous habit when he saw one.

"I got a job picking up used grease from fryers around town. Nastiest fucking job you can imagine, but it paid well enough for a black kid who didn't know any better. I got a room at the YMCA and pretty much made it on my own for about six months. The managers there also paid me a little bit to help clean up the gym at night. It wasn't much, but it was better than nothing." He took a long drag off of his cigarette and slowly blew it out through his nose.

"One night, I was shoving the basketballs into the closet when two guys started fighting outside the front door. I was big for my age, but my attitude was even bigger. I ran out there to put a stop to it. One of the guys was renting a room there so I knew him, but I didn't know the other guy at all. I ran up and told them to take it down the street.

"The stranger looked at me, and his eyes were red. And they were…empty. It was spooky. Before I had a chance to back off, he swung at me. I managed to duck most of it, and I'm glad I did because what little did make contact nearly ripped my head off. His fingernails cut like razors and hit like hammers. My head felt like it was on fire.

"I woke up in the hospital the next day with bandages all over my head. My parents were there. Let me tell you, I was never so glad to see someone in my life than I was right then. I told them what happened, said I was sorry, and asked if I could come home. I hadn't realized how lonely I was until I saw them." He stared off into space for a spell and then jumped when his cigarette burned down to his fingers. He flicked it out the window.

"The doctor released me after a few days, making a comment about the healing abilities of the young, and we went home. The police had already been there and had taken a statement, but they didn't seem too concerned. I was just another black kid with knife wounds as far as they were concerned.

"During the ride home, Mom kept asking for details on the man who struck me. Did he have a weapon? What did he look like? Did he say anything? What did he sound like? I didn't remember much so I couldn't answer all of her questions.

"When I got home, things were great for the first few days. Then things went to hell again. I was constantly fighting with my parents, my dad mostly. I spent quite a bit of time on the streets because I didn't want to go home. I was too smart to get into too much trouble, but for a teenager in New Orleans, it isn't hard to get into *some* trouble. I met a couple of guys down by the docks I took a shine to. I spent more and more of my time at their place.

"One night, they asked me if I wanted to head out to the swamp for some hunting and drinking. What the hell? It sounded like fun. I performed my first *renovatio* that night—along with them, of course." He pulled out another cigarette and lit it.

"When I got home a few days later, my mother asked me how it felt to be a *Loup Garou*? I nearly shit a brick, I tell you. I asked her how she knew, and that's when I learned there was more to my mom than I thought I knew. She told me what she knew of *Lupus sapiens*, which wasn't much, but it definitely filled in the gaps left over from what my *grex* members told me."

"I guess *Loup Garou* means werewolf?" Aaron asked.

"Yeah, it's the Cajun word for it."

Angelina had woken up and was leaning over the back of the front seats. "You've never told me this story, Jose."

He reached back and squeezed her arm. It was the best hug he could give her inside Devil Car. "I know. I'm sorry. Meeting Aaron, and since he knows my mother...Well, it's brought up a bunch of memories I thought I had forgotten."

Jealous of the attention Angelina was showing Jose, Elwood must have thought Aaron needed some too. He reached up and licked his master's ear.

Angelina warned, "This dog is crazy about you, Yuma. Don't you ever mistreat him, or you'll have to answer to me."

Jose turned from Angelina and stared out at the highway again as the miles slid under the car one after the other. "Things slowly returned to normal over the next few months, other than having to join my *grex* on the full moon. I finished school and was looking at colleges when I got into an argument with my Alpha. He didn't think I was spending enough time with the pack during the month. Personally, I wasn't that interested in being *lupus*. I considered it a nuisance. Well, things came to a head, and he put a bug in Ricardo's ear. Before I knew it, I was shunned."

Aaron interrupted. "Ricardo?"

"Yeah, he was Clan leader. Still is, I think."

"He is," Aaron confirmed.

"Anyway, a couple of weeks later, my dad and I were coming out of a movie theater. We were both science fiction fans so we decided to put our differences aside for a while and watch *2001: A Space Odyssey* together. Outside the theater, as we got to the car, a couple of guys jumped us. They said they were only there for me and if my dad backed off, he would live. My dad's right cross snapped one's neck before I knew what was happening. Then he jumped on the second one and told me to run. The second guy pulled a knife and shoved it into my dad's ribs, but not before my dad got his hands around his neck. My dad broke the guy's neck as he fell on him. He gave his life for me that night.

"When the police showed up, they listed it as a gang fight and put me in jail. My mother showed up with her law license in tow and got me off. We didn't go home, though. She took me to the edge of town, gave me $516.32, a suitcase full of my clothes, and told me to run and never look back. Those were Fectors my dad killed. I knew about the Fectors, but I didn't know they were after me. She also gave me that necklace—told me to wear it and that I would understand later why.

"I hitched a ride east, toward Florida. Going north was out of the question for me. Too damned cold up there. I spent a few months doing different jobs, basically keeping my head down, and I eventually ended up in Miami. I met *Viam Lupus* and joined up." Jose laughed under his breath. "Being *Lupis solitarius*, it seemed ironic we formed a pack. We were a pack of Lone Wolves. We were never as close as a true pack, though. We were joined at the hip purely for survival purposes."

Aaron asked, "How many *grexes* like yours are out there do you think?"

"I don't know. Anyway, over the next ten years or so, I moved up in the ranks. I had learned to *frenis* about two months before I joined, so I was naturally looked at as a leader."

Aaron nodded his head. "You were probably a welcome addition too. It helped the pack stay hidden by helping with the wildlings."

"Oh, absolutely," Jose agreed.

"So, when did you meet Angelina?"

"A couple of years ago. I was shopping, not paying attention to what was going on around me—good way to get killed, by the way—and I walked around a corner, and there I was, staring at her. We both knew the other was *lupus*, but we were still cautious. Being shunned makes you that way; you don't know if the *lupus* standing across from you is shunned or not. I took a chance because we were both too scared to say anything. I pulled open the front of my shirt and showed her my scars." Jose turned around and grinned at Angelina. She rolled her eyes, sat back, and started petting Elwood again. There was obviously some private joke there.

"Anyway, we started talking and one thing led to another, and then she joined our pack. It was a good thing too. When we went to our hunting ground at the next full moon, the Fectors attacked. They were after her and had tracked her to the *grex*. I managed to get her out of there before they could kill her. Unfortunately, our Alpha was killed. I had no strong urge to be Alpha, but I was the only one left who could *frenis*. Everyone naturally looked to me."

Aaron asked, "Was that attack led by Father Thomas?"

"I don't know about that one, but the one before that, definitely."

"I'm still having a hard time wrapping my head around that by the way.

I'm a good judge of character usually. I can't believe I was so far off base with him."

"Like I said, they're sneaky," Jose grumbled. "Anyway, in time Angelina and I fell in love. We married each other under the stars. Florida may not recognize it, but she's my wife. I also started going by her last name, Suarez—I wasn't sure if *they* would look for me under my real last name or not. They found the *grex*, and I didn't know how much information they had on me by that point. Just to confuse things even further, I told everyone outside our *grex* she was my sister."

Aaron asked, "How did you learn to *frenis*? I was under the impression that it isn't something easily learned, that it has to be taught."

"I'm not sure." Jose furrowed his brows as he dug up an old memory. "I just woke up one morning and realized I remembered everything from the night before." He stopped talking long enough to get another cigarette out. "One of the strange things I found out when I learned to *frenis* was that I was able to communicate with my mom. We couldn't talk, like I am right now, but we could pass on our feelings to each other. That seemed to be enough for us. As long as each of us knew the other was safe, the distance between us didn't matter. The necklace allows that—or at least I think it's the necklace. By the way…during my last *renovatio*, she left me with the feeling we would see each other soon."

"Your mom has tricks on top of tricks."

Jose chuckled and nodded his head. "Tell me about it."

"You think you could talk with her now?" Aaron asked. "I'm understandably concerned about the whole Father Thomas problem. Part of me still wants to believe he's not trying to fuck us over. But another part of me keeps pointing to the evidence."

"No." Jose shook his head. "I have to be *lupus*. When we stop, I'll give it a try."

"Okay." Aaron peeked into the backseat and saw Angelina gently stroking Elwood's head. "Jose, I'm sorry about the salami comment I made. You too, Angelina. I didn't know. I can't even imagine what y'all have been through."

Jose chuckled darkly. "Don't worry about it. We get it a lot."

"And I'm sorry about your *grex*. I wanted your help, but I didn't want it this way."

"Yeah, I know you didn't," Jose offered. "It's still hard, though. We were as close to being friends as possible under the circumstances. We had a system, and it seemed to work for us. We hadn't had an attack in close to a year. *Viam Lupus* has had more than its share of death, though. We always watched out for each other because we knew we were living on borrowed time."

"I'm afraid I probably brought them to you."

"Probably. If you weren't wearing that necklace, I'd probably have killed you by now." He ran his hands through his hair. "Time for some payback, though. I've been waiting for an opportunity to get back at them for my dad's death."

Aaron said over his shoulder, "What about you, Angelina? Care to share?" Aaron didn't think she would; she was pretty tight-lipped. So when she did start talking, Aaron didn't interrupt her once.

Chapter 38—Angelina Suarez

Angelina Suarez was born in Cuba in 1951 to Luis and Amelia Suarez just a few years before the entire island erupted in revolution. Although she and her younger brother, Raul, never experienced the war directly, it was on the periphery, always close. Castro may not have realized it when he seized the reins of power, but he set in motion events that would have wide-ranging effects, not just on his island or between the Soviet Union and America but on the *Lupus sapiens* race as well.

Angelina's parents, though part of the "worker" class, believed in individual freedom and a strong education. They worked endlessly to ensure their two children were brought up in that environment. However, with the takeover of the government, Castro was intent on ensuring the youth of Cuba were given a "State Education."

The Cuban people looked to America as the shining example of what their lives should be. The study of America's Founding Fathers was part of that example. But that was before the revolution. Hitler, Jefferson, Stalin, and most every other powerful leader knew an education supplied by the State inculcated the youth to the needs and wants of the State and was the best way to ensure the longevity of the State and its political theories. Fidel Castro, being a lawyer, was not stupid; he knew it, too.

Cuban parents, fearing Marxist-Leninist indoctrination and that the government would eventually remove their parental authority, sent their children to America. In February 1962, Angelina and her brother were two of approximately 14,000 unaccompanied minors who immigrated to America under Operation Pedro Pan. Monsignor Bryan O. Walsh, an Irish, Catholic priest spearheaded Operation Pedro Pan and arranged for over half of these children to be placed with relatives or foster homes around the country. Angelina and her brother were not so lucky. They grew up under the Catholic Welfare Bureau in a group home in Miami. Still, in their parents' eyes, it was better than growing up in Cuba under Castro. Their parents died in a failed counter-revolution, knowing their children were safe, three years after sending them to America.

Angelina worked hard to honor her parents and their decision to send them to America by dedicating her life to learning and earning a full college scholarship through the Catholic Welfare Bureau. She ultimately received her Doctorate from the University of Miami Medical School in Psychology in 1978.

She spent her first year and a half after college working directly for the Bureau at the Miami Bridge, a program for run-away teens; she wanted to give something back to the organization that spent so much time and so many resources on her and her brother's behalf. As a professional counselor, she oversaw scores of kids and young adults, helping them overcome drug addictions and other problems.

Angelina's life came crashing down around her on October 20, 1979.

Angelina had a surprise for her little brother. She had a new boyfriend, Eddie Ramirez, and wanted Raul to meet him. With Raul's studies in school and her time working at the Bridge, the siblings were finding it hard to stay in touch. Still, they finally managed to snag some time together. They decided to meet at the Club Alexandre, one of the newest and trendiest clubs in the area.

Raul was already there and standing near the end of the bar nursing a drink when Angelina and Eddie arrived. Angelina couldn't help but grin with wry humor when she saw a few women hovering around in his general vicinity, stealing glances at him. She could hardly blame them. Raul kept himself in shape and was educated. Both showed in his demeanor and poise. She snuck up on him and poked him in the ribs, and he nearly spilled his drink when he jerked around to face her.

He smiled, opened his arms, and gave her a long, brotherly hug. "Ang! It's good see you. Heck, look at you, all cleaned up. Eddie must be important!"

"Thanks a lot, Raul," she howled in mock anger but hugging him back anyway. She knew she was considered good-looking but didn't advertise it. Tonight, however, she wanted to make an impression on Eddie. She fixed her long, black hair into the latest Farrah Fawcett fashion and wore a dress showing her ample cleavage. She was short, so she hoped Eddie would get an eyeful when he looked down to her.

They broke the hug. "Raul, this is Eddie," she announced. "Eddie, this is my pain in the neck kid brother, Raul."

Eddie stuck his hand out. "It's nice to meet you, Raul. Don't let her get you down. She talks highly of you."

Raul laughed when she elbowed Eddie in the ribs.

Angelina and Eddie danced while Raul was a few feet away with two different women. The dance floor was crowded, but that only added to the excitement, because it forced Angelina to rub up against Eddie to keep from bumping into the other dancers. He smelled nice, but it wasn't artificial, and it made her want to stay close to him. The lights from the dance floor flashed to the beat of the music while a sweaty-cologne emanated from the dancers surrounding them. They combined to form a hypnotic experience, simultaneously relaxing and exciting the senses at the same time. The song ended, and the DJ mixed in the next one, almost beat for beat. Angelina leaned toward Eddie and yelled, "I'm thirsty! Let's get—"

Eddie doubled over in a painful convulsion, nearly knocking Angelina off of her feet. She hunched over him, placing her arm over his back to support him. "Eddie, you okay?"

Eddie only growled in response; it was guttural and animalistic. He dropped to his knees, hugging his arms around his stomach.

Angelina screamed, "Eddie, what's wrong?"

Raul rushed over and yelled over the loud music into her ear. "What's wrong with Eddie?"

"I don't know!" she screamed back. "He just dropped to the floor!"

Without warning, Eddie stood up, pushing Angelina away.

Raul yelled, "Hey, man! Watch out!" He grabbed Angelina, keeping her on her feet. "Nice mask, asshole, but Halloween isn't for another couple of weeks yet!" Raul wasn't laughing at his own joke, though. He raised his fists and struck Eddie across the side of his head.

It was a solid blow, but Eddie didn't go down. In fact, the blow didn't shake him at all. He slowly turned his gaze to Raul and growled around curled lips. Raul and Angelina stared into the face of horrid malevolence, and it stared back with eyes not quite human. Suddenly, Eddie rose to his full height and ripped his shirt off of his chest, transforming into something terrifying, something out of a nightmare. He grew a long snout and pointed fangs, his legs and arms extended out of his pants and sleeves, and his hands sprouted long, razor-sharp talons. Raul quickly pushed Angelina behind him and then ran to Eddie's other side. Eddie started to turn toward Angelina, so Raul struck him in the head again, grabbing his attention.

Angelina wanted to yell, "*Raul…No!*" but time slowed as she watched the horror show unfold in front of her. Eddie lashed out with his claws, carving Raul from mid-stomach up through his throat and lower jaw, spraying his blood on her and some of the less attentive dancers around them. His other hand swung back, not deliberately but as if balancing, and scratched Angelina's side, slightly ripping the dress and leaving small, bloody grooves along her ribs. They burned like fire. The handful of people dancing around the carnage shrieked and scrambled away in all directions, but their cries of alarm disappeared in the strobe of the lights and the *boom, boom, boom* of the music and the laughing and joyful screaming normal for a dance floor.

"Eddie" dropped to all fours, raised his snout into the air and howled. Angelina stood frozen. Her mind screamed for release, screamed at her to hide, but the analytical part of her mind was captivated. This was a part of her she knew existed but had only studied in school. She was experiencing raw instinct!

A man seemingly made of shadow deliberately strode out of the crowd and sidled up next to Eddie. He wore all black except for the dazzling white square of a priest's clerical collar. He reached over his shoulder, pulled a sword, and with practiced precision brought it down in a silky-smooth arc across the back of Eddie's neck, severing his head and cutting off the waning howl. The man's attention immediately settled on Angelina's wound. His gaze shifted to her face, and she stared back in numb fear. A mask covered his head and face, leaving only his eyes exposed where a burning sadness mixed with an aged hatred lived. Angelina crossed herself and he hesitated. He blinked watery eyes at her and then gently returned the cross, nodding to her before disappearing into the crowd as fast as he had appeared.

She was standing there staring at her dead brother and the naked, headless human body of Eddie when the police and the paramedics arrived. She ignored them. Her mind was a jumble of psychology terms and personal feelings. She tried to separate them. Her primitive side knew what she saw, but her training tried to classify it under a neat and tidy medical diagnostic category. The paramedics got to her first, but they found no wounds, only light scars. "You got off easy, Ma'am. That dog ripped your dress but missed your skin."

The police were sympathetic to Angelina, but they also expected her to answer a lot of questions. "Who were Eddie's friends?" "Where was he from?" "What was his address?" "How long did she know him?" "How did she meet him?" There were a dozen others, but Angelina couldn't remember them all. By the time they were done with her, she realized she didn't know Eddie that well at all. The hardest questions to answer were the ones where they wanted her to describe what she saw. She repeated it over and over, and by the end of the night, she was so tired she would have said anything just to go home and sleep.

Dr. Hernandez, the police psychologist on duty that night, sat down with her. "Dr. Suarez, you are aware of Occam's Razor just as surely as I am. What makes more sense to you? That Eddie was a werewolf or that this was a mob hit, and you've had a psychotic break after seeing your brother, the only other surviving member of your family, killed in front of you?"

She let them convince her someone snuck a large dog into the club, and it was that dog that attacked and killed Raul. That someone then killed Eddie. Miami Vice took over the investigation at that point because it was now classified as a drug mob hit. Raul's death was classified as collateral damage.

Late November 1980

Craig sat in his chair next to his swimming pool. He wore a heavily starched button-up shirt neatly tucked into a pair of slacks that were so tightly pressed the creases would cut a finger. The folded cuffs of his slacks landed lightly onto a pair of black leather shoes that could have been made of glass. Every light in the courtyard reflected back off of them.

Angelina stood before him, nervous but confident about her situation. She was here so Craig could investigate the circumstances surrounding the death of her pack Alpha, Larry Rhodes. Lisa and Mary Rhodes, Angelina's pack female Alpha and Larry's wife, sat in chairs a few feet away.

Craig started off. "Angelina, you are accused of violating the Pact, of killing a *lupus* without permission of the Conclave. How do you plead?"

Angelina gave him a shrewd glance. "How do I plead?" she asked, with a little more attitude than she probably should have. "Are you serious? This isn't a court of law. That son of a bitch tried to kill me. You've read the police report."

Mary jumped up from her chair. "He did not! Larry was a good man. He would never try to kill someone unless it was in self-defense."

Craig directed a dark look toward Mary. "Please sit down." He turned back to Angelina. "The police are not a concern here. Did you or did you not kill Larry Rhodes?"

Angelina straightened her back, put her hands on her hips. "Yes. I didn't want to, though. Mr. Minor, I'm *not* a murderer."

Craig nodded his head. "Why don't you tell us your side of the story? Perhaps that will clear some things up."

She'd already been through this with her Clan head, James, and if he referred it up the chain, then he wasn't convinced of her innocence. She didn't think this boded well, but she refused to be railroaded. She planned on telling it exactly as it happened. She didn't think Craig had risen to the rank of *Lupus Rex* without having an objective mind.

"All right," she optimistically agreed.

November 1979

Angelina was in her office at the Bridge. It was just large enough for the battered desk she was sitting at, her chair, a large filing cabinet, and two smaller chairs reserved for her patients. The Bridge did good work, but it was under-funded. The office still smelled of the old, musty carpet that had been ripped up months ago regardless of the number of cans of air freshener she sprayed. She swore it had gotten worse while she was away.

She had a picture of Raul in one hand and a damp tissue in the other. It was her first day back at work since Raul's funeral, and she was having a hard time knowing where to start on the stack of folders that had piled up while she was gone. A knock on her door brought her out of her trance.

A tall man walked in, dressed in a cheap, grey suit with a loosened, blue tie. He was Caucasian with black hair and brown eyes, and although he was dressed sloppily, Angelina could tell he took care of himself; he had a spring in his step one usually only saw in younger men. He held a police badge open in his hand. "Dr. Suarez?"

"Yes, may I help you?"

"Yes, Ma'am. I'm Detective Larry Rhodes. I'm with the Miami Metro Police." He stepped the rest of the way into the office and put his badge away. "If you have the time, I would like to ask a few questions regarding the investigation into your brother's and boyfriend's deaths."

Angelina shook her head. "Now is not a good time, Detective." She put Raul's picture back in the corner of her desk. "This is my first day back, and as you can see—" she pointed to the stack of case files "—I've got a lot of catching up to do. Besides, I've already repeatd the story twenty times it seems."

He frowned at being put off, but then his eyes brightened up. "Would you be willing to let me buy you lunch? It would be on the police department, of course." He had a friendly enough smile. "I don't have a large expense account, but I can swing for a decent burger and a large soda."

"Okay," she sighed, nodding her head. "Meet me out front at noon."

The morning went faster than she expected it would. Her stomach rumbled, and when she checked the clock on the wall, she was astonished to see it was two minutes after twelve. She picked up her purse, rushed out of her office, and down the hall to the front door, her high heels clacking on the wooden floor.

Detective Rhodes was standing patiently next to a large, black sedan that visually screamed, "Police!" He stubbed his cigarette out under the toe of his shoe and smiled when he saw her come out through the door. "Hello, Dr. Suarez. Thanks for agreeing to meet with me." He opened the passenger door for her and then jogged around the front of the car and got in himself. As he pulled into traffic, he asked, "How's your first day back at work turning out?"

"Busy. And I'm hungry." His smell was quite noticeable under the smell of the cigarette he just finished. She hadn't realized it until now, but she could also smell him all day in her office, as well. It wasn't an unpleasant odor, but virile and musky. It reminded her somewhat of Eddie, and she was surprised at herself for not being uncomfortable with that strange coincidence.

"Well, you'll like lunch." He showed that friendly smile of his again. "I promise."

They drove out of the city and into the suburbs to the west where they pulled into a small mom and pop hamburger stand. It had been a camper at one point in its life, as evidenced by the towing tongue on one end, but its days of rolling down the road were over. It was sitting on cinder blocks now and had a window cut into the side, ruining its structural stability. A large canopy was taped to the main structure, sheltering the window from heat and rain. There was no inside seating, and an extremely large, greasy-looking woman took orders at the window.

Detective Rhodes ordered for the both of them. "Two cheeseburgers all the way with fries and large cokes."

Angelina countered, "No tomatoes on mine. Hate 'em."

He turned back to the lady. "Hold the tomatoes on one of them."

A few minutes later, they were sitting down at one of the picnic tables outside and eating their cheeseburgers. A few bites later, Angelina admitted, "You were right. This is a good burger. Thanks, Detective. I needed this. I needed to do something different, get away from the routine and the triggers."

He smiled around a large mouth of food. "You're welcome!"

They ate the rest of their burgers in silence. When they sat back from the table, Detective Rhodes started in with some questions. She was right; they were the same ones she'd answered twenty times before. The last question caught her off-guard, though.

"Why do you think the scratches the dog made healed so quickly?"

Suddenly, in her mind's eye, she saw the scratches on her side the night they were put there. She had been bleeding, but they weren't serious, so she didn't worry about them. When the paramedics inspected her and found them to be scabs, they naturally assumed they were old. She was too numb from the events of that night to contradict them.

She snapped her head up at him sharply. "What are you talking about?"

"When Eddie scratched you. You were healed before the police arrived. Why do you think that is?"

"How did you know?"

Detective Rhodes rolled his sleeve up. Along his left forearm was a series of long scratches. "Because the same thing happened to me...and to Eddie as well."

"I don't understand what you're trying to tell me." Angelina's heart rate jumped up, and the world around him disappeared, leaving her staring at him through a tunnel.

"Angelina, what do you think scratched you that night?"

"It was a dog," she recounted, trancelike.

"No, it wasn't," he objected, shaking his head. "You know what it was."

The tunnel vision turned into a kaleidoscope. There were two, then four, then eight versions of Detective Rhodes spinning around in it.

Angelina woke up on a small cot surrounded by the pungent smell of raw and cooked meat, fresh vegetables, sugary drinks, and a dozen other smells she couldn't place. Detective Rhodes was sitting next to her in an old, wooden folding chair. The greasy, order-taking-lady walked across an aisle a few feet away from the end of the cot.

She sat up. "What happened?"

"You fainted," he sassed with a gentle smile. "Don't worry. It happens sometimes."

Angelina let the memories of her last few conscious minutes run through her head. "You think I was scratched by a werewolf." It was a statement of fact.

He raised his eyebrows in apparent surprise. "I know you were because I'm a werewolf too. Eddie was part of my pack. And now you are."

Angelina laughed maniacally. "You're nuts. Take me back to my office."

He stood up and offered his hand. "Let's go."

On the way back, he reached into his coat pocket and pulled out a business card. "This is my home address and phone number. I hope you decide to join us at the next full moon."

"You aren't letting this go, are you?" she sarcastically asked.

"Listen, Doctor. If you are not with us when you change, you'll go on a rampage and kill innocent people. There are those out there who want to kill us. You saw who killed Eddie. They'll come after you next if that happens. We can protect you. Think about it. Please. The next full moon is in two weeks."

Over the next couple of weeks Angelina thought about what Detective Rhodes told her. The repressed memory of how she got those scratches kept floating to the top of her conscious mind whenever she caught herself daydreaming. She was familiar with repressed memories. She just didn't think she had any. She looked up the date of the full moon. She pulled out her map and looked up the address on Detective Rhodes's business card. At noon on the day the full moon would arrive, she found herself sitting in her car in Detective Rhodes's driveway.

She sneered at herself in the rearview mirror and exclaimed, "You've got to be kidding me! There are no such things as werewolves!"

She started the car and was about to put it into reverse when Detective Rhodes knocked on her door's window. He had his friendly smile painted all over his face. "Are you coming in?" he asked. "Everyone's here and keen on meeting you!"

Angelina didn't remember anyone she met that afternoon. It was like another kaleidoscope of featureless faces and forgotten names. Of what little she did remember was that around 5:00 o'clock that afternoon, they all jumped into different vehicles and drove out to the country. Her strongest memory of her first *renovatio* was a burning pain suddenly being replaced with waking up nude in the woods, lost and confused. Detective Rhodes showed up with a bathrobe for her. He didn't make any effort to hide his leer as she wrapped herself in the robe.

Early November 1980

Angelina came to know her *grex* mates as she settled back into her life, but she didn't feel the overriding need to establish strong ties to them. She buried herself in her work and did the best she could for her patients. Detective Rhodes went out of his way to teach her the ropes of being *lupa*, because he had high hopes for her and wanted her to learn to *frenis*. He strongly believed there was a place for her in the *grex* leadership. Educated *lupis* were highly sought after as recruits. He also bought her a pistol for protection and taught her how to use it. He said, "I would prefer you shoot any intruder rather than perform a *renovatio* and eat him. Less paperwork." She enjoyed his company but knew he was married, so didn't let their relationship ever go beyond lunch once or twice a week.

Besides, he was sneaky.

She couldn't nail it down, but something about him didn't sit right with her. He was manipulative and harsh when he didn't get his way. It might have been the Alpha mentality mixed with being a cop, but he wasn't the type of man she wanted to spend her life with. He was her Alpha, not her boyfriend.

One night, shortly after the anniversary of Raul's death, Larry weakly knocked on her door. She opened it a crack, and he stood there, shrunk in on himself, and smelling upset and uncertain.

"Larry! What's wrong?" She finished opening the door the whole way.

"Mary and I got into a fight." He sagged even farther as he said it.

"Come in. Can I get you anything?" She grabbed him by the arm and pulled him into her house.

"No." He shuffled in and his confusion deepened. It was the first time he had been at her house, so he was in unfamiliar territory. "I just didn't know who else to talk to."

"Come sit down in the living room." She led him to the sofa, and he sat down. She sat down next to him and her training kicked in before she realized what was happening. Regardless of level of training though, talking about a problem is usually the first step to solving it. "Tell me what happened."

He leaned forward, knees on his elbows, head bowed. "She's jealous of you."

Angelina exclaimed, "Me? Why in the world would she be jealous of me?"

He didn't answer.

Angelina got up and paced around the room. "She knows we aren't an item, right, Larry? She's my female Alpha, dammit! She could make all kinds of trouble for me. What did you tell her, Larry?"

"I didn't have to tell her anything. She knows I'm in love with you."

Angelina stopped pacing immediately. If she had been running, she would probably have tripped and fallen it was so abrupt. "What do you mean you're in love with me? You don't know me!" Angelina's blood pressure started rising and her *lupa* stirred, but when she concentrated, she could smell the truth on him. He honestly believed he was in love with her.

He stood up and took a step toward her. "I can't help myself. The heart wants what the heart wants, Angelina. You could kill Mary, take her place as female Alpha! I could arrange— "

"What kind of mushy bullshit is that, Yuma?" she flung at him. "You been reading romance novels or something? Get out. Go home. Tell her it's all a big misunderstanding. I'll call her now." She picked up the phone and started calling his house—and stopped before she dialed the last digit. *I've got his number memorized! How many times have I called him in the last year?*

She was putting the phone down when he snatched it out of her hand. She sensed a change in his demeanor. Unrequited love, hurt, and anger blackened the areas around his eyes. "Go home? I have no home to go to because of you, Angelina! You lead me on for a year and then tell me to get lost? You've ruined my marriage, you bitch!"

"I'm sorry, Larry. What can we do to fix this?" Angelina backed away from him because she knew what was next. She mentally kicked herself for not seeing the warning signs. She had counseled enough battered women to know where this was heading.

"This can't be fixed. You've already told me how you—hey! Where are you going, you bitch?!"

Angelina sprinted into her bedroom and slammed her door closed. It wouldn't stop him, but it might slow him down. She needed to get her pistol out of the night stand, all the way on the other side of her room. She scrambled over her bed, and a familiar growl rumbled from the hallway. *He's performed his* renovatio! *So the* frentatus *aren't as civilized as they've led us to believe.*

She got to the other side of the bedroom and opened the nightstand drawer. She pulled her pistol out just as he crashed through the door. He took a split second to orient himself, and that split second gave her the time she needed. She raised the revolver and emptied it into him.

His last *vagor* conveyed surprise.

She slowly walked over to his dying body and coldly watched the life leak from his scared eyes. "Did you forget you were the one who gave me the silver-tipped, hollow points? And insist I keep them loaded in my pistol at all times?"

Late November 1980

Mary jumped to her feet again and yelled, "That's bullshit! Larry and I may have had our problems, but he would never have planned to kill me. Craig, she's lying!"

This time it was Lisa who shot her a dark look. "Mary, sit down!" she growled, the *lupa* quite evident in her voice. "Don't interfere again!"

Craig stood up from his chair and slowly paced around, arms half crossed, rubbing his chin with one hand. "I have to admit, Angelina, it does look like he attacked you first."

"What do you mean, it looked like? He busted down my door. He was *lupus*. He was coming after me!"

Craig shook his head. "There could be any number of reasons for him coming through the door like that. Sure, he was upset, but still…any number of reasons."

Angelina glared at Craig. She couldn't believe what she was hearing. "Like what?"

"He might have been coming in to try and reason with you. He wasn't a wildling. He was well aware of his abilities. Maybe he was just trying to scare you."

Angelina scoffed. "Well, he certainly did that!"

By now, Craig had slowly worked his way over to her. Before she had a chance to react, he lashed out with his culas, and scarred her with the mark of *Lupa solitarius*. She fell to the ground in agony. "I'm sorry, Angelina, but the law is the law. We have no proof it was self-defense. And killing your pack Alpha on top of that? Well, let's just say you're lucky I don't declare you *Utlagatus* as well."

Lisa and Mary got up and marched out of the rear foyer.

Craig looked down at her. "You may leave when you are feeling better."

He followed Lisa and Mary out.

Chapter 39—St. Joseph Church, New Orleans

Aaron Darveau, June 25, 1983

The rest of the trip to Pensacola was quiet, other than two rest stops for gas, food, driver switching, and bathroom breaks. Everyone concentrated on their own thoughts and what the future was holding for them.

Aaron pulled into a gas station just as the sun dragged the last of its light with it below the horizon. Angelina was sleeping in the backseat while Elwood was sprawled along the rest of it, asleep with his head on her lap. Since she had climbed into the back in Miami, the dog hadn't whimpered once. His wound had healed up sufficiently, so she had removed the stitches and walked him when they stopped for gas and bathroom breaks. She might not have liked Aaron, but she loved Elwood.

They filled up the tank then pulled around to the back of the gas station to where there was a small stand of trees. Jose needed some privacy to transform, and with the sun already down, the woods were perfect cover. While Angelina took Elwood out to do his business, Aaron leaned against the hood of Devil Car and watched Jose perform his *renovatio*. He disappeared into the woods, leaving Aaron alone with nothing more than a guttural growl.

It was the first time Aaron had heard *lupus* talk while he was human. It wasn't quite as smooth as when he was *lupus*, but he got the drift of what Jose said. "***Be back shortly.***"

Jose stepped out of the woods in human form about ten minutes later. Aaron jumped off of the car and asked, "Did it work?"

"Yeah," Jose informed them. "I got the feeling she was all right and that we should trust *your* instincts."

Aaron blinked. "That's it?" he asked cynically. "That doesn't help us one damned bit. I don't know *what* my fucking instincts are telling me right now!" He paced around in a circle. "I need to talk to him."

"Who?" Angelina asked.

"Father Thomas."

Jose asked, "Are you sure that's wise? You might tip our hand."

"We don't have a hand!" Aaron exclaimed. "We've got five different suits and no face cards. Are we walking into a trap or not? I hate mysteries, Jose, and this is a jim-dandy."

Aaron made the phone call to Father Thomas. "Father, how are things going?"

"Okay right now, but they know we have her. They haven't found us yet, but it's only a matter of time. They'll track us here eventually. Where are you at?" He sounded tired.

"Pensacola. Be there around midnight." He waved for Jose and Angelina to come closer to the phone booth. "Father, how do you know they know you have her?"

"One of my friends hung out in the bar across the street from her apartment. He saw them go in."

"Oh." Aaron paused. "Tell me, how did a priest know they were *lupus*? I don't think they walked in there in *lupus* form, did they?"

Father Thomas got quiet on the other end of the line.

Aaron decided to confront the issue head-on. "Father, are you a Fector?"

Father Thomas didn't hesitate. "Yes and no. I'm retired. I don't hunt *lupis* anymore."

"I'm having a hard time believing that right now," Aaron insisted.

"Why? What's happened?"

"*Viam Lupus* was wiped out by Fectors this morning. Only Jose and his wife survived. It's dreadfully coincidental they attacked right after I found them." Jose was nodding his head. Angelina was absent-mindedly stroking Elwood's ears, her eyes white. She was using her Gift, taking in the information from the phone call to try to see through the uncertainty.

"Aaron," Father Thomas pleaded, softly, "you have to believe me when I say I had nothing to do with that."

"I want to, Father." Aaron paused for a few moments. "You say you used to be a Fector? What happened?"

"You have to ask?" Father Thomas asked incredulously.

The answer left Aaron's lips before he knew he had it. "Kyle."

"Yes, Kyle." Father Thomas took a deep breath. "When he became infected, I no longer saw howlers in the same light. When I looked at Kyle, I didn't see evil. I saw that little boy I helped raise. I knew someday I might be ordered to kill him. He was as close to a son to me as possible without being from my own loins.

"We're not all cold-blooded killers, but that was what the Order had become filled with. One day I got word Kyle had been infected. Aaron, I was shocked to find out the Order knew about it. I began to wonder just how close the Lamp of Truth was to the Race. How would they have this kind of information? I was wise enough not to raise that question out loud.

"I went through a few weeks of anger and confusion and fear, but in the end realized I could never kill Kyle if ordered to. I requested a release from the Order in 1981. I told them I was getting too old to be effective. Rather than boot me entirely out, they moved me to inactive status and reassigned me to that church there in Orlando."

Aaron listened to what Father Thomas said without interruption. He wished he had been in front of the priest so he could have used all of his *lupus* senses to look for deception, to see his way through any trap that might be set for him. Unfortunately, the only one he had was hearing. He found nothing in Father Thomas's speech to indicate anything other than honesty. "Father, this sounds too neat and tidy."

Father Thomas asked, "Aaron, do you believe in fate?"

"As in 'I don't have a say in what my future holds for me?' No, I do not. I refuse to believe I don't have a say in how my life turns out."

"That's good. I don't believe in it either. But I do believe we all have a purpose. We may live our entire lives never realizing that purpose. But when someone gets an inkling of what it is, that person can change the world. It might be something as simple as hugging a child who's fallen and scraped his knee who is destined to grow up to be a great teacher. Or it may be something as fantastic as saving a voodoo witch from being ripped to shreds by werewolves."

"What are you getting at Father?"

"I used to think my purpose was to kill howlers. After Kyle, I realized that wasn't it at all. I drifted from day to day because I didn't know what my purpose was anymore. Then I met you and realized I'd been wrong again. I did know my purpose.

"Every decision I've made in my life has led me to this spot, right now, consorting with you, Aaron, a shunned *Lupus Rex*. And every decision you've made in your life has led you here to me, a member of *Lucerna Veritatis*. You're not evil. I see that in you. Nobody evil could care as much about his fellow man as you do. God's not yet done intertwining our destinies.

"But that doesn't mean we have to work toward them. We can ignore them if we wish. I can walk out of this church and never look back. You can turn your car around and head another direction. To me, those would be the greater sins."

Aaron measured what Father Thomas said. His *lupus* senses picked up the Father's heartbeat. It never wavered. He was telling the truth.

He raised his brows at Angelina and Jose. She was nodding her head and Jose, too, nodded his, but reluctantly.

"Okay, Father, we believe you." Their conversation briefly lingered in silence before Aaron demanded, "No more secrets, Father. I don't have time to be second guessing every decision I make because I'm dealing with incomplete information. You got that?"

"Understood. And I apologize for misleading you. Now hurry up and get here."

"We will. Have you settled on a safe location yet?"

"Yes, St. Joseph on Tulane Avenue. It's as safe as can be under the circumstances. Can you find it?"

Aaron asked Jose, "Do you know where St. Joseph is on Tulane Avenue?"

Jose answered, "Yes."

"Jose knows how to find it. See you soon—wait, hold on, Jose wants to speak with Jajine."

Aaron didn't hang around and eavesdrop.

Aaron pulled over and let Jose drive when they reached the outskirts of New Orleans. He was familiar with the streets and would be able to get there more quickly without having to give commands from the passenger seat. Elwood was sitting up. He knew things were coming to a head and was whining in spite of Angelina's cooing and petting.

Aaron asked her, "This intuition of yours, can it give us a little help on how we should proceed?"

"Yes. It says to kill them all."

"That's the strategy, obviously, but any details on tactics?"

She consulted her Gift again. "No. There are too many possible outcomes. I can't see it clearly. My intuition isn't that strong. But I do feel we are going to need that *lupus* of yours, the one that killed a would-be Queen. Nothing else is going to help us."

"What do you mean, 'too many outcomes?' How many do you see?"

"I don't know. I'm not that good at this. I can't seem to keep things straight in my head. Most *lupas* are good at making educated guesses without known facts. I don't like doing that. Maybe it's my medical training, but I need something to work with. How many *lupis*? Who's there? Are they expecting us? How many priests? Are there any Fectors there? Right now, we don't know anything other than the fact there are *lupis* involved."

"You saw we needed my *lupus*, at least."

She laughed cynically and Elwood barked playfully at the commotion. "I didn't need my Gift for that, Yuma," she informed him. "You kicked Jose's ass without trying. Regardless of what we're facing, we'll need that kind of skill on our side."

Jose didn't appear to appreciate Angelina's comment; his jaw muscles bulged out when Aaron glanced at him. He decided to change the subject. "Jose, your mom got any mumbo-jumbo she can throw around?"

Jose just snorted. "Who the fuck knows? I haven't seen her in years."

Aaron watched the lights of New Orleans get brighter the closer they got. He rubbed his sweaty palms on his jeans. "Would it freak y'all out if I said I was scared shitless?"

Jose's face darkened. "Only a fool wouldn't be scared right now."

Craig Minor, June 25, 1983

Craig and Lisa stood across the street from the church, staring at the triple arch design of its front entrance. It was a nineteenth century American cathedral, ninety years old, built to show the glory of God, the God who cursed them with this disease, the God who set the Fectors onto them.

Craig sighed, **"It's a shame we have to destroy some of this. Such beauty."**

Lisa growled at him, **"The witch is inside, and she has to die."**

"I know that," he snapped back, **"you don't tell me my job."**

Lisa snarled, **"Someone has to. You let Karen get killed, and you lost the bastard who did it. At least you found the witch, so you're not a complete loss."**

Craig was quite upset when he found out Ricardo shunned someone with a witch for a mother. He insisted he'd done the necessary background checking, but it was not a well-known fact. Jajine was smart to keep it hidden. She moved around quite a bit, and didn't go by her given name, so the local pack couldn't find her at first. Supposedly, every house in New Orleans with a door on it had a fortune teller living inside, and without a description, not even the sex, they spent quite a few resources looking for one who gave out silver, wolf fang necklaces.

Craig and Lisa were still in Orlando yesterday when Ricardo called. "The Fectors found her first," he reported. "I'm not sure how they found out about her, though. And I don't know why they would be protecting her. Catholicism and Voodoo isn't exactly a mainstream mix, if you know what I mean."

"Fectors? There's no fucking Fectors in New Orleans. These are just some friends Aaron managed to pick up. He's from Louisiana, in case you forgot. Did you even read the damned report I sent out? He annihilated an entire monastery *and* killed their North American Commander. By himself! There's no way they would work with him."

"So you don't know where he's at?"

Craig lowered his voice. "We barely missed him in Miami. The police found his car at a dealership in Orlando, but no one knows what he's driving now. He's lying low or the Fectors have already gotten him."

"Hmm." Ricardo wouldn't let it go. "Well, they looked like Fectors. And smelled like them, too."

Craig wasn't in the mood to argue with him. "Then you better get her," Craig ordered. "And then kill her."

"Craig, I would love to, but I've got another crisis on my hands. I've got wildlings running all over south Arkansas, and I'm up to my ears trying to clean that mess up. I've even got Hollywood movie producers in Fouke, Arkansas interviewing everyone they run into. I think they're going to make another Boggy Creek movie there—like I don't have enough shit on my plate already. I'll send Hank and Kenny down, though. They're my most trusted enforcers. They'll be able to handle it."

Craig's admission to Aaron had been right. *We've grown too complacent.* "Well, if you're too tame to handle one little ol' black woman, I guess I'll have to take care of it for you. Don't bother sending anybody. My *grex* will handle it."

So Craig was now standing out in the drizzling rain, getting ready to storm a church.

He was glad he decided to come himself once he got to New Orleans and saw the situation first-hand. The local *grex* might be capable, but they were a little too informal for his tastes. They called themselves *Loup Garou* and considered themselves better than the rest of the Race. He established himself as Alpha and put a stop to that notion right off the bat. Just to drive the point home, he put Bill and Glen over them. There were a few fights, but in the end things were going to be done his way. He split the pack up into three groups, with Bill, Glen, and himself in charge of a group each.

The first group, consisting of two plus Bill, was on the roof of the church in *lupis* form. They reported eight human priests plus the witch. The priests appeared to be armed like Fectors, but Craig found that unlikely. The closest Fector monastery was in Jackson, Mississippi, and they didn't know what was going on down here.

The second group, consisting of five plus Glen, patrolled around the church, also in *lupis* form. Traffic was light this time of night, so they didn't have to duck into the shadows that often.

The third group comprised two *lupis* plus himself and Lisa. They stood in reserve across the street in an empty lot, a construction site for a new hospital going up. Summer and Autumn were there as well, but they were Lisa's bodyguards in case Craig was forced to engage the enemy.

At 11:47, the drizzle turned to rain. Three minutes later, the midnight church bells rang, the last for the day, and he gave the word to attack, using the tolling of the bells to cover their entrance. Bill's group crashed through the windows along the upper balcony, and Glen's group ran through the front entrance. Craig and his group sprinted across the street and stood outside the front door once everyone else was inside. He was only there as back-up and had no intention of risking his own life unless absolutely necessary. He planned to have this taken care of tonight and be back in Orlando tomorrow.

Lisa stayed across the street with Summer and Autumn.

Craig sent the two *lupis* with him in through the front doors to report on what they saw. One of them came back out a few moments later. "**They're shooting silver-tipped crossbow bolts,**" he reported. "**We have two down. I don't know how many of theirs are down. They've built some kind of barricade near the choir section. Glen and his guys appear to be mixing it up back there with them.**"

"**Silver? Damnit, they might be Fectors! Keep me informed.**" The howls and growls of the *lupis* echoed from the church along with the crashing of furniture and human screams. He hoped this would be over soon because too much noise would bring cops. He chastised himself for not thinking about that. Cathedrals were built of stone and designed to carry sound. Ignorant, medieval country-folk would break out in tears the first time they heard a choir singing in a cathedral. Hearing those beautiful sounds provoked an emotional response when the only ones you had heard up until then were those you spent your entire life listening to in the middle of a field. The Catholic Church got many converts that way.

One of his sentries came back out. **"Glen appears to be down—he isn't moving—and we've lost another from Bill's group. And the noise is getting worse."**

"I can hear it, you fool. Let's move in and help. We have to finish this now."

Summer Levi, June 25, 1983

Summer, Autumn, and Lisa watched Craig rush inside the church. Lisa started to run after him, but Autumn held her back.

Summer, eyes white, whimpered with glee, **"He'll be fine. We're winni—"**

A bright orange Ford Mustang roared down the street toward them and screeched to a stop in front of the church. Aaron had arrived, and he brought help; two other people jumped out of the car with him, and they all immediately performed a *renovatio*.

Summer whined and panted, **"He must have driven straight through from Miami to make it here by now."**

Autumn and Lisa whined with uncertainty. This was an unexpected and wholly unwelcome turn of events. None of them had taken into account Aaron showing up tonight in their predictions.

They consulted their Gift again, and all came to the same conclusion. If they ran in now, they would all three die. They had to wait. Nothing else was certain other than that.

Aaron Darveau, June 25, 1983

Aaron saw three *lupis* run in through the front door of the church as Jose pulled Devil Car to the curb. The three of them jumped out and performed their *renovatio* before the car doors closed, ripping their clothes off in the process. Elwood was still in no condition to fight, so Aaron told him to stay. As they leapt up the steps, he told Jose and Angelina, **"Keep your wits about you. Don't release your *lupus* unless you have to. I'll create a distraction. Our goal is to save Jajine. Nothing else matters. Both of you head to her and protect her."**

Aaron raced Jose up the steps and ran into the church. There was dust in the air, musty, along with the smell of sweat and blood, leather, wood, and oiled iron. He saw Father Thomas and the other priests holed up behind the choir wall, shooting self-loading crossbows at the attacking *lupis.* He saw Jajine behind them and Jose and Angelina as they tried to fight their way to her.

Aaron let loose a *vagor.* "**Catch you shitheads at a bad time?!**"

Aaron's bloodlust bubbled to the surface. His *lupus* wanted to be free. Sixteen hours on the road, crammed into Devil Car, had led to this. His *vagor* was more than a taunt; it was a challenge to whoever thought they were Alpha. It was answered by two *lupis,* and he partially tucked his tail in surprise when he saw one of them was Craig, hiding behind some flunky.

The flunky's first swipe glanced off Aaron's chin. He recognized the feint too late though, when the second swipe doubled him over and expelled the last bit of choked air from his belly.

He hated having the air knocked out of him. Fortunately, he knew how to defend himself, and rolled somewhat with the attack. Still, it was a hell of blow, probably the hardest he'd ever experienced. He wasn't used to that. Other than the few fights he'd been in since Florida, his only other experience was in the ring. It was only his training that kept him on his feet.

The flunky stood there in amazement that Aaron was still standing. He took a step back when he saw Aaron rear up, lips snarl with rage, knees bend for balance, and a deep and guttural growl thunder from his chest.

Craig exclaimed with a hollow rumble, "**Kill him, you fool! That's Aaron!**" The flunky took one hesitant step and then rushed the rest of the way in. Aaron smelled the sickly-sweet smell of fear on him.

Aaron howled with anger, "**You…dare…attack…**" as he stepped to the side and two steps forward, saying each word with each step until he was inside the flunky's circle. Aaron brought his arm up and twisted to the right, intent on using it as a lever to throw the flunky to the ground. He punctuated the last move with "***me!***" and his arm hit empty air.

Aaron's eyes widened as he saw too late the flunky counter his attack. Aaron knew the instant he didn't make contact he was in a weak position. Before he could defend himself, Craig engaged by jumping into the air and landing a kick high to his shoulder blade, sending a numbing pain up through his shoulder and down his arm. He willed his feet to maintain his balance. If he fell now, he was dead. *I hope Master Chen never finds out about this fight. He would be ashamed of me for rushing in all balls to the wall like this. Will I ever learn?*

The flunky came in with a follow up to Craig. Aaron deflected it easily enough, allowing him to move a few steps out of reach. He took advantage of the break and caught his breath.

He pulled Chi from around himself, and the noise of the battle disappeared, and the smell of death turned sweet. Only he and his adversaries existed—and the pain in his shoulder and the numbness in his arm. Seeing both of them warily approaching him was confusing. *How did it come to this?*

His lupus rumbled indifferently, ***"It doesn't matter. It is here."***

They both swung at Aaron as soon as they came within range. He used his numb arm to block Craig's blow—he knew he wouldn't feel it—while he dodged the flunky's haymaker, sending him out of range. Craig jumped into the air and came down with his cula extended, intent on raking Aaron from nose to belly. Aaron was wrong about not feeling Craig's blow. His arm turned to jelly under the blocked attack. *Should have deflected!*

Craig grinned, knowing Aaron was in a weak spot. Aaron squatted down—not completely under his own will—and stepped into Craig's circle. Using his good arm, he shoved his talons into Craig's lower gut, and using the strength of his legs to stand, ripped his cula up through Craig's belly and into his chest. Craig's eyes widened with pain and fear.

Aaron lifted his cula to Craig's eyes and showed him his still beating heart.

Craig airlessly muttered, **"They were right, you ascend—"** He crumpled to the floor as the heart in Aaron's hand pumped its last drop of blood and stopped beating.

Aaron rapidly turned to his left and relief washed through him when he saw the flunky staring in open-mouthed disbelief at the bloody heap of *Lupus Rex*. Aaron swiped his cula across the flunky's throat and dropped the mushy mess to his feet next to Craig's heart.

Suddenly, Jajine cried out, "Joey, no!" Jajine was between a couple of the displaced pews near the front, rushing for the middle. She kneeled down out of sight.

Aaron's culas dug into the wooden floor as he used his *lupus* strength to leap to Jajine's side. She was covered in blood trying to staunch the blood flow from Jose's neck, chest, and abdomen. Jose had taken a blow similar to what Craig just received; he was slashed open from groin to neck.

Jose's glassy eyes found his mother. With a weak smile he gurgled, "I told you to call me Jose, Mom. After Dad."

Aaron took a quick glance around the church. The fighting was over. There were a few priests left, but all of the *lupis* were down or dead. He looked down at Jose and tried to find the source of the blood. He didn't know what to do, but he knelt down anyway to do something, anything. His arm was still numb, but he willed it to work.

He changed back to human form and reached for Jose's chest, but Jose stopped him by grabbing his hand. "You can't save me," he choked out, "but you can save my mother. They won't stop looking for either of you. Especially after this." Eyes wild and unfocused, he turned his head looking for someone, someone not there, and called out "Ange—!" but a series of wet coughs cut him off.

"I'll watch out for them, Jose. You have my word." Movement to his right snatched his attention away from Jose. Angelina darted toward them on all fours. "Angelina's coming, Jose!"

Jose pulled on Aaron's hand again, and he choked out through racking coughs, "Finish *cough* what you started *cough* *frenator*. Don't let *cough* bastards win." Blood bubbled from his mouth along with a string of gurgling coughs. Aaron turned him onto his side to help with his breathing, but it was useless. Jose died in his arms while Jajine and Angelina wailed in grief.

They were interrupted by a shriek from the front of the church. **"Craig!"**

Aaron snapped his head around. *Lisa? She's here, too?* She launched herself from the doorway, flying in an arc that ended in a scrambled landing by Craig's side. **"Nooo!"** she screamed as she threw herself over him.

The *lupas*, Summer and Autumn, stood in the doorway, and when they saw Aaron, dropped to all fours and sprinted toward him. He wasn't in any shape to take on two, possibly three, *lupis*. He quickly looked around for help. Half the priests were dead, and the other half weren't in position. Angelina was useless with Jose lying dead next to her, and Jajine was merely human. He was about to die, and he couldn't do a whole lot about it.

Jajine placed her hand on his arm, and the church grew quiet. The dust hung suspended in the air, and the crossbow bolts floated by slow enough to count the hairs on their fletching. Aaron turned to look at her and saw her attention was still on Jose. She spoke, but her lips didn't move. "Aaron, now is the time to fulfill that destiny I warned you about. This is why I've led you here, boy. This night is what they've feared since you first changed. I can't help you anymore. It's up to you now."

He glared at the enemies bearing down on him. *It's time to end this!*

He performed a *renovatio* and rose to his full height. The pain in his arm and shoulder disappeared, his joints loosened, and his muscles crackled with renewed energy. He now understood why it was a called a *renovatio*, a rejuvenation.

The *vagor* he let loose the night Kyle was shunned was borne of necessity and fear.

The *vagor* he let loose when he ran into the church a few minutes earlier was borne of desperation.

The *vagor* he let loose when he stood up from beside Jose's dead form was borne of nature, of seizing one's rightful dominion. It reverberated throughout the church, shattering all of the remaining windows.

And it bore one distinct concept: *I! Am! Rex!*

History changed. Summer and Autumn skidded to a halt two steps before Aaron, their anger rapidly transforming to fear.

He took a single step, closing the gap between them, towering above them, muscles tense, culas extended, face twisted with malevolence. Saliva streamed from his fangs. They were one heartbeat away from death. He proclaimed, "**Challenge me and die!**"

Their fear and anger swiftly changed to belief as Aaron saw the effects of their Gift cascade through them. Their world just changed, and they acknowledged it—and him—by looking at the floor in front of his feet.

The battle was over.

Aaron looked around the church. *Too much death. Why does it have to be this way?*

Father Thomas appeared at his side, holding a sheet. Aaron took it and wrapped it around himself. "We found two *lupis* still alive—" he pointed at the front door "—other than those three." He was eying Summer, Autumn, and Lisa. They were wrapping their own sheets around themselves as two priests guarded them, silver-tipped crossbow bolts aimed menacingly. "All things considered, we won."

Aaron regurgitated his Tai Chi lesson in a detached voice, "Nobody ever wins a fight."

"Perhaps. But those who don't fall carry on."

"For a man of God, you sure have a brutal way of looking at things. But I guess that's the Fector in you, right?"

Father Thomas slowly nodded his head. "Yeah."

Aaron watched the remaining priests. If someone had told him a few days ago he would be in a church with a bunch of Fectors who weren't trying to kill him, he would have laughed. "It was you who sent the newspaper clipping about Kyle and Sally, wasn't it?"

"Yes. How did you know?"

"The smell of leather, wood, and oiled iron; the smell of your equipment. The only time I ever ran across that smell was when I was fighting for my life—other than the letter in my barracks. No one would have left something that obvious unless it was either a warning or an invitation."

Father Thomas smiled with a knowing look on his face. "It was both. Kyle told me what you did for him at Craig's house the night he was shunned. It impressed me. I wanted to meet the man who defied *Lupus Rex* before he was terminated."

Aaron raised his eyebrows in surprise. "Before I was terminated?"

"From what Kyle told me, I knew you wouldn't last long." He chuckled wryly. "You were too strong-willed for them. And when you did get shunned, the Order was abuzz."

"I didn't defy him," Aaron groaned, he eyes suddenly turning warm and blurry as he remembered the closed caskets.

"But you didn't submit. You argued with him. You wanted to ignore the Pact in favor of what was right. It might have been because of your inexperience, but I think there's something else in you. You know what's *Right* and what's *Wrong*. Unfortunately, there's more *Wrong* in this war than *Right* on both sides."

Aaron changed the subject because he didn't like praise he didn't think he deserved. It embarrassed him. And right now, a lot of people were dead because of him. "Are all of these former Fectors?"

"No, they are all active. But they tend to empathize more with me than with the strictures they've sworn to uphold to the letter. The Order could put them to death for what they've done here."

Aaron tensed up. "I thought the Order was no longer crusading against us," he quipped bitterly.

"How long did you think the Order would abide by that?" Father Thomas's tone reminded Aaron of his eighth grade math teacher. Anytime Aaron asked a silly question, she would look at him like he had just fallen out of the sky. "We've sworn to do whatever it takes to destroy every last one of you, even if it means working with you for a time. In fact, I could be put to death just for telling you *that*. Anyway, Father Ignacio was close to starting the crusades again."

"Wow. How close?"

"Next Easter Sunday."

Aaron spoke with determination in voice. "I hope we've stopped that."

Father Thomas looked sympathetic. "Me, too."

"So, what's with the crossbows? Why not rifles?"

"Too much noise. We'll use them when we know we won't attract much attention, but in a cathedral in the middle of a city? No, we don't want the attention any more than you do."

The priests finished administering last rites on the bodies and then one of them introduced himself to Aaron. "I'm Father Samuel. If you wish, we'll take care of the burial arrangements for your dead along with ours."

Aaron was humbled by the offer that came from this complete stranger. "Yes, thank you very much for that. I want Craig in an unmarked grave for now though."

"Done. So you're the *Lupus Rex* who would bring down the Race, huh?"

"That's me, but I'm not bringing it down. That would be impossible. But I am going to transform it. I'm not exactly sure how just yet, but that's my goal. And I want Father Thomas to help. The senseless murders have got to stop." He watched Father Samuel's face. "Are we going to have trouble with each other?"

He shook his head. "Probably not. Father Thomas speaks highly of you. And I, in turn, highly respect his opinion. But we'll be watching. If you can't keep a handle on things, we will not hesitate to grab that handle ourselves."

Aaron added, "And the quota stops tonight."

Father Samuel gave Aaron an appraising look. "How are you going to keep the wildlings in line?"

Aaron ran his fingers through his hair. "By teaching them to *frenis*."

Both Fathers showed surprise. Father Thomas asked, "You know how to do that?"

"I think so." Aaron was watching Jajine as he spoke to them. "Once they can *frenis*, they'll be able to control their passions, be able to tell right from wrong while changed. That's the only reason they go crazy. The ones who can't tell the difference—" he shrugged his shoulders "—I'll deal with personally and harshly. If I can't catch them, I'll call Father Thomas."

"Okay. For now though, we're looking at it as 'The enemy of my enemy is my friend.' We'll still continue to track and kill any who have slipped through the cracks though, the ones who are killing humans. We have no choice."

"Fair enough, as long as they're necessary, but I'll no longer send you names," Aaron countered. "And stay in touch with me. Let me know when you get one. I'll do the same. Communication between us is important. I know we'll never be accepted one hundred percent, but I don't think we need to war with each other. Please, don't start the crusades again. Give me time to make this work."

Father Samuel shared a neutral look with Father Thomas. "Agreed. I'll reinstate Father Thomas. He'll be your contact."

Father Thomas released his breath. Aaron hadn't been aware he was holding it.

Aaron told Father Samuel, "I'm surprised you aren't any more upset with me than you are, considering what I did in Orlando."

"You mean to Father Ignacio and his men? He's actually wiped out monasteries he judged to be too liberal in their pursuit of howlers. He wasn't quite a rogue agent, but he was close. The Superior, that's the head of our Order, tended to give him lots of leeway because he lived through the Calamity. Father Ignacio was a good man at one time, but lost his way. He actually trained me, but we parted ways years ago." He shook his head in sorrow. "His heart was so eaten up with hate. Still, I'm sad he's dead." Both Fathers made the sign of the cross.

Aaron was trying to reconcile what Father Thomas told him and what Father Samuel just said. "I thought he was starting the crusades again?"

"Oh, he was. But it was going to be without the *official* consent of The Superior. Plausible deniability. I suspect they were going to give him enough rope to hang himself—or you. It was a win-win situation for the Order. If he failed, they could retire him and deny they knew anything about it. If he succeeded, they'd have welcomed him with open arms."

Aaron's face scrunched up in disgust. "Politics."

Father Samuel displayed a barbed grin. "Better get used to it, *Lupus Rex*. You're about to experience it all first hand."

"Yeah, probably." He saw the other Fectors were cautiously watching him. "Am I going to have any problems with the rest of the Lamp of Truth over that?"

"Most certainly!" His face beamed ironic humor. "We take an oath to kill all *lupis* on sight, and Father Ignacio personally rebuilt nearly every monastery in North America to his specifications. But there comes a point where you have to question your motives. Most of us know *Lupis sapiens* aren't the result of some evil curse as we once believed, yet we still perpetuate that belief. Father Thomas and I are going to appeal for calm, though. Just watch your back in the meantime."

"Thanks. And thanks for helping with Jajine."

"Let's keep that our little secret. If the powers that be found out we worked with howlers to protect a voodoo priestess…well, I'm not sure what they would do to me." Father Samuel got a pained look on his face. "Probably pull out some old and dusty inquisition tome."

Aaron chuckled. "Deal. Well, I have some official business of my own to attend to. If you'll excuse me."

He turned to Autumn and Summer. Bill and Glen were now standing there as well. All four were human and obviously not as damaged as first thought. He went over to them, and they all submitted to his authority by looking at the floor. Lisa was still lying across Craig, in human form too, but she was no longer crying.

"So, tell me, guys. What am I to do with you? You tried to kill me. Should a king show mercy, or should he make an example of you?"

Bill spoke up first. "Aaron, man, me and Glen didn't want to do this. But Craig said if we didn't, he'd shun us. We didn't even know you'd be here. We're okay with you being the head honcho. Right, Glen?"

Glen nodded his head heartily, "Damned straight. No problems out of me. Hell, Kyle was our friend too. I infected him myself. I was trying to teach him to *frenis*. And when Bill told me what you told him—that Craig turned him over to the Fectors with address and photo—it made me sick to my stomach."

Bill added, "Craig ruled while over five thousand innocent people were sent to their deaths. We didn't sign up for that shit, man."

Summer and Autumn grabbed Glen by the arms and asked in unison, "Told you what?"

Aaron let them talk it out amongst themselves while he went over to talk with Lisa. He squatted down in front of her. "Lisa?" She either didn't hear him, or she was ignoring him. "Lisa, I need you to look at me. Right now!"

She turned her face, a mixture of daggers and pain, up to him. An unfathomable grief radiation from her. The loss of her *Postpartor* and *Lupus Rex* were too much, even for *Lupa Reginam.* "What? What do want, Aaron? This?" She raised her hand into the air. It held a crossbow bolt, a silver tipped one. He grabbed her arm before she was able to drive the bolt into her chest.

"You have one last duty to perform first." He took the bolt from her hand and stood up. "Then you can kill yourself."

She shot an angry look at him, "What duty?"

"You're going to help me ascend as *Lupus Rex.*"

Chapter 40—Scansio

noun [skan'-sē-ō]
1. Ascension.

Aaron Darveau, June 27, 1983, Florida

Convincing Lisa to go along with Aaron's plans was a testament to the females' intuition. He knew what he needed to do, but the idea was so farfetched, pure logic said it wouldn't work. However, Summer and Autumn said they were sure he could pull it off—if they had Lisa's cooperation. The first day back in Orlando, he told Lisa his plans.

"If you think I'm going to cooperate with you in this mad scheme," she proclaimed with regal confidence, "you're sorely mistaken."

"Why not?" he asked. "It's for the best of the Race and you know it. Summer and Autumn can see it. I know you can too."

"You killed Craig, you sonuvabitch!" she screeched. "And you killed Karen. You're *Utlagatus*, to boot." Then she stared out the small porthole he left for her in her bedroom window and ignored him.

That's when he went to the girls for help.

Autumn freely admitted, "I didn't believe it would work either until you explained it. But my Gift shows it clearly. I'm surprised Lisa doesn't see it too."

"She doesn't want to," Summer griped. "That's the problem."

"Don't worry, Aaron," Autumn added. "We'll convince her. It's just too soon after losing Craig." She shook her head in distaste, her curls wrapping around her face and then whipping out. "You should have come to us first."

Summer agreed. "Yeah, you should have."

"I did!" Aaron exclaimed.

"No, you told us your plan," Autumn objected.

"Yeah," Summer added, "you didn't tell us you were going to ask Lisa so soon."

Aaron sighed. "Okay, girls, I'm leaving it in your hands. I'm putting my neck on the chopping block. Don't let it get cut off, okay?"

Aaron sent out a fax to all of the Clan heads that afternoon. He was taking a huge risk based on the girls' perceived confidence they would be able to convert Lisa, but he had no choice.

To All Concerned,

Lupa Reginam will appoint her Postpartor at the next Caeruleo Lunaris. The Utlagatus, Aaron Darveau, is still at large. He escaped capture in Miami. The New Orleans witch, Jajine, is dead.

During the next two months, Lupus Rex's estate is off limits to all lupis, other than those currently living here and hired guards. It is possible Darveau may make an attempt on Lupus Rex's or Lupa Reginam's lives. Any lupis found on the grounds without permission will be assumed hostile and a threat to the Race and dealt with accordingly.

As with tradition, during the Ascension Ceremony, each Dux Lupus may bring only his Ducissa Lupa.

Please do not arrive earlier than August 23ʳᵈ. There are no housing arrangements available at the estate.

Sincerely,

Lupus Rex

He hoped that would keep Craig's frequent visitors from dropping in unannounced.

He put Holly, a young wildling, to answering the phone. His instructions were simple. "If any of the Clan heads call, be polite, tell them no one is currently available to speak to them, and you have no information you can give out. Take their phone numbers. I don't care what they have to say, make no promises of a call back. And you can ignore any threats. They won't break the Pact over being snubbed. Think you can handle that?"

"Yes, Mr. Darveau. What if they ask who the new *Postpartor* is?"

"You don't know. Lisa hasn't decided yet, so you won't be lying. You do nothing more than I told you. Just play dumb. It's easier than trying to talk around the subject."

"Yes, Sir."

She did an admirable job. The phone rang a couple of dozen times a day, each day, during the following week. Then the call volume dropped to a couple of times a day for the next month. Then they stopped altogether.

Aaron called Bill and Glen into his office. "Glen, I need you to start spreading the word. We're accepting any *Lupus solitarius* back who wishes to come back."

Glen's face opened up with surprise. "Any?"

Aaron was firm. "Yes, any," he informed them with certainty. "All they

301

have to do is ask you personally. I trust your judgment."

"All right. I'll get on it." He scratched his head, trying to figure out how to go about it. "I know a few I can talk to who might be able to help."

Aaron turned to Bill. "I need you to find fifty *lupis* we can trust with our lives. I don't care what *grex* or clan they're in. We need them patrolling the grounds."

Astounded, Bill asked, "Fifty? That's a lot. Why? Expecting trouble?"

"Yes. I sent out a fax today telling everyone to stay away. I don't trust them to do so, though." He handed them the fax.

They both tried to grab it and read it at the same time. Bill exclaimed, "Whoa, fuck, man! Why the hell did you go and do that? What are you up to?"

"I plan to go through the Ascension Ceremony. Lisa is going to appoint Angelina as *Lupa Reginam*, and then Angelina is going to choose me as *Lupus Rex*."

Bill and Glen stood there in silence. Aaron could smell the confusion on them; they didn't know how to respond. Bill finally spoke up, but he had doubt in his tone. "Lisa agreed to this?"

"Not yet. The girls are working on her."

Glen asked, "To hell with Lisa, you expect the Conclave to agree to this? Aaron, you aren't just shunned. You're outlaw, man. They'll kill you as soon as you walk into the circle."

"If my plan plays out right, they won't touch me. You remember Marlon Brando from *The Godfather*? Yeah? Well, I'm gonna make them an offer they can't refuse."

Glen asked, "Are you going to fill us in on this plan of yours?"

"Not yet. I'm still working out the details."

Bill piped in. "If they can't talk to Craig, they're gonna get suspicious. They know you're outlaw. They know Karen is dead. You've taken Jajine off of their radar, but they'll still wanna know who the new queen is going to be. You're right. They're gonna try to sneak in to find out what's happening. We can't keep the fuckers out for long."

"I know," Aaron grunted. "But I don't need 'long.' I just need two months. That's why I want this place crawling with *lupis* loyal to us. Any *lupis* who isn't, I want them killed on sight. I know it's a Pact violation, but we're dead if we're caught anyway. We're fighting for our lives here. I don't want any information leaking out. We should be able to keep a lid on things for that long."

Bill was shaking his head. "I don't think we'll get away with it."

"Me either," Glen argued. He was pacing around the office, clearly scared of the future. "Once the word is out on the repatriations, they'll know something is fishy." He muttered, "I'll have to set up a meeting place and bring in the ones I trust—and hope I don't get caught consorting with *Lupis solitarius*."

Bill and Glen nodded to each other and came to an unspoken agreement. Bill finally spoke for the two of them. "We'll do it. We should've died in New Orleans, so we're living on borrowed time anyway. 'It's better to burn out than fade away,' right?"

"Good," Aaron said, relieved. "And, guys, I need this to go off without a hitch, or we're all dead. Get Frank involved. Heavily. He knows the estate like no one else. We don't sleep until we've got fifty pissed off *lupis* running around and digging up the yard, you got it?"

Glen ceded, "Yeah, we got it, man."

They walked out, and Bill asked Glen, "Did he say 'digging up the yard?'"

Glen explained, "Yeah, you know like dogs."

"I know what he meant, but—never mind."

Bill found his fifty in short order, but most of them were wildlings, and the majority of *them* were at Kyle's shunning. They knew Aaron stood up for them, so they came onboard happily. But a few *frenatus* showed up too, all married to *lupas* or with girlfriends who were *lupa*. Aaron suspected the *lupas* saw which way the wind was blowing and decided against tacking into it.

Aaron used his Navy experience to set up a watch rotation, keeping twelve *lupis* patrolling the grounds at any given time. The rest were either watch commanders or off duty. None were allowed to leave the grounds, and all were available within a few minutes' notice to respond to any incursions.

Unfortunately, Bill was spending more time out there patrolling with the wildlings than Aaron wanted him to. Aaron talked to him about it a couple of days later. "I would prefer more *frenatus* in the patrols so that you don't have to be out there so much. I need your help with other things."

Bill raised his hands in the air in frustration and a bit of anger. "I would too, but you didn't leave me a whole lotta fuckin' time, man. I got what I could. Somebody has to keep an eye on them."

"You're right. You're right." Aaron then introduced Part Two. "Now, as the repatriates come in, any who can *frenis*, put them out there on patrol. Start swapping out the wildlings. Get Frank to help you. Besides, I want him to start running with us during the hunts from now on. This will be a good way to introduce him as a leader to the rest of the *lupis* here."

Bill was clearly relieved. "Will do."

For Glen's part, during the first couple of weeks only a few of the shunned showed up. Then they showed up in droves as the word spread. Glen asked Aaron, "The clans may send some spies. We can usually detect deceit, but not all the time. How do we handle that?"

Aaron brought Jajine in. "She can tell."

And tell she could. Out of the first couple of dozen to show up, she found three spies. The first two were killed on the spot. The third one lunged at her, yelling, "Die, witch!" Glen and the two other *frenatus* tore the spy to pieces before he finished his *renovatio*. After that, they had no more problems with spies, so either the word got out that *Lupus Rex* was serious, or they just got lucky.

Everyone was surprised at the number of *Lupis solitarius* that rolled in. There were more than anyone realized and the majority of them were never been part of the Race to start with. They belonged to *grexes* outside the Race's control.

Within three weeks, Aaron had fifty *frenatus* patrolling the grounds. Bill, Glen, and the girls were further astounded because they couldn't figure out how so many had learned to *frenis* without help from the Race.

The girls, using this new information, finally convinced Lisa to go along with Aaron. At least she convinced Aaron she would. She was hard to read, but the girls said they believed her.

Then he filled Bill and Glen in on his plans. They must have had the hearts of riverboat gamblers because they acted like they would live through this; they both grinned in approval.

Aaron Darveau, July 21, 1983

Once Lisa agreed to the plan, Aaron approached Angelina. If he thought convincing Lisa to go along with his plans was hard, trying to convince Angelina was like trying to brush alligator teeth—neither party was going to enjoy it, and someone was going to get bitten.

"You're asking me to marry you, Yuma? I'm already married!"

"Jose is dead, Ang. I wish he wasn't either. But he is. I didn't know him that long, but I like to think we were friends."

"Fuck you! I'm not doing it."

"Angelina," Aaron pleaded, "with you as *Lupa Reginam*, everyone would think twice before trying to kill you. And with me as *Lupus Rex*, I can keep a close watch on you, just as Jose wanted. This is the best solution! You don't have to love me. You don't have to have my children. We don't even have to share the same bedroom. But the Race needs stability. I can't stop the killings without you."

I can't believe I'm saying this. This is practically the same argument Karen used.

"Pick someone else. Summer and Autumn seem taken with you. Maybe you could have two queens."

"I've thought about it. But I want you." He put his hands on both of her arms, forcing her to look him in the face. "*My* intuition says you would be better at it. If we're going to start bringing in shunned *lupis*, they would feel better if they knew their queen was like them."

She shook him loose and yelled, "No! Now get out of my room!"

So Aaron, again, turned the convincing over to someone who he hoped was better at it than he was. Jajine.

Aaron threw himself into the chair in her bedroom. "Technically, you're still her mother-in-law. Maybe you'll have better luck."

"Boy, I don't know dat girl."

"You can drop the accent around me." He smiled. "I know better." Then his smile turned into a grimace. "Listen, you both loved the same man. That's a bond."

Jajine had recovered from Jose's death faster than he thought she would. Once they were on the road back to Orlando, she came out of her stupor. She wasn't talkative, but she was responsive. Aaron was happy to see that. Once Father Thomas had all of her belongings delivered to the estate, including one pissed off python, the healing process proceeded at a much faster rate. She didn't talk about Jose, but his ghost always seemed to be in the room when they were both there.

"You want I put a love charm on her for you?" she asked with a little mischievous grin.

Aaron exclaimed, "What? No! Hell, no!" Then a little quieter, "Wait, you can really do that?"

Jajine's musical laughter filled the room. "Of course, I can, boy!" she exclaimed. "It's the hardest voodoo I know, but I can do it. Hate's the easy one. It's always easier to destroy than create."

"I would prefer she did it of her own accord," he decided.

"Good! I'm proud of you, boy!" she exclaimed with a vigor that reminded him of her from ten years earlier.

"Why?" he asked.

"You know the easy way is there, but you also know it's wrong."

Aaron muttered. "It just seems like it's cheating." He didn't want to get into a discussion on right and wrong, so he changed the subject back. "So, does this mean you'll give it a try?"

She sighed. "Yeah, I'll give it a try."

He exclaimed, "That was easier than I thought it would be. Thanks! I was afraid I might have to bring someone in to convince *you*."

"I owe you," she whispered, suddenly serious. "You killed Craig."

"Not really. If you hadn't helped me, we wouldn't be here at all. There's no telling where I'd be. Hell, I'd probably be Karen's punk right now." He half-grinned at her. "Technically, we're even. But, hey, I don't want to keep score." He saw Craig crumple to floor in his mind's eye. "And besides, I didn't kill him for you. I killed him because he was trying to kill me, you, and everyone I cared about."

"Hmp. I still think the charm would be easier," she complained with sarcastic energy. "And you should have waited a while before approaching her. She's still grieving. Men always screw things up."

"You're right; I should have waited. I'm just worried the wheels are going to come off this wagon if we don't move soon." He got up to leave, but she ran up to him and hugged him.

"Aaron, thank you," she sobbed.

Taken aback, he asked, "For what?"

"For being a friend to Joey." She pulled back, tears in her eyes. "He'd been on his own for so long. Angelina helped, but he couldn't bring her to me. There was no link between her and his family. You became that link. He died knowing he wasn't alone. That's comforting to me."

Aaron shuffled his feet. "You may not realize it, Jajine," he replied with tenderness, "but you're probably the closest thing I have to a mother right now." He gently placed his hands on her cheeks and kissed her lightly on the forehead. "You've been in my dreams for quite a bit of my life."

"Never saw dat one coming," she grumbled under her breath. "A white boy for a son. Must be losing my touch, Luna."

He didn't have anything else to say, so he hugged her back and left.

Aaron Darveau, August 18, 1983

Aaron read up on the details of the Ascension Ceremony and realized he needed six people he could trust to help him handle part of it. Lisa and Angelina were onboard, so those positions were filled. But the other four were important too. He called Bill, Glen, Summer, and Autumn into his office.

"I need four hunters for the ceremony," Aaron informed them. "They're really only ritual positions, but I suspect they'll probably be the first ones attacked after my name is called out. Know anyone willing to put their lives on the line for me?"

They all looked at each other with something between disbelief and amusement. Summer cackled, "Yes, us. Who else did you think would do it?"

Aaron took a deep breath in relief. "Thanks, guys. I hoped you would volunteer, but I didn't want to ask you outright. You did hear the part about them probably being the first ones attacked, right?"

Angelina swept into the office. "First ones killed, you mean, Yuma!" She'd been correcting him quite a bit since she accepted his proposition.

"We know that, Angelina," Autumn shared. "But we're doing it anyway."

Summer picked up where Autumn had left off, "If we don't succeed, we're all dead anyway."

"Yeah," Autumn held, "I would rather die quickly than suffer the torture they would subject us to. And—"

Bill interrupted them, "Hey, slow down, Season Girls! Let's just forget about the fuckin' death talk, all right?"

Glen finished for him. "Yeah, let's not let it get that far, okay?"

They all got quiet and looked at Aaron, awaiting his command.

Aaron began explaining the details of his plan to them. "I hope it doesn't come to a fight, but if it does, here is what I want you to do…."

Aaron Darveau, August 23, 1983, *Caeruleo Lunaris*

Bill came into Craig's old office. Aaron had turned it into his over the last couple of months, and everyone knew this is where they would find him if wasn't out doing his Tai Chi forms. "Everyone's ready, man. They're all in position."

Aaron glanced up from behind the desk. "Good. Thanks, Bill. Any problems?"

Bill shook his head. "None."

"Well, let me go get Lisa." He stood up, and Elwood jumped to his feet too, ready to follow Aaron. "Elwood, go find Jajine. Stay with her tonight."

Elwood gave Aaron a dirty look, whined, and then turned and trotted out the doorway.

Bill watched Elwood. "How the hell do you do that, man?"

"Do what?"

"Like what just happened, dude," he explained. "You give him this complex fuckin' order, and he just does it."

"Oh, that," Aaron murmured, arching his eyebrows. "Ever since the junkyard, he just knows what I want. I thought he was just smart, but Jajine says he's my familiar."

"Like a witch's familiar? Black cats and shit?"

"Yeah. Supposedly, there are other things I can use him for, but I haven't figured them out yet. Been too busy with the Ascension plans."

"Well, that's hands down the damnedest thing I've seen in a long while. I thought I'd seen it all when Glen first changed, but now familiars?" Bill gave Aaron a nervous look. "Fuck, dude, are you a werewolf or something else?"

"I'm a werewolf. But right now I'm a worried werewolf. I'm worried about Lisa," Aaron divulged. "I hope she understands her part in this tonight. She may not know it, but everything depends on her. She could wreck it all."

"I don't think she will. Summer and Autumn have been working hard with her. I think she's simply ready for this shit to be over. Even she knows there ain't no goin' back."

"Do you trust the girls, though? They've spent quite a bit of time in there with her. How do you know they aren't scheming behind our backs?"

"Man, you don't know *lupas* that well, do you? Their instincts are to protect the Race first, themselves second. If Angelina can see it, you can bet your lily-white coon-ass they do too."

Aaron sighed slightly. "I hope you're right. The last two months have been crazy. I would hate to see it all end because she's got an ax to grind on my skull."

"Dude! Everything's gonna be just fine. You'll see. Besides, it's too late to turn all chicken-shit now."

Aaron unlocked the door to Lisa's room. He had kept her confined in there ever since they got back from New Orleans. It wasn't solitary confinement, but it was close. Her meals were delivered to her, and her clothes and linens were washed when she wanted. She was allowed to roam the grounds as long as she had her guards with her, Luke and Michael.

Luke and Michael were both formerly *Lupis solitarius*. They learned to *frenis* on their own, so Aaron repatriated them. Luke told Aaron when they first met, "We're tired of sleeping under a different bridge every night. If it means three squares a day and a soft place to sleep, we'll do whatever you need us to do." Michael heartily nodded his head in agreement, so they took shifts standing outside Lisa's door. They were both there when Aaron arrived, though.

"Lisa, it's Aaron. It's time."

"I know," she whispered quietly.

He stepped through the doorway and asked her, "You ready?"

"Yes." She was naked, ready for the ceremony, and looked down at her feet when he stepped into the room. "Let's get this over with."

He led Lisa out the back foyer onto the patio with Luke and Michael following them. Bill, Glen, Autumn, and Summer were already there waiting on them to arrive. They were *lupus*, dressed in Ascension Cloaks—long, flowing cloaks with baggy sleeves and large hoods that completely covered their faces. Angelina was there, but human, wearing a cloak as well. Lisa nodded to everyone and then performed a *renovatio*. She grabbed one of the two remaining cloaks lying across the table and put it on. Aaron put his on as soon as he stripped his own clothes off.

They formed up into a straight line. Lisa led the pack followed by Angelina, then Aaron, and then the remaining four *lupis*. Luke and Michael remained behind. They had other things to attend to.

Aaron thought, *Two months of preparation. I hope I don't die tonight.*

They marched solemnly across the estate to the Ascension Circle, the location where the ceremony would take place, just as the sun was dropping below the tree line. A moist, stiff breeze stirred up the smell of freshly cut grass from within and out beyond the circle. It was this circle where Lisa would name her *Postpartor*, the *lupa* who would replace her as *Lupa Reginam*.

The circle consisted of thirteen points, twelve of which were for the Conclave, and each point represented the equal stature of each member. A flaming torch stood between each position in the circle. Each *Ducissa Lupa* stood to the right of each *Dux Lupus*. Thus, two people stood between each torch. All present were swathed in Ascension Cloaks as well.

The thirteenth point was reserved for *Lupus Rex*. Lisa stood to the side while the six cloaked figures following her walked into the center of the circle. Bill, Glen, Autumn, and Summer formed a square, facing outward, while Angelina and Aaron stood in their center, facing the thirteenth point. Lisa took her position as if Craig were in attendance, to his right, leaving the thirteenth position empty. This brought a hushed exclamation from all the members present.

One of the Conclave, Ricardo, stepped forward and removed his hood. "**Where is** *Lupus Rex***?**" he demanded with a low, raspy growl.

Everyone around the Ascension Circle echoed Ricardo's question. "**Where's Craig?**"

Lisa raised her right cula into the air. "**Silence!**" she commanded. The circle fell silent. She held her cula there, above her head, until Ricardo replaced his hood and returned to his position.

Lisa dropped her cula to her side and proclaimed, "***Lupus Rex* is dead, killed by Aaron Darveau,** *Utlagatus* **and former consort of Karen Argali.**"

The circle erupted into chaos as the news of Craig's death took them completely by surprise. This was exactly what Aaron wanted. Over half of the *lupas* were on their knees, eyes misty white, keening and whining and howling, trying to see what was going to happen. Some of the Clan heads were kneeling next to them, trying to comfort them or trying to get answers themselves.

James stepped out of the circle and let loose a *vagor*. "**Silence!**" he growled. When everyone quieted down, he asked, "**When did this happen?**"

Aaron tensed up. *She could offer me up right now if she wished.* He hoped his cloak would hide his discomfort.

Lisa's voice cracked when she answered. "**It doesn't matter. What matters is the continuation of the Pact. Please return to your positions. I'm ready to begin.**" Everyone was muttering and grumbling, but they moved back into their positions.

The ceremony, a script that hadn't changed in nearly five hundred years, began. Lisa stepped forward to a location just in front of where Craig would stand and raised her culas in the air. "**Bind the prey!**"

The two human figures in the middle, Aaron and Angelina, the prey, appeared to give a start as the four *lupis*, the hunters, turned to face them, producing chains from within their cloaks. They moved inward together, while the prey tried to "escape." The hunters "captured" the prey and bound them with their chains. Aaron knew the prey represented the unwanted position of *Lupa Reginam* and *Lupus Rex*. The Race considered it a duty to be chosen, and the chains represented the idea the new rulers didn't really want the position. Aaron knew it was all hogwash, but appearances are everything—perception is reality. *Well, that's the idea, anyway. All ceremonies are filled with pomp and circumstance.*

The *Dux Lupus* to the immediate right of the *Lupus Rex* position stepped forward and asked, "**Are you *Lupa Reginam*?**"

Lisa responded, "**Yes, I am.**"

Satisfied, the *Dux Lupus* stepped back while the second one stepped forward. "**Do you speak for the Race?**"

"**Yes, I do.**"

In turn, each *Dux Lupus* stepped forward and asked his question.

"**Do you stand for the Race?**"

"**Yes, I do.**"

"**Do you cry for the Race?**"

"**Yes, I do.**"

"**Do you bleed for the Race?**"

"**Yes, I do.**"

"**Do you fight for the Race?**"

"**Yes, I do.**"

"**Do you suffer for the Race?**"

"**Yes, I do.**"

"**Does your *Lupus Rex* lead with honor?**"

Lisa hesitated, and with a crack in her voice the size of the Mississippi River, yowled, "**Yes, he did.**"

"**Are you pure of heart?**"

"**Yes, I am.**"

"**Will you choose a *Postpartor*?**"

"**Yes, I will.**"

"Will you choose this *Postpartor* under duress?"

"No, I will not."

"Name her."

Lisa strode into the center of the circle and stood before Angelina. "**Will you ascend to *Lupa Reginam*?**"

Angelina shouted, "No, I will not!" To Aaron's ears, it sounded too real for comfort.

"**If you do not, I'll let the hunters have you.**"

Angelina brilliantly acted the part by appearing to struggle with the decision before answering. "Then, yes, I will guide the Race to the best of my abilities."

Lisa reached up and pulled the hood down, revealing the new *Lupa Reginam*. "**I choose Angelina Suarez!**"

James stepped forward and out of the circle again, angry. "**What is this? Craig declared her *Lupa solitarius*! She killed the Alpha of her pack! One of my packs! What are you pulling, Lisa?**"

"**You are out of line, *Dux Lupus*! I choose my *Postpartor*, not you, or have you forgotten that? Technically, the Pact does not exclude *Lupa solitarius*. I have chosen to recognize her, therefore she is no longer shunned. She's *frenatus*, and she has accepted the position.**"

James hesitated, looking around at the circle for support. He found none that would speak up and openly defy *Lupa Reginam*, so he bowed his head and scurried back into place.

Lisa motioned to the four hunters to remove Angelina's chains. Once free, she removed her cloak, revealing her naked human body to the circle, and performed a *renovatio*. Her skin was flawless in the flame light except for the crossed scars on her chest. They were clearly visible as they followed the curves of her breasts. She let loose a *vagor* as she rose to her full height.

"Angelina Suarez," Lisa asked, "**will you take the oath to prove your worth?**"

Angelina responded, "Yes, I will."

The first *Dux Lupus* stepped forward and asked, "**Will you speak for the Race?**"

She responded, "Yes, I will."

The following *Dux Lupis* all took their turn asking a question.

"**Will you stand for the Race?**"

"Yes, I will."

"Will you cry for the Race?"

"Yes, I will."

"Will you bleed for the Race?"

"Yes, I will."

"Will you fight for the Race?"

"Yes, I will."

"Will you suffer for the Race?"

"Yes, I will."

"Are you pure of heart?"

"Yes, I am."

"Have you chosen your *Lupus Rex*?"

"Yes, I have."

"Have you chosen your *Lupus Rex* under duress?"

"No, I have not."

"Will your *Lupus Rex* lead with honor?

"Yes, he will."

"Call him forth."

The circle was quiet. Everyone was waiting to see who the next *Lupus Rex* would be. Angelina motioned to the hunters and waited while they removed Aaron's chains. The hunters retook their positions and she shouted, **"Come forth, my *Lupus Rex*! It is time to take your position next to me, but not in front of me, to take your oath to defend and uphold the Pact."**

Aaron stepped up next to Angelina and became the center of attention. This was the most dangerous part in the ceremony. He performed a *renovatio* inside his cloak, instead of removing it first, tearing it off as the fabric rubbed his skin like acid. He gripped Angelina's left cula with his right.

She raised them both over their heads and proclaimed, **"I choose Aaron Darveau!"**

The Ascension Circle was quiet for a few heartbeats and then disintegrated into a typhoon of *vagors*. Everyone was howling their disbelief and disapproval in fury. A few of them rushed the center in full bloodlust while the rest built up the courage to do so themselves.

Aaron let loose his own *vagor*, **"Now!"** He was afraid it was drowned out by everyone else's noise.

Father Thomas called a few times over the weeks leading up to the ceremony to inform him the Lamp of Truth had been more active than normal recently. "It's the same faction Father Ignacio belonged to. They're on the warpath, Aaron."

"Father, I'm between a rock and hard place. If I fight back, the word would get out that Craig isn't controlling things anymore. And his reputation isn't that great right now; he's supposedly lost Karen and let me get away. If I do nothing, the Clans might decide to fight back on their own." He sighed. "All I can do is hope things don't escalate much past where they are now."

"I understand, but if you don't do something, it could blow up in all of our faces. Father Samuel is concerned, too. He's willing to give you the benefit of the doubt, but if it comes down to humans and *lupis*, he's not choosing you."

Aaron thought about possible solutions. "I'll send out orders, under Craig's letterhead, for everyone to keep their heads down even more than they usually do. I'll say I don't want it to interfere with the upcoming ceremony, that I'm working with the Fector leadership, blah, blah. That might delay them long enough."

"Okay. I'll let Father Samuel know."

"Thanks," Aaron offered. "Hey, how's that little project of ours coming along?"

"I think we'll be ready. Where do you want them delivered?"

"To the front door. Make sure they are in big boxes, though. I don't want anyone knowing what we have until the last minute."

"Understood."

In the aftermath of the *Battle of New Orleans*, as Bill and Glen were calling it, and the remaining *lupis* in the church had submitted to Aaron's will, he immediately knew what he needed. Curing the Race was out of the question, and letting them die off in a generation was a pipe dream. That left him with no choice but to Ascend and lead the Race into a peaceful future. For that to happen, he needed the Race to submit to him as a whole. That was the easy part—saying it. The hard part was figuring out how to do it. Going around the world and expecting each *lupus* he ran across to submit was pure fantasy. He needed it to be recognized by the Clan heads. In the Navy they say, "*Shit rolls downhill.*" If the Clan heads accept it, everyone else will too.

How do I convince the Clan heads to accept me as their Lupus Rex? With an Ascension Ceremony, of course. And it just so happens we have one scheduled in two months.

He commended himself on the brilliant plan, but it had one glaring hole. Once his name was called out, any number of the Conclave would rush the center intent on killing him. He needed some way to get more help into the circle to force the issue.

How do I get enough lupis in there with me without it being obvious a coup is in progress? Have them run up at the last minute? No, that won't work. Lupis senses would detect the approach of anyone long before they made it into the circle. So, how do I get them in without the Conclave seeing, hearing, or smelling them? WWKD? Steal a Romulan Cloaking Device, of course.

Sadly, I'm fresh out of Romulans. I guess I'm on my own here.

He relied on his Tai Chi to give him the answer he needed. Everything in Tai Chi was about redirecting force. But it could also redirect attention—while your opponent is concentrating on your right arm, strike with your foot. He could use the same technique here. Tai Chi would allow his army to move up without being seen or heard.

But it wouldn't cover their smell.

How did those Fectors at Craig's hide from me? And how did they hide from a whole pack at Jose's in Miami? They were undetectable. With a sudden flash of insight, Aaron knew the Fectors had a method of masking their scent that allowed them to hide from *lupis.*

The Fectors have a cloaking device! Way to go, Kirk!

So while the circle was worrying about Craig's death and Angelina's selection as *Postpartor,* they wouldn't be paying attention to what was hiding behind them out beyond the waist-high, *purposely uncut* grass enclosing the circle. While the circle was screaming and crying and yelling and howling, they wouldn't hear the *lupis* sneaking across the *freshly cut* grass out beyond that. And by the time Aaron's name was mentioned, they certainly wouldn't know he had forty-eight *frenatus* within ten yards of the twenty-four members of the circle.

The morning he left New Orleans for Orlando, he told Father Thomas, "I need enough of your scent masking technology for fifty *lupis.* And I need it before August 22nd."

Father Thomas leaned back, eyes wide, and exclaimed, "In two months?! That's not much time, Aaron! The Order isn't going to hand that over to howlers, ahem, *lupis*. I'll have to steal it."

"Can you get it for me?"

"I'll do my best."

His best turned out to be a real nail biter. It showed up on August 20th, three days before the ceremony.

When Aaron's name was announced to the Conclave, the forty-eight *lupis* hiding behind the tall grass made one leap half-way to the circle, dropped their scent-masking blankets, and attempted to reach the inside of the circle with a second leap. They'd practiced this over and over until everyone knew exactly what to do and how to do it together. Each member of the circle had two of Aaron's *frenatus* assigned to them. It was their responsibility to keep the Conclave contained, to subdue them if possible, kill them if not.

None of this would have been possible without the blankets. Aaron still wasn't sure exactly how they worked, but they did a fairly decent job of masking scent. They reminded him of the ghillie suits he had seen S.E.A.L. snipers use during his time in the Navy, but these had a special liner made from a new material developed by N.A.S.A. that absorbed odors.

He and Angelina wore Ascension Cloaks made from the same material. He didn't want to tip his hand to any of the Conclave who was under the cloaks. Quite a few members of the Conclave would recognize him by smell, and the hoax would be up as soon as he stepped into the circle.

By the time Aaron yelled, *"**Now**,"* his army was already in the air, leaping over the outer ring of any stragglers who had not immediately rushed the center while the four hunters surrounding him and Angelina pulled their robes off and faced the onslaught of bloodlust-enraged *lupis*.

Aaron was right about the hunters being the first ones attacked. Warren and James made for Bill and Autumn at the same time. Glen and Summer stayed on the other side; they had their own problems running at them. He hoped they would remember what he told them. *"Don't try to stop them. Redirect. Move out of the way. Stay alive. Wait for the army. The purpose is not to show we can kill. They already know that. Our end game is to stop the killing."*

Aaron stepped up next to Autumn when he saw Warren had targeted her. Warren's face twisted with unadulterated hatred when he saw Aaron step from behind the hunters, and shifted the direction he was sprinting, targeting him instead. Aaron needed Warren down, incapacitated if

316

possible, dead only if necessary. Aaron timed Warren's approach and jumped to the side just before they clashed, leaving his left leg out. Warren didn't anticipate Aaron's sudden dodge and tripped over his leg, flying face first toward the ground. Unfortunately, Warren hadn't totally given up on attacking Autumn. Aaron watched, unable to do anything, as Warren jabbed his right arm out, talons extended like meat hooks, ripping the right side of her neck and throat to shreds. She reached up with both culas, trying to stop her life from draining away. Warren went down and Aaron followed him with his own handful of angry razors, bouncing his talons across Warren's ribs like a spoon on a Mardi Gras washboard—*bap, bap, bap, bap!* Warren howled in agony—his spine filleted opened up for everyone to see.

Meanwhile, Bill goaded James, "**Right here, mother fucker!**" James rushed into Bill's circle and disbelief sprang onto his face as Bill dropped to the ground and let James run over his head. Bill reached up and goosed him, forcing him to turn head over heels. Bill yelled, "**Holy fuck! It worked!**" Bill must have remembered his lesson from Aaron's first full moon with them.

Aaron responded to Bill's deflection too late—he was close to laughing at James because he had fallen for the same trick twice—when James crashed into him, back first and head down. They both fell to the ground, and Aaron expectantly found *lupus* tail in his jaw and scrambling *lupus* talons all around him. James's left leg found traction on Aaron's ribcage and tore it to ribbons before he could push and kick James off of him.

Madame Jajine was sitting at her rickety, old TV tray, while Elwood sat at Luna's terrarium, watching the snake slither from one end to the other. "I'm glad dat nice church goin' fella—Thomas his name?—packed dis up for me, Luna. I'd be completely lost without it." She was staring into her blood-smeared mirror, watching the fight unfold.

She saw Aaron go down. "*Ah Bondye! Oh, God,* don't give up now, boy! Get up! Kill that evil *con lungyet!* Kill that sonuvabitch!" She knew what Aaron wanted, but she also knew it wasn't going to end as bloodless as he hoped.

She adjusted the mirror, moving her point of view out a bit, and the entire battle appeared before her. Aaron's plans were paying off. All but six of the visitors were under control, Aaron's *lupis* captors standing over them. Of the six, one was down with serious wounds and another one was being chased across the field, a *lupa*.

Four more were rushing toward the center.

She saw that sweet little girl standing next to Aaron go down, holding her throat while Aaron sliced her attacker's spinal column wide open, and one of those two big rednecks—Glen, she thought—went down too, gutted like a Mississippi River catfish.

Aaron thought, *It's over. One last thing to do. Die.* Though Aaron had learned to stay on his feet, he was averse to getting up. He didn't want to look at his side. As much as it hurt, he knew his guts had to be running out between his ribs.

His *lupus* shouted at him, **"Get up, dammit!"** He rolled over to look at James.

This was bizarre. Bizarre because the two *lupis* were staring at each other from the ground—James, who wanted Aaron dead for a multitude of reasons: he'd killed Karen, he'd killed Craig, he was upsetting the balance. Take your pick. Then Aaron, who wanted to transform the Race, prevent the needless killing…by killing those who didn't agree with him. *Maybe I'm no better than they are after all.*

His *lupus* mocked him. ***"So what are you gonna do, surrender?"***

Aaron howled, **"No!"**

Aaron and James both jumped to their feet at the same time. James was all killer and lean muscle. He leapt catlike toward Aaron, a different tactic from their sparring matches a few months ago, swinging his culas like meat cleavers multiple times before touching down where Aaron was no longer standing. Aaron's face cracked into a snarl, and he made eye contact, going against all rules of close combat because you can't see your opponent's entire body. But he wanted James to see the determination in his face. **"You know you can't win, James. Help me! The Race needs you! I need you, dammit!"** Time seemed to freeze as James hesitated. Aaron dared to hope he might actually avoid a fight; his side still felt like it was opened up, but he refused to look at it for fear of giving James an opening.

James made up his mind. He charged at Aaron with his talons out and up, swiping with his right and closing in with a left. Closer. Closer. Aaron ducked the first and met the second with his own right. The power of Aaron's block sent James's arm up, up, up—but not far enough to throw him off balance.

Whoosh! James's lightning fast swing sliced through the hair on Aaron's stomach, the flesh underneath saved by no more than a deep breath. His follow-up strike was a sledge-hammer backhand blow to Aaron's head that blurred his vision. He countered by hooking his left foot under James's knee.

James staggered, off-balance finally, and Aaron dug with his left cula, attempting the same move he killed Craig with. James caught Aaron by surprise by revealing he wasn't as off balance as he had let on. James's feint was exposed when he dodged to the left, and Aaron's cula buried itself in nothing but air. James's face shined with glee when he realized Aaron was no longer within his circle. Aaron liked gloaters because they got clumsy. *Would James, though? He's probably the most dangerous enemy out here—he's fought me before.*

Swipe. Smack. Bash. Aaron's first two swings went wide. His vision was still blurry from the head blow, but the third, a lucky blow from his elbow, found James's mouth. James's lower jaw slammed closed, mercilessly trapping his tongue between his teeth. Blood spurted from his mouth as the front half of his tongue dropped to the ground. His eyes clouded over with tears, not from fear, but from pain. He tried to take one last swipe at Aaron but he didn't see the rock at his feet and tumbled to one knee.

Aaron stood straight and cast an appraising look down at his foe. He saw Karen. He saw Craig. He saw James. James peered up at Aaron through bloodshot and blurry eyes. They both knew this was the end. James lifted his snout into the air, and like Karen and Craig before him, refused to yield with that one, final, simple act.

Jajine couldn't turn away from the scene on her mirror. It was like watching a train wreck. She knew there would be death, but she was still shocked to see it played out. She watched in horror as Aaron raised his cula and dropped it down and to the side of James's neck for one final blow. James's head rolled across the ground, out of sight of her mirror. Aaron dropped to all fours, raised his head into the air, and let loose a long, piercing howl. Although she couldn't hear anything through the mirror, the howl came through the walls and door of her room.

Elwood jumped up and ran toward the door, whining and with hackles raised. He pawed at it, but Jajine ignored him.

"Do you hear dat, Luna? Dat is da cry of a man suffering a pain dat'll never heal. I felt dat pain de day my Joey died. Aaron makes it now." She stopped and listened to something only she could hear. "'cause he don't like de killin', girl? Ain't you figgered dat out yet?" She listened again and chuckled some. "Oh yeah, he definitely be good at it though, you got dat right. Dat's what makes him so special. He doesn't want to do it, but does it anyway 'cause he knows it has to be done. Lao Tzu said, 'From caring comes courage.' Dat's my Aaron, Luna. Dat's him."

All of the *lupis* in the circle stopped whatever they were doing and turned their heads to Aaron as his *vagor* dwindled to a ragged breath. He bowed his head and struggled to stand up. As if his joints were filled with gravel, he wavered under the effort. But the higher he raised himself, the stronger he became, as if the wounds from a hundred battles were leaving him all at once.

Aaron inspected the circle. Warren and James were dead. Half a dozen of his army was dead. He saw at least a half dozen of the Conclave, *Dux* and *Ducissa*, dead or dying. Glen was dead. Autumn was dead. Bill and Summer stood over the cowering form of Ricardo, stealing glances at their fallen siblings but not daring to grieve; everyone understood what was at stake. Two of Aaron's *frenatus* were protecting the prone but live and healthy forms of Angelina and Lisa.

But no one was fighting any more. Aaron had control of the circle.

He helped Angelina and Lisa to their feet. He grasped Angelina's culas in his own. "**Continue, please,**" he growled, looking at Lisa.

She stepped next to him, eyes downcast. "**Will you take the oath to prove your worth?**"

Aaron responded, "**Yes, I will.**"

At this point, a member of the circle should have stepped forward to ask the next question. None did. Aaron stood there looking into Angelina's eyes while everyone else watched him. Angelina and Aaron both knew the same thing. *They have to make the decision on their own. We cannot force them or everything that has happened tonight has been for naught.* He still held her culas in his, but she wasn't trying to free herself. Aaron experienced eternity in those few minutes, buried in Angelina's eyes. She matched the depth of his burial, and he saw something appear there, something he had never seen there before. He had seen it in his mother's eyes when she looked at his father. Respect, understanding, tolerance. Love.

Ricardo cleared his throat, and Aaron and Angelina jumped as if someone had stuck them with a needle. Aaron was surprised Ricardo was the first to make up his mind.

He stood up and asked, **"Will you speak for the Race?"**

Aaron never took his eyes off of Angelina's. **"Yes, I will."**

The two *frenatus* guarding Ricardo let him resume his position in the circle, cautiously following him. Then they took up positions behind him as the other guards were doing to the other members.

A few more minutes passed before another one stepped forward. **"Will you stand for the Race?"**

"Yes, I will."

Then the rest of them performed the ceremony, each one taking less time to decide to do so than the one before them. Where some were no longer able to do so, either because they were dead or incapacitated, the *Ducissa* would do it. Or an empty position was skipped and the next one would ask a question again.

"Will you cry for the Race?"

"Yes, as I do now."

"Will you bleed for the Race?"

"Yes, as I do now."

"Will you fight for the Race?"

"Yes, as I have done and will continue to do."

"Will you suffer for the Race?"

"Yes, as I do now."

"Are you pure of heart?"

"I strive to be."

"Have you taken this position by force?"

"No, I have not. But I have maintained the sanctity of the ceremony with it."

"Will you lead with honor?

"Always."

Lisa had one more question to ask. **"Will you abide by the Pact and enforce it for all *lupis*?"**

"Yes, I will."

Lisa turned to Angelina. **"He has taken the oath. He has proven his worth."**

Angelina gently squeezed Aaron's culas. **"You are my *Lupus Rex.*"**

Aaron quietly responded, "**You are my *Lupa Reginam*.**"

Aaron let loose a *vagor* as he slowly turned and faced all members of the Conclave still alive. "**I am *Lupus Rex!***"

Jajine picked up a large, nasty looking, smoldering Howie Wowie cigar from an ashtray. "Okay, Luna. It's our turn, girl. Let's make him shine." She took a long drag off of the cigar and then slowly blew the greyish-white smoke at the mirror. "Let's show doze witches what da future looks like! Or as Aaron put it, 'Hit the override button on their intuition.'"

The silver fang hanging on Aaron's necklace shined with a brilliant, silvery glow only the *lupas* could see. The glow dimmed and brightened, synchronized to the rhythm of his heartbeat. *Duh-bump-bump. Duh-bump-bump. Duh-bump-bump.* He held his arms out to his side, parallel to the ground, turning around in a circle. He saw the *lupas' Mulieres intuitionem* take hold—their eyes shined with the same intensity as his necklace, and their bodies swayed to the same beat as the flashing fang. The *lupis* gawked in intense curiosity. They had never seen their *lupas'* eyes glow so brightly when using their Gift before. Aaron completed his turn and the light winked out, releasing the *lupas* from its hold, and ending the vision he and Jajine had crafted for them.

This was why the Race hated witches—Jajine could cast a spell that would give them visions of whatever she wanted, and they would take them for the truth, never knowing they came from a witch.

Voodoo mythology though, said the Race hated witches for other reasons. Supposedly, the first witch killed some god's favorite pet, a wolf, and in retaliation, this god created the first werewolf and told him to kill all the witches. Jajine though, was a product of the twentieth century and understood that mythology wasn't history, so she tended to believe the Race's version. In either case, the feud went back to before recorded Race history, so no one really knew the true reason.

Of course, casting that spell and sending visions wasn't as easy as the Race believed it to be. It couldn't be done at the witches' leisure. Jajine wanted to keep that a mystery, so she swore Aaron and Angelina to secrecy; they were the only two members of the Race who knew this.

The spell required, among other things, a *lupus* wearing a silver talisman, at least one *lupa* to receive the vision, a blue moon to cast the spell under, and smoke from burning hemp that had been harvested under a full moon with a silver blade. The hemp was procured courtesy of Howie himself. He wasn't sure why he needed to use a silver knife under a full moon to get it, but knowing his sons were werewolves, he didn't argue the point.

The final component of the spell was the most esoteric of them all. Jajine needed to sacrifice a hellhound, a spiritual creature, and she hadn't been sure how she was going to accomplish that when she sent Aaron on his quest all those years ago. Summoning a Hellhound was not something that was good for the soul. Sacrificing one? Maybe not that either, but summoning one would surely be a black mark against her when she finally shrugged off her mortal coil. She needed to find a replacement. Voodoo was good at finding sympathetic replacements.

Or so she thought.

She traveled home to Haiti to consult with different priestesses there, scouring their libraries for anything that would suit her purposes. She found nothing.

She traveled to the different Caribbean islands, consulting with witches there too. Again, she found nothing.

She traveled to Africa, her ancestral home. Most of the lore there had been lost with the modernization, Christianization, and Islamization of the continent, but there were still isolated pockets where the old ways were preserved. She came up empty there too. There *was* a story about some priests writing down various rituals and taking them back to their libraries in Italy, but there was no way she was going to get access to those books.

She arrived back in New Orleans a few years later, destitute and frustrated. She needed a hellhound, and that's all there was to it. She talked it over with her familiar, Luna, and decided that if a spiritual creature was required, something that didn't exist in the material world, then the sacrifice didn't need to take place in the material world, either. Luckily, the only stipulation on the sacrifice was it had to occur before the rest of the ritual. Voodoo was funny that way.

Aaron's necklace had voodoo on it to give him dreams of fighting a werewolf. If she had the necklace, it would be a simple matter to change those encounters to be with a hellhound instead. The effect would be the same on his end. He'd have to fight for his soul, and she would have her sacrifice assuming he was able to win the fight, killing two birds with one stone, so to speak. Unfortunately, her scrying mirror showed him surrounded my machinery onboard a ship in the middle of the ocean. Changing the magic on something she wasn't touching was something she had never tried. She spent the next two months studying the spell and gathering her components. Most of the components she had on hand. What she didn't have was a mouthful of water from the bottom of the ocean, the hair from a fly killed by a wolf, and a piece of yellow amethyst. An arduous writing campaign to her friends in Haiti asking for help in locating the components produced what she needed.

Under a full moon, out in the swamp, she performed her ritual. She burned all of the dry components, and using the water, mixed the ash into a paste. She smeared the paste on her face and recited the verbal components. When she was done, she didn't feel any different, and nothing spectacular happened other than producing a particularly noxious odor that she suspected no amount of soap would wash off for the next week. *Oh, well! That's voodoo for you!* Overall, it was fairly anti-climactic in her opinion. Luna agreed with a scoff and slithered back into the car.

By her estimation, she finished the spell about three months before the hellhound would be scheduled to show up in Aaron's dreams.

Aaron waited a few minutes after the vision ended because he wanted the *lupas* to dwell on what they saw. He didn't intentionally speak loudly, but when he addressed them, his voice thundered across the field and echoed from all directions at once. "***Lupas*, say what you know**."

One of the *Ducissa Lupas* stepped forward. "**We see death for any who oppose you, *Lupus Rex***."

That was not exactly what he wanted to hear. His voice thundered again as he asked, "**But do you believe it?!**"

Every *lupis* present except Angelina turned their gaze to the ground in front of Aaron. Another *Ducissa Lupa* answered for them all, "**Yes**."

Aaron nodded his head in regal approval.

Angelina stepped up as the new *Lupa Reginam*. "**Our *lupa*s have spoken. This ceremony is now at an end. There will be no hunt tonight. We must collect our dead**."

Part V—Lupus Rex

noun [lü'-pəs()reks]
1. Wolf King.

Chapter 41—Inperium

noun [in-pir'-ē-əm]
1. Authority. 2. Commandment.

Aaron Darveau, August 24, 1983

Aaron was up early and in his office, trying to get a handle on what to do his first day on the job as *Lupus Rex*. The first thing he did was put Kyle's cherrywood box on the desk to remind him what it took to get there.

Besides ensuring lunch was served in a few hours for the Conclave, he had a few positions to fill. Six *Dux Lupis* were dead. Their *lupa*s would pick another one when they returned to their clans, or pick a *Postpartor* and retire. Among those six were James and Warren. James wasn't married, so clan *Gloriosi* was leaderless. *Luna Amator* was leaderless as well, because when Warren went down under Aaron's scythe-like talons, his wife, Riley, rather than submit to Aaron, attacked her two captors, knowing they would kill her. They did. Aaron had to respect her for wishing to die on her own terms but wished she would have chosen life instead. He called Bill and Summer into his office.

"Hey, Chief." It wasn't Bill's usual, jovial greeting. He and Summer were both grieving the loss of Autumn and Glen.

"Hey, Guys. Have a seat. I know this is too soon, but I need something from you."

Summer asked, "What?"

"James is dead. You're both members of Clan *Gloriosi*. I need you to take over. If I show my support, the families should fall in line."

Summer snapped, "Fine," stood up, and walked out. Bill and Aaron stared at her as she left, afraid to say anything further, even something as simple as, "Thank you."

"That leaves just you. I know you two get together sometimes on the hunts. I'm not sure what your lives are like away from here, though. Will she pick you?"

"If you tell her to."

"I would prefer you guys made that decision on your own. I'll find someone else if I have to, but I could really use a friendly *Dux* on the Conclave over the next couple of years."

"I'll do it if she asks me."

"Thanks. Now, *Luna Amator*. Any ideas who I can trust there?"

"None. That clan is mostly based out of New England. I don't get up there that often. Actually, never."

Nervousness swiftly descended onto Aaron. He could think of no way to bring up the next bit of business gently. "How are we dealing with the bodies? And aren't they going to be missed?"

"Turns out the estate has a commercial-grade freezer. We've got the bodies in there. How about an accident? That's how things are usually covered up. As far as people missing them, yeah, they'll be missed. Craig, especially. He has, or had, contacts, and some of them were good friends of his. They're gonna be sniffing around more than a hound dog sniffs after a bitch in heat."

Aaron had been thinking about how to hide their deaths. "We need a yacht accident somewhere, big fire, explosion. Know anybody who can arrange that?"

In a burst of agitation, Bill yelled, "Fuck, no! Do I look like the yachting type?" He leaned back in his chair and sighed. "Sorry, man." He looked at the ground, not in submission to Aaron but in grief. "I'll ask around. Glen would know. Wait, yeah, he works—used to work on yachts up in Jacksonville. I'll ask his old boss. He's *lupus*. He'll cooperate." He stared off into the distance for a few seconds, his face in turmoil. "Is that the story? They're out on a boat trip?"

"It's the best I can think of right now. I'll talk to Lisa too."

"I can't tell my parents that bullshit, though," Bill contended. "They know the truth about us, so they deserve the full truth about how he died."

Aaron sighed. "I understand. I guess that was the hole in my plan, huh? I should have thought of something before now." Aaron threw his pencil down on the desk. "I wasn't expecting so many to die. One or two. Not a dozen." He rested his head in his hands. "*Mea culpa*. I really fucked it up, didn't I?"

Bill sprayed out an uncontrollable snicker. "No fuckin' way, man. You pulled off something nobody ever thought possible."

Aaron gaped at Bill. "What are you talking about?"

"Dude, haven't you read the history books? Hundreds, sometimes thousands, would die during a coup, and not all of them were *lupis*. That's why the Fectors got involved. We were killing humans too. Only losing a dozen *lupis* is nothing short of a fuckin' miracle."

"He's right, boy!" Jajine surprised them both by coming into the office unannounced. "So, what you gonna do with all dis here power?"

"Save as many lives as possible." Aaron sat back in his chair and took a deep breath. "I think I can do that if I teach everyone to *frenis*. And that brings me to my next task. I'm glad you're here because that's what I need from you. How did you teach me? And how did you make me immune to silver? Those would be nice skills to possess."

Bill was looking confused. "What do you mean she taught you? She isn't even *lupus*."

Jajine threw a tickled look at Aaron. "Boy, I didn't teach you anything you didn't already know how to do. And the silver? I couldn't do that if I tried. That came naturally."

A confused expression crossed his face. "What do you mean? You gave me this necklace." He pulled it out from under his shirt. "It must do something."

"It sho do!" she cackled. "It gots some bad dream voodoo on it."

"Why is it a wolf's fang, then?"

She winked at him and asked, "Don't dey teach irony in schoo' no mo?"

Aaron muttered, "Well, so much for the silver angle." Suddenly, he exclaimed, "Hey, you know something!?" He held the necklace up, watching it glint under the office lights. "I haven't had any of those dreams since I first transformed!"

"Of course not!"

Exasperated, Aaron ranted, "All right, Jajine, I'm really confused now. Explain it to me."

The thickness in her accent changed to something more respectable again. "Aaron, the dreams did nothing more than show you how to respect yourself. You knew the dog was bad. You didn't want it to win."

"I didn't want it to kill me!"

"Of course! And I didn't either! There was too much at stake. If you hadn't have had a sense of self-worth, you wouldn't have cared if you had lost or not. You have to like yourself before you can like others. If you can't respect yourself, you can't respect anyone or anything."

"Now you're talking about self-confidence, right?"

"Yes and no. Self-confidence can be faked. People confuse arrogance with self-confidence. The *frenatus* have been doing it for centuries. But if you respect yourself, *real* self-confidence comes free. Real self-confidence only comes if you value yourself. If you don't value yourself, you don't value anything. That's the secret, Aaron. Teach people to respect and value themselves, they'll learn to control their passions."

"I still don't understand."

"*Ah Bondye*, boy, you gonna give me a migraine." She sat down in the chair next to Bill. "You remember that day you helped pick up my groceries?"

"Yes, Ma'am."

"Why did you do it?"

"You needed help." Aaron nervously shifted in his seat. "People were being rude."

"Exactly. You didn't care I was black. You didn't care if anyone would have called you 'nigger lover.' You wouldn't have been able to live with yourself if you had let a wrong go unrighted. *That*, boy, is integrity and self-respect. And because of that, you showed me respect."

"Okaaayyy." Aaron dragged out the word. "So how do I teach wildlings self-respect?"

"Hell, boy, I don't know. Dat's yo' job." Her accent was back, but she grinned and winked at him. "But I would start with finding out how the *frenatus* kept them down."

Aaron pointed his raised eyebrows at Bill.

Bill squirmed in his seat. "Well, I don't rightly know myself. I just know it's hard to *frenis*."

Jajine raised her eyebrows that time. "Is it, Bill? Aaron did it on his first time. How hard can it be?"

Aaron snapped his fingers and sat up. "That's it! I know how to do it."

Jajine just smiled while Bill asked, "Well, don't just sit there jawin' about it. How you gonna do it?"

Aaron leaned forward in his chair. "Like this…."

Angelina Darveau, August 24, 1983

Angelina set her glass of tea on the table and reached down to scratch Elwood's ears. The Conclave, or what was left of them, were all sitting around the table, eating a steak and lobster lunch they weren't really enjoying. But as Aaron was *Lupus Rex*, and he had invited everyone to lunch, they were obligated to show up. She watched him study everyone at the table. When his eyes met hers, her heart pounded with a couple of extra thumps. He smiled and winked at her. *What a Yuma!*

Father Thomas strode up, his leather shoes clicking on the stone slabs, and stopped next to Aaron. She smelled the mixture of angst and amazement amongst them all. A Catholic priest usually meant Fectors.

Aaron smiled and stood up. "Welcome, Father Thomas!"

"Thank you, Aaron." He smiled at Angelia. "Good afternoon to you, too, Angelina. It is good to see you again."

She smiled back at him. "Buenos diás, Padre'."

Aaron turned and addressed everyone at the table. "Everyone, I would like to introduce to you Father Thomas of the *Lucerna Veritatis*." Aaron could tell the Conclave was not happy with a Fector showing up for lunch, but the presence of the four dozen or so *frenatus* comprising his personal *custodia* standing along the loggia kept them in line. "Father Thomas and I have come to a new arrangement. All previous deals with the Lamp of Truth are hereby cancelled. We will no longer shun *lupis* to ensure peace with the Lamp of Light. From this day forward, we will take responsibility for our own actions."

Everyone at the table, save Angelina and Aaron, burst out in an uproar. "What?" "How do we punish them?" "Sometimes they don't work out." "What do we do, rub their noses in their piss and swat their bottoms?"

Aaron shook his head and raised his voice. "We aren't getting rid of shunning!" He waited for everyone to quiet down. "The Pact is still intact. I've sworn to uphold it, and I plan to keep that oath. We just aren't going to adhere to the quota Stoddard arranged for." Aaron took a deep drink of his tea. "As a race, we've gotten lazy. We infect people and then throw them to the wolves, so to speak, when they don't work out. Or when we're short for the year. That's murder, and that stops now. For centuries we've tried to tell people we aren't evil. How can we expect them to believe us if we're sacrificing our own for a little safety?!"

Antonio Spedada, the South American clan head, asked, "How do we keep the Fectors off of us?"

Aaron grinned at them. "We're going to teach the wildlings to *frenis*. All of them." He waited until the laughing died down. "Father Thomas, I know you're interested in how I plan to do this. That's why I invited you to lunch today."

Everyone was looking at the both of them in anticipation. Aaron strolled along the length of the table. "Everyone's been brainwashed by centuries of tradition. Everyone tries and tries to *frenis*, and some get lucky. Then the Race treats it like it is some kind of miracle. It's not a miracle, and it's not really hard." He got to Angelina and put a gentle hand on her shoulder, kneeled down, and scratched Elwood's ears. "It's only hard because the wildlings have been told it's hard." He stood back up and continued his trek around the table. "And because they think it's hard, they don't think they can do it. So they fail. And when they fail, it eats at them, makes them feel unworthy. And because of that, it *becomes* hard. It's a positive feedback loop!" As he made it back to his own seat, he turned and faced everyone again. "All we have to do is show them it isn't hard to break the cycle of failure. Let them know they are just as good as the rest of the *frenatus*."

Bill, sitting in James's old spot, smirked. "Just that simple, huh, Chief?"

Angelina knew Bill's snide remark was preplanned. Aaron needed someone to ask the dumb question, to get it out on the table so they could talk about it. It worked like a charm. He had everyone's attention.

Aaron grinned a bashful smile. "Well, the devil is in the details."

Father Thomas, on cue, interjected. "I know something about tradition. The church is rife with it. 'We can't do that. It's not done that way.' You may be onto something here, Aaron." He addressed the Conclave. "I can assure you that the official position of *Lucerna Veritatis* would be to live and let live if the wildlings could control themselves as easily as you've been controlling them up to now."

Antonio asked, "Why? Why would *frenatus* be more acceptable to the *interfectores*?"

Father Thomas rubbed his crucifix as he put his thoughts together. "Because if you can *frenis*, you are controlling your passions. If you can control your passions, you won't go on murdering sprees. Granted, you will have some who are evil by nature as with any population, and they will have to be dealt with, but the general consensus would be that you aren't a bunch of bloodthirsty demons created by Satan. The only reason for the crusades against the Race in the beginning was to prevent the needless killings. If you can stop the killings by controlling your passions, we wouldn't feel the need to wipe the entire Race out."

Antonio spoke up again, "Aaron, we've been trying to teach them to *frenis* for centuries—"

Aaron cut him off. "Not really. You've been telling them how hard it is."

Antonio shook his head and sighed. "I suppose you have a plan then? How to teach this magic trick of yours?"

"I do. I bridled on my first *renovatio* because I was confident in myself. I plan to instill that same sense of self-worth into the wildlings. Unfortunately, it will take some time to get it up and running. In the meantime, I'll be sending my envoys to you, ambassadors if you will."

A couple whispered to each other, "Spies."

Aaron slammed his hand down on the table and everyone stopped talking. "If you want to consider them spies, then so be it! However, I will expect nothing but the best treatment for them."

One of the *Dux* Angelina wasn't familiar with asked, "Why would we want to do this?"

Angelina saw Aaron bristle slightly, but he held his peace. He had a temper, but he knew how to direct it. He shot it at them like a crossbow bolt. His voice thundered. "Because I will declare you *Utlagatus* and kill you if you don't. Now, if you prefer, or in your sleep later. I'll even let you choose the way you prefer it right now."

He waited. "No takers?" he asked. "Great! Now, if one of my envoys so much as bites his tongue while eating, I will not be pleased. If they pull a nail while running during your hunts, I will consider it an assault upon my person."

A couple more voiced some concerns, but the *lupas* quieted them down.

When everyone was looking at him again, he smiled. It was not a friendly smile, though. He might not be in *lupus* form, but the smile was as predatory as if he were. "Listen, people. I already have spies in all of your clans and packs. The *lupas* have spoken. This is not a negotiation. This is the way it is." He took the time to enunciate each word so it was not misunderstood. "So do *not* fuck with me by thinking you have a say in the matter." Everyone submitted by looking at the table in front of him.

"Settled? Good." Aaron then turned to Father Thomas. "One last thing. Father Thomas is also here so you all know that our new arrangement is not with you. It is with me. If you step out of line or permit one of your clan to step out of line, Father Thomas has my permission to take care of the situation in any way he sees fit.

"If I die, there will be war," he vowed. "If Jajine or Angelina dies, the Conclave will only have eleven places at my table, because I'll wipe your entire clan out of existence." He gently sat down and took a sip of his tea. "Talk to your *lupa*s if you have any doubt."

Orlando Sentinel, August 25, 1983, Page 21

An Orlando couple, Craig and Lisa Minor, are dead following an explosion onboard their yacht, Lupus Rex, one mile off the coast near Savusavu Bay marina in Fiji on Wednesday.

Craig Minor died instantly while Lisa Minor is still missing.

Fiji Times says the couple were the owners of Sun State Meat, Poultry, and Fish, based in Orlando.

It is believed there were others onboard with them.

Fiji police have confirmed the incident adding investigations are continuing.

Orlando Sentinel, August 26, 1983, Page 21

Fiji police have confirmed that Craig Minor, who was killed when his yacht, Lupus Rex, exploded one mile off the coast near Savusavu Bay marina in Fiji on Wednesday, was not alone. Visiting Mr. Minor were James Gondolfin of Pensacola, Warren and Riley Freeman of Maine, Glen Benson of Atlanta, Autumn Levy of Bradenton and fiancé' to Mr. Benson, Walther Brinkerhoff of Germany, Tàmhas Hamilton of Scotland, Esmond Heath of Australia, and Chidike Afolayan of South Africa.

Lisa Minor had not yet joined her husband and is safe in Orlando at her estate.

Family spokesman, Aaron Darveau, asked for everyone's prayers for the victims' families.

Chapter 42—Epilogus
noun [e-pə-lŏg'-əs]
1. Conclusion.

Aaron Darveau, September 9, 1984

Aaron stood on the hillside, looking down at the Race's newly constructed Confucian monastery. It was sitting in the middle of the field where Aaron woke up from his first *renovatio*. *This has been long time coming.*

It had been a little over a year since his Ascension and quite a bit had changed. Lisa sold the entire estate and her business to Aaron and Angelina for a paltry sum, with the understanding he build her a house on the far side of the property where she could live out her days. She also introduced him to her banker, lawyer, and accountant; they were the ones who ran the operations of Craig's and Lisa's public lives. They had no problem working for Aaron as long as the checks continued to clear the bank. Still, Aaron didn't know the first thing about running a meat wholesaling company. In fact, he harbored no perceptions whatsoever he would be able to run a multi-million dollar company of any type. That was easily solved the Navy way; he delegated. He hired two men from Kansas City who were ready for a promotion and gave them lucrative benefits tied directly to the company's performance.

With that out of the way, he got busy on his *frenis* training program. He used some of the estate's acreage for a temple to house that Tai Chi Studio he always wanted. He needed the studio because he planned to train wildlings from the different clans in Tai Chi—not in combat, but in the art form. His hope was that as the students became more confident in their abilities, they would learn to respect themselves. With that self-respect would come their ability to *frenis*.

This was not a new idea, and Aaron was the perfect example. He was a Tai Chi Master, regardless of what he told people. He knew it. He knew what his abilities were. He was confident in them, so he had no reason to brag about them. He didn't require respect from others because he respected *himself*, and that was all that mattered.

However, wanting to do something and knowing how to do it are two different things. Master Chen had a saying, *"You cannot travel a path unless you know how to walk."* Aaron invited him down to help with the small detail of starting a Tai Chi monastery.

Master Chen was reluctant to believe Aaron was *lupus*. He'd heard tales and myths about *Lang-ren*, the Chinese word for werewolves, but like Americans, he didn't put much faith in them. He continued to think Aaron's mind had *bent too far in the spring wind*—until he saw his first *renovatio*. Between the two of them, they put together an intense training schedule, and with Angelina's Gift as a guide, they selected twenty-four students. Master Chen was hoping Aaron would be able to teach a class himself, but Race business was keeping him too busy.

Aaron knew what *defrenatus* were capable of when they got pissed off. Master Chen did not. Still, he flatly refused Aaron's offer of having a couple of *frenatus* available during class time. "Students must respect sifu, not soldier behind tree," he reminded Aaron. Master Chen didn't need to know anything about *lupus* to train them. He did what came naturally to him—he was a Sifu. He spent four hours a day with the students over the next year, excluding weekends. He taught them the forms, and through the forms, meditation, and through meditation, self-discipline.

The students were responsible for more than just learning and practicing the forms. They were also charged with building the monastery, growing their own food, and making and repairing their own clothes. Of the original twenty-four students, sixteen learned to *frenis* within the first six months. They were free to return to their clans at that point—they had passed the class—but they chose to stay and finish the work on the monastery instead, putting their graduation off a few months. The remaining eight students did not quit, and Aaron and Master Chen did not give up on them. Their lessons would continue under Master Chen's tutelage while Aaron became Sifu for the next beginner class.

All in all, Aaron considered his experiment a success. Sixteen wildlings from clans who had all but given up on them were now *frenatus*.

The clans were non-committal in their responses to the report.

Master Chen wasn't happy, though. "If pilot lands good sixteen of twenty-four times, plane go *boom* on road eight times!" He considered it a complete and utter failure.

However, he was visibly pleased to see his former student finally taking the reins of his own class. He caught up with Aaron meditating at the monastery's altar on the morning before the first graduation ceremony. "Aaron, I have sumting for you."

Aaron brought himself back to consciousness and stood, foregoing his normal stretching after meditation so as to properly address his Master. "Good Morning, Sifu." He put his right fist into his left hand and bowed.

Master Chen returned Aaron's bow before reaching down for a small package sitting by his feet. "Tis was my first Gung-fu Saam. My Sifu give to me when I become Master. My son no want old clothes. Ha Ha!"

Aaron unwrapped the paper from his new uniform, and then held it up and admired it. It was white with black piping and had traditional wooden toggles to hold it closed. It was made from fine silk.

Master Chen asked, "You like?"

"Hell, yes! I thought I was going to have to give my graduation speech in blue jeans and sandals. These are beautiful. Thank you." Aaron bowed to him.

"You are most welcome, Master Darveau."

The sudden appearance of Master Chen's excellent command of the English language caught Aaron off guard. "Hey! Where's your accent?"

Master Chen grinned. "I leave it in front of my students."

At the first graduation ceremony, Master Chen awarded badges of completion—a stainless steel wolf fang on a leather thong, silver being poisonous as *Lupus sapiens* jewelry. Aaron's hippy necklace was the symbol of their success.

Aaron, as *Lupus Rex*, gave a short speech.

"Before I embraced being *lupis*, I used to think we were all two people: Who we think we are, and who we truly are. But now I know I was wrong.

Each of us are three different people: Who we think we are. Who we truly are. And who other people think we are. It is our purpose in life to find the center between those three people. I hope at that center you'll find you are a warrior-scholar.

"The Warrior-Scholar relies on and strives to excel in a wide variety of skills to a much greater degree than a generalist. Songster and pugilist. Doctor and swordsman. Writer and cavalier. One cannot exist in abundance without the other. It is only through self-respect and confidence in your abilities that a future free from fear exists. The Race needs *lupis* willing to bravely lead it into this new, fearless future.

"We have done our best to show you the path to this center. Today, it all comes to fruition. Will this fruit rot and drag the Race down into anarchy? Or is today the beginning of the end of the war between *lupis* and their own race?

"Today, you will return to your clans. If you choose to remain on this path, in time, you will become leaders. Some of you may even continue what you have learned here and become masters. And someday you may even return here to the *Viam Lupus* Academy to teach. Just remember, always, you are the future of the Race. It lives or dies with the decisions you make."

Afterward

When people read this book, people who know me, they ask where I came up with the idea. That is a story in itself and included in this book. Read Chapter 4—*Luto Via* again. Other than a few details that have been changed for cinematic enhancement, that chapter is a true story.

In addition, Karen, Lisa, and Craig are real people, although their last names have been changed as well as the circumstances surrounding their living environment. I thought, "What if those really were werewolves chasing us, and my girlfriend, Karen, was a werewolf, and her friends, Lisa and Craig, were werewolves, and...."

Everything else built from that.

Dr. Mike O'Neal, a good friend of mine and one of my former college professors, had an interesting comment after he finished reading *Lupus Rex*. Paraphrased, "I love the book, Tom. But Aaron is a Louisiana born, car loving, tai chi practicing, US Navy enlistee, Captain Kirk fan who also happens to be a werewolf. Is the Captain Kirk thing too much?"

I don't know. You be the judge.

Latin to English Translations

To assist the reader, below are English translations of the Latin phrases and words used throughout this tome. Translations and pronunciations may not be exact, but this is how the Race has handed them down from generation to generation; as with any language, there is drift in meaning and pronunciation.

Acer Dens
Noun, Phrase: āsər()denz

1. Sharp tooth.
2. Clan Name.
3. The *Acer Dens* Clan originates from Germany and surrounding areas.

Antelogium
Noun: an-tē-lä'-ji-əm

1. Beginning.

Ambrosius
Adjective: am-brō'-zhuhs

1. Divine.
2. Clan Name.
3. The *Ambrosius* Clan originates from Western Asia.

Astutia
Noun: ə-stü'-shə

1. Clever Persuasion.
2. Diplomacy.

Caeruleo Lunaris
Noun, Phrase: ke(ə)- rül'-ē-ō()lü-nar'-əs

1. Blue Moon.
2. A blue moon has cultural and mystical properties for *Lupus sapiens* and witchcraft.

Celeriter

Adverb: səl-ər-ī'-tər

1. Swiftly.
2. Clan Name.
3. The *Celeriter* Clan originates from Spain and surrounding areas.

Concoquo

Verb: kän'-kō-kwō

1. Boiling or seething together into a concoction.
2. Figuratively: Assimilate through hardship.
3. Figuratively: Learning things the hard way.

Confido

Noun: kən-ˈfīd-ō

1. Confide.

Coquo et Comedo

Verb, Phrase: käk'-kwō()ə()kä'-mə-dō

1. Prepare and eat.

Custodes

Noun: kus'-tō-dəs

1. Custodians
2. Keepers of the lore.

Custodia

Noun: kus-tō'-dē-ə

1. A company of guards, usually military in origin.

Defrenator/Defrenatus

Noun: dē-frə-nā'-tor/dē-frə-nā'-tus

1. A *lupus* who has not learned to control his or her emotions or make conscious decisions while transformed.
2. Slang: Wildling, Unbridled.
3. Plural: *Defrenatus.*

Ducissa Lupa

Noun, Phrase: duk-is'-sə()lü'-pə

1. *Lupus sapiens* female Clan Head.
2. Literally Duchess Wolf.

Dux Lupus

Noun, Phrase: duks()lü'-pəs

1. *Lupus sapiens* male Clan Head.
2. Literally Duke Wolf.

Epilogus

Noun: e-pə-lög'-əs

1. Conclusion.

Familia/Familiæ

Noun: fə-mi'-ljə/ fə-mi'-ljā

1. A family of *grexes.*
2. Plural: *Familiæ.*

Fel saccula

Noun, Phrase: fel()sak'-ü-lə

1. Venom sac.
2. Slang: Cula, when combined with *manicula.*

Forma

Noun: fòrm'-ə

1. Form, shape, fashion, plan, mold.

Fortitudo Incarnatum

Noun, Phrase: fort-ə-tü'-dō()in-kär-nā'-tum

1. Strength Incarnate.
2. Dominate form presented by a *lupus* when forcing another *lupus* into submission.

Frenator/Frenatus

Noun: fren'-ə-tor/fren-ät'-tus

1. A *lupus* who has learned to control his or her emotions and make conscious decisions while transformed.
2. Slang: Bridled.
3. Plural: *Frenatus.*

Frenis

Verb: fren'-is

1. To control one's emotions and make conscious decisions while transformed.
2. Bridle, control, restrain.

Gloriosi

Adjective: glôr-ē-ōs'-ē

1. Glorious.
2. Clan Name.
3. The *Gloriosi* Clan originates from North America with no defined boundaries.

Grex

Noun: greks

    1.   Pack, typically of *Lupus sapiens*.

Historiae Nostrae

Noun, Phrase: his-t(ə-)rā()näs-trä

    1.   Our history or past.

Illustratio

Noun: il-lus-trä'-tē-ō

    1.   Enlightenment.

Illustro

Verb: il'-lus-tro

    1.   Enlighten.
    2.   Make clear.

Imaginatio

Noun: i-mä-ji-nä'-tē-ō

    1.   Dream.
    2.   Imagination.

Inperium

Noun: in-pir'-ē-əm

    1.   Authority.
    2.   Commandment.

Interfectore

Noun: in-tər-fek-tor'-ə

    1.   Killer.
    2.   Murderer.
    3.   Slang: Fector. A member of *Lucerna Veritatis*.

Iustum

Adjective: yüs-tüm

1. Justice.

Loup Garou

Noun, Phrase: lü()gə-rü'

1. From the French, werewolf.
2. Name for *lupis* in the South Louisiana region.

Lucerna Veritatis

Noun, Phrase: lü-ser'-nə()ver-i-tā'-tis

1. Lamp of Truth.
2. Ancient order of priests formed to fight *Lupus sapiens*.

Luna Amator

Noun, Phrase: lü'-nə()ä-mä-tor'

1. Moon lover.
2. Clan Name.
3. The *Luna Amator* Clan originates from the northeastern portion of North America.

Lupa/Lupas

Noun: lü'-pə/lü'-pəz

1. Slang for female *Lupus sapiens*.
2. *Lupas*, the plural form, is used when referring to multiple females.

Lupa Reginam

Noun, Phrase: lü'-pə()rəg'-i-nəm

1. Wolf Queen.

Lupum lues
Noun, Phrase: lü'-pum()lü'-əs

1. Wolf's Bane.
2. Under certain conditions it can force an early *Renovatio*. *Lupis* find its smell particularly pungent and offensive in its raw form.

Lupus/Lupis
Noun: lü'-pəs/lü'-pis

1. Slang for male *Lupus sapiens*. May refer to males or females.
2. *Lupis*, the plural form, is used when referring to multiple males or males and females together. Does not typically refer to the individuals of the entire Race.

Lupus Rex
Noun, Phrase: lü'-pəs()reks

1. Wolf King.

Lupus/Lupis sapiens
Noun, Phrase: lü'-pəs/lü'-pis()sā'-pē-ənz

1. Wise wolf.
2. Scientific name for the werewolf species.
3. Used when referencing the entire Race as a whole.
4. *Lupis*, the plural form, is typically used when referring to the group of individuals comprising the entire Race.
5. Slang: Howler, Race, werewolf, *lupus*, *lupa*.

Lupus (Lupis)(Lupa)(Lupas) solitarius
Noun, Phrase: lü'-pəs()sä-lə-ter'-rē-əs

1. Lone or solitary Wolf.
2. A *lupus* who has been shunned by the Race, or one who is not recognized by the Race.

Luto Via

Noun, Phrase: Lü-tō()(v)(w)ē'-ə

1. Dirt Road.

Manicula

Noun: mə-nik'-ü-lə

1. Hand.
2. Slang: Cula, when combined with *fel saccula*.

Mors Atra

Noun, Phrase: morz()ā'-trə

1. Dark death.
2. Clan Name.
3. The Mors Atra Clan originates from Africa.

Mulieres Intuitionem

Noun, Phrase: mü-li'-er-əs()in-tü-ish'-uhn-əm

1. Women's intuition.
2. The Gift that all *lupas* possess.

Natus Ululare

Noun: nā'-təs()ü-lə-lar'-ē

1. Created to howl in dominance.
2. Literally, born to howl.

Necar

Noun: nē'-kar

1. Killing.

Non Evitabilis

Noun, Phrase: nän()ev'-ə-tə-bil-is

1. Unavoidable.

Os Ruptor

Noun, Phrase: oz()rup'-tər

1. Bone breaker.
2. Clan Name.
3. The *Os Ruptor* Clan originates from Eastern Europe.

Paedagogus

Noun: pe-də-gäg'-əs

1. Tutor.
2. Guide.

Pilo Crasso

Noun, Phrase: pī-lō()kras-ō

1. Thick hair.
2. Clan Name.
3. The Pilo Crasso Clan originates from Australia.

Plenilunium

Noun: ple-ni-lü'-ni-um

1. Full moon.

Postpartor

Noun: pōst-par'-tər

1. Successor.
2. Typically refers to the incoming *Lupa Reginam*.

Præda

Noun: prā'-də

1. Prey.

Prensio

Noun: prən'-sē-ō

   1. Capture.

Princeps Lupus

Noun, Phrase: prin'-səps()lü'-pəs

   1. Wolf Prince.
   2. The *lupus* chosen by the *Postpartor* to ascend to *Lupus Rex*.

Pulsante Ungue

Noun, Phrase: pul-sän'-tē()un'-gü

   1. Striking claw.
   2. Clan Name.
   3. The *Pulsante Ungue* Clan originates from China/Eastern Asia.
   4. The Chinese name roughly translates to *Ji Zhua*.

Quadrivium

Noun: kwä-dri-(v)(w)ē-əm

   1. Crossroad.

Reges

Noun: rē'-jəs

   1. Kings.

Renovatio/Innovationes

Noun: re-nə-vä'-tē-ō/in-ə-vā'-shən-əs

   1. Rebirth, rejuvenate, or renewal.
   2. The transformation from human to *lupus*.
   3. Plural: *Innovationes*

Sans Peur

Noun, Phrase: sänz()pyür

1. Without fear.
2. Clan Name.
3. The *Sans Peur* Clan originates from the British Isles.

Scansio

Noun: skan'-sē-ō

1. Ascension.

Sequentia

Noun: sē-kwən'-shə

1. Continuation.

Sui Deceptio

Noun, Phrase: sü'-ī()di-sep'-tē-ō

1. Self-deception.

Suscitatio

Noun: sə-se-tā'-tē-ō

1. Awakening.

Tiro

Noun: tir-ō

1. Recruit.

Tonitrua

Noun: ton-ē-trü'-ə

1. Thunder.
2. Clan Name.
3. The *Tonitrua* Clan originates from South America.

Utlagatus
Noun: üt-läg'-ə-tus

1. Outlaw.

Vagor
Noun: vā'-gor

1. A howl, typically a commandant.

Venatio
Noun: və-nā'-tē-ō

1. Hunting.
2. Clan Name.
3. The *Venatio* Clan originates from North America with no defined boundaries.

Venator
Noun: və-nā'-tər

1. A hunter.

Veneno
Noun: və-nē'-nō

1. Infect.

Venor
Verb: vē'-nōr

1. Stalk.

Viam Lupus
Noun, Phrase: (v)(w)ē'-əm()lü'-pəs

1. The Way of the Wolf.

Bibliography

1   *Lucerna Veritatis* oath adapted from The Jesuit Oath of Induction as recorded in *Subterranean Rome* by Charles Didier translated from the French and published in New York in 1843.

Author's note:

Many of you may question the sanctity of this vow. Remember that the Fectors have been around for a long time. The Catholic Church was responsible for the Inquisition, and they were not very nice to those who didn't toe the company line. In order to appreciate this vow, you have to remove yourself from the modern version of Catholicism and imagine what a vow would look like from the Dark Ages when Church history was rife with superstition and cruelty.

I didn't make this vow up. In a different form, it was published in 1843 as indicated above. There are questions as to its authenticity. Indeed, I make no claims one way or the other, but it was too good not to use for a bunch of blood-thirsty bible-thumpers.

The vow:

"My son, heretofore you have been taught to act the dissembler: among Roman Catholics to be a Roman Catholic, and to be a spy even among your own brethren; to believe no man, to trust no man. Among all other heretical faiths, to be of the heretical faiths; obtaining their confidence, to seek even to preach from their pulpits, and to denounce with all the vehemence in your nature the extermination of *Lupis sapiens*, that you might be enabled to gather together all information for the benefit of your Order as a faithful soldier of the Pope.

"You have been taught to insidiously plant the seeds of jealousy and hatred between communities that harbor *Lupis sapiens*, provinces that harbor *Lupis sapiens*, states that were at peace that harbor *Lupis sapiens*, and incite them to deeds of blood, involving them in war with each other, and to create revolutions and civil wars in countries that were independent and prosperous that harbor *Lupis sapiens*, cultivating the arts and the sciences and enjoying the blessings of peace that harbor *Lupis sapiens*, to show how harboring Satan's Spawn brings down all men. To take sides with the combatants and to act secretly with your brother *Lucerna Veritatis*, who might be engaged on the other side, but openly opposed to that with which you might be connected, only that the Church might be the gainer in the end, in the conditions fixed in the treaties for peace and that the end justifies the means.

"You have been taught your duty as a spy, to gather all statistics, facts and information in your power from every source; to ingratiate yourself into the confidence of those who harbor *Lupis sapiens*, as well as that of the merchant, the banker, the lawyer, among the schools and universities, in parliaments and legislatures, and the judiciaries and councils of state, and to be all things to all men, for the Pope's sake, whose servants we are unto death.

"You have received all your instructions heretofore as a novice, a neophyte, and have served as co-adjurer, confessor and priest, but you have not yet been invested with all that is necessary to command in the *Lucerna Veritatis* in the service of the Pope. You must serve the proper time as the instrument and executioner as directed by your superiors; for none can command here who has not consecrated his labors with the shedding of the blood of *Lupis sapiens*; for "without the shedding of impure and evil blood, no man can be saved." Therefore, to fit yourself for your work and make your own salvation sure, you will, in addition to your former oath of obedience to your Order and allegiance to the Pope, repeat after me:

"I, John Billings, in the presence of Almighty God, the Blessed Virgin Mary, the blessed Michael the Archangel, the blessed St. John the Baptist, the holy Apostles St. Peter and St. Paul and all the saints and sacred hosts of heaven, and to you, my ghostly father, The Superior General of the Society of *Lucerna Veritatis*, founded by St. Ignatius Loyola in the Pontificate of Paul the Third, and continued to the present, do by the womb of the virgin, the matrix of God, and the rod of Jesus Christ, declare and swear, that his holiness the Pope is Christ's Vice-regent and is the true and only head of the Catholic or Universal Church throughout the earth; and that by virtue of the keys of binding and loosing, given to his Holiness by my Savior, Jesus Christ, he hath power to depose any king, prince, state, commonwealth, or government that harbors *Lupis sapiens*, all being illegal and that they may safely be destroyed. Therefore, to the utmost of my power I shall and will defend this doctrine of his Holiness's right and custom against all who harbor *Lupis sapiens*. I do now renounce and disown any allegiance as due to any who may harbor *Lupis sapiens*.

351

"I do further declare that I will help, assist, and advise all or any of his Holiness's agents in any place wherever I shall be.

"I do further promise and declare that notwithstanding I am dispensed with, to assume my religion heretical, for the propaganda of the Mother Church's interest, to keep secret and private all her agents' counsels from time to time, as they may entrust me and not to divulge, directly or indirectly, by word, writing or circumstance whatever; but to execute all that shall be proposed, given in charge or discovered unto me, by you, my ghostly father, or any of this sacred covenant.

"I do further promise and declare that I will have no opinion or will of my own, or any mental reservation whatever, even as a corpse or cadaver, but will unhesitatingly obey each and every command that I may receive from my superiors in the Militia of the Pope and of Jesus Christ.

"That I may go to any part of the world withersoever I may be sent, without murmuring or repining, and will be submissive in all things whatsoever communicated to me.

"I furthermore promise and declare that I will, when the opportunity presents itself, to make and wage relentless war, secretly or openly, against all who would harbor *Lupis sapiens*, as I am directed to do, to extirpate and exterminate them from the face of the whole earth; and that I will spare neither age, sex or condition; and that I will hang, waste, boil, flay, strangle and bury alive these infamous *Lupis sapiens*, rip up the stomachs and wombs of their women and crush their infants' heads against the walls, in order to annihilate forever their execrable race. That when the same cannot be done openly, I will secretly use the poisoned cup, the strangulating cord, the steel of the poniard or the silver bullet, regardless of the honor, rank, dignity, or authority of the person or persons, whatever may be their condition in life, either public or private, as I at any time may be directed so to do by any agent of the Pope or Superior of the Brotherhood of the Holy Faith, of the Society of *Lucerna Veritatis*.

"In confirmation of which, I hereby dedicate my life, my soul and all my corporal powers, and with this dagger which I now receive, I will subscribe my name written in my own blood, in testimony thereof; and should I prove false or weaken in my determination, may my brethren and fellow soldiers of the Militia of the Pope cut off my hands and my feet, and my throat from ear to ear, my belly opened and sulphur burned therein, with all the punishment that can be inflicted upon me on earth and my soul be tortured by demons in an eternal hell forever!

"All of which, I, John Billings, do swear by the Blessed Trinity and blessed Sacraments, which I am now to receive, to perform and on my part to keep inviolable; and do call all the heavenly and glorious hosts of heaven to witness the blessed Sacrament of the Eucharist, and witness the same further with my name written and with the point of this dagger dipped in my own blood and sealed in the presence of this holy covenant."

About the Author

Tom Sutherland is a Louisiana reared, car loving, Tai Chi practicing, U.S. Navy veteran, Captain Kirk fan who also happens to be a licensed pilot and software engineer. He lives with Angela, his wife of 23 years, in north Texas with their dachshund, Lex the Wonder Dog. Both their daughter and son have moved out, leaving the house feeling empty. He owns his own industrial software engineering company because he can't stand having only one boss.

22705606R00205

Made in the USA
San Bernardino, CA
17 July 2015